The Last Romantics

The Last Romantics

A Novel

Tara Conklin

wm

WILLIAM MORROW
An Imprint of HarperCollins*Publishers*

HarperCollins books may be purchased for educational, business, or
sales promotional use. For information, please email the Special Markets
Department in the U.S. at SPsales@harpercollins.com or in Canada at
HCOrder@harpercollins.com.

FIRST EDITION

Designed by Fritz Metsch

Library of Congress Cataloging-in-Publication Data has been applied for.
Library and Archives Canada Cataloguing in Publication information is
available upon request.

ISBN 978-0-06-235820-2
ISBN 978-1-4434-3630-4 (Canada)

19 20 21 22 23   LSC   10 9 8 7 6 5 4 3 2

Dedicated to the memory of Luella Briody Conklin
and Kenneth Jerome Conklin

For my sisters

Behind the cotton wool is hidden a pattern; that we—I mean all human beings—are connected with this; that the whole world is a work of art; that we are parts of the work of art. *Hamlet* or a Beethoven quartet is the truth about this vast mass that we call the world. But there is no Shakespeare, there is no Beethoven; certainly and emphatically there is no God; we are the words; we are the music; we are the thing itself.

—Virginia Woolf, *Moments of Being*

Wait, they don't love you like I love you.

—Karen O, Yeah Yeah Yeahs

The Last Romantics

Year 2079

AT FIRST I believed the girl to be an apparition. A ghost. She rose from the crowd in the auditorium and walked to the microphone.

I remained very still. For the past ninety minutes, I had been seated onstage to discuss my body of work. As much as I dread large crowds, the event had been a success. The audience was respectful, intelligent, curious. I'd even made them laugh. That joke about the frog, of all things. We heard the sirens only once, a brief wail during which I paused my reading. We all waited, the thousand here in the auditorium and the thousands more watching via satellite and DTR. We waited, and then the sirens quieted, and I resumed with my poem.

Afterward the questions. So many questions! My first public event in twenty-five years—of course there would be questions, but I was not prepared for the intensity, the thoroughness with which these people had read my work. It still surprises me now, eighty years into this literary experiment, that my words might mean something to anyone other than myself.

I am 102 years old and a poet of some renown. My name is Fiona Skinner.

When the girl stepped forward, my attention was elsewhere.

My energy low. I wondered what snack Henry had waiting for me backstage and hoped it was the candy with the peanut butter in the center, my favorite. My thoughts fixed on other comforts: the tall, soft bed in my house in the mountains; the river stocked with trout; the deep, cold well; the generator with its soothing hum. We never heard the sirens there, no, the nearest town was too far. It was a safe place, our house, a place beyond the reach of politics and rising oceans. At least that's what I chose to believe. It's possible to exist under any number of illusions, to believe so thoroughly in the presence of things you cannot see—safety, God, love—that you impose upon them physical shapes. A bed, a cross, a husband. But ideas willed into being are still ideas and just as fragile.

The girl at the microphone was an arresting sight: slender and tall, a dark bob cut short and sharp to her chin. She looked eighteen, perhaps twenty years old. Not a girl, then, nearly a woman.

The crowd was silent. She coughed into her hand. "Ms. Skinner," she began. "My name is Luna."

"Luna?" I said, and my voice caught, my breath stilled. For a moment I traveled back all those years to a different place and time. At last, I thought. Luna has returned.

"Yes. My mother named me after the last line of *The Love Poem*," she said.

"Oh, of course." I smiled. Henry had told me about this, the popularity of the name. *The Love Poem* had that effect on some readers. They wanted to keep a piece of it. And here was one of those babies, now grown, standing before me. Another Luna.

The girl's face was half in shadow. I saw a mole high on her right cheek. About the size of a dime. A birthmark. A dark kiss.

"My mother always wanted to ask you about the name," Luna continued. "She'd memorized the last pages at school. When my brother and I were little, she'd recite them at dinner if we were feeling down." Her face became soft with the memory. *"The Love Poem* meant so much to her. I want to know, for my mother. Who was your inspiration? Who was Luna?"

The auditorium went still. Onstage the lights had become hot, but a cold spread through me, ice flooding my veins. I shivered. A sweat rose along my hairline. It was a question I'd always refused to answer publicly. And privately; even Henry didn't know the truth. But of course I should have expected it tonight. Isn't that why I'd agreed to speak one last time? Isn't that why I was here? To finally tell this story.

An old regret lodged in my throat, blocking my voice. I coughed.

"Luna is the Spanish word for *moon,* of course," I said. "In the poem itself, there are many metaphors, many symbols that mean different things. I wrote it seventy-five years ago, my dear. Your mother, you, anyone here"—I waved my palm at the audience—"you know what the poem means more than I do now."

The Luna standing before me shook her head in frustration. A lock of hair fell into her eyes, and she pushed it away. "No. I mean the real woman. My mother always said there was someone named Luna."

I straightened my spine and heard the bones crack, a minor internal disruption. I wasn't often put on the spot. At home I had a gardener, a personal assistant, a housekeeper, a cook. I lived with my second husband, Henry, but I ran the house and gave the orders. Some might say I'm imposing. I prefer to think of it as self-assured. This girl was also self-assured, I could see it in the set of her shoulders, the purse of her lips.

How to describe the first Luna? I met Luna Hernandez only once. On a night when the wind threw tree branches onto the road and leaves whirled in crazy circles. Decades ago, a lifetime ago. That Luna had grown and changed in my mind until I hardly saw her anymore. Were her eyes brown or gray? The mole, was it high on the right cheek or the left? Had it been remorse I saw on her face that night or merely dismissal?

"I wrote a poem about love," I began, addressing the crowd. "But there are certain limitations. There are certain *failings*. I've always been wary of love, you see. Its promises are too dizzy, its reasons too vague, its origins murkier than mud." Here I heard a chuckle from the audience. "Yes, mud!" I called in the direction of the laugh. "When I was young, I tried dissecting love, setting it up on a table with a good strong light and poking, prodding, slicing. For years I believed it possible to identify the crux, the core, and that once you found this essential element you might tend it like a rose and grow something beautiful. Back then I was a romantic. I didn't understand that there's no stopping betrayal. If you live long enough and well enough to know love, its various permutations and shades, you will falter. You will break someone's heart. Fairy tales don't tell you that. Poetry doesn't either."

I paused.

"You're not answering the question," Luna said; her arms were now crossed against her chest, her chin down.

"Let me tell you a story," I said. "In these difficult times, stories are important. In a sense, stories are all we have to tell us about the future."

Luna moved away from the microphone. She was listening intently, everyone was, shoulders pitched just slightly forward, curious and alert.

"Once upon a time," I began, "there was a father and a mother and four children, three girls and one boy. They lived together in a house like any other house, in a town like many other towns, and for a time they were happy." I paused, and all those faces in the auditorium stared down on me, all those eyes. "And then—" I stopped again, faltering. I sipped my glass of water. "And then there was the Pause. Everything started there. Our mother didn't mean for it to happen, she didn't, but this is a story about the failures of love, and the Pause was the first."

PART I

Bexley

Chapter 1

IN THE SPRING of 1981, our father died. His name was Ellis Avery Skinner, thirty-four years old, a small bald lozenge at the back of his head that he covered every morning with a few hopeful strands. We lived in the middle-class town of Bexley, Connecticut, where our father owned and operated a dental practice. At the moment his heart stopped, he was pulling on a pair of blue rubber gloves while one of his afternoon patients, a Mrs. Lipton, lay before him on the padded recliner, breathing deeply from a sweet mask of chloroform.

"Oh!" our father said, and toppled sideways to the floor.

"Dr. Skinner?" Mrs. Lipton sat up. She was unsteady, groggy, and afraid as she looked down at our father on the floor. He twitched once, twice, and then Mrs. Lipton began to scream.

The look on his face, she later reported to our mother, was one of surrender and absolute surprise.

Our mother was thirty-one years old. She'd never held a full-time job and possessed a degree in English literature from Colby College in her home state of Maine that sat unframed in an upstairs closet. Her dark hair hung like two pressed curtains framing the window of her face. Her eyes were wide and brown, with sparse lashes and narrow lids that gave an impression of watchfulness and exposure. Her name was Antonia, though everyone called her Noni, and it was decided long before my birth that her children should call her Noni, too.

The day of our father's funeral was dank, mid-March. Ronald Reagan was president, the Cold War dragged on, *Star Wars* had made us all believe in forces we could not see. At that time Bexley was a town where people greeted each other by name at the post office or the bank and no one cared who had money and who did not. The doctor and the mill worker both visited my father for root canals, and both drank beer at the same drafty tavern. The dark Punnel River meandered along the east side of town and gave us something to do on summer days. This was still the era when a ninety-minute commute to New York City seemed absurd, and so the people who lived in Bexley, for the most part, worked in Bexley.

It was no surprise when the whole town turned out for our father's funeral. Hundreds, it seemed to me. Thousands. Noni led us through that awful day with an iron grip on two of our eight hands. She alternated, she did not play favorites. She had four children, and we all needed to feel the warmth of her palm.

Renee, the eldest of us, was eleven years old. Long, thin limbs, chestnut hair she wore in a single braid down her back. Even as a child, Renee exuded competence and self-containment, and at the funeral she was no different. She did not cry or make a fuss when her tights ran up the back. She helped Noni with us, the younger ones, and tried not to look directly at the casket.

After Renee came Caroline, who was eight, and then Joe, who was seven. Caroline was the fairest of us, with cheeks pink as bubble gum and hair that streaked blond in the summers. Joe was the boy, the only boy, with floppy hands and large feet and a stubborn right-side cowlick that he was forever flipping away from his face.

Joe and Caroline both had a tawny glow and quick, broad grins and were mistaken so frequently for twins that sometimes even they forgot there was a year between them.

And then came me, Fiona, the youngest, four years and eight months old on the day our father died. I was a pudgy child with soft, dimpled knees and unruly reddish hair that frizzed and flamed around my freckled face. My looks contrasted so vividly with those of my lithe, golden siblings that neighbors raised eyebrows. A tilt of the head, a shadow of gossipy doubt passing behind the eyes. Bexley, Connecticut, was like that. Working-class New Englanders starched in Puritan ethics. Their nails were dirty, but their souls were clean. After our father's death, the gossip stopped. Widowhood trumped the suggestion of infidelity. In her grief Noni became infallible, untouchable.

I remember very little about my father while he was alive, but the day we buried him I recall in great detail. At the cemetery a racket of crows flew above the casket. Our priest, Father Johns, delivered remarks in tones that rose and fell like a fitful storm; I could not understand a word of it. The ground was mushy with thaw, but crusts of snow still lurked beneath trees and along the shadowy side of the marble mausoleum that sat up on a low hill behind the grave site.

The mausoleum resembled a house: front steps, a peaked roof, the appearance of windows. It was so much larger and more impressive than the tidy headstone Noni had chosen for our father's grave. I was more interested in the mausoleum than I was in Father Johns, and so I ran away from the funeral, around the back of the crowd, and up the hill. The mausoleum stones were a deep gray, speckled with rain spots and age, significant and somber. Along the top I sounded out the name GARRISON H. CLARK. And then: BELOVED FATHER, HUSBAND, SON, BROTHER, COLLEAGUE, FRIEND.

Down the small hill, Father Johns spoke in a dull, deep voice. From a distance, finally, I could make out the words:

"Too soon . . ."

"Great burden . . ."

"Do not ask . . ."

Noni's head was bowed; she hadn't noticed my absence. Noni was Catholic and felt it in her knees that ached from all the praying but not, she realized that day, in her heart. This was the last time she would entertain the rituals of organized religion, the last day she would bow her head to the words of a man wearing white.

From my position on the hill, the mourners looked similar to the crows, only bigger and quieter, perched on the yellowish green of the spring grass that cut abruptly to the darkness of earth beside the casket. I thought of how little space there was on our father's stone. How unassuming it was, how meager, nothing like Garrison H. Clark's showy marble mausoleum. Standing beneath a stranger's name, gazing down at my father's funeral, for the first time that day I began to cry.

* * *

WE LIVED IN a yellow house, a three-story Colonial on a street lined with arching maples and oaks that threw down acorns in the spring and curling red and orange leaves in the fall. There was a steep, clattery staircase leading to the bedrooms upstairs and a basement that smelled faintly of mold and scorched sheets. In the backyard we had a metal swing set, and a sandbox used regularly by the neighborhood cats, and flower beds of nasturtium, lavender, gardenia, and clematis tended diligently by Noni.

After our father's funeral, people began to arrive at the yellow house. Everyone from church and others, too, people I had never seen before, people who knew my name and crouched to say it: "Fiona! Darling Fi!"

Our next-door neighbor, Mrs. Granger, took the plates covered in plastic wrap, the Tupperware containers in pastel shades, and bustled away to place them on the dining-room table. It struck me as odd to see Mrs. Granger perform this role, which seemed more properly to belong to Noni. But she remained on the orange couch, a white handkerchief moving from face to lap, face to lap, as strangers knelt before her, bowing their heads as though she bestowed upon them some sort of honor. She had never looked less like our mother.

The black of Noni's dress, the orange of the couch, and the white of the handkerchief reminded me of Halloween, and I felt a strange, empty excitement. A near hysteria. Plus all the food. Everywhere! Bowls of green grapes and Chex Mix and hard butterscotch candies and potato chips. Platters of ham-and-cheese sandwiches cut into neat triangles, cubes of watermelon that leaked pink juice onto the white tablecloth. I grabbed what I could and ate it quickly, unsure as to what was permitted here, what would be allowed.

It soon became clear that anything was allowed when your father has died. I spied Joe beneath a table with an entire bowl of hard candies and three cans of Coca-Cola. Caroline took off her tights and sprawled on the floor, singing to herself; Renee sat on a rocking chair and picked with great concentration at an elbow scab, ignoring the adult who stood before her, saying her name again and again in a calm, sympathetic voice.

I ran crazily around the room. I slapped various bottoms and did not apologize. I picked my nose and wiped my finger on the coffee table. No one stopped me or spoke to me or noticed me at all. The freedom was exhausting. I climbed unsteadily into Renee's lap. She wore a stiff black dress and black tights that she pulled at as I settled against her. With a shoeless toe, she rocked the chair back and forth, back and forth. The movement soothed me like a ship on the sea or a car on a bumpy road. This is how I would always imagine Renee: as a steadiness in times of turmoil.

I was on Renee's lap when it began. I don't know what triggered Joe's fury. I know only that he got hold of a fireplace poker, sooty at its tip, cast iron, heavy. About the length of a baseball bat.

Joe began in the dining room and moved steadily, ferociously through the house. He did not strike people, only things. There was the sound of wood splintering, glass shattering, dull thumps and sickening crashes as he brought the poker down again and again on a table, a chair, those many bowls and platters of food. The noise startled me, but I didn't cry. I listened. We all listened. Muted conversations and quiet tears gave way to a nervous, cowardly hush.

Crash. Into the living room he came. The crystal bowl full of hard candies, the porcelain table lamp with a linen shade, Noni's collection of delicate glassware cats—all crashed and shattered to the floor. Joe paused before the piano, and then he took aim at the photographs that stood on top: pictures of what we, the Skinners, had been until that day. Six together. Ellis and Antonia, Renee and Caroline and Joe and little Fiona. *Crash.* Six together on windswept New England beaches and before tinselly Christmas trees, grinning and mugging, arms over shoulders, holding hands. *Crash.* We were gap-toothed children and anonymous infants, full-cheeked within our swaddles. Our parents were proud and exhausted, bright, blameless, beautiful even in their polyester and plaid. *Crash.* All of it, gone.

I waited for someone to stop Joe, but no one did. The room

echoed with the noise of his destruction, grunts and strained inhalations, but otherwise there was silence. No one spoke. No one moved to stop him. Even Noni remained on the couch, her face pale and stricken. I wondered then, and I would wonder for the rest of my life: why did our mother not take the poker from Joe's grasp, wrap her arms around him, tell him that everything would be okay?

Finally Joe paused. At seven years old, he already stood four feet tall. A borrowed black suit showed his pale ankles and pale, knobby wrists. Plaster dust had settled in his hair, onto the shoulders of his suit, ghosting his skin. With a free hand, he wiped sweat from his forehead.

Then a man's voice called out. To this day I have no idea who spoke, but one could say he changed the course of Joe's life, of all our lives. "Antonia," the voice said. "Your boy's got quite an arm. It'd be a shame if he didn't play some baseball."

Someone chuckled. A child began to cry. With a dull thud, Joe dropped the poker. Renee removed me from her lap, and went to him. "Joe," she said. His hands shook, and she took one in her own. Caroline sprinted across the room in her bare feet and threw her arms around him. I followed, stumbling like a drunk from sleepiness and overstimulation, and wrapped myself around Joe's calves and feet.

I believe this was the moment when we each assumed responsibility for our brother, Joe. A lifelong obligation of love that each of us, for different reasons, would not fulfill. We would try: Renee in her studied, worrisome way; Caroline carelessly with great bursts of energy followed by distraction; and myself, quiet and tentative, assuming that Joe would never need me, not in the way that I needed him. Years later this assumption would prove to be wrong. But by then it would be too late.

* * *

THE FIRST THING Noni did after all the funeral food was eaten and we had returned to school was to inquire about Little League baseball for Joe. She could focus on one thing at a time, she thought. If she tried to fix everyone all at once, she would fail, she would fall to the floor and never get up again. It's important to take small steps. This was what Mrs. Cooperton, our neighbor the social worker, told her at the funeral. One day at a time. Cross one thing off your list at a time.

Noni worried that Joe would lack a strong male presence in his life, and that worry eclipsed all others. Her inquiries returned the name of a baseball coach, Marty Roach, who was famous in Bexley. For twenty-three years he'd taught young boys the nature of teamwork and the beauty of a well-thrown ball. His office, Noni had heard, was festooned with birthday cards sent by former players, men now, who had moved on to cities and careers but harbored an enduring affection for old Coach Marty. This was what Noni wanted. Someone who would endure for Joe.

"Looks like the roster's already full," the man on the phone told her. "But for you, Mrs. Skinner, we can fit one more."

Noni brought us all to that first practice. The team met at the Bexley High School playing field, which was rough, chewed-up grass bordered to the north by a chain-link fence. Beyond the fence lay thick scrub, densely packed bushes, brambles, and spindly pines that eventually thickened and stretched into the forest that covered Packensatt Peak, the closest thing to a mountain that Bexley could claim. High-school kids liked to jump the fence and wander into this wilderness to smoke and drink and light fires and have faltering, unforgettable sex. Noni looked across the field to the tangled trees and saw a defensive line holding steady against an encroaching disorder.

On the field a dozen boys stood in a row, a loose knot of fathers beside them. The air smelled of wet leaves and sweetness from the mulch that sat in huge piles around the field's southern perimeter, spring preparation for later plantings. Off to the side was Marty Roach. Maybe it was the suggestion of the surname, but I had never before seen a man who so closely resembled an insect. He was short and stocky, with burly shoulders, a dark, ample mustache, and large meat-hook hands. Sparse black hair striped the white dome of his scalp, and I thought that at any moment antennae would sprout from his forehead. He looked designed to survive in hardy conditions, to find forgotten crumbs in a clean kitchen. Noni shook his hand uneasily.

"Hiya, Joe," he said, leaning down to look my brother in the eye. "Ready to play?" He inclined his head toward the row of boys.

Joe nodded once and stepped away from Noni, took his place in line.

"Now, boys," Marty said, stretching his arms out wide. "Today is our first day as a team. We are all learning our roles. As teammates you will come to rely on one another. You will come to know one another like brothers." Coach Marty paused. "But for today let's just have some fun."

We sat in the stands with Noni and watched as boys threw balls to their fathers with loose, inelegant gestures. Marty stood alone with Joe and showed him how to hold a bat, swing evenly from the waist, trap a ball within the webbed leather of his glove. After a spell the boys divided into teams and began to scrimmage. Joe positioned himself in center field, just behind second base, where he looked both in the thick of it and dismally alone. Poor Joe, I thought. He stepped from one foot to the other, rubbed his nose, took off his hat and put it on again. The other players laughed or talked or waved to their fathers. Oh, poor Joe.

Batters took their turns at the plate. There were futile swings, dropped bats, tears. Finally a round-bellied blond stepped up. He was short but powerful, clearly experienced. A father lobbed a gentle pitch, the boy swung hard, and—*crack*—the ball arced forward into the field. And then, all at once, it was Joe like a toy on a spring who came up high to catch the ball. The force of the ball hitting Joe's glove—*whomp*—took me by surprise.

The blond boy pulled up from running, a look of shock and dismay on his face.

"Wow! Great catch!" Marty called to Joe.

We clapped wildly, my sisters and Noni and I. Joe gave us a small wave. He smiled. Beside me on the bleachers, I felt Noni expand in the way of a hungry lung filling at last with air. She waved back at Joe.

*　*　*

AFTER BASEBALL BEGAN for Joe, one worry relaxed but others rose up to replace it.

Sometimes after dinner I heard Noni muttering. "One thing at a time," she would say. "One thing. One thing."

The casseroles stopped appearing on our doorstep. Our teachers stopped asking how we were holding up and gazing at us with grave, kindly faces. I slept soundly now. Joe and Renee, too. Only Caroline still suffered nightmares, terrifying dreams of darkness and a child with evil eyes. But after a spell, we became accustomed to Caroline's bad dreams, and so it seemed, in a way, a return to normalcy.

One thing at a time. One thing.

Sometimes Noni yelled and threw objects at the wall—pencils and books and staplers. Papers littered the kitchen table and the study and Noni's bedroom. At night Noni worried over a big gray calculator. We wandered in and kissed her and asked her to put us to bed, but she would say, "In a minute, just give me a minute," and so we put ourselves to bed. We fell asleep atop the covers to the sound of Noni punching numbers with a jagged index finger, sharp and insistent.

Three months after our father died, we moved from our yellow house to a gray one-story ranch six miles away. This house had no stairs or swing set or much of a backyard, only a strip of gravel and a rectangle of sparse, yellowed grass that backed against a tall wooden fence. In the front yard sat a single tree, a large, humbling locust that threw a rough blanket of shade over the house. We loved our yellow house and cried more bitterly for this loss than we had for our father.

"We have no money," Noni explained. "I'm sorry. Your daddy never told me we were out of money."

It was June when we moved. School was out. Low-relief mounds of mosquito bites marked my legs, red and itchy and bleeding from my attentions. On that sticky, heavy day, we all rode with Noni in the long front seat of the U-Haul. Joe sat closest to the window, and he alone craned his neck to watch the yellow house disappear behind us.

We helped Noni unpack the towels and sheets, the plates and silverware, our summer clothes, our books. Renee and Caroline would now share a room. Joe was down the hall, closest to the bathroom. I would sleep in a small, tucked-away space that had a low ceiling and no windows. Our old things looked wrong in the new rooms. At any moment I expected someone—our father perhaps—to pop out from behind a door and say *Surprise!* or *What a hoot!*, which were things our father used to say.

For dinner that first night, we sat on the couch and ate spaghetti with sauce from a jar. Accidentally we had arranged ourselves by age: Renee beside Caroline beside Joe beside me. I was wearing my nightgown, a short one, and the nubby orange upholstery itched against the backs of my thighs. The skin around our mouths was stained pink from the tomato sauce.

"Kids," Noni said. She was standing in front of the couch. Unpacked boxes lined the walls. In the kitchen dirty dishes filled the sink.

"Yes?" said Renee.

"Kids," Noni said again. "I'm feeling tired. Very tired." Her hair hung lank around her face, her eyes gazed out from deep inside her head. The bones around her neck were thin and pronounced. They looked delicate, easy to break.

"I need some rest," Noni said. "Okay?" She gazed from one of us to the other, her eyebrows up.

Caroline, Joe, and I all turned to Renee: she was the eldest, she was the one who knew how to answer our mother.

"Don't worry, Noni," said Renee. "I can do it."

Noni nodded once as though something had been decided. She bent to each of us and hugged us, kissed us on our heads. There was a tickle of hair against my cheek, and then she disappeared down the long, dark hall to her bedroom.

Our mother did not emerge for three days. Then six. Then four. Then six again. This continued. Occasionally she would appear to cook dinner. Or ask us about our day. Or preside over a cut knee, a sunburned shoulder, a snotty nose. But primarily she rested in her room, door closed, curtains drawn, lights off. A bubble of darkened quiet that we feared to disrupt. How long did it last? Renee later claimed three years, give or take. Joe put it closer to two. When we were older, we called this period "the Pause," but back then we had no words to describe it. We pretended that it was okay. This was temporary, we told ourselves. We must wait for Noni to finish resting. We must wait patiently for her to return.

Chapter 2

THAT FIRST SUMMER we went feral. Joe and I became wild things, twigs in our hair, skin brown and dirty and scraped. Renee and Caroline tried to remain more respectable, more mature, but they, too, bore the marks of neglect and adventure. The house was never clean. We pulled what we needed from the cardboard boxes but did not unpack them fully. We played games, built forts, constructed castles that stayed up for days and then scattered underfoot as we played indoor tag or wrestled or fought. We slept in the clothes we wore all day, we did not brush our teeth, we bathed only when we began to smell ourselves or when Renee stripped off our clothes, pushed us under the shower, and turned on the tap. We ate food with our hands straight from the refrigerator or from the box of groceries that arrived every Friday, delivered by the stock boy, Jimmy, from the Bexley corner store. The food we received was odd or close to spoiling—leftovers, we came to see, unsellable. Charity. We were often hungry. We were always barefoot.

Joe and I explored our new neighborhood: only six miles from our old house, but it felt foreign. Another state, another country. There were people with brown skin, head scarves, tattoos. The houses were small, and domestic life spilled from windows and doors in ways that would have been unthinkable in our old neighborhood. In front yards men sat on beach chairs and drank from dull brown bottles. Women yelled at their children, who ran naked through a flicking sprinkler. A teenage girl blew smoke in practiced rings up toward the summer sky.

In twenty years Bexley would be deemed a commuter town and new expensive homes, new box stores, would arrive, but in 1981 it was small, forgotten, besieged by inflation and unemployment. On Bexley's east side sat an abandoned mill where industrial furniture was once made for colleges and hospitals. Decades before, the company brought in workers from the city, settled them in cheap houses outfitted with the company's own cheap wares. Now the mill stood empty, brooding, a sprawling, static octopus with graffitied tentacles of red brick and cracked windows and one tall, grimy smokestack for a head. All around the perimeter were scattered raw wooden boards, chairs with stuffing torn from seat cushions, tables with splintered stumps instead of legs.

Before the Pause, Noni often drove past the building, and always I would gaze at it with the fear and delight of a cowardly voyeur. During the Pause, Noni no longer drove, and so we had no occasion to pass the factory. But sometimes in bed at night, I imagined it: moonlight hitting the broken windowpanes, rats and cats and raccoons nosing through the interior, biting one another, fighting, scratching the furniture, defecating in empty rooms. I imagined a busy darkness, a dismantling that must be carried out under cover of night. The mysteries of the factory seemed to me similar to the mystery of Noni. Inside, invisible forces were at work, and they were full of a secret rage.

Our friends receded that summer. We couldn't walk to the old neighborhood. Noni had instructed us to use the telephone only for emergencies. And besides, it soon became clear that our friends had returned to their normal lives, lives where groceries must be bought, dinners cooked, television shows watched, where loved ones were bothersome but healthy and alive. We reminded them of the constant threat of calamity. How quickly it could all go to pieces.

* * *

ON THE MORNING of my fifth birthday, Noni emerged to bake me a cake. We all watched as she lined up the ingredients on the kitchen counter: an ancient tin of baking powder, a wrapped square of hardened brown sugar. We did not volunteer to help. It seemed too risky. To us our mother was an exotic animal, a gazelle perhaps, that might startle if we moved too fast, spoke too loudly.

There was the soft drop of the sifted flour, the crack of the eggs, the steady buzz of the mixer, and then—*ping*—out of the oven came the cake, all golden and puffed up like my own private sun. We each ate a thick slab of cake, Noni, too, and then she kissed me and walked again down the hall, the thready hem of her bathrobe skimming the floor.

She closed the door to her bedroom.

I burst into tears.

Renee, Caroline, and Joe exchanged looks. Caroline hid a smile with her hand.

"Fiona," Renee said, "Joe's got a surprise."

Out the front door Joe disappeared, and when he returned, in his arms was a small rabbit. It struggled with kicking surges to escape, but Joe held it close to his chest.

"Happy Birthday, Fi," he said.

My heart surged with excitement as Joe brought the rabbit to me. Gently he placed it into my arms. I stroked its soft fur, its beating heart a rapid tapping against my palm. The fur was black and gray, except for white around the rabbit's eyes and on its stomach. The rabbit looked very scared, but Joe talked in a slow voice and I used my softest hands, my gentlest touch.

"Where did she come from?" I asked.

Joe whispered, "A secret."

Outside in the backyard, Joe helped me set up an enclosure of sorts with some broken-down boxes for a fence, a wooden crate propped on its side for shelter, and one cereal bowl for water, another for food. I named the rabbit Celeste after the elephant queen in the Babar books.

Every morning I fed my rabbit carrots and wilted lettuce and the small green apples that fell from the trees in the park. Celeste was not a delicate eater. Her nose moved together with her mouth in a grasping motion, and the food vanished quickly. I loved the quick motion of her eyes. I loved her long legs with their loping, circular movement like she was riding a bicycle. I loved her smell of musk and clean, fresh grass and even the dry, perfectly shaped pellets of dung that sat in tidy piles around her pen.

Joe loved Celeste, too. For weeks we studied her. We determined what she liked best to eat, where she most enjoyed a scratch, when she was most amenable to a cuddle, and when she preferred to play. Joe liked to feed her long blades of grass, the ends disappearing smoothly into her mouth as though she slurped spaghetti.

We doted on Celeste for one month, maybe two, and then she vanished. When I arrived one morning to feed her as I always did, her pen was empty. It was August, the days slow to start, humidity thick as fudge. Joe helped me search the bushes in the yard and took me down the street, calling "Celeste! Celeste!" until the dew burned off and we were both sweaty, pink-faced, still wearing our pajamas.

I wept as Joe carried me home.

"Fiona, listen," Joe said. "Celeste had to go back to live with her rabbit brothers and sisters." He set me down in the front yard. My tears had wet his pajama top. Stripes of snot glistened on his shoulder.

"Really?" I said. I hadn't considered this possibility.

"Have you ever heard the term 'reproduce like rabbits'?" said Joe. "All rabbits have so many brothers and sisters! The most of any species." Joe was eight and wise in every single way.

I stopped crying. I believed my brother. All at once I felt ashamed for keeping Celeste imprisoned for so many weeks. I was glad that now she had returned home. It would be a terrible thing, I thought, to be separated from your siblings.

* * *

MY GRIEF FOR Celeste lasted exactly five days. Then Joe brought me to the pond.

It was another hot, sticky morning, and I lay on the couch reading *War of the Worlds* and imagining where I would hide from an alien invasion. I was a precocious and prolific reader, often stealing Renee's books or ones from the cardboard boxes we had yet to unpack, generally preferring to exist within my own made-up world rather than the real one that surrounded me.

"Come here," Joe said, standing in the doorway. "I want to show you something."

I narrowed my eyes, examining his face, and then put the book down.

He led me along the sidewalk, through a neighbor's backyard, over a low fence, and down a steep, wooded hill. The going was rough—no real path, heavy vegetation, and fallen tree trunks. Shifting spots of sun played with my eyes, and I tripped and fell.

Joe helped me up, then swung me onto his shoulders, and I rode like this down the hill, ducking sharp branches, holding tight with my legs around his shoulders, my arms around his neck.

Finally the woods thinned, and Joe lifted me down. Before us was a shallow, sun-speckled brook that twisted through the trees.

"Ta-da!" Joe said, as though he were a magician and this his finest trick. It was cool here, calm, the water talking quietly to itself, the fizz of dragonflies and the airy whine of mosquitoes.

"Let's stay," I said.

For the next few hours, we played on the rocks beside the brook. We did not speak. We threw stones. We crouched and watched the spindly-legged water bugs skitter across the surface. We fashioned fishing poles from sticks and bits of long grass tied to the ends, but we had no bait and the quick, darting minnows ignored our efforts, instead flashing silver as they poked and picked algae from the rocks like housewives choosing melons. We walked downstream, the brook widening as it went. The sound of rushing water grew louder, and then the woods cleared and before us shimmered a small green pond set like a jewel amid the trees and the long cattails. On the far side was a dam with water rushing beyond it in turbulent free fall.

Duck grass and bunches of loosestrife grew along the perimeter, lily pads, too, with their hand-size leaves and stiff flowers like divination rods. There was a low grassy bank, perfect for sitting, and a small beach area of gray sand and pebbles. No one else was here, but I saw evidence of activity: a battered little rowboat overturned on the grass, a crushed soda can, a few orange cigarette butts, one marked with the dull red of lipstick. It was the most beautiful place I'd ever seen.

"Joe!" I called. "Can we go in?"

Joe didn't answer, just pulled off his shirt and jumped from the bank into the water. I stripped off my sundress and tiptoed across the sand. My feet, ankles, knees, thighs entered the water, and the cold advanced with an excruciating certainty that was lovely and painful all at once. Beyond the narrow strip of sand, the bottom of the pond was thick with mud and slime. I felt it squirt between my toes, my feet sinking deeper with each step. The cold clutched at my hips, my stomach, my bare chest, and it was only then I remembered that I could not swim.

My feet lost their grip on the slippery bottom. My head slid under smoothly, silently. My mind registered only surprise: at the cold, at the heavy silence, at the quality of the underwater light—green and glancing gold—and the fine algae that drifted like mossy snowflakes in the water. I waved my arms, and the algae spun crazily, an explosion of green particles unburdened by gravity. In the distance I made out the bulging eyes and long, spiked mustache of a catfish.

I wanted to stay here. It was beautiful and strange in a way that the gray house and our new life were not. That life was only strange, only coarse and dirty. Underwater in the pond was the first time I felt wonder.

And then Joe's strong hand gripped my shoulder and he hauled me up out of the gold and out of the wonder. I inhaled, and the cold water invaded me. I thought I'd swallowed a minnow, a whole school of minnows, and their sharp silver bodies cut deeply into the interior spaces of my nose and chest.

"Fiona!" Joe cried. I coughed and sputtered as Joe pulled me onto the grass. I lay on the bank heaving and then vomited in one satisfying, emptying gasp.

The look on Joe's face was terrible. "Fi, are you okay? I'm so sorry.

This was so stupid. So stupid. Noni never taught you to swim, did she?" He hit his forehead with his hand.

"I'm okay." My voice was a rough croak. I cleared it and repeated, "Joe, I'm *okay*." It felt odd, me reassuring Joe who so often reassured me. The pain in my chest expanded at the sight of my brother in such distress. "Joe, you saved me," I said.

Joe had already started to grow into himself. In one short season, he'd become a standout on his Little League team. His hands were huge, his feet huge, too, his shoulders skinny and boyish but broad, his waist narrow. He was shaped like a kite trailing streamers of pond water as he stood above me. He looked at me with his dark blue eyes and slicked-back hair, and his face transformed into a sort of relief.

"Save you?" he said. "I guess I did." And Joe smiled.

*   *   *

THAT SUMMER JOE taught me how to swim. Every day we walked to the pond with towels and swimsuits and sandwiches. We started slowly, Joe's hands on the small of my back, my arms circling, legs kicking up a flurry of water as I struggled to suspend myself. It took one week, and then I was floating on my back without assistance, my arms outstretched like the points of a star, hair spread around me.

"Next, dog-paddle," Joe directed, and I knew that he was proud of me. I was not a quick study. I did not take easily to physical activity and was disposed to fall back on complaints of a sprained ankle, a shortness of breath.

One of the many miracles of the pond was that here, in the water, my physical self disappeared. The feeling was delicious. As I tilted my head back atop the surface of the water, a cold rushing filled my ears and I became weightless. This was a sensation I would remember some twenty years later, when I at last would lose the weight that since childhood had circled my body like a sleeping python. *Unencumbered* is the word I would use in poems to describe it. And also: *Untethered. Unrestricted. Expansive. Free.* I felt it first in the pond with Joe beside me in the water.

Renee soon turned suspicious. "Where are you guys going?" she asked one morning. She walked to Joe and sniffed his hair. "You smell fishy," she said.

Renee and Caroline spent their days primarily indoors in front of the fan, where it was cool. They braided each other's hair and made papier-mâché bowls and beads and masks by wrapping gluey strips of newspaper around the various items they wished to replicate. When they were tired of making things, they watched *The Brady Bunch* or *The A-Team* on rerun or sometimes a program that showed a man painting oil landscapes, his voice so calm that it stupefied them. They learned from this man nothing about painting, only that it was possible to spend your entire day in a sort of daze, half awake, half asleep, and at the end of it to feel jumpy and restless but entirely worn out from heat and boredom.

Renee sniffed Joe's hair again. "Take us," she said.

Joe and I led our sisters down the road, down the steep hill, along the bank of the brook through the woods until we reached the pond. The day was very hot, and the mere sight of the dark water cooled me off. The rushing sound operated as a hush on us all. Maples and slender birches arched over the pond. The current was weak and nearly invisible. Over the dam the water spilled like a silver cloth pulled through a wringer.

Renee let out a whistle. "Awesome," she said.

Immediately I resented the presence of my sisters. This was our place, mine and Joe's, and their intrusion altered the feel of it. Caroline wore a bikini and spread her towel in a sprinkling of sun. Renee began to patrol the bank in search of frogs. Yesterday I'd seen a large one, a bullfrog with a call like a rock dropping down a well, but I didn't tell Renee. I let her search.

"Fi, let's practice swimming," said Joe. I scowled at him, but he lifted his eyebrows, and his face said, *This is still our place. We can share with the others, it doesn't change what we have found.*

And so I relented. I let Joe place me into the water, stomach down. His hands buoyed me up, and I kicked my legs, circled my arms. I didn't swim that day or the next, but it happened soon, that perfect moment when my body stopped being mere weight and became like the water itself: fluid, joyful, effortless. It was Joe who made this happen, Joe who clapped the loudest as I swam from bank to bank.

Over the course of that summer, Caroline and I developed a game. Inside the gray house, we rarely played together, but outside at the pond the rules shifted, expectations changed. She and I would scour the brook for water-rough pieces of broken glass or other strange treasures. The rocky bottom was full of odd detritus, perhaps castoffs from the old furniture mill or wayward bits from the town dump. Once we found a large silver spoon, then a crusty broken bicycle chain, then a small green bottle. We would arrange these treasures carefully and make up elaborate stories about their provenance and the lengths to which their previous owners would go to reclaim them. Before the Pause, Noni raised us on fairy tales and fantastic stories. Princesses and queens, mothers and trolls, a dashing prince, salvation, and a perfect everlasting love. The pond offered the perfect backdrop for magical possibility.

For weeks Caroline and I discussed the owner of the spoon,

a wily queen from a distant, frozen place who became angry at her daughter and threw the spoon at the poor girl. The daughter ducked, and the spoon sailed over her defenseless head, across nations, oceans, time, and landed here in our brook.

"And then the daughter disappeared," Caroline said solemnly. "The queen believes the girl's spirit is hidden inside the spoon. She searches, but she can't find it. The queen vows to search forever. Until her dying day."

We gazed into the tarnished silver of the great spoon's bowl and saw the barest dull reflection of our own faces staring back.

*   *   *

IT WAS THE second summer of the Pause when our game ended. This was when we first met Nathan Duffy. One morning we tramped down the hill and heard splashing, giggles, whoops. We emerged from the woods to see a gaggle of kids, each brown from the sun and shaggy-haired, different heights and genders but all variations on the same essential theme. Nathan was one of six siblings, looked after during the summers by their babysitter, Angela, who long ago had come to the pond when she was a kid. Now Angela spread out a flowered king sheet and sat smack in the middle with a crossword as the Duffy siblings swam, played, ate, and fought around her. Nathan was middle of the pack—two older brothers, three younger sisters—and the quietest. I hadn't even noticed him until later that day when he appeared beside our blanket.

Nathan crouched on his haunches in the grass and asked Caroline about her book.

"Is that Nancy Drew?" he said. "Do you read the Hardy Boys, too? I like *The Tower Treasure* best." It was overcast that day, a dull, heavy sky. Thunder was coming, rain too.

Caroline lifted her eyes from the book and studied Nathan.

They were both long-legged and skinny, both dirty blond, both bronzed and squint-eyed in the sun. Nathan wore gold glasses that matched his hair. His gaze was careful and serious.

During the Pause, Caroline was the one who missed our parents the most. She cried easily, silently, at the kitchen table while we ate breakfast or later in the living room when we played Monopoly, even if she was winning. Her bad dreams raged for nights, then subsided, then took hold again without any apparent pattern or cause. She'd awake screaming and crying, and none of us could comfort her, not even Renee.

Now she coolly returned Nathan's gaze and shrugged her shoulders. "Hardy Boys are okay," she replied. "But Nancy is braver."

Nathan tilted his head, considering. With his long, careful fingers, he picked at the edge of our quilt and at a collection of small, warm pebbles I had gathered and placed on a leaf.

"Wanna swim?" he said suddenly. He moved quick as a darting minnow, jumping away from us, running along the bank, from one side of the pond to the other, in and out of the water, atop the dam (although it was slippery and Angela yelled at him to come off), up a tree and down. At last he returned to Caroline. He shook his wet head at her, and she angrily slammed her book shut and stalked off to sit on the sand. But she looked back at him. I saw the glance, her interest in this pale, quick boy clear on her face.

It wasn't long before we learned all about Nathan. He had a mother named Jeanette, a father named Cyrus, and five siblings who became known to us as a single unit: DouglasTerryMaddyEmilyJen. We called them the Goats, because their last name was Duffy, which reminded us of the Billy Goats Gruff from the fairy tale, and also because there was something goatlike about them, with their long, curious faces and all that shaggy hair. Each of them appeared strong-willed, utterly confident, fighting loudly with the others over questions of Eggo preparation and volcanic eruptions and Michael Jackson song lyrics.

The day after we first met Nathan Duffy, we met Ace McAllister. Ace came crashing down the path to the pond wearing head-to-toe camouflage and holding a BB gun.

"Bang, bang, bang!" he yelled, startling us from our games and books.

"That's Ace," Nathan declared without emotion as Ace pretended to shoot him again and again.

Ace was short and thick in the torso, with heavy limbs and broad features. He had an abundance of dark, shiny hair that fell into his eyes. He and Nathan were not friends, but they were neighbors and only one year apart in age, and so their mothers had thrust them together since their earliest days of playground visits and birthday parties.

"Angela, gotcha!" Ace yelled, and directed his attention toward the babysitter. Angela flapped a hand at him but did not lift her eyes from her magazine. Once she'd been his babysitter, too, and brought him on summer afternoons to the pond, but she'd quit to work for the Duffys. Now Ace's parents left him alone with a ten-dollar bill, a house key, and instructions to keep out of trouble.

Within days it became clear that Ace was the wildest of us all. He cannonballed off the dam into the pond and whooped so loudly that even Nathan's big brother Terry told him to quiet down. Nathan was in sixth grade, Ace in fifth at a private day school in Greenwich called Pierpont Academy. We all went to public school, and the idea of Pierpont—with its uniforms and lacrosse fields—struck me as impressively mature and intellectual, but Ace went there only because his parents had money and they didn't know what else to do with him. He boasted that he'd been kicked out of a fancy boarding school in New Hampshire, suspended at public school, and Pierpont Academy was the only place that would take him. He talked of fights won, beers drunk, cigarettes smoked. We doubted the truth of these claims but listened nonetheless to the stories. He often brought his BB gun to the pond, or a loud boom box he claimed to have stolen. He captured frogs and crickets and once a small green garter snake, keeping each for a spell in a shoe box. I suspected he longed to poke these animals, or hurt them, but he didn't dare with us there.

When Ace learned that Joe played baseball, he began to treat him with more interest and more aggression. He began to say things like, "Look, here comes Joe DiMaaaaggio," drawing out the *ah* as a croak. But there was also the slightest hint of deference, of awe. Joe was one year younger than Ace but taller, stronger, with an athlete's calm.

Joe regarded Ace cautiously. They were friendly, but, I believed at the time, they would never be friends. Ace was an unwanted but unavoidable summer accessory, and we accepted him as we accepted the humidity and the mosquitoes, with only mild complaint.

The six of us—me and Joe, Nathan and Ace, Caroline and Renee—formed a gang of sorts. We weren't always together, not every day, but most days we swam at the pond or played Twenty Questions on the grass or watched TV at Nathan's house while the Goats milled around and slammed doors and talked on the phone in loud, amused voices. In the early evening, once the sun began to drop, we would play baseball at the park. We always handicapped Joe—*Only your left hand! No mitt! Close your eyes!*—because otherwise the games were short and humiliating. We also wanted to see what Joe could do, and so we pushed him to perform in wilder, more ridiculous scenarios. He did so gamely, laughing, always succeeding at the trials we set. Sometimes we sat in the stands and watched as Ace pitched ball after ball and Joe hit each long and high, a dreamy, lazy smile on his face. An effortless look, as though hitting the ball like that required only the smallest piece of himself.

"Your brother will be famous," Nathan said to me one afternoon in his careful, considered way. "He's already like a superstar."

I don't remember replying. I might have said, *Of course.* I might have simply shrugged. It seemed so self-evident, there was no need for a reply. Joe *was* already a superstar. Back then did he know what people expected of him? At the field the look on his face was always dreamy, his movements casual, but it must have cost him to play like that. To give us the spectacle we craved.

* * *

IN THE LAST week of the summer of 1983, Joe and Ace fought. It was because of me, or rather what had been done to me. It was about, of all things, my rabbit, Celeste.

"You live in that gray house, right?" Ace asked me one afternoon. We'd been at the pond all day, and my skin was itchy and sticky from swimming and drying in the sun and swimming again. I felt slightly bored, definitely hungry, wondering what Renee would make us for dinner and whether the book I'd dropped accidentally into the water would dry in time for me to finish it tonight. I was six years old, chubby, pink-faced, and never without a book in hand. Recently I had started to keep lists of words in the black-and-white composition notebooks Renee used for school. They were not poems, not yet, merely catalogs of my feelings and sensations, things I had seen, events that had transpired.

Green, gold, fish, water, sun, grass, sisters, brother, swimming, free, warm, soft.

Ace looked at me now with intense interest. "The gray house?" he prodded.

I looked up from my notebook and nodded.

"Do you have a pet rabbit?"

I put down my pencil and closed the book. "She ran away," I explained, "to be with her brothers and sisters."

Ace began to laugh, great big peals. He held his stomach for effect and rolled over onto his back.

"Run away?" he said. "She didn't run away. I took that rabbit."

"But why?" I asked. I wasn't angry yet, only confused.

"She was a mighty fine rabbit. Mighty. Fine." Ace licked his lips with a slurping sound.

"Oh, stop it, Ace," Nathan called. He was swimming, treading water as he listened. "Don't tease Fiona."

"I'm not teasing! I'm just telling the truth! 'Don't tease the girls, Ace. Don't tell lies. Be a good boy like me.'" The last he said in a mocking, high voice. Nathan didn't respond. He ducked his head beneath the water.

"You didn't," I said to Ace. "You did *not*."

"I didn't eat her, no. I'm just kidding. What I did was I took her over to the railroad tracks, down the other side of the hill, and played with her a little. I just left her there. On the tracks, I mean."

Brown freckles marked the high point of Ace's cheeks. They seemed to darken as he spoke.

"I tried to tie her to the track, put a rope around her leg," he said. "I mean, so I could go back for her, bring her back to your house, but I think she must have gotten away. There was only a little bit of fur when I went to find her. Just a teeny scrap."

My face grew hot, a pressure rose behind my eyes. I believed that Ace was lying, that he wanted to see me cry, and I didn't want to give him the satisfaction. But I couldn't help myself. I remembered Celeste and her clean fur, her twitching triangular nose.

Soft, lovely, new, alone.

Joe saw me crying. "What did you do to her?" he called across the grass to Ace. Joe's voice was sharp. He was playing solitaire, the cards spread in front of him, half a deck still in his hands.

I wanted to say, *I'm fine, Joe,* but the words wouldn't come. The humid air moved thickly through my lungs. And then Ace answered for me. He repeated everything he'd told me about Celeste and the train tracks. Joe's face went still as Ace spoke. I remembered how Joe had loved the rabbit, too.

"You're lying," he said to Ace.

"I'm not," Ace answered. Now everyone was listening. Renee had stayed home that day to bake a pie from the raspberries that grew like weeds in the alley behind our house, but the rest of us were there: me, Caroline, Nathan, and two of the Goats. At the pond the lack of parental oversight made us wild in one way but conservative in another. We did not swear or fight with one another. We avoided conflict. Only Ace seemed intent on something more destructive. This would be true his entire life.

Ace was shorter than Joe, but heavier and thicker. He played no sports; he seemed to exist only on cans of Orange Crush and cellophane packages of Hostess doughnuts he would eat in three bites, powdered sugar ghosting his mouth.

"What are you going to do?" Ace said. "Huh, Joe? Big strong Joe?"

We watched Joe: he was very tan, which made his eyes more blue and his hair more gold than brown. All the swimming and hiking up and down the hill had melted away his baby fat. You could see in Joe now the beginning of his broad, muscular shoulders, the athlete's chest and stomach that years later he would rub with baby oil as a lifeguard at the Bexley rec center's pool, surrounded always by a cadre of high-school girls who looked like women.

But today he was still a boy. At his eyebrow one slender muscle twitched.

Joe did what I remembered instantly Noni doing from before the Pause, before our father's death, when she was still our mother and engaged in the task of taking care of us. Joe counted down.

"If you don't take it back in five seconds," Joe said, "you'll be sorry." He swallowed and flicked his cowlick back from his eyes. "Five. Four. Three. Two—"

Before Joe could finish, Ace turned and ran. His legs carried him up away from the bank and around to the slippery top of the dam where the water rushed over concrete gummed with green algae. He pranced along the top. "Come and get me, Joe," he said.

Joe didn't go to the top of the dam. None of us did. Renee told us it was too dangerous, we could fall, and we believed her. We all watched Ace jump on one leg, then the other, taunting Joe, daring him. Ace's feet were wrapped in silver as the water rushed over them.

"Come on, Joe," he said. "You pussy."

And then Ace slipped. One foot dropped over the far side of the dam. He landed heavily on a knee, which cracked with a sickening sound just before he slid off. For an instant Ace's hands hung grasping onto the lip, water pushing into his face, but the force of it was too strong and the hands disappeared.

This happened so quickly that we barely registered his absence. Ace was there on the dam, and then he was gone. The still, hot air remained the same, the sound of rushing water, the buzz of a sapphire-blue dragonfly that started and stopped across the surface of the pond. It seemed possible that Ace would return, pop up again, that the thrust of those seconds would unfurl and bring us back to the start. But of course that can never happen.

Ace fell, and no one spoke, and then Joe ran up the path and into the woods surrounding the pond and down the hill on the other side. I heard the crash of underbrush, the thud of his feet. The drop on the other side of the dam was the distance of a three-story building to the ground. The pool into which the water fell was dark, rocky along the edges, and who knew how deep? The pool swiftly became a thin, roiling stream bordered by thick undergrowth and tall, shaggy trees. For us the pond marked the edge of our world. Beyond the pond, below the dam, stretched an unknown wilderness.

Joe called for Ace, his voice growing weaker as he traveled farther into the woods. Nathan began to follow Joe, and I stood, ready to join them, but Nathan told me harshly to sit down. "Joe and I can do it," he said. "Girls stay here." And then he, too, was gone, bounding into the brush.

Five hours after Ace fell from the dam, Joe stepped through the door of the gray house. He was sweaty, feet muddy, face and hands scratched from branches and brambles. Ace was fine, he told us, fished from the stream by Joe about half a mile from the pond. He'd swallowed some water, Joe said, and had been struggling when Joe found him.

"Was he drowned?" I asked.

"Not exactly," Joe said. "He puked up half the pond once I pulled him out." Joe was smiling, but his face was tight and nervous.

Ace's ankle had twisted in the fall, the knee was grazed raw and swollen, but he was able to walk with Joe and Nathan half carrying him back up to the road and to his house. Only Ace's mother had been home, Joe reported, a woman none of us had ever met. She was tall and skinny, and she didn't look like Ace one bit. She was sitting on a flowered couch and smoking a cigarette when they pushed open the front door. Ace's house looked shiny on the inside, and Joe had been afraid to touch anything or even to place his feet on the pale carpet and so they'd hovered half in, half out of the door, holding Ace.

Ace's mother blew smoke from her nostrils like a dragon before asking, "What happened this time?"

Joe and Nathan deposited Ace onto the couch and then waited as Ace's mother poked and prodded at the ankle.

"Just a sprain," she declared, and gave Ace a bag of frozen peas and the TV remote control. She pulled two crisp dollar bills from her wallet, handed one to Joe, one to Nathan, and said, "Thank you for bringing him home. Run along now." So they did.

It was another week before we saw Ace again. One morning he returned to the pond with a slight limp, his left ankle wrapped in a putty-colored bandage, the laces of his left sneaker loose. He sat beside me on a towel.

"Mom says I can't go swimming for another week," Ace told me. He pulled a deck of cards from his pocket. "Rummy?" he asked.

Soon it became clear that Ace had changed. The challenge that he'd worn like a badge was gone. The bite of aggression between Ace and Joe evaporated. In its place was a new, cautious friendship. Joe treated Ace with kindness and some pity, almost as though he were a much younger child. Ace followed Joe, he courted him with a sort of stifled awe. Finally Ace understood, I thought, that Joe was special.

This continued for the rest of the summer, until we arrived back at our different schools, each of us locked in our own grade and class and routine. Sometimes during the winter, I'd catch a glimpse of Ace at the grocery store with his mother or gliding through town in the blue BMW his father drove, sleek and shiny as a slow-moving bullet. Always Ace looked small and shrunken beside his parents, who were both tall, graceful people. Later I understood how every day Ace disappointed his parents simply because of who he was: unambitious, easily distracted, petty-minded. Even then I recognized the signs of that disappointment: the way his mother did not look directly at her son. The way his father walked a pace in front. I found myself feeling sorry for Ace. I found myself unable to recall the Ace that once had seemed like a threat.

Chapter 3

THE PAUSE COULD not go on forever. We knew this. There were dangers. We were children alone, the four of us, without protection or instruction, and while Renee played the part of quasi mother, she buckled under the weight. *Unsustainable,* I wrote later. *Unsupportable, hazardous, perilous, unsafe.*

The year that Renee turned thirteen, she grew high, round nubs on her chest and hair that went lank and greasy just days after her bath. She exuded a musty, earthy smell and was inhabited by a new atmosphere of churning activity like a spirit possessed. We had all seen the movie *Poltergeist,* and I thought that this was the only explanation for my sister: an otherworldly occupation.

One night Renee was late coming home. After cross-country practice, she always caught the late bus at five thirty, but it was now six fifty and dark, and still no sign of her. Joe and Caroline and I made ourselves cheese sandwiches for dinner and chewed silently on the couch, plates on our laps, watching the door. Twice Joe said he should call the school, but he hadn't, not yet.

"What if she doesn't come back?" Caroline said. She was ten years old and afraid of spiders, the kitchen garbage disposal, and the *grrr* sound Joe made only to frighten her. Nightmares still plagued Caroline and would well into her twenties.

I was undisturbed by Renee's mysterious absence. Life without Renee was simply impossible. She made charts that listed our chores, homework, Joe's baseball schedule, Caroline's flute concerts, her own cross-country practices and meets. Renee ensured that we wore clean clothes to school, brushed our teeth, brushed our hair, caught the school bus, did our homework. Renee relit the pilot light on the furnace when it sputtered out. She forged Noni's signature on checks and permission slips. She cooked spaghetti and frozen peas and pancakes from the Bisquick box. We had learned to exist without our mother, but we could not exist without Renee.

"Maybe," Caroline said, "we should wake up Noni." We hadn't seen our mother today. We hadn't seen her yesterday either.

"No," said Joe. "I'll go find Renee." I saw in him the same air of responsibility, of taking charge, that he'd worn when Ace fell off the dam.

"I want to come," I said.

Joe crouched down to look me in the eye. "Fiona, it's better if I go alone. I'll go faster. And you need to keep Caroline company. Keep her safe."

I expected Caroline to dispute this, but she only nodded. "Yes, Fiona, stay with me. Please." Caroline's eyes were going red, her voice shook.

And so I stayed as Joe disappeared out the door, into the night. Caroline and I sat on the couch to wait. We did not talk or turn on the TV; we finished our sandwiches and listened intently for a sound, any sound, to come from Noni's room.

Forty-five minutes passed, perhaps an hour, and at last the front door opened and Renee and Joe, both breathless and agitated, tum-

bled inside. Relief flooded me, a rush I had not known I was waiting for. Caroline burst into tears.

"What happened?" I asked. "Where were you?"

Renee pulled roughly at the curtains, clicked the lights off, and
chased us all into the kitchen at the back of the house. Her manner was short and urgent. On her left cheek, there was a bloodied scrape, the skin swollen, and all at once, for the first time that
night, I felt afraid.

"Sit down," she ordered, and we sat at the kitchen table.

A car had been parked at the bus stop, Renee told us, a brown
car with a man in the driver's seat. An elbow out the window, sunglasses although it was dusk, the sun nearly gone.

"Baby," he called to her. "I've seen you. Want a ride?"

It was a fifteen-minute walk from the bus stop to our house.
Renee did not want a ride, not from this man, and she told him
so, but he began to follow her, the car inching along the road. No
other cars passed, and Renee felt cold and very weak.

"I didn't think I could run fast enough," she said. Renee, who
was a natural runner, whose thighs were the circumference of my
arm, who galloped along the rocky cross-country trail in meet
after meet, winning medal after medal, the child of a mountain
goat and a gazelle. She had never before said there was a race she
couldn't win.

"I didn't know what to do," she continued. "I was afraid he
would follow me here, so I went down another street and then
another, and then he stopped the car behind me, and I ran and hid
in the Hunters' backyard. There was a swing set with a slide—like
in the yellow house, remember? I hid under the slide until I heard
Joe calling for me."

Joe had wandered the neighborhood, walking in circles away
from our house, he told us, calling Renee's name.

"But what about your cheek?" I asked. "Who hurt you?"

Renee gingerly touched the spot on her face as though discovering it for the first time. "Oh. I . . . um . . ."

"She scraped it on the slide," said Joe. "She ran out so quickly she didn't duck low enough. So she hit it."

Renee nodded tentatively, then with more force. "Yes, that's it," she murmured, again touching her face. "The slide."

The man who called Renee "baby" never returned. It was an isolated incident, but it infected us in a way I didn't understand until much later. Renee stopped taking the late bus and would now wait until her coach was finished for the night and could drive her home. Caroline's nightmares doubled in frequency and ferocity. I stopped roaming the neighborhood as freely as I once had. Perhaps this was for the best—a check on our behavior, a lean toward safety—but I remember it only as a chill up my spine, a dampness to my palms. The idea that someone was watching us. That we were unsafe.

The incident made us all feel vulnerable, although in different ways. For Joe it was fear of what might happen to us, his sisters. But for us, Joe's sisters, it was fear for ourselves. The man might come again for Renee or for me or for Caroline, but he would not come for Joe. Only girls remained at the mercy of men with bad intentions. Men in cars that were brown or red or gray, who wore sunglasses or didn't, who were young or old, white or black, strangers or known to us.

This fear uncovered the tenuousness of our position during the Pause. The cracks became evident, and I watched them widen. Caroline and Joe began to fight frequently, Renee to cry without reason, to serve us dinner with shaking hands. Joe spent more time with his friends, girls in particular. He was the tallest boy in fifth grade, and girls took a spirited, wholesome interest in him as though he were a fuzzy stuffed animal in need of cuddling. Kim, Ashley, Shannon, Julie. I remember their ponytails and squeaky Keds and sticker collections in hard-backed photo albums with plastic pages. In school they would tease Joe gently and give him the Oreos and juice boxes from their lunches. They refilled his water bottle at baseball practice. They told their mothers that their friend Joe needed a ride to the movies, or a new pencil case, or construction paper for the science report about mammals, and could they please help? Joe accepted their attentions. He began to spend more time with these girls, away from the house and me.

In my notebook I wrote the words *dust, dirty, drafty, alone, Gilligan, cold, island, tv, shipwrecked.*

* * *

NOT LONG AFTER the man followed Renee, Joe took me to the old yellow house. It was only after the accident that I placed the two events together, not in the way of cause and effect but a more amorphous push-pull. A sense of growing unease. A secret interior turmoil finding its way into the open air.

The day we walked back to our old neighborhood was beautiful: sunshine and crisp air, clear sky, the rustle of flaming leaves underfoot. Autumn in full bloom. New people lived at the yellow house, a family with boys and girls, apparently. Joe and I stood for a spell on the sidewalk and surveyed the bikes, footballs, Frisbees and hula hoops that lay abandoned across the front lawn.

"There's no car," Joe said. He was holding my hand. "They must not be home."

"But what about all this stuff?" I replied.

Joe shrugged. "Let's go check."

He led me around to the back door—down the side alley, past the garbage bins, turn left, cut across the lawn, over the patio, and there, the back door painted a bright white. I knew that door so well. It took my breath away to see it again.

"Maybe we could go in and look around," Joe said.

"But, Joe . . ." I protested, though weakly. I wanted to go inside, too. I liked the idea of freely examining other people's things, taking time to sort through the mother's makeup bag, to check the Scrabble game for marked-up score sheets. Maybe I would find a journal, a notebook like the one I kept, filled with the secret thoughts of another girl. The possibility gave me a shiver of delight.

I followed Joe as he pushed open the back door and called "Hello! Hello!" We stood in the kitchen, our old kitchen, and listened to the quiet ticking of the clock, the silent settling of the house. The room looked the same, different only in small, frivolous ways. A new round table. Photos of unfamiliar faces pegged to the fridge. The smell was different, too, heavier than I remembered it, and more chemical.

"Let's go upstairs," Joe said.

Slowly we climbed the creaking steps. I went immediately to my bedroom but paused in the doorway. Unlike the kitchen, this room was fundamentally changed: bed, curtains, stuffed animals, all different, and, strangest of all, in a corner stood a bubbling fish tank that glowed blue. I saw no board games, no tantalizing notebooks. I stepped inside my old room and watched the fish dart in a mindless dance. They were the same size as the minnows from the pond, but these fish were brightly colored with stripes and spots, and they moved faster, with less purpose. There was nothing for these fish to do, nowhere for them to go. They were trapped.

"Fiona!" Joe called from the hall. "Fiona! Come here!"

I found him standing in what had been our parents' bedroom. This room, too, was unrecognizable, with glossy furniture set in odd places and a large abstract painting on the wall.

"I thought he'd be here," Joe said.

"Who?" I asked.

"Dad. We're looking for Dad. That's why we're here."

"Dad?" I barely remembered our father. I thought of him rarely and only with reference to Noni and all that she'd endured. "Joe, are you sure?"

"Yes I'm sure," he whispered fiercely. "Now, *shhh*. I know he'll come."

The yearning in Joe's voice shattered the still air into a million pieces. It shocked me into a stunned silence.

And so we waited, standing in the middle of a room that no longer belonged to our parents. The air became heavier, the walls moved inward. I could hear Joe's labored breathing and the faint *tick-tick* of a clock from another room. The moments lengthened and spun like a carnival ride. I chewed the inside of my cheek and waited for Joe to be finished. Everything about this made me light-headed, vaguely nauseous. Back then I didn't believe that we would ever see our father again.

Without warning I began to giggle. The silence, the discomfort, the ache in my knees, the outright strangeness of it all. I couldn't contain myself any longer.

"Joe—ooooh—" I held up my arms and wiggled my fingers. "Look, I'm a ghost Joe! Look!"

I moved toward him with arms outstretched. On my brother's face, I saw an immediate deflation and a flicker of shame.

"Yeah, a ghost," Joe said gruffly, and laughed. "Got you, didn't I?"

The slam of a car door startled us both. There were voices outside in the driveway, then footsteps at the front door. Joe grabbed my hand, and together we ran down the stairs and out the back. We were breathless and scared, both of us laughing as we made it through the side gate and across our old neighbors' lawns and eventually home to the gray house.

I never told anyone about this episode, although later I came to see it as a marker of the end of the Pause. Certain things had become unsustainable. Certain pressures threatened to explode. Renee's responsibilities, Caroline's nightmares, Joe and his . . . I didn't know what to call it. His lack. The way he had everything and nothing. The way he smiled and flicked back his cowlick and said everything that everyone wanted to hear, and yet it seemed that his manner began outside himself, externally, with the wishes of others who wanted something from him. Coach Marty, Noni, the team, his friends, his teachers, the girls. Even us, his sisters.

What did Joe want for himself? I never knew. It was only years later, after the accident, that I realized I had never thought to ask.

* * *

AFTER THE EPISODE with Renee, it was ironic that a man in a car at last brought us salvation. The Pause ended because a man in a car slowed and stopped.

It was Renee, of course, who saw to it that Joe attended every baseball practice and every game. This was Joe's fourth year of Little League. His progress in the sport was a rare orchid that we tended with careful watering, pruning, reverence. "Tell your mother Joe is doing great," Coach Marty would say to Renee. "Tell her he's one in a million."

Twice weekly the four of us walked from home to the Bexley playing field. The route consisted of one mile of calm, tree-lined residential streets followed by one and a half miles of flat, fast Route 9, a four-lane highway running through empty fields of tall, yellowed grass and splintered old fences, the occasional neglected house, and one you-pump gas station. There was no sidewalk, so we walked in the breakdown lane or in the grass. Surely we looked curious to passing cars: Renee striding forward with her solid, sure-footed step; Joe pristine in his baseball gear, bat slung over a shoulder; me with curly hair crazy in the wind, skipping beside Joe to keep up; Caroline wearing a long skirt, singing to herself, lagging behind. The trip took over an hour.

One morning a car slowed beside us. A man leaned over to peer through the open passenger window. It was Coach Marty.

"What are you kids doing?" he asked. "Joe Skinner, is that you?"

"We're on our way to practice," Renee answered, still walking. "I'm taking Joe to the field."

Coach Marty's car inched along beside us as he considered this answer. He looked at me chewing a wad of bubble gum too big for my mouth, and then he pulled to the side of the road just ahead.

"I'll take you," he said. "Get in."

Renee hesitated. Later we would come to know Marty Roach very well, but on that morning he was only Joe's coach, the funny man with the dark mustache whom we glimpsed from afar on the field.

"We're good at walking," Renee said carefully. "We do it every week."

It was a cold spring day, and the wind whistled along the road and the grassy fields and reached through our thin coats. We were all shivering, hands in pockets. Caroline's long hair whipped around her face.

"Please, Renee," said Caroline. "Let's go with him." There were dark half-moons beneath her eyes. Her tolerance for this life had reached its limits.

Renee looked at the road, she looked at Joe, who nodded, and then she said to Marty, "Okay."

Marty's car smelled of mint and tobacco, not cigarettes but the ripe, woody scent of pulp tobacco, and it seemed to me a cozy place, like a room with a fireplace in the days before Christmas. Years later I would date a much older man who smoked a pipe—

pure affect, we didn't date for long—but the first time he took the pipe out and lit it, I returned again to the back of that car. Coach Marty's huge, meaty hands on the wheel, the back of his head a white dome striped with the dark brown of his comb-over. Gray vinyl seats, a pull-down armrest in the center that he pushed up to accommodate us, releasing a grainy silt that he wiped away with the back of his hand onto the floor of the car.

"There you go," he said, and the four of us packed thigh to thigh into the back seat.

Some say there are no secrets in small towns, but I believe this to be false. There were people in Bexley who knew about Noni—I'm sure of it—but they kept the matter to themselves. Noni was a secret; Noni was something no one discussed. Back then there was no "reply all" or neighborhood message board. You had to pick up the phone and hope that the person to whom you wished to speak would answer. You had to walk out your front door and start up your car and drive to the Skinners' new house and knock on the front door and hope that Antonia Skinner would not send you immediately away, as she did to Mrs. Lipton when she tried to drop off a tin of cookies that first Christmas.

The Skinner children went to school. We were fed. It was a difficult time—of course it was, everyone understood that. No one wanted to intrude. We were left alone.

Only Coach Marty did not leave us alone. Maybe it was the week after that first ride to the field, or the next month, or next season. I don't remember exactly, but I do remember that one day Marty Roach came home with us.

That night there was a baseball game, a midseason corker between the Mavericks and the Eagles from neighboring Milford. Joe scored three runs, committed no errors, caught a high fly ball to close out the sixth inning, and you could see the hope drain from the faces of those Milford boys. The sun lingered in the sky after the game, bright pinks and orange, and in the air there was a buzzy warmth. My hands were sticky from melted ice cream. Joe's purple-and-green uniform looked regal in the dying light, a worn-out king touched with glitter and dirt.

After the game Marty drove us home. I remember standing with him at our front door, which was painted the same dingy gray as the rest of the house. Our screen was torn, broken long ago during a game of pirates between me and Joe. The corner hung down, nearly touching the ground.

Renee used her key to let us in. She did not hesitate. She threw open the door as if to say, *Here it is. Look and tell me, is this okay?*

Coach Marty stood in the middle of the living room—a mess of unpacked boxes and dirty dishes, games, forts, discarded clothing, a trail of checkers I had laid days ago for a lost stuffed bear—and called for our mother.

"Mrs. Skinner? Mrs. Skinner? Antonia?"

No answer. And so Renee yelled, "Noni! Noni, come here!"

After a spell we heard a creak of floorboards. Noni emerged at the end of the hall in her bathrobe, which was dirty, her long hair wild around her head, and in that moment we saw her anew. Her face was indoor pale, her feet bare. I noticed the musty stench of the house, of unwashed floors and dirty dishes, damp towels, dusty corners. What before had been only Noni resting, always resting, now appeared to me terrible.

Our mother looked at Marty and said, "Oh. Hello."

* * *

NOT LONG AFTER this, our Aunt Claudia arrived from Cleveland. She was childless, our father's much-older sister whom we had met only once before at his funeral. She had tightly curled gray hair that sat like a bathing cap on her head and a long, horsey face. Claudia brought with her one pink suitcase and an air of rigorous competence. Our mother left the house; our mother returned; the house became clean; we became clean. Our mother left the house again, only this time she wore a neat blue skirt suit and lipstick colored a race-car red. Claudia told us that Noni was looking for a job, and about time, too.

"You've got to get on with things," Claudia said as we watched Noni drive away. "Too much laying around isn't good for anyone. Remember that. Keeping busy is the best defense against feeling sad. It's simple, but it's true."

Aunt Claudia was proof of this lesson. She was the least sad and most busy person I had ever met. She swirled around our house with a cloth and a spray bottle like a bird looking for an exit, and everything she bumped into became clean, tidy, sparkling. Back home Aunt Claudia worked as a teller at a bank in North Royalton, Ohio, a Cleveland suburb. She described for us the intricate details of her job, the piles of twenties wrapped in special paper, the safe as big as a room, the secret slots of the safe-deposit boxes where people placed the oddest things.

"Once a man came in and rented one for a pair of shoes, ladies' shoes," she told us. "Now, why would anyone do such a thing?"

For four weeks Claudia cooked large, well-balanced meals that we ate until our stomachs groaned; she cycled load after load of dirty clothes through the washer and dryer; she read aloud books we had read before, but still we listened; she bought us art supplies, and we colored diligently the pictures of forest animals and trees, though we were far too old for coloring books.

I wrote *muscle, broom, thick, bristle, warm, squeak, soap, gravy, meat, full.*

What we liked best of all was Claudia telling stories about our father when he was a boy: his extreme fear of ants, his favorite food (meatballs), the operation he had when he was ten to fix the knuckle of his right thumb (trigger thumb, she called it). When she recounted these episodes, her eyes would become glassy and she'd dab at them with a tissue she pulled from a small plastic pack that accompanied her everywhere.

One day we were eating lunch when Aunt Claudia said, "Joe, you look just like your father." She paused to blow her nose into a tissue. "*You're* the man of the family now. Don't you forget it."

We had never before considered the word *man* with reference to Joe. When Claudia said this, we all turned toward him. We were eating pink boiled hot dogs with white buns that disappeared like cotton candy in your mouth. Noni was out on another interview.

Suddenly Joe seemed altered. He felt it, too. He stiffened his shoulders, brought up his puffy chest. "I'm the man of the family," he repeated, and I giggled because it struck me as both absurd and momentous. Joe was ten years old. A man.

Although we basked in Claudia's attentions and listened avidly to her stories, inside we remained watchful. There was so much information, so much nutrition and stimulation that we barely spoke during the month that she stayed with us. We did everything she told us to do. We did not fight or talk back or make large messes because we were too exhausted by her capable, forceful presence. But secretly each of us wondered: what will happen when Aunt Claudia leaves?

On her last night, Aunt Claudia took us all to the International House of Pancakes. We were celebrating Noni's new job as a receptionist at Dr. Hart's dental practice across town. Dr. Hart, our father's old competitor, had been looking for someone like our mother, someone who knew the ins and outs of the business, the peculiar dental vocabulary, the complexities of a dentist's life.

Noni had cut her hair short with little wings on the sides like Billie Jean King, and it gave me a shock of strangeness to see her without a mass of dark curls. As she chewed her blueberry pancakes, her hand stole up to her neck to finger the sharp line where hair met skin.

"Thank you, Claudia, for taking such good care of us," Noni said, and raised her glass of orange juice. We all clinked and called "Cheers!"

"Of course," Claudia answered. "I only wish I'd come sooner. I just thought you needed some space, Antonia. That was really it."

Noni only nodded.

"But I didn't realize both your parents were dead. And no siblings. I hadn't realized you were so alone, Antonia. Really, I hadn't."

"It's okay. We're fine now. Right, kids?" Noni looked around the table at each of us. Our fingers were sticky from maple syrup, our teeth and blood tingly with sugar. We had eaten stacks of pancakes, and yet our stomachs still felt empty. Were we fine? Yes. One by one we returned Noni's gaze and nodded. Even Renee nodded. *Yes,* we said. *We are all fine.*

"Good," Noni said. "Good." She smiled a firm little smile.

And that was how it happened: we forgave our mother. We forgave Noni not because she was all we had, although this was true, but because we shared her. She belonged to the four of us, and for one not to forgive her meant that the others couldn't either, and none of us was willing to shoulder the burden of that decision. None of us could bear to take Noni away from the others again.

* * *

AFTER AUNT CLAUDIA left, Noni returned with a vengeance. She began to call herself a feminist and to call us, her daughters, feminists, too. She bought books by Gloria Steinem and bell hooks and Germaine Greer that she read aloud at the dinner table. The year was 1984.

"Better late than never," Noni said.

Only a few of my friends' mothers worked. One was a professor at the University of Connecticut who wore half-glasses on a string of purple beads around her neck. Another, a family lawyer who rented an office in Bexley with her name printed in gold on the window. But for the most part, the mothers remained at home and oversaw play dates and drove us to the movies and lurked in the kitchen, where they banged pots and spread peanut butter onto saltine crackers for us to eat after school. While our father was alive, Noni had been this kind of mother. But after she began working for Dr. Hart, Noni changed. She would describe for us her day at Dr. Hart's office, the patients and their troublesome dental quandaries, the new system of color-coded file notes, the car accident just in front of the building that closed the street for hours. We saw in these stories a Noni who enjoyed her life away from us. This life of drama and intrigue that existed far from the confines of the gray house and us, her children.

When I was in third grade, I memorized for the class Sylvia Plath's poem "The Applicant," which traumatized my poor teacher, Miss Adelaide. ("A living doll, everywhere you look. / It can sew, it can cook, / It can talk, talk, talk!") Fourth grade, I dressed as Gloria Steinem for Halloween and spent the entire night explaining the significance of my bell-bottoms and turtleneck. Fifth grade, Noni volunteered to assist in my puberty and health class, and I walked through the class handing out tampons and pads in purple plastic wrappers.

Noni regretted the Pause, she told us. She wanted to make it up to us, all those lost days while she rested. The missed baseball games and teacher conferences and Caroline's flute concerts and Renee's cross-country meets and dinners and bedtimes and love.

"I am so sorry," she would say. "I am so, so sorry. I should have gotten some help. Thank goodness nothing horrible happened."

We would look at one another and say nothing about the pond, or Ace's accident, or the man who followed Renee from the bus stop. In fact, we told Noni nothing about the Pause. Wordlessly we agreed that it was better to keep these events secret. We saw this as protecting ourselves from discipline but also as protection for Noni. We believed that she required care and shelter, that we must not subject her to upheaval or stress. Our mother was a temperamental furnace, a rescue dog once hostile but then subdued.

Now Noni explained her own early life and marriage as a cautionary tale, the period of her paralyzing grief the price we all paid for her foolishness. In these stories our father emerged as a dashing but hapless prince, one who lulled the good princess into a life of fat complacency deep within a castle of tricks and mirrors. When the prince disappeared, the castle was revealed to be only a cardboard shell; there was no coach, no footmen, only the pumpkin and the simpering mice. The shock of it all sent the princess into a deep sleep, until a good fairy godmother—not another prince, please, anything but that—roused her. And what did the princess see when she first awoke? What greeted her and stirred her fully from the glass chamber? Why, it was the mice, of course. They clambered atop the wreckage of the castle and reminded her that she could build it herself again.

Chapter 4

THE YEAR WAS 1989. The first George Bush was president. The previous month on TV, we'd watched as young men and women with outdated haircuts and funny clothes took sledgehammers to the Berlin Wall. There was a sense of radical change and diminished threats. It was June, a beautiful warm night, and we were eating dinner with the back door open. Light-hungry moths fluttered against the screen. The night air smelled of dew and pavement.

"I don't want you girls making the same mistakes I did," Noni was saying. "I loved your father, I did, but you must not rely on a man. You must have your own money. Your own direction in life."

By now we were accustomed to this line of discussion. We all nodded. We were eating pork chops, steamed broccoli, underdone rice that stuck between our teeth. Tonight Joe had played baseball, and he still wore his uniform, which was dirty across the front from when he slid into home in the seventh inning. A nick of mud marked his chin.

When Noni discussed feminism, Joe remained cautiously curious, wide-eyed, mostly silent. He was afraid to ask the wrong questions, ones that would invite our mother's disdain, and also he sensed—correctly—that these discussions were not for his benefit.

They were intended for us, the girls. Noni believed that the world was harder on women than it was on men, particularly women without men, and you could become one of those in a heartbeat. Noni wanted us to be ready in the ways that she had not. Joe's passage would be smooth, paved with the wishes of all those who loved and admired him and wanted only to see him succeed.

Renee and I listened avidly to our mother's lectures, tonight and every night. We nodded and used words like *patriarchy* and *privilege* and *gender*. Shortly after the end of the Pause, Renee had announced that she would become a doctor, and now all her efforts pointed to this goal. AP chemistry, biology, and calculus; her part-time job at the lab in New Haven; her dominance on the Bexley High cross-country team.

Only Caroline, at sixteen, yawned or examined her fingernails or tried, occasionally, to dispute Noni's lessons.

"But what if we want to be married?" Caroline asked tonight. "What if we *want* other people?" Caroline's hair fell long across her back and was streaked a whitish blond from the Sun In she used every morning with the blow dryer. We knew that she was thinking of Nathan Duffy and the Goats, who now called Caroline an honorary Duffy. In the afternoons Nathan would ride his bike slowly past our house and leave on the front steps odd little gifts: one silver stick of dusty Juicy Fruit, a silky brown horse chestnut big as a child's fist, a lone pink carnation frilly as a tutu.

Noni answered Caroline's question in the abstract. Even if she knew that the front-door gifts were for Caroline, she believed them irrelevant.

"Fine. Have other people," Noni said. "But remember that they can be gone—poof! In an instant. Gone. So be prepared."

This answer did not satisfy Caroline, who shifted and fidgeted on her chair. She blinked rapidly, her entire face reddened. She looked ready to weep.

"Oh, Caroline," Noni said, and her voice softened. "I'm sorry. I don't mean to scare you, really, I don't. I just want to *prepare* you. So you won't have to suffer. So you'll have an easier, better time than I did." She took hold of Caroline's hand. We had finished eating our pork chops; on each of our plates lay a ragged, moon-shaped bone.

I wanted to believe that Noni's suffering would not be our own, but her lessons seemed difficult to place within the context of our actual lives. Noni herself had sworn off dating and all men. For her, easier and better meant being alone. We watched *The Love Boat* every Saturday night with a mixture of delight and unease as the new cadre of attractive passengers flirted and kissed and paired off in the few short days of their tropical cruise. Was this supposed to happen? Caroline seemed to me the purest example of true love: worshipped by Nathan in a factual, fateful way. But even their relationship was dependent on parental whims and the absence of snow, which in the winters made the roof too precarious for Caroline to shimmy across and down to Nathan's waiting car.

Caroline, still sniffling, turned to Noni. "Can I ask you a question?" she said gently.

"Of course," Noni answered.

"I was wondering if I could have a slightly later curfew. Just on Saturdays. Or Fridays. One day." Caroline's eyes glistened, still wet from her tears. "Please," she said.

I almost considered Nathan to be one of us, the Skinners. He loved the secret, rushing green of the pond; he knew about the Pause. I'd watched him grow just as I'd watched Joe, with his sudden height and the rough spots of beard that appeared in patches across his cheeks and neck like camouflage. But Noni knew noth-

ing about that. To her, Nathan presented the same risks and lia-
bilities as a stray dog brought home from the park. Would it bite?
How long would it stay? She looked at him askance no matter how
strenuously he tried to impress her.

"I'm going to study biology," he had told Noni earlier that year,
"be a university professor. I'm particularly interested in amphibi-
ans, frogs mostly. They're disappearing. We need to save the frogs."

It was the pond that had started this for Nathan. The baritone
bullfrogs and the smaller ones, green as a new leaf. The *plunk-splash*
sound as they leaped into the water. The bulging, lidless eyes, jel-
lied, glistening.

But Noni had no use for frogs, or for Nathan. She had imposed
a strict 11:00 P.M. curfew on Caroline, Renee, and me, although it
was clear that only Caroline truly needed it. I was in sixth grade,
twelve years old, and had nowhere to go, nothing outrageous to
do. My most scandalous behavior involved sneaking into movies I
hadn't paid for at the cineplex with my friend Violet and eating far
too much buttered popcorn.

At night Renee studied organic chemistry and compared medical schools. After one brief romantic fiasco last year involving our
high school's star wrestler, Brett Swenson, Renee now ignored boys
altogether. She was too busy, she said, for distractions. She accepted
Noni's curfew with a shrug.

On this spring night, all of us together at the dinner table, Noni
tilted her head and narrowed her eyes as she considered Caroline's
request for a later curfew.

"No," she said. "We've been over this, Caroline. You have a curfew for a reason. I want you home."

"But what about Joe?" Caroline asked.

It was true that Joe glided through the gauntlet of Noni's discipline unmarked. Noni let him go to parties, date widely, deeply.

And—this was the kicker for Caroline—stay out as late as he wanted. By the time Joe reached Bexley High School, he was a six-foot-four center fielder with the reach and charm of Willie Mays, the goofy grin and sleepy eyes of Joe DiMaggio. Girls swooned over him, boys followed him down the hallways and invited him to parties. Teachers indulged him whether they realized it or not. His dimples, the soft swell of his walk, the subtle crack in his voice, the tall golden promise of Joe Skinner. Parents congratulated Noni routinely, because they understood that just to have a son like Joe—simply to be the origin of whatever DNA soup produced a boy like that—was something to celebrate.

Noni said that Joe didn't need a curfew. He was always up early for baseball practice anyhow. He hated alcohol. Hated the taste, hated the way it made him feel: out of control, bumbling, fuzzy. And think about the public service he performed as the reliable designated driver, the lone sober man among a battalion of high-school drunks. Why would Noni put others at risk just to make a point?

"But Joe is younger than me!" Caroline exclaimed.

Noni sighed. "Listen, if Joe needs one more hour to keep some other kid from driving home drunk and killing himself—Caroline, I'm going to let him do it."

The rest of us remained silent. This scenario had played out before, always with the same result. Now, predictable as Christmas, Caroline would push away from the table, pound down the hall, and close her door with a wall-shaking slam.

But this time she didn't.

"You play favorites," Caroline accused. "You let Joe do whatever he wants, and you take it out on us."

I inhaled sharply. Renee was looking down at the table. Joe's eyes were closed, as though he could remove himself from this fight by refusing to acknowledge its escalation.

"That's not true," Noni said.

"Yes it is." Caroline's cheeks deepened to red. There was a reck-lessness in her voice. "And we have to go to every single baseball game. And you don't care about his grades. And he gets to stay out late, and he's sleeping with girls. Older girls. Did you know that? Jeanine Bobkin, Christi from Hamden High. That exchange stu-dent from Italy. And he's only fifteen!"

"A lot more can happen to you, Caroline Skinner, when you stay out late." Noni said this quietly, and it was the softness of her voice that made us all listen harder.

Caroline pushed her chair away from the table and stood up, her eyes blazing. Until this moment I had always seen Caroline as a mild person, someone who squealed rather than yelled, who labored over friendship bracelets pinned to her knee. But here she was, animated by her sense of injustice, training the full force of her fury onto Noni, whom we generally shielded from any con-flict or emotional excess. Now, nearly six years after the Pause had ended, such precautions were perhaps unnecessary, but they had become routine.

"I . . . I . . ." Caroline stammered. Her resolve, so firmly stamped on her face, was not finding its way to her mouth. We watched our sister struggle for the right words. "I . . . I . . . I hate you," Caroline said to Noni, and then she burst into tears and ran to her room.

A dangerous, damaged silence descended. I glanced sideways at Noni, trying to gauge her mood. But Noni merely sipped her wine, chewed her chop. Our mother was opaque to us, a combination of stubborn principles, disciplined instruction, and distance. It was Caroline who wore her heart on her sleeve. Our mother taught us how to protect ourselves from hurt but not how to determine what might be worth the risk.

Joe was the first to speak. He opened his eyes and said, "Should I apologize? This feels like my fault."

"No, you should not apologize," Noni replied in her no-nonsense way. "Just give her some time." She sipped the last of her wine, then brought her plate to the kitchen and followed Caroline to her room. I could hear her knocking on the door and her patient voice. "Caroline, please let me in. Caro?"

Renee began to clear the table. I helped until the plates were stacked in the dishwasher, the wood wiped clean, Renee in her chair, pulling an acid yellow highlighter thick as a cigar across a page of her calculus book. The smell of meat and steam still lingered in the room. The front door was closed now, the house shut up tight, battened against the buggy spring night. Noni had gained entrance to Caroline's room at last. I heard an occasional muffled sob, a brief angry shout.

Joe had finished his homework on the bus, he claimed, and stood in the hall, ear pressed to phone. I was on my way to the kitchen to find something more to eat. My chronic hunger was a residue from the Pause. It didn't matter how much I ate during the day; always at night I'd feel an empty rumbling. As I passed Joe in the hall, he held his hand over the mouthpiece. "Battleship?" he asked me.

I heard a flash of feminine mumble, a giggling laugh.

Fragrant, flounce, hair, tease, pretty, smile, wink, sugar, sweet.

I shrugged. "Sure."

I set up the game there on the floor of the hall, and we played, sitting cross-legged, facing each other. I ate a salami sandwich. Joe drank two glasses of milk and remained on the phone. He gave the conversation only the barest attention. D9. F10. A13. With each coordinate he placed his hand on the mouthpiece.

"You sank my battleship," he told me.

"Yee-haw!" I whooped loudly.

Joe frowned and told the girl he needed to go. Feminine protest erupted on the other end. I could hear the tone but not the words: pout, cajoling, *Jooooe*. I widened my eyes and twirled an index finger at my forehead. *Cuckoo,* I signaled to Joe. *You and all these stupid girls.* I vowed then never to be like them, frivolous and weak-willed, with their glossy lips and padded bras, speaking for hours to a boy who only pretended to listen.

Joe kept my gaze. "Holly—" he said into the phone, but she kept interrupting him.

"I'm—"

"Listen—"

"Wait—"

And then he simply hung up.

"Your turn," I said.

As we continued the game, Joe jiggled a knee, tapped an index finger against the floor, squinted and frowned. Back then some part of Joe was always in motion. A leg, a finger, a crack of the neck, a roll of the shoulders. He was still growing, his bones lengthening, skin expanding, his whole person surging forward into a bright unknown. Joe's vitality seeped out of him, uncontainable. I felt it all the time.

"Fiona," he said as we were clearing away the pieces of the game. He had won, but barely.

"What?"

"I'm glad you're my little sister."

I shrugged. "It's not like I have a choice," I replied, but I felt my big, hot heart spreading through my chest like a starfish, like a many-fingered creature that had finally found its treasure. "Noni wouldn't let you trade me in anyhow."

"True," Joe said, and he grinned back at me, a faint milk mustache still clinging to the delicate blond hairs of his upper lip. He looked beautiful and sated and spent.

* * *

AND THEN, IN a heartbeat, with a rattle of Caroline's armful of bracelets, the squeak of Renee's running shoes, the funny hiccup of Joe's laugh, my siblings were leaving home.

—cold, lonesome, lone, together, mother, brother, sister, other—

Picture the day: late summer in New England, humid and close, the lawn thick as shag from Noni's tending. A day when we would have been at the pond. The year was 1992, and eighteen-year-old Joe was piling suitcases and plastic crates, a secondhand microwave, four pillows, three baseball bats, a life-size cardboard cutout of Bill and Ted into Noni's Volvo station wagon.

"Do you really need the cardboard thing?" Noni asked, squinting into the sun. Dog-day cicadas whined with a high-pitched keen, a cyclical sound so pervasive you didn't even notice it until it was all you noticed, and then, at that very moment, the sound began to fade.

"Yes," Joe said solemnly. He was sweaty, wearing blue nylon shorts and a purple-and-green Mavericks tee. "I need them. I'm pretty sure it was on that list they sent. Books, sheets, Bill and Ted . . ."

"Okay, okay," said Noni. "Bring Bill and Ted. But don't blame me if your new roommate asks to switch." She winked at Joe and slid the poster into the back of the car.

All morning Noni had pranced around like a golden retriever. Alden College! Our mother had won the parental college lottery: not Ivy League but close, with a full financial-aid package. Given

Joe's mediocre grades, no one thought he had a shot at a school like Alden, but Coach Marty knew the baseball coach. Alden needed a freshman center fielder, and Joe Skinner was it.

"Joe, don't take Bill!" I called from my seat on the front lawn. "I love him!" For the first hour of packing, I had helped, sort of, but the tolerable morning temperature had given way so quickly to a sludgy, heavy heat that I'd declared myself overwhelmed and found a place in the shade. "Just cut Ted off," I called. "Take Ted, but leave Bill."

My childhood baby fat had not melted away as we all (or at least I) had assumed it would. That summer I was fifteen years old, alarmingly pudgy from puberty and Coke and frosted doughnuts and a general aversion to physical effort. For three long months, I'd moped around the house, reading too much sexed-up Updike and working a stinky, mindless job at a burger place in Bexley that paid me eight dollars an hour to cut tomatoes and onions and lift buns off the grill before they burned. I felt a persistent exhaustion brought on by the act of pushing my body through the days. My knees ached, my back ached, my fingers stank, my friends all annoyed me. I had no desire to grow older; I was already old enough.

I had started work on a dandelion chain when Nathan Duffy's dented old VW pulled up to the house. The passenger door opened with a rattle, and out tumbled Caroline in a short flowery dress, her waist-length dirty-blond hair falling like a cape behind her.

"I'm so glad you guys haven't left!" Caroline called to Joe. "I thought we'd missed saying good-bye." She scanned the lawn. "Where's Renee?"

I pointed: Renee was sitting on the bumper of the rented U-Haul, the U-Haul she'd packed up the night before with everything she'd need for her first year of medical school at Boston University.

A fine sheen of sweat covered her tan limbs, legs in micro running shorts. Her arms were crossed against her stomach, her long brown hair pulled back in a ponytail that bobbed slightly as she tapped her foot. Renee, impatience personified.

"We're still an hour away from leaving," Renee told Caroline. She checked her watch, then looked pointedly at Joe. "At *least.*"

Joe grinned back. *Look after your brother,* Noni had said when it became clear they would both be going to school in Boston. And Renee had answered, *Have I ever not?*

Nathan ambled around to sit next to me on the grass. "Morning, Fiona," he said.

"Renee, should we bring the snow boots now or wait till after Thanksgiving break?" Joe called across the lawn.

"Bring them," Renee answered, examining a cuticle. "It might snow before we get back home."

Back home. They were leaving, all of them. In one two-week stretch, I was losing Joe to college, Renee to medical school, and Caroline to Lexington, Kentucky. That spring Nathan had graduated early from University of Connecticut and was set to start a biology Ph.D. program. Caroline would transfer schools. Although there was still some question about her credits, there was no question that she was going with Nathan.

Noni and I would remain alone in the gray house.

"I'll miss you, Fi," Joe said. Sighing, he lay down beside me on the lawn and shaded his eyes with his hand. "A lot."

"Me, too," I said.

"You'll be happy we're gone. Really, you will. No more noise. No more of that awful Indigo Girls." The last he said loudly in Renee's direction, but she ignored him apart from a quick flip of her middle finger.

"Or farting," said Caroline, staring pointedly at Joe. She lay down and settled her head on Nathan's thigh. "The house will be a lot less stinky."

"Um, Caroline," said Joe, "perhaps you haven't noticed, but our mother can pass gas like a champ. Right, Noni?"

"What? Joe?" Noni was coming out the front door carrying another box. "Joe, why are you lying down? Why is *everyone* on the grass? Aren't we still packing?"

"I'm taking a break," said Joe. "Fiona looked sad."

"I am not sad," I said quickly. It was a lie, of course, but I objected to the idea that I was so easy to read. The truth was that I didn't want this, us here sprawled on the lawn, to end. I wanted this miserable, hot day to go on forever. I wanted Joe beside me, Caroline and Renee within earshot. All of us close enough to touch.

"Noni," said Joe from his prone position, "I just want you to know that I plan to be home a lot, so don't forget the Dr Pepper and the sour-cream-and-onion Lay's potato chips, not that Pringles bullshit, and those peanut butter M&M's and mint-chocolate-chip ice cream—any brand is okay, but it must be *green*."

Noni stood above Joe, hands on her hips.

"Are you taking notes?" he asked. "Mental notes?"

"That's exactly what I'm doing. Now, would you get up and help me finish here?"

"Fiona needs me more," Joe said, but he pushed himself up just enough to throw his arms around me and kiss me on the cheek, and then he was up, running back into the house.

"Yuck." I rubbed Joe's spit off my face. Nathan smiled, but there was tension and distraction in his face.

"Caro," Nathan whispered to Caroline. Her eyes were closed. "Now?" he asked.

"Oh, I don't know," she answered without opening her eyes.

"Now *what?*" I said. I'd heard a tremor in Nathan's voice, an unmistakable wobble of excitement.

"I think we should get your mom," Nathan said. Caroline's eyes fluttered open.

Soon all of us stood in a loose circle in the shade thrown by the towering locust I had never been able to climb, all of us looking at Caroline and Nathan.

"Caroline, what is it?" asked Noni.

Nathan looked to Caroline, who smiled and nodded. Nathan cleared his throat, but it was Caroline who spoke. "We're married!" she said, and clapped her hands quickly like a child.

The words dropped quiet as a cloud into our circle, and for a moment we all stood muzzled, stunned. A crow called across the empty street. Somewhere, a lawn mower started up with a bewildered buzz. Caroline was nineteen years old.

"Oh, Caroline," Noni said, her voice thick, her face fallen.

"We did it last week, at the courthouse," Caroline said, ignoring Noni. "Here's the ring." She held out her hand, and yes, there it was, a thin silver band with a stone so small it seemed merely a nick in the metal.

"And I thought I would be the last," Noni said.

"The last what?" asked Caroline.

"The last to . . . to decide something like this. For a man."

Caroline said nothing. Nathan shifted, his discomfort clear. We all waited as our mother considered the news of Caroline's marriage. She shook her head and looked up at the sky, which was flat and heavy and absolutely blue. I thought she might yell or begin to cry, and for a moment all four of us stood poised to receive that, ready in that far-off, distant way we would always be ready to lose our mother again to turbulent, unbearable emotion.

Noni exhaled. She shook her head and grimaced and wiped her eyes. "Well, at least you're not *pregnant*," she said with a laugh. And then, anxiously: "You're not pregnant, are you?"

Caroline giggled and shook her head no. "Well, congratulations, then," Noni said. "This is . . . exciting!" And with that we all breathed once again.

"Congratulations!" I said. "What a surprise!" I hugged Caroline and stepped back to examine her. She didn't look any different. I almost expected the weight of this event to show on her face, alter the light in her eyes. But no, the same limpid blue, the same pale smattering of freckles. Only Nathan seemed physically altered: he stood straighter, it seemed to me, shoulders more square. The responsibility perhaps weighed on him, or maybe it simply made him proud. Husband. Wife. Despite our mother's lessons, or maybe because of them, I believed secretly and fervently in the heady promises of love. I believed it would mark us all in some irreversible, wonderful way. Even me someday.

And then, before I knew it, Renee and Joe were in the car, the sun falling in long lines through the low branches, Noni calling out last-minute driving directions, and Renee nodding and yelling out the window, "Don't worry!"

"We'll see you next week!" Noni called. In a few days, when Noni could take time off work, she and I would drive to Boston for the end of Joe's orientation week. Then I would see his drafty dorm room, Alden's emerald quad and sparkling baseball field, and meet a few of the boys who would become his teammates and fraternity brothers, his best friends. They all seemed cut from a mold: strong-boned, clear-eyed, with shockingly good posture. Joe looked like them. He fit in, I thought then; he had found his natural place. We would meet Joe's coach—a tall blond man with dazzling teeth who spoke very fast and made me long for Coach Marty—and eat tepid pasta in the cavernous freshman dining hall. Throughout, Joe would usher us from one event to the next, building to building, with a sort of good-natured bafflement, as though he were as surprised as anyone to find himself here, amid the ivy-covered walls and straight-A students.

As Renee carefully released the parking brake and eased away from the house, I saw Joe freeze: a thin smile, a hand in mid-wave, a length of tan, strong arm.

"Good luck!" I called. This seemed the right thing to say, although I considered Joe already the luckiest, the most charmed. It seemed inevitable that all he wanted would line up before him like the balls that long ago Ace would pitch, pulling them one by one from his bulging pockets as we watched breathless from the stands.

Crack, crack, crack, crack!

Each hit was followed by a startling, whole silence as we watched the ball travel up into air and then breathlessly down, down, down, until it would land with a final dull thump in the grassy field.

PART II

New York City

Year 2079

THE LIGHTS IN the auditorium flickered once, then again. The microphone cut out and I stopped speaking. Henry, dear Henry, stood up from the front row and made his way onstage. He was only eighty-four, but his knees were bad from riding horses all those years, and so he limped a bit, winced as he climbed the steps. There was an empty chair beside me, vacated hastily by the venue organizer, and Henry took it and then took hold of my hand and brought it to his lips. In the second row, a young man and woman watched us. She had vivid red hair, the color of a flag, and the man's arm circled her shoulders. Her hair fell across his chest. They, too, were holding hands. *Entwined,* I thought. *Knotted, woven, linked.*

And that was the moment the room plunged into darkness. I felt the pressure of Henry's palm. There was one short, sharp scream from the balcony, but otherwise the crowd remained calm. No rush for the exits, no hysteria. This kind of thing happened too frequently now for it to rouse much of a panic. Still, I felt the heightened tension in the room. The shallow breathing, hands squeezing hands, sweat rising on palms, eyes staring into nothing. Whispers of confusion and comfort.

We waited in darkness for one minute, three, five. My thoughts turned to Luna, the young Luna here in the room and the other Luna out there somewhere. Was that Luna still alive? Did she ever wonder about me, too? Did she wear a diamond ring on her finger? On a chain around her neck? Or was it hidden away in a drawer, unworn and forgotten?

My eyes adjusted. A few exit signs glowed orange. The greenish hue of screens flickered like fireflies on a summer night. I remembered the security check: DEVICES STRICTLY FORBIDDEN INSIDE THE AUDITORIUM! But of course there are always people who will find a way to break the rules.

"The whole city is out!" one woman declared, reading from a bright light.

This information provoked more agitation, groans, and some hurried, hushed conversations. *Who cares if the city is out?* I thought. Perhaps it was one of those megastorms, or a tremor deep underground, or a hurricane off the coast of Borneo. The news exhausted me. The news bored me. What did it matter? Here we sat, the proverbial ducks. We might as well just reach for the chocolate candy in our pockets, hold the hand of the one we love best, and smile.

Backstage I heard the rustle and hurried footfalls of venue staff doing their best to turn the lights on again.

"We've got it," a voice called, "the generator." There was the thump of a heavy lever being pulled and dim yellow lights emerged along the base of the walls and along the rows between seats.

Suddenly the space was transformed. It was no longer dark and menacing, nor was it a grand auditorium divided between stage and audience. It was now simply a room, a large, cozy room with an arched ceiling and many, many chairs. *Oh, this is something,* I thought. *Now we can have a proper chat. Now we can get down to the things that matter.*

The young woman Luna had been perched on a folding chair.

Now she again stood. She tapped the microphone gently, but it was dead, of course, and so she called out, "Ms. Skinner?"

I felt a surge of great affection for her, irrational in its intensity. That mole, high on her right cheek. I struggled to recall the other Luna, the Luna from a lifetime ago.

"Yes, dear," I said. "Please go ahead." I wanted to scoop her up and protect her, to ferry her out of here and back to my house in the woods with its fence and bunker and generator and fresh-spring well. There I might convince myself that we were safe.

"When did the unraveling begin?" Luna asked.

"The unraveling?" I repeated.

"You said this was a story about the failures of love," said Luna, her tone accusatory. "That's what you said."

"Yes. I did say that."

"You repeat the word *unraveling* several times in *The Love Poem*. You said there was happiness in your family, and then—" Luna did not finish the sentence. She left the question hanging over me, over us all.

"And then," I repeated. I cleared my throat. I glanced at Henry, and he winked, nodded for me to continue. If there is one thing I have succeeded at in life, I thought then, it's choosing husbands.

When did Joe's unraveling begin? I considered how to answer Luna's question. When he met Sandrine? Or took the job at Morgan Capital? Or was it when his baseball career ended with one slide into home? Maybe it began even earlier, when he was still a child who looked like a man, tall and golden, watched and worshipped in Bexley like the local god of any small village. Later, when I asked my sisters, Caroline believed that it began during the Pause, when the ways in which love might disappear first became known to us. We were too young, Caroline said, for that kind of wisdom.

Renee said no, the Pause didn't do that to Joe. Look at the day of our father's funeral when he raged and howled. Renee believed that the unraveling began then, in the yellow house, Joe with the fireplace poker, surrounded by all those who loved him and no one, not one of us, able to help. From that moment, she believed, it was written across his skin, embedded within the veins.

To unravel is to unknit, disconnect, untangle, separate. To fall apart.

"I will tell you this," I replied. "The love of your life is always the one you have betrayed the most. The love that defines you is the one upon whom you once turned your back." I was speaking directly to Luna now, not to the woman with the red hair and her partner, not to Henry, not to the faceless masses here in the hall who had paid money to see me speak. Only to Luna. "The unraveling began—" I said, but then stopped myself, tilted my head. "I don't know when it began, I'm afraid. But I do remember when I first became aware that it was happening."

Chapter 5

IT WAS AUTUMN 2004. An election year, long enough after 9/11 that we no longer spoke of it every day but close enough that the Manhattan skyline still looked broken. I had agreed to help Caroline clean out her new rental house in the small town of Hamden, Connecticut. I'd seen Caroline and her family infrequently since she and Nathan had left Bexley. In twelve years they'd moved four times, from one university town to the next in search of Nathan's Ph.D. in biology and a permanent teaching position. The Skinner-Duffys now numbered five: Nathan, Caroline, ten-year-old Louis, and the twins, six-year-old Lily and Beatrix. Their most recent moves had been to cities where one of Nathan's siblings lived—his brother Terry in Columbus, his sister Maddy in Austin. We'd assumed they'd settle there in Texas, the kids growing up with drawls and a fondness for BBQ, but last month Nathan had received a tenure-track offer from Hamden College, a cozy liberal-arts school located thirty minutes from Noni in Bexley and an hour's train ride from me, Renee, and Joe in New York City.

Caroline was finally coming home.

"I'm happy to help with the move," I told Caroline. "Whatever you need me to do."

"Oh, Fi, thank you," said Caroline. We were on the phone, Caroline in Austin, me in my apartment in Queens that I shared with Jenji and Beth, two friends from Vassar and a third, Umani, we'd found on Craigslist. I was twenty-seven years old and worked as an editorial assistant at an environmental NGO called ClimateSense-Now! My job sounded good at dinner parties, but it required little more than correcting the maddening typos of my boss, Homer Goshen, Ph.D., and writing the occasional high-minded press release. Because of this, and because I was paid less per hour than an adolescent babysitter, I felt justified in taking regular sick days. Inexplicably, Homer allowed it. *Hope that ankle heals up,* he'd say over the phone, or *That must be a nasty bug.* A guilty pang always followed these calls, but rarely was it strong enough to make me go to work.

"The Goats are useless," Caroline continued. "No one can come, even for a few hours. They're all so busy getting married or finishing their dissertations or whatever. Emily showed at New York Fashion Week, did Noni tell you?"

Emily was Nathan's second sister, a recent graduate of FIT, prone to wearing foodstuff as clothing.

"She hasn't mentioned it," I said, although of course Noni had. "It's hard to keep up with the achievements of those Duffys." In the background I heard one of the twins singing a nonsense song and Louis calling, "Mom, where's my oboe?"

"I'm glad you're moving back east, Caroline," I said.

"God, so am I." There was a muffled pause as she spoke to Louis, and then she returned. "And, Fiona," she said, "we need to talk about Joe."

"Sure." I was hungover, eating potato chips out of the bag, and I paused to lick salt from my fingers. "Joe, sure," I said, and then we spoke a bit longer about flight arrivals and train times, and then I hung up the phone.

I didn't think much about why Caroline had mentioned our brother. It was one week before Joe's engagement party, and I assumed she wanted to discuss the wedding. He was set to marry Sandrine Cahill, a popcorn blonde who worked as an accessories buyer at Barneys. Sandrine grew up outside Chicago, the only child of an industrious midwestern family that presided over the manufacture of something ubiquitous but boring, like computer paper or parts of a car. Sandrine was not objectionable in any obvious way. She came from sensible money, and she worked hard to build on it, yet there was something ruthless in her pursuit of the good life. New York did that, I think, to some people. Sandrine wanted prestige and fancy things. She wanted recognition, and she wanted you to know exactly what she possessed: a front-row seat at Marc Jacobs, perfect abdominals, a position in the Junior League, a dinner reservation at Nobu. I couldn't stand her, nor could Renee, but Caroline the eternal optimist insisted we were being unfair. Surprisingly, Noni tolerated her, too. I think our mother secretly admired Sandrine, even after the engagement fell apart, for her collection of achievements. I couldn't help but feel Noni's comparison and judgment: If only Fiona were such a go-getter! Think what she might accomplish.

On Tuesday morning I took the train from Grand Central Station through the city bustle and vacant lots and gray, low urban sprawl, out past the suburbs proper, and into the wider expanses of green until we reached the small middle- and working-class towns like Danbury and Woodbury and Hamden.

Caroline, in a red coat, waved at me from the platform. "You're so skinny," she said as we hugged, and it was neither a compliment nor a complaint. I'd lost another twenty pounds since she'd seen me last Christmas. It was now October.

"Just wait until you see the house," Caroline said. "It looks exactly like a castle. I think this will be it. Our forever home!" She winked. The forever home had been her black swan for years now. After the third move, from Mississippi to Ohio, Caroline began talking about the forever home the way first-graders talked about the tooth fairy. Could it possibly exist? Would she ever see it?

We drove alongside the Metro-North train tracks and rows of beaten-down bungalows, through Hamden's low-lying downtown, then past the green college quad and sports fields and into the residential neighborhood where professors lived in rambling old homes with poster boards of KERRY-EDWARDS '04 perched on every lawn. Caroline accelerated and slowed as she squinted at house numbers. It was late morning, sunny and crisp, trees capped with bright orange leaves. Hamden reminded me so much of Bexley: the same splintery homes, pavement surging with tree roots, the same pumpkins with the same toothy faces. Along the sidewalk, a girl kicked sullenly at leaves, her body thick beneath a pink parka, her legs stout and round as logs. As we passed her in the car, I felt an ache not of nostalgia or grief but something in between the two.

"*Here* it is," Caroline said at last, and pulled in to a short, gravelly drive.

The front yard of Caroline's forever home was covered with damp, unraked leaves and flanked by a row of overgrown shrubs. A fallen tree branch long as the car. A side bed of brittle, brown daisies. A white plastic bag stuck on a bush that flapped in the breeze. Caroline's eyes swept over the mess, but she didn't comment on it, just tilted her head back to take stock.

The house was a pale lavender with yellow trim, the paint faded and flaking. Green clumps of moss clung to the steeply pitched roof, and the front steps were grayed and sagging with age. But the place was large, a true Victorian, with tall windows, gabled molding, and, best of all, a rounded towerlike structure with its own pointed roof rising from the second story.

"It's just like a castle," Caroline said, turning to me, eager as a puppy for affirmation. It was a look I'd never seen before. I was so young when Caroline left Bexley, and then she'd always lived so far away. And all those blond, clever Goats took possession of Caroline in a way that I understood and resented only years later. They helped her through pregnancies and childbirths. They advised on what kind of minivan to buy, would Montessori be a good fit for Louis, do the twins really need that DTaP vaccine? She let herself be folded into the Duffys, and who could blame her? Two bright, chirpy parents, cousins and family football games at Thanksgiving. The Skinners were too few and too complicated to compete with all that photogenic togetherness.

But now here she was. Her hair hung lank from airplane air, her red coat was too thin for this chilly day. She'd arrived into JFK at five fifteen that morning, traveling all this way for a house she'd seen only in photographs.

"You're right, Caroline," I said, and smiled. "A castle."

We opened the front door and stepped into a damp and penetrating cold. I shivered. We stood at the foot of a wide staircase that led up into darkness. To our left, the large living room was bare, with a sooty fireplace on the far wall that gaped dark and menacing as a wound. There was dust everywhere and a dry brown substance crusting the shadowy corners of the room. The place smelled of mold and something else. Something closed-in, musty, animal.

Caroline dropped the bag of cleaning supplies to the floor.

"I think we might need some help," I said. "What about Renee or Joe?"

"Renee's taking on extra ER shifts," Caroline answered in a

monotone. "As if the surgical fellowship isn't enough. And Joe . . . I don't know. I didn't ask him." The last she said vaguely, walking away from me into the dim interior of the house.

We went room to room, the only sound our dull footsteps and Caroline's occasional sharp intake of breath as another mess or sign of age came into view. In the kitchen there was a squat white refrigerator with a long silver handle and a walk-in pantry, its shelves lined with scraps of greasy paper, smelling of old bacon and ammonia. In the hall we found one half bath with an unspeakable toilet. In the dining room, cobwebs intricate as chandeliers hung from the ceiling.

We finished our circle and arrived back in the living room.

"Caroline, can the college find you another house?" I asked gently. The kids and Nathan were set to arrive from Austin in two days.

"Oh, no, this is the only one," she replied. "It's rent-to-buy. It's all we can afford." Her eyes were bright. "But I love it. It's perfect. That big front window? These original floors?" She rubbed a toe along a floorboard to reveal a grainy, dark wood beneath the dirt. "Let's get started."

And so we began to clean with spray bottles and brushes and paper towels, wearing unwieldy yellow gloves and those small paper masks I associated with Asian flus and hypochondriacs. As we worked side by side, I realized how good it felt to have her back. I'd missed Caroline for herself, but what I'd missed more was the idea of us, the four Skinner siblings, together. She was the missing piece of the puzzle of adulthood that I'd been trying for years to put together here in New York with Joe and Renee. Now I could be the quirky aunt to Caroline's kids, taking them to gallery shows and poetry readings in the city, teaching them to swear, and buying them candy. Renee would be the role model who showed them how to work hard and succeed, who examined their cut knees with professional concern. And Uncle Joe would tell them fart jokes, give them extravagant electronics for their birthdays, teach them to catch and throw. Joe still loved baseball, even if he no longer played, and who knew? Maybe Louis would be a natural. And here in Hamden, Caroline would host family dinners where we'd all gather and make toasts and drink and eat cake and play Scrabble. At last we would be siblings who were no longer children.

I was musing about all this, scrubbing with a hard plastic brush the dried-on something from a corner of the kitchen floor, when Caroline pulled off her paper mask and said,

"Fiona, when was the last time you saw Joe?"

I sat back on my heels. "Well, I . . ." I tried to remember the last time I'd seen our brother. It was a month ago at least. An uptown French place with wicker chairs, stiff white napkins at 11:00 A.M. Sandrine had been there, too.

"I met him for brunch," I told Caroline. "I can't really remember when exactly. He's been so busy with work and wedding stuff."

"Did you notice anything? I mean, anything off about him?"

I struggled to remember the details of that morning. They'd arrived late, both of them hungover, too thin, undeniably glamorous. They had asked me to write a poem to commemorate their engagement, a poem to be read at the party next week, and I'd said yes. I'd been flattered and immediately nervous. What if they didn't like it? I had never written a love poem before.

I told Caroline about the poem for Joe and Sandrine. I'd brought a copy with me to Hamden, hoping I could do a test reading for my sister. But Caroline wasn't interested.

"Fiona. We're talking about *Joe*," she said. "How did he seem?"

"He seemed fine," I answered. "He's lost some weight, but he works too hard. You know that."

"Renee is worried about him. She saw him a couple weeks ago

about an irregular heartbeat. She thinks we should all speak to him. Together."

"Heartbeat—" I began, but just then we heard noise from upstairs, a high-pitched animal sound. Across the ceiling a creak of floorboards traveled from one side of the room to the other. Then the noise stopped.

"What was *that*?" Caroline whispered.

"It's okay," I said. "I'll go check it out." I still remembered the ferocity of Caroline's nightmares, the bruised shadows of sleepless nights beneath her eyes.

But Caroline shook her head. "No, we should both go."

*   *   *

AS AN ADOLESCENT Caroline believed what Noni told us about independence and self-reliance and strength. More than anything Caroline did not want to disappoint our mother. But putting Noni's lessons into action proved more difficult for Caroline than for the rest of us. She could do nothing to impress Noni. It had been clear for so long that Joe and Renee were the impressive ones, and for this Caroline felt a certain jealousy and resentment but also a deep, abiding relief.

What remained for Caroline was to surprise our mother. And she did.

As she moved with Nathan for his summer research opportunities and guest teaching positions, Caroline stayed in school. She studied anthropology, history, art history, biology, Spanish, theater. With each move the transfer of credits became more difficult, the registrars more impatient, the path to an actual degree more complex. Caroline persevered. She was not an academic star, no trophies lined her dresser, but our mother valued tenacity.

And then, back in Kentucky, Caroline became pregnant. She

was twenty-one years old. Nathan was three years into his graduate research on Central American tropical frogs. In their rented bungalow, one entire room was devoted to a series of plastic kiddie pools joined together by a complex filtration and pumping system, lit by heat lamps, the temperature maintained at a steamy ninety-five degrees Fahrenheit. Inside this ecosystem lived plant life indigenous to a tropical climate and eight tiny Panamanian golden frogs.

On the day Caroline finally disappointed Noni, she left Nathan at home with the frogs, crouched before the pools, notebook in hand. He nodded absently as she kissed him on the cheek. Caroline was running late for class, again. This one—Ancient Chinese Ceramics—was located across the wide green campus lawn, up a short punishing hill, through a heavy door, inside a room that looked like a doctor's waiting room or a preflight boarding area: white and gray and brown, full of people who slouched and yawned.

At seven months pregnant, Caroline felt unwieldy as a cello. She was panting slightly, her face hot, as she pushed open the classroom door. The teaching assistant glanced up and then away with a roll of his eyes. Although she knew she had nothing to be ashamed of, Caroline felt ashamed. For being late to class, for being married and pregnant, for being distracted and sleepy, for being herself.

"Ms. Duffy," the TA said.

"Yes?" answered Caroline as she settled into a chair without a desk; she no longer fit behind a desk.

"Can you please comment on the ceramics of the later Ming years and their use of the symbol of the bee?" A tattoo of a rose crawled up the TA's neck. He gazed at her with tight, small blue eyes.

"The bee?" she repeated.

The TA nodded. The A/C unit abruptly shut off, plunging the

room into silence. Around her, Caroline felt the swollen anticipation of the group, all fifteen, maybe twenty students. Where before they had been inattentive and uninterested, now, with notice of her humiliation, they became alert.

"Um, I don't know," Caroline replied.

The TA moved immediately on. "Mr. Purcell?" he asked the boy sitting to Caroline's right and Robbie Purcell explained to the class the significance of the bee.

As Robbie rattled on, Caroline felt strangely buoyed by the TA's dismissal. Here she sat in a bland room with bland desks and bland chairs, surrounded by bland people who were not pregnant, who were not harboring life within. Now these people were discussing avidly the importance of the bee. At that moment, deep within her, the baby moved, an elbow or a knee just below her left ribs, and Caroline was transported. There existed nothing so momentous as this feeling of intimacy and distance, the strangeness of it and the atavistic understanding. The TA had no idea. Caroline felt a surge of pity for him. Pity and impatience.

Caroline picked up her notebook and pen and returned them to her bag. She stood and moved toward the door.

"Um, Ms. Duffy," the TA called. "You just got here."

Someone in the class snickered.

"I'm leaving," Caroline said, and she did.

Caroline went directly to the registrar's office and withdrew from the University of Kentucky. The registrar's assistant gazed at her belly and accepted the paperwork without comment. When she arrived back home, Nathan was sitting in the same position as when she'd left. He looked up as she entered the room.

"No more college," she announced breezily, standing in the doorway. "I quit."

Nathan watched her for one long moment, chewing a pen cap. On his lap was a black-and-white composition book, the kind he used for observations on the frogs. He had dozens of them, shelved carefully in the den, the raw data for his dissertation. Caroline felt her breath shorten and catch. For the first time in their relationship, she feared his rejection. Nathan, steady as a heartbeat, had never wavered in his own professional vision and her place beside him, sharing that life. But a college professor married to a college dropout? The vision tilted and shook. An Etch A Sketch in the hands of a restless toddler. What would Caroline do if she wasn't with Nathan? What would she *do*?

Nathan removed the pen cap from his mouth and shrugged. "You can always go back after the baby," he said. "It's just one semester."

"Exactly," she said, exhaling. Her breath returned. The vision stabilized. "I'm so uncomfortable, Nathan. It just seems so pointless."

"I agree," he said, and rose from the chair. "I love you, Caroline." He kissed her and took her hand and led her into the room. "Did you know that the frogs communicate with gestures?" His face was hazy with wonder. "They wave their hands."

"Hands? Is that really the right word?"

"Yes. Hands."

Together they crouched over the pools, lit up like a tropical night by a red heat lamp, and studied the frogs. Their skin was a bright banana yellow spotted with black, the eyes a deeper yellow, nearly gold, and split by a pod of black pupil. Caroline counted the long, thin fingers, each shaped like a tiny upside-down spoon.

"Don't they look like the baby's hands?" Caroline said, turning to Nathan. When their doctor had performed the twenty-week scan, Caroline and Nathan both had gasped. The images offered a revelation of bone and form and quick, jiggery movement.

"They do," Nathan said to Caroline. "See? Life."

* * *

INSIDE THE HAMDEN house, I followed Caroline up the stairs. We moved slowly, cautiously. Ferrets, foxes, even bears lived in the woods around here; or maybe the house had a squatter. We stood for a moment on the landing to listen. And then we heard it: a high-pitched, mewling sort of noise like a newborn's cry. We followed the sound to the master bedroom, where a metal bed frame bereft of mattress sat smack in the middle. Yellow autumn light filtered through the dirty windows, giving the room the feel of an old photo, something ghostly printed on tin. And there in the far corner, splayed atop a pile of old newspapers, was an enormous orange tabby. Her long stomach bristled with pink, distended nipples, and surrounding her were a dozen newborn kittens, each one no bigger than an infant's fist and just as soft, round, and useless.

We stood motionless in the doorway. We made no sound, but the cat saw us. Her ears went rigid. When Caroline began a slow approach, the cat pulled back its head and hissed, showing four pointed white teeth, two up and two down. She looked reptilian, or like a small, vicious monster from a fairy tale. A few of the kittens mewed faintly. One struggled to open its eyes, and then it did and they were the hueless blue of water, and they stared straight into me.

"Uh-oh," I said.

Caroline didn't answer straightaway. "Well, that's unexpected," she said, her voice strained but cheerful. "Of *course* there's a family of cats in the master bedroom."

"At least they're cute." I moved closer to touch one, but the mother reared up its head and hissed. I stepped back. "I bet the girls would love a kitten," I said. Other than the rabbit Celeste, I'd never owned a pet, but the same childish yearning returned now, an echo of an ache so potent I imagined the girls must feel it, too. How could you not want something to care for?

"Well, we've got Milkshake," Caroline replied, referring to their yellow Lab who poured like sticky liquid over every visitor. "And the girls have their gerbils."

"What about Louis?" I suggested.

"He's got Stu the chameleon. And a tankful of saltwater fish."

"Well, we could put up signs. Give them away." I was trying to salvage Caroline's mood, which I could see was declining rapidly and perhaps irreversibly. She was the camel, and this was the straw.

"No." Caroline shook her head. "That would take too long. And Nathan will be here in two days. He'll want to keep them all. *Trust me.*" She said the last with a certain testiness.

"Let's just clean the downstairs first," I said. "Let the cats sleep. We'll decide later." Postponing a difficult decision was a specialty of mine. I found that often the difficult part evaporated into the haze of delay.

But Caroline didn't answer. She was staring at the cats with a mixture of disgust and exhaustion; her mouth had a pulled-down quality, a tired little frown. At this moment all of her family's worldly possessions were packed into a U-Haul being driven from Austin, Texas, to Hamden, Connecticut, by two men named Sasha. The Sashas had claimed they would make no stops. Probably they were in Pennsylvania by now, home of the Amish. Perhaps stuck behind a family in a horse-drawn carriage. Perhaps already running late. Caroline's children, staying the night with a kindergarten friend in Austin, were undoubtedly eating too much sugar and playing with toy guns. Nathan was living out of a suitcase; he'd packed only one pair of pants. Everyone was waiting for Caroline to proclaim the new house ready.

There were times—at Christmas, say, or the day we all took Noni to the shore for her sixtieth birthday—when I envied Caroline's centrality. The way her children bounced around her with their giggles and sticky lips and Nathan rubbed her shoulders as she closed her eyes and sighed: it all looked so fine and sweet. But sometimes it looked simply crushing. A straitjacket of her own making. Every morning she packed three school lunches, each one requiring a different sandwich. Every night three different bedtime stories.

"Listen, I'll take the kittens," I offered. "My roommates keep saying we need a pet."

Caroline sighed. "Fiona. You'll have thirteen pets."

I shrugged. "I'll find homes for some of them."

"That's ridiculous. You don't know how to take care of a cat."

"Of course I do," I said. "Cats are easy."

"They're living things."

"I know that."

"They need food and water."

"I know that, too."

"Consistent care."

"Caroline. *Stop.* I'll keep a few, find homes for a few more. And the rest I'll take to a shelter."

"But they'll die at a shelter."

I tilted my chin, considering. "Yes, that's probably true."

"No." Caroline shook her head. "I can't do that. I'll keep them. I'll figure it out."

"Why don't we give one to Joe and Sandrine!" I said. "A wedding present!" This struck me as an inspired idea, but Caroline shook her head.

"Not Joe," she said, and paused. Something flickered on her face, not the cat or the house, something deeper and older. "Listen, let's go outside for a minute." She kept one eye on the cat as she backed out of the room.

At the end of the hall, I glimpsed the tower's rounded interior wall, painted the same lavender as the house exterior. One small window cast a block of sunlight onto the floor. The space looked utterly beguiling, magical, fit for a princess. "Caroline," I said, "remember our game with the queen mother, from the pond? Remember the spoon? Do you think she ever found her daughter?"

Caroline looked at me with confusion and shook her head. "Fiona, I'm sorry, I don't remember."

"You don't?" I remembered distinctly the curve of the spoon's handle, the bubbles trapped within the green glass bottle. All the stories we had once told each other. How could she have forgotten?

"Fiona, come here, I need to talk to you about something."

I sat beside Caroline at the top of the steps.

"Renee thinks it's happening again," she said. "That Joe's in trouble. The drinking, the drugs, the visions or whatever it is he calls them. We didn't tell you last time."

For a moment I thought Caroline was talking about someone else, a different Joe, not our brother. But there were no other Joes.

"What? What last time?"

"When he was in college. When he quit baseball."

"You mean his knee," I said, not as a question. I remembered the day Joe called Noni to tell her about the knee injury. I'd been at the kitchen table eating lunch. Noni had answered the white wall phone with the long curly cord. "Joe!" she said, and then, "What's the matter?" I watched her face animate, then fall.

"Fiona, there wasn't a knee injury," Caroline said gently. "He was kicked off the team."

I shook my head. "But . . . what about the coach's letter?"

"Renee wrote it."

"And the surgery?"

"Never happened."

"But Joe was on crutches."

"He borrowed them. Only for those days when you and Noni were visiting."

"I don't believe you," I said.

Caroline was watching me. "Renee was worried about this," she said. "Renee thought you'd be mad."

"I'm not mad. I'm—" I stood up and walked away from my sister, down the hall, toward the tower room. Inside, it was smaller than it had seemed from the outside, and draftier, danker. The ceiling did not rise to a point but had been sealed off flat at a height of only seven or eight feet; the plaster was mottled with water stains. It felt confining, not a magical tower at all but a cell. I left the room quickly and stood for a moment in the hall, listening to the mewling kittens.

How to describe the feeling of suddenly not knowing something that you knew? After that call from Joe, Noni had cried for hours, I remembered. She'd tried to reach the coach, the team doctor. Then she called Renee, and it was Renee who explained everything. The ACL tear, the meniscus, how fragile these ligaments were, how difficult to repair fully. Noni had come away from that call no longer tearful but resigned. Her dream, Joe's dream, gone with one slide into home.

But there hadn't been a slide into home. Or an ACL tear or a surgical repair. I shook my head.

"You must have gotten it wrong," I called now to Caroline, who turned to face me. "I don't see how you could have done it. Joe would have told me. Or Noni would have found out—" I stopped. Suddenly I knew that Caroline was telling the truth. Of course they'd done it. The four of us had kept Noni's secret for all those years of the Pause. I was the one keeping secrets now, about the blog, how I spent my time away from the office. The Skinners excelled at secrets. Honesty was where we always fell short.

"I wish you'd told me then," I said.

"You were too young."

"I was seventeen."

"You always idolized Joe. And all his friends. We thought . . ." Caroline paused. "Renee and I didn't think it was a good idea to tell you. That's all."

"I wouldn't have told Noni," I said. "I would have kept the secret."

Caroline watched me for a beat. "Joe said that Dad told him to stop playing baseball," she stated without emotion. "Dad said that Joe's throwing arm wasn't what it used to be. *Dad* told him this."

"Dad?" All at once I remembered that long-gone afternoon from the Pause when Joe took me to the yellow house and we stood in our parents' old bedroom and waited for our father. I had never told anyone about that day, and I did not tell Caroline now. The memory felt like a small, terrible bomb I was holding in my hands.

* * *

FOR WEEKS CAROLINE did not tell our mother that she'd quit school.

"You should tell Noni," Nathan would say over breakfast or as they got ready for bed. He would always touch her in some way as he said it—take hold of her hand, stroke her forearm—but it made no difference.

"I can't," Caroline always answered. "She'll be so disappointed."

"Maybe. But you should still tell her."

Through the years Nathan had finally won Noni over and now had an easier relationship with her than Caroline did. But he didn't know Noni as Caroline knew her. He didn't understand the peculiar combination of history both small and large that animated Noni's parenting. Caroline remembered all the discussions of feminism at the dinner table, the college-fund jam jar on the windowsill that bristled with dollar bills. Nathan's success was not symbolic; it was merely success.

One month after withdrawing from college, Caroline was settled in the braided hammock strung between two sturdy aspens in the backyard when Nathan brought her the phone.

"Call your mother," he directed. "I can't keep lying to her."

Caroline accepted the phone but did not dial. She lay back and watched a white butterfly flounce from one droopy daisy to the next.

Perhaps, Caroline thought, Noni would remember her own pregnancies. The backaches, the troubled sleep, the brain that flitted and flew from one subject to the next while beneath it all droned the urgent soundtrack of one small heartbeat. How could Caroline concentrate? How could she possibly fit in among a bunch of adolescents who partied all weekend and believed a seventeenth-century bee worthy of discussion? People who thought only of themselves? Caroline was beyond all that; already she existed beyond herself. Caroline's thoughts and ambitions extended wider, broader, further into a peopled future, the branching limbs of family expanding above and beyond, with herself at the center, the powerful, nurturing trunk.

The butterfly flapped out of sight, and Caroline picked up the phone and dialed her mother.

"Oh, Caroline," Noni said after Caroline had explained. "You are not a tree! You are twenty-one years old."

"But I know what I want. I don't need a degree to do it."

"But what you want might change. That's all I'm saying. Prepare for the future." Noni paused. "Have you talked to Renee about this?"

"No." Caroline felt the familiar prickling of resentment. "I don't need to talk to Renee. It's one semester, Noni. I can always go back."

"But you won't."

"How do you know that?" Caroline asked.

"I know," Noni answered. "I just know you won't do it."

And Caroline, who considered herself to be good-natured and easygoing, an optimist with a sunny disposition, became enraged. Without another word she hung up the heavy, cordless phone and threw it down to the ground. Caroline was breathing heavily, hotly. She placed a hand on her chest and leaned back into the hammock. It was unseasonably humid, even for Kentucky, and today Caroline wore only a pair of Nathan's boxer shorts and an old bikini top that allowed a clear view of her bare belly. As her breath raced, she felt beads of sweat accumulate on her upper lip, at her temples, and across the taut skin of her stomach.

"Baby," she said to her belly, "sometimes your Noni is rude and mean. Sometimes she's a bitch. But she loves us. Really she does. She loves us the same as the others."

Caroline closed her eyes and drifted into a strange half sleep where she dreamed that she was hitting a tree over and over again with her fists. The tree of course did not respond; the tree simply stood there impassive, resolute as any tree, which only spurred Caroline to punch harder, kick and scream, anything to provoke a response, but all she managed were fists and feet that were sore and bloody.

Then she woke up. The phone was ringing, ringing, ringing. Renee's number appeared on the screen. For one long minute, Caroline opened and closed her hands, thinking of the dream and her sore knuckles. She was still angry at Noni, who had always demanded so much of her children, so much, and yet refused to recognize Caroline's genuine efforts. Noni believed so fervently in the lessons of her own experience that she could not envision a scenario where they might fail to apply. Had Noni ever loved her husband the way she, Caroline, loved Nathan Duffy? Doubtful. Had Noni ever chosen her life the way Caroline has chosen hers? Absolutely not. Noni's life had been poured over her head like a bucket of milk.

The phone continued to ring, but Caroline still did not answer. She knew already the purpose of Renee's call: Noni had asked Renee to persuade Caroline to stay in school, to hew her life more closely to the marvel that was Renee's. Caroline and Renee could have this particular discussion next week or next month or next Christmas, or they could have it now. Caroline picked up the phone.

"Caro," said Renee. She was crying.

"I've decided," Caroline said in a rush. "You can't talk me out of it."

"What?" Renee paused. "No—it's Joe."

"Joe?" Caroline sat up, and the sudden movement of her ungainly weight upset the hammock. For a moment she teetered, and then she tilted out, landing heavily on all fours, her stomach grazing the grass. She grabbed for the phone. "What's the matter with Joe?"

As Renee explained, Caroline moved herself slowly to a sitting position. She'd scraped her knee, but she did not wipe away the blood that ran down her leg.

Joe, Renee told her, was in trouble. There had been a fraternity party at Alden College with an overabundance of vodka punch, various illegal drugs, and some three hundred undergraduates. Two dozen people were taken to the ER. One girl had nearly died. Joe was one of the party organizers, Renee told Caroline, and so the dean was coming down hard on him. He was off the baseball team. He might even be expelled.

"Noni can't know about this," said Renee, and there was an old desperation in her voice that Caroline hadn't heard in many years. "I'm supposed to meet with some people at the college later today, but I've got exams. I'm supposed to be studying for the boards."

"Oh, Renee, I'll help," Caroline said, and she remembered her dream about beating the tree. She'd assumed the tree was Noni, but perhaps instead it was Joe. No matter the disruptions that swirled around him, he remained the same: imperturbable, stubborn, oblivious to the sky and earth and rain that nurtured him every day.

Caroline and Renee talked for nearly an hour, circling what they knew and what they could reasonably keep from Noni. They made a rough plan: Renee would attend the meeting, gauge how serious the college was about expelling Joe, and try her best to talk them out of it. Then together she and Caroline would devise a story. Why was Joe off the team? An injury seemed the most plausible explanation; he'd sprained an ankle late last year, and Coach Marty had always been concerned about that left knee. They would protect Noni. Isn't this what they'd always done?

Caroline clicked off the phone. Still sitting on the grass, she realized that her lower back ached, her legs hurt. She tried to stand but stopped herself. She felt . . . what exactly? An internal stirring, a glancing discomfort. She became aware of an insect hum in the air and the swirling pollen that floated lazily across her vision and that peculiar fecund fullness to the trees and grass, even the clouds overhead, that seemed to Caroline uniquely southern. Bexley would never see a rosebush like that rosebush. Ripe. Bursting.

Again Caroline tried to stand, and again the discomfort was

enough to make her pull back. She wondered if Nathan was within earshot. No. He was inside with the frogs. It was time, Caroline believed, for their supper.

And then she noticed a dark wetness on the grass and on her legs. More than a scraped knee.

Using the hammock as a shaky support, she pushed herself to standing and immediately felt a rush of liquid between her legs and a tight, twisting pain. No, she thought. No. She was thirty-four weeks pregnant. It was too early.

"Nathan!" Caroline called, and folded into herself.

*   *   *

"SO THE DAY Louis was born was the day they kicked Joe off the baseball team," Caroline told me. "Renee came up with the knee-injury story. Renee dealt with the college."

We were sitting at the top of the stairs. I had been running a fingernail over a groove in the molding, marking a line in the thick white paint, and now I stopped.

"And how is all this happening again?" I asked.

"Well, Joe's drinking too much. Cocaine, other drugs, too, probably. He had some kind of heart episode recently. Renee is worried he's putting himself at risk, but he denies it, of course. She thinks Joe needs an intervention. And she wants the three of us to do it together." Caroline paused. "I think he just needs to grow up. He needs his own doctor for starters. Why does Renee keep *doing* this?"

"Joe doesn't do coke," I said.

"He's done it for years," replied Caroline. "You never noticed?"

I shook my head. But maybe. What had I seen? Joe's repeated trips to the bathroom, a joke about too much coffee, his runny nose and bloodshot eyes. A jumpiness, an elation. In college there had been plenty of pot, that musty-sweet smell in his hair and on his clothes. Last Christmas at Noni's house, Joe always with a gin and tonic in hand, sodden lime slices on every table, every countertop.

"Ace gets him the drugs," Caroline said. "That's what Renee says."

In the past few years, Joe and Ace had become friends once again. During college they'd drifted, but now both lived in New York, both worked long hours inside towering office buildings. Joe had described Ace to me as a different person since our summers at the pond. No longer aggressive and lost, no longer trying to impress with bravado and risk taking. I had believed my brother.

In the space of this past hour with Caroline, a gaping hole had opened. Joe and Renee and Caroline stood on one side, me on the other, the youngest, the baby, alone.

A surge of feline whimpers came from the bedroom, and Caroline and I looked toward the door.

"We need to deal with the cat," said Caroline.

"Okay, I'll wait out here," I replied, not looking at her.

Caroline sighed and closed her eyes and then immediately opened them again. "I know! I've got some oxy," she said.

I raised my eyebrows.

"Chronic back pain," Caroline said. "*You* try carrying two babies in your uterus for thirty-nine weeks. Let's go find some tuna."

Caroline and I left the house and drove to the Hamden main street in search of cat food. In the cramped, dusty aisles of a corner grocer, we found two tins of tuna fish. Caroline also bought a pack of Marlboros.

Inside the parked car, Caroline lit up.

"I didn't know you smoked," I said.

"In high school," Caroline replied. "I still think about it. I've been thinking about it a lot recently. Just don't tell Nathan. He'd probably divorce me. Too *unwifely*." Caroline inhaled deeply and exhaled out the window in a long, forceful column of smoke. "Oh," she said, and closed her eyes.

With her eyes closed, head back, my sister looked different. *Surrendered*, I thought. *Abandoned, adrift, lost.* She'd given in to the pull of the nicotine, the problem of the cats, the stress of the new house. Caroline was always so cheerful and in control, secure in the way of life's major acquisitions—love, children, home—that her good mood seemed to me a given. What reason could Caroline possibly have to doubt anything, to spend even one night staring at a dark ceiling? But of course she had her breaking point. We all did.

I considered Joe's job at Morgan Capital: his dazzling office, the boat parties and bonuses. And Sandrine. A yearlong courtship capped with that engagement ring, an acorn-size solitaire that sat high on her finger and seemed to suck all the light from any room. Next week Joe's boss, Kyle Morgan, was hosting the engagement party. One hundred guests had been invited, a jazz quartet hired, caterers and waiters, bartenders and florists, and a color scheme of green, pink, and white. It was an event almost as grand as the wedding itself. That's what Sandrine had wanted. Sandrine and her ponytail, her pale pink nails. At that brunch last month, she'd absently pushed the diamond in circles around her finger. With each pass I'd wondered what it felt like to play with a ring that beautiful, to understand its promise and possess it so completely.

"We don't need to worry about Joe," I said now to Caroline. "I'm not Sandrine's biggest fan, but he loves her. He's getting married! His job is demanding, but it's what he *does*. And he's got tons of friends. Renee is overreacting. Maybe he smokes some pot or drinks too much on the weekends, but give him a break. He works a lot of hours. He's an adult. We all have our vices."

Caroline sat up, raised the cigarette with a wry twist of her mouth.

"See?" I said.

"But Renee thinks he's spending too much money."

"He's *got* so much money."

"He bought a car and a parking space. Did he tell you? And they're looking at four-bed apartments on the Upper West Side. Central Park West. Do you have any idea what those cost?"

"He works in banking. It's a different world. Renee spends all her time around sick people. Of course she'll think he's sick. Joe is not sick."

I saw Caroline hesitate. We had always followed Renee on questions of significance. It wasn't that we saw her as infallible, only less fallible than we were.

"I know Joe better than Renee does," I continued. "If something bad were happening, he would have told me." Even as I said these words, I knew they weren't true, not anymore. When had Joe and I last seen each other alone, without Sandrine? Or Noni? When had we talked about something other than his job, my job, how much money I needed to borrow?

Caroline sighed. "Oh, I don't know," she said, and rubbed her eyes. And in that moment my sister Caroline, who wanted always to assume the best of a house or a person, began to believe me. Joe was okay. An intervention was completely unnecessary.

"Well, you'll have to convince Renee," she said. "You'll never reach her on the phone. Talk to her at the engagement party. She promised Joe she'd be there."

As Caroline weakened, I felt a sort of relief, that I had saved Joe and he would in time be grateful. It was also a reprieve from an understanding that had begun to sink in: That what I thought was true about Joe was not true. That I was a little sister who worshipped her big brother and would never see him clearly. I could barely admit this to myself; I would never admit it to Caroline.

We sat in silence for three minutes, five, ten, as Caroline smoked another cigarette.

"Caroline, the cat?" I said at last. I inclined my head toward the house.

"Oh. Right." She flicked a butt out the window. "Let's go deal with the fucking cat."

In the kitchen Caroline pounded three oxycodone tablets with her shoe and sprinkled them over a plate of tuna.

At first the cat ignored the plate.

"Come on, it's *tuna*. When have you eaten this well?" Caroline said.

Some of the kittens were asleep, translucent lids covering eyeballs the color of sky, their bodies downy and plump. Others kneaded the cat's belly as they nursed. Caroline waved the plate beneath the cat's nose, and at last it lifted its head and sniffed the tuna. Delicately it nibbled, and then, with a handful of bites, the plate was clean.

"Now we wait," said Caroline.

"How long?"

"Well, with me maybe fifteen minutes. But that's just one pill." Caroline paused, considering the three. "I hope we didn't kill it," she said.

It took five minutes. The cat's eyes wavered, then closed. Its head tilted back.

I found a cardboard box, and together we picked up the cat, its body heavy and difficult to grip, liquid concrete in a sack of fur, and dropped it inside. We loaded up the kittens, and then Caroline carried the box downstairs and slid it into the back of the car. Clouds had moved in. Across the lawn fallen leaves jumped and spun with the wind. One lodged in my hair, which was longer than it had been at Christmas, dyed a deep brownish red that was richer and darker than my natural color. Caroline plucked the leaf from my hair.

"So are you dating?" she asked.

"Um, yeah, you could say I'm dating," I answered. Maybe Caroline would have understood about the blog, but I wasn't ready to tell her. Not yet. I needed some unmistakable, tangible sign of success to put before my family. I had never played a sport or excelled academically or been popular in school; I had only ever written words into secret books, and now this, *The Last Romantic*.

"Anyone special?" Caroline asked.

"No, definitely not."

"You'll meet someone soon enough," she said in a soothing way, "don't worry."

"Oh, I'm not worried," I said. "I'm not really looking for someone special."

Caroline raised her eyebrows. "How did you get your cheeks to look like that?" she asked me. "Makeup?"

"No," I said. "Not makeup."

"And your eyes look different, too."

"I've lost weight, Caroline. Almost fifty pounds"

"Oh." Caroline gazed at me, standing in the overgrown yard of this dirty, disappointing house, and I saw on her face a jealousy so pure it took my breath away. By the time Caroline was my age, she'd already had three children and been married to Nathan for eight years.

"Let me take the cats, Caroline," I said. "You've got enough to deal with."

"No," she said. "I'll take them."

I saw my sister struggle, the rubbing together of two versions of herself. The first was Caroline the mother, the nurturer, a woman who wanted the kittens to live, who cared for her family and bestowed emergency hugs and made pancakes from scratch, who was worried about Joe and wondered why he did the things he did, who was trying to protect him. But the other Caroline was worn out. She wanted to get rid of the kittens; she wanted Nathan to make the pancakes for once; she wanted nothing more than to sleep a full night in a hotel bed covered with sheets that someone else had washed. She wanted Joe to take care of himself. Why should she take care of everyone? When had she signed up for *that*? It seemed that every year her scope of concern grew wider and more unmanageable. Preschool, elementary school, home school, the new towns, the new mothers' groups, Nathan's new colleagues, Nathan's new class schedule. No. Enough was enough. Caroline needed to draw a line or she might explode. She might lie down beside the mother cat and its dozen dozing kittens and never get up again.

*　*　*

AFTER NATHAN HEARD Caroline's calls, after he found her lying on the grass, curled around her stomach as though it were something she was holding rather than something that was part of her, after the paramedics arrived (faster than Nathan thought possible), after the blessedly calm ER nurse told Nathan that the baby was coming now, he's crowning now, Mr. Duffy, Caroline Skinner Duffy screamed a great loud *"Fuck!"* and pushed baby Louis into the world. He was messy and bloody, purple, crying his head off, with a mop of dark curly hair and a nose the size of a pencil eraser. Caroline held her son to her chest and began to cry, because she knew with absolute clarity that she had been waiting her whole life to meet this boy. Every minute had been leading her to this one now, minute falling into minute, pushing her forward, and thank goodness. Thank *God* (although Caroline had never before believed in God) she had done everything just as she'd done it so that she might be sitting here now in this achingly bright room, surrounded by these two miraculous women wearing yellow scrubs and rubber shoes that made the smallest, most pleasing squeaks as they moved around the bed, and in her arms holding this tiny, perfect body.

With her thumb Caroline rubbed a bit of blood off her son's cheek. His eyes were the darkest blue, almost black, and he gazed at her with a seriousness that seemed nearly wise. But how? Caroline thought. How could he already be wise?

"Look at him." Nathan's voice at her shoulder so startled Caroline that she almost released her grip on Louis. She had forgotten that Nathan was here, too.

"Oh, Nathan," Caroline said. "Look at him!"

"He's amazing."

Caroline did not even nod, the statement being so self-evident. Together they watched Louis breathe.

Then one of the miraculous women told them that she needed to take Louis away for respiratory tests and monitoring because his Apgar score was low. "You can visit him in a few hours," the nurse said, and gently removed Louis from Caroline's grip. As the nurse wrapped him efficiently in a yellow flannel blanket printed with small blue elephants, Caroline began to weep. Nathan took her hand, but he too was crying, and they gripped each other with a desperate strength as their son was carried from the room.

Twenty-four hours later, Caroline opened her eyes in her hospital room that was painted the same chalky pink as calamine lotion. Baby Louis, swaddled up tight as a sausage, was asleep beside her in a rolling cot. He had been discharged already from the NICU; in two days they would both be going home.

Sitting in a chair beside the cot was Renee.

"Renee!" Caroline said.

"Congratulations sleepyhead," said Renee. "I finished my board exams and thought I'd come see you."

Maybe it was the post-delivery drugs or her general state of sleepiness or the new-mother hormones, but Caroline had never before been happier to see another human being.

"I'm so glad you came!" she said. "I'm really touched."

"Of course I came. Noni was worried about you."

"When does she get here?"

"Oh— Well, she had to work. She'll come down next week. Nathan told her that would give you guys a chance to settle in first."

Caroline wondered when this conversation had taken place and why Noni hadn't come immediately. If a first grandchild didn't merit a day off work, then what did? And what time was it? What day was it?

It was then that Renee smiled and laughed. "How lucky that Louis came when he did," she said.

"Lucky? But he was too early," said Caroline, confused.

"I mean on the same day as Joe's trouble with the college. Noni was so distracted. I don't think I could have gotten away with it otherwise. She'd still be asking questions and wanting to talk to the coach. Now she's buying onesies. It worked out perfectly."

"Oh, of course," Caroline said; now she understood. "Joe. Perfect timing."

Renee peered into Louis's cot. "He's cute," she said without touching him, and then she sat back down in the chair.

They talked for a bit longer, though later Caroline would not be able to recall the details of the conversation. Undoubtedly they talked about Joe. Probably the delivery, the ER doctor, burping, diapers.

What Caroline would remember was that after Renee left, she closed her eyes and she thought about Joe and about baby Louis. She thought about Noni, her sisters, how we were raised, who we'd all become, and Caroline decided then that everything she knew about parenting was misconceived. That she and Nathan would start fresh. The past didn't matter, it didn't, as long as you were aware of its reach. If you possessed that self-knowledge, you would not fall down the same holes. That day in the hospital, alone with her newborn son, Caroline promised him that she would be a better mother than the one she'd had. And it would be this imperative, flawed and guilt-ridden and imbued with Caroline's own sense of personal history, that would propel my sister through the next fifteen years of her life. Only after Joe's accident would she realize the futility of her mission. Better was largely irrelevant when it came to mothering because the entire enterprise relied on the presumption that one day, sooner than you thought, your child would become an entirely self-reliant, independent person who made her own decisions. That child wouldn't necessarily remember the Halloween costumes you made from hand six years running. Or maybe she did, but she resented you for it because she'd wanted store-bought costumes just like all her friends. It didn't matter how great a mother you tried to be; eventually every child walked off into the world alone.

* * *

WITH THE CATS finally out of the way, we moved our cleaning operation upstairs. We scrubbed and wiped and swept up the cat hair, the droppings, the dust, the worst of the linoleum stains in the bathroom. We threw away the kittens' newspaper nest. The October sun through clean windows made the bedrooms glow as though a giant candle burned somewhere within the walls.

"I'll sew some curtains, maybe paint a mural for the girls," mused Caroline as we stood in a doorway surveying our work. I narrowed my eyes, and yes, I could see it, Caroline's vision. The forever house.

And then Caroline declared it enough, sufficient for today. She would spend the night at Noni's, then return tomorrow to oversee the cleaning service she'd decided to hire. They'd descend in the morning with power vacuums and a team of ten. The house wouldn't be perfect before her family arrived, but it would be clean. It would be enough.

It was late afternoon when we emerged outside again. Sun slanting through orange leaves, a deeper chill in the air.

"Thanks," Caroline said. "I appreciate you coming, Fiona. And just watch Joe at the party, okay? See what you think. Talk to Renee. I don't know. Maybe he doesn't need any help. Maybe he's okay." Caroline shrugged. "Wait—I haven't even asked you about work or your poetry or anything."

"All fine," I said. I smiled at my sister. "All great."

Caroline nodded absently. "Good," she said without looking at me. "And do you need any, you know, money or anything?"

"Funding for the arts?" I said, and shook my head quickly. "Nope. Thanks, Caroline." I was a socialist at heart and took my siblings' money as I imagined the executive director of ClimateSenseNow! accepted donations from guilt-ridden corporate CEOs. We all valued the same ideals; we just had different ways of expressing those values. But her assumption that I needed cash, her reluctance at offering it, embarrassed me. I knew that my siblings saw me as irresponsible, but wasn't I here today, helping her? Didn't that count for something?

I peered into the back of the car; the cat's body was splayed, limbs at odd angles, motionless.

"Still out cold," I said.

"I can't keep them," Caroline replied. "You're right, it's too much. Let's do a shelter."

"Are you sure?"

Caroline nodded. "They won't die. I'm sure they'll find nice homes. They look like high-class cats. People are bound to see their potential."

"I think that's the best thing," I said. "There's a place in Milford. We can make it there before six o'clock."

Caroline hesitated. "Fiona, can you do it?"

"Do what?"

"Can you take them to the shelter? I can't. I know I won't go through with it."

"How? I don't have a car. I'd have to leave you here."

"No. Take them with you to the city. On the train. They'll be knocked out for a few more hours. I'll give you money for a cab from the station. You can go straight to a shelter. Okay?"

What Caroline was suggesting struck me as slightly preposterous— me, on a Metro-North commuter train on a weekday afternoon, rush hour, with a box full of kittens and their fat, mean, drugged-out mom—but I didn't want Caroline to change her mind. My sister needed someone to help her, and that someone was me.

"Okay," I shrugged. "I'll do it."

"And one more thing," Caroline said with a sly smile. "Will you read me the poem you wrote for Joe and Sandrine?"

"Really?" I said. Earlier in the day, she'd been so dismissive. Plus, as far as I knew, Caroline had never read a poem in her life, let alone one of mine. "Isn't it late? Don't you have to get going?"

"No, not yet," she said. "I can't come to Joe's party, you know that. I want to hear it."

A breeze came up and blew hair around my face. I felt a tremor of self-consciousness and embarrassment, residue of my adolescence and all its awkward wishing. It seemed ridiculous that I would still yearn for my siblings' approval, but here it was.

"You look amazing," Caroline said gazing up at me. "Have I told you that? So strong and beautiful. Please read the poem. Honestly. I'd love to hear it."

"Okay."

I pulled the scribbled sheet of paper from my purse and stood before Caroline. She sat unsteadily on the front steps of the house, wood creaking as she tried to find a comfortable spot. Here was her family's new home: its sweeping wide porch, the delicate molding on the railings, the paint flaking but the exact shade of purple found on the inside lip of a seashell. The peaked roof of the tower, its shingles shaped like half-moons, pierced the blue sky.

"Caroline, it *does* look like a castle," I said. "Really."

She stopped her fidgeting. "I'm ready. Read to me."

"This is called 'He and She,'" I began.

While I read the poem, a crow squawked only once and the wind quieted down so that Caroline heard every word. At the end my sister clapped wildly and said, "It's wonderful, Fiona. Joe will love it."

Chapter 6

ON THE NIGHT of Joe's engagement party, Renee was working overnight in the ER. She was a fellow in transplant surgery, but Jaypa, the attending physician, was short-staffed and had asked her to take a shift. As a medical student, Renee had always loved the ER—it was quick, urgent, dirty, the opposite of transplants—so she told Jaypa, sure, but if she wasn't out by seven for her brother's engagement party, she would send his fiancée down to mess Jaypa up.

"Do you promise?" Jaypa said; he'd met Sandrine before. "Sounds like fun."

The first ten hours of the shift were hectic—a gunshot wound, two heart attacks, three broken bones, a schizophrenic off his meds—but then Renee managed to sleep a couple hours in one of the rickety resident cots. She woke up, ate a bagel, drank some coffee, and the last hours proceeded with a snoozy calm. Now she had only ninety minutes to go. A heart monitor beeped. A nurse's clogs squeaked. The external glass doors heaved open, and two paramedics entered, talking about the Giants and what a season. They laughed. Renee yawned.

All week she'd convinced herself that the party would be fine, maybe even fun, but in moments like this—her defenses lowered by exhaustion, her mind unoccupied by sewing stitches or drawing blood—she could be honest with herself. No, she did not want to celebrate Joe and Sandrine's engagement. Two hours of feigned delight at Joe's unfortunate selection of Sandrine Cahill as a wife. Two hours of forced conversation with bankers, lawyers, and aging frat boys from Alden College. Two hours of answering questions about her marital status—nope, still single, nope, no kids!—and two hours of forgetting that Joe teetered on a ledge of his own making.

Or did he? It was so hard to tell what was simply Joe being Joe—charming, affable, careless—and what was a problem. Renee had struggled to recognize the distinction before. In college she'd misread the signs and thought he'd be fine. Just fraternity partying, that's how she'd described it to Caroline. But then, so quickly, Joe had spiraled out of control.

Her sisters thought she was overreacting.

Yesterday Caroline had called Renee to tell her this. "Don't you think Fiona would know if something was going on?" she'd said. Renee had not responded. It was true: Fiona and Joe had always been close, she looked up to him so much. These days Renee saw Joe infrequently. They were both so busy with their work. Even rarer was seeing Joe without Sandrine.

"I can't come to the party," Caroline continued. "I've got my hands full with the move and the new house. When would we even do this intervention thing anyhow?"

"As soon as possible. We need to act before it escalates," said Renee. "You can't leave me alone on this, Caroline. Not again."

For a moment there was silence on the line. "I was having a baby, Renee. I did not mean to leave you alone."

Renee recognized that her resentment was unfair. She knew that Caroline had wanted to help that last time. But still. Caroline pushed Renee's most sensitive buttons. Because Renee did not have children or a family, she was always expected to step in when stepping in was required. Baking the pies at Thanksgiving. Talking to Noni about her will. Giving Fiona money for a security deposit on her apartment. And Joe. Always Joe. Once Renee had relished this responsibility, had prided herself on being the one in charge. Not anymore.

Renee closed her eyes, tilted the phone away from her mouth, and exhaled slowly. Noni had sent her an article about meditative breathing, how it calmed the central nervous system. Whenever Renee thought about her brother, a hectic thrum started in her chest, and now the thrum was galloping. Joe had been working brutally long hours. She wondered if he would be high at his own party. Probably. Ace would be there.

Renee counted to six, inhale, seven, exhale.

"Renee?" said Caroline. "Are you there? Are we finished?"

Renee opened her eyes. The breathing exercise was bullshit, she decided.

"Okay," she said. "I'll talk to him at the party. Just talk, and then we'll see. I'll let you know how it goes."

They'd ended the call, but the thrum in Renee's chest had persisted, an urgent staccato beat of *Joe-Joe-Joe* that followed her through the rest of that day and the next, and now, tonight, while she sat with her coffee in the ER, the beat grew louder as each passing minute brought her closer to the engagement party.

Jaypa sidled up to the nurses' station and set his iPhone on the desk. He winked at Renee, then pressed Play. As the opening notes of Beethoven's Fifth filled the space, Jaypa loudly cracked the knuckles on each hand and began to conduct. Eyes squeezed shut, arms pumping, a trail of blood faint on the front of his sky-blue scrubs. He'd almost attended music school, Jaypa had told Renee, but his parents would pay for school only if he switched to medicine. And so he'd switched.

Renee liked Jaypa, though she did not trust him. Once he had said to her, "Renee, you're not like the other girl residents. I don't mean that in a bad way. I mean it in a good way." Currently he was dating a nurse, a lovely twenty-two-year-old brunette from Arkansas.

Renee watched as Jaypa reached the first-movement crescendo. He should really be meeting with one of the residents or catching up with paperwork, she thought. The attending had responsibilities; he made more money than any of them. But Jaypa liked to put on a show. Renee knew this about him. The nurses, the residents, the EMTs, they all knew this about him, and so now they all stopped to watch. Renee saw Jaypa open one eye just a crack to assess his audience; then he continued with a dramatic flurry of hand movements.

Men, thought Renee. How many hours had she spent tolerating the ridiculous behavior of disappointed men?

The ER's external doors slid open, and a gust of cold street air traveled through the waiting room, admissions office, triage, all the way into the examining rooms. Renee shivered and pulled on her cardigan.

"Help!" called a man's voice. "Help my wife!"

Immediately the sleepy order of the late-shift ER splintered into a dozen different moving parts. A nurse rushed forward with a gurney. Jaypa switched off the music. A first-year resident grabbed her stethoscope and walked-ran toward the entry. Renee yawned again and checked her watch. Forty-five minutes until the end of her shift. Forty-five minutes until the party. She sat back and waited for the patient to arrive.

It didn't take long. The door burst open with Jaypa and two trauma nurses pushing a gurney. On top lay a hugely pregnant woman, her legs striped with blood, stomach raw and exposed by the lift of her shirt. Holding the woman's hand was a middle-aged man in jeans and a faded Nirvana tee, his face pale and drawn, eyes red.

Immediately Renee knew what had happened: an attempted home birth. The woman's long hair was wet from a tub. The smell of sweat and incense came off the man in waves.

"You're her husband?" Jaypa asked the man, who nodded. "Ma'am, how many weeks? Do you have any health conditions?"

"Forty-one weeks," the husband answered. "And she's diabetic."

"Diabetic?" Jaypa stopped and placed his hands on the taut risen skin of the woman's stomach. He pushed, assessed. "Macrosomia," he said to Renee. "We need a C-section."

Renee picked up the receiver on the wall to call upstairs to surgery.

The woman began to cry. "Don't let them take me," she said to her husband. "Don't leave me."

"I'll stay with you," he answered.

"Don't let them take me—" The woman inhaled sharply as another contraction hit.

"I'll find you," the man said, stroking his wife's hair. "I'll always find you."

Renee was on hold when he said this. She felt the receiver knock against her ear and realized that her hand was shaking.

"Hello? Hello?" said a nurse on the other line. "We've got a room, you can bring her up. Hello?"

*　*　*

I'll always find you.

Renee never knew his name, she never saw him again after that night, but for many years she thought every day about the man in the car. Every quickening of her heart as she walked along a dark street; every surge of fearful adrenaline; every hiccup of tension or worry when she found herself alone with a strange man for however brief a time—on an elevator, in a waiting room, walking in opposite directions along a quiet sidewalk. All of this, her acute awareness of everyday vulnerability, she blamed on the man in the car.

That long-ago night, Renee stepped off the school bus and there it was, a car she'd seen before. Brown two-door, long and low to the ground, its hood shaped like the snout of a fox. She didn't know about cars, couldn't say what make it was, but the shape was distinctive enough that she remembered it from the week before, and possibly the week before that. When had Renee first seen the brown car waiting by the school bus? She couldn't say exactly. It hadn't seemed important.

The bus lights blinked ruby red in the early-evening dark. It was a few days into November, a week past Halloween. Fallen leaves dull in their colors lined the sidewalks in sodden drifts and clogged the sunken runoff grates. The trees were stark, empty birds' nests stuck like clots in the veined webs of branches.

From the school bus, a creaky metal arm extended into the opposite lane, but cars kept right on going.

"You gotta stop, it's the law," the driver called weakly out the window.

Renee waved good-bye to Missy and Katie and Theresa, each of them hurtling off onto different streets toward home, shoulders pulled forward with their backpacks. Missy with her flute case knocking against a hip.

Renee, alone on the sidewalk as the bus pulled away. Across the street, the car. Lights off, but Renee saw a figure in the driver's seat. A male silhouette. One elbow out the window. Sunglasses, despite the dark. She noticed the man, but she was not afraid, not at first. This was year three of the Pause. Renee was too busy to be afraid. Track practice, homework, Joe's baseball, cooking dinners, running baths, washing dishes and clothes. Any childhood fears had been so fully realized—darkness, death, solitude—that she saw them now almost as comforts. Obstacles she had surmounted. Fears converted to routine.

Renee began walking fast, she always walked fast, thinking of the frozen pizza she would put in the oven for dinner—or had they eaten that on Monday? She recalled also a box of mac and cheese, an orange the color of a highway worker's vest. She was hungry. She picked up the pace.

It was then she heard his voice.

"Hey, baby. I've seen you before."

The car was there, right beside her, inching along the road. His voice was not threatening, not loud. He spoke so faintly she almost didn't make out the words. She looked ahead: No one on the sidewalk. No cars passing. It was dinnertime. Lights blazed in the windows of every house she passed. Each one its own private universe.

Renee turned her head and smiled—why did she smile? *Smile at the nice man.* It was an instinct, a directive from childhood, and she regretted it as soon as she felt her lips split.

"Yeah, baby," the man said. "You've got a pretty smile. Want me to drive you somewhere? Come on, get in. It's cold."

Renee shook her head. "No thanks," she said. Home was still four more blocks east, then three north, up the hill, second house on the right. Her brother and sisters were waiting for her. They had not seen Noni for five days. Or was it six?

"I think you should get in. I think you want to get in. Come on. You're pretty, does anyone ever tell you that? You're such a pretty girl. I like pretty girls." His voice was almost soothing in its repetition. But beneath his words, Renee felt more than heard an electricity of purpose. An urgency. The drip, drip of a faucet into a sink that has only just begun to overflow.

Renee didn't look at the man. She pulled up her backpack, thrust her hands deeper into her pockets, walked faster. The car matched her pace.

Later she couldn't say why she decided to run. Something flipped, a chemical reaction, a flight instinct, a realization that she was in fact in danger.

Running was something that Renee did very well. Cross-country was her event. She loved the variety of it, the spills and jumps. Now she sprinted, imagining that this was a course, the rutted sidewalk and slippery leaves, a jump from curb to street and back again. Backpack banging against her lower spine, lungs firing with the cold. She ran and turned, and the car turned with her, tires squealing. It was like a movie, unreal, absurd. She heard the car brake hard, and she glanced behind to see the man open the door, hurl himself onto the sidewalk. He was shorter than she was expecting, scrawny, except for a ball of a stomach that strained the white button-down shirt he wore. His hair neat and brown as the car. He looked like a banker or a teacher, utterly benign. He began to chase her.

Renee ran faster, ducked into a yard, crossed that one, then another. She should have stopped to knock on a door—of course that's what she should have done. She would spend months, years really, wondering why she hadn't, but in the moment, as she ran, it seemed impossible to breach those closed front doors, the warm glow of those windows.

Renee's breath came in an urgent white column from her mouth as she ran. Behind her she heard the man's footfalls, his labored, reckless breathing. One house was dark—the Hunters, out of town for a family wedding—and it was here that she turned. Into the front yard, around to the back, to a yard that looked like their old yard at the yellow house. A swing set, a rectangular sandbox, the lawn lined with flower beds that now lay dormant, clipped to the sleepy essentials to wait out winter. Sometimes Renee babysat for the Hunter twins, girls with brown ringlets. She liked to play with them out here, no matter the weather.

Now Renee looked for somewhere to hide, under the swing, behind the shed. She crouched beneath the low, sloping plastic slide, trying to make herself small. Invisible. The man entered the yard, still breathing hard. He slowed, stopped. There was no easy way out of here, Renee realized. The man roamed the yard, his eyes scanning. How long did it take? The yard was small. Of course he found her.

The man from the car grabbed Renee's arm and pulled her from beneath the slide. She turned her head, and—*bam*—he punched her, his fist glancing off the left side of her head. The force made her lose her footing. How did it happen that he was on top of her? Her backpack had come loose, spilling pens and stickers and erasers across the lawn. A note from her friend Dawn, folded into an origami star.

"Don't run from me," the man was saying. "Don't you ever run away from me again, do you understand? I will find you. I will always find you."

Renee was fighting, but his hands were on her shoulders and he was strong, his breath in her face. "I will *always* find you," he said again, and spit rained onto her face, into her eyes. He was hurting her, she was blinking, blinking, trying to clear her sight.

And then she heard Joe's voice.

"Renee? Renee!"

"Joe—" Renee tried to yell, but she couldn't. The weight of the man compressed her chest, her stomach, and she couldn't speak, but she saw him, her brother, Joe. He was standing behind the man.

"Get off her," Joe said. He growled the words, a sound Renee had never heard before and would never hear again. He kicked the man hard and then again, kicked against the man's body as though it were a locked door Joe was trying to open. At ten years old, Joe was shorter than the man but stronger from all the baseball work-outs. And he was wearing his spiked cleats, the ones for baseball practice. One more kick and the man's weight rolled off Renee.

The man lay panting in the dirt beside the swing set. "Hey, kid," he said, and held up his hands. "What the—" Joe kicked the man once, twice in the stomach, and then in the head. Again and again and again.

"Joe!" Renee screamed. She pulled herself to standing and ran to her brother.

"You can stop now," she said. "Stop."

The man's face was bloody. In her memories Renee would never recall what the man in the car looked like. She would remember only a bloody blur, nose smashed, chin collapsed.

Joe was shaking.

"We have to go," Renee said. "Leave him."

"Is he okay?" Joe asked. "Is he—" His voice had returned to normal. It was again the voice of a boy.

"It doesn't matter. We need to leave. Let's go home." An essential calm took hold of Renee then. Her heart beat solid and cold inside her chest. Her fear of the man was immediately gone. Nothing bad had happened, nothing worth mentioning. The only true thing was that she needed to remove herself and Joe from this yard, from this place beside the bloodied man. They needed to leave no trace of themselves behind.

"Help me clean this stuff up," she said to Joe, and they began to collect her school things: the purple zippered pencil case, the red binder, two notebooks, her geometry book, a plastic protractor. The star note was muddied, torn by Joe's cleat. Carefully Renee refolded the note and slipped it into her back pocket.

And then Renee took her brother's hand and they walked to the front of the Hunters' house and to the sidewalk. The brown car was pulled to the curb, its driver's door open, headlights on, a tiny electronic beep alerting its owner of things gone awry. Joe and Renee walked past the car at a normal pace. They did not hurry, they did not call attention to themselves. They walked three more blocks east, then three more north, then up the hill, through the front door of the gray house. Home.

When they crossed the threshold, Renee finally let go of Joe's hand.

"Where were you?" I was the first to ask. "We were so worried!" Caroline sat on the couch with wide, frightened eyes.

"We're fine, everything's fine," Renee said. But then she told us to close the blinds, to gather in the kitchen.

Renee told us half the story, as calmly and clearly as she could, but she did not tell us everything. She knew with an insight beyond her thirteen years that we would always remember this night. The lesson she wanted us to retain was one of caution. Of fear, but not terror. Of a lesson learned, a near miss, so that we might avoid what had happened to our sister. Renee bore the brunt of it so that we wouldn't have to.

This was how Renee saw it. And I was grateful to her, I am grateful to this day. The man in the car is the reason as a young woman I always carried Mace in my purse, the reason I learned self-defense in college, a class taught by an ex-marine who called us "ladies" but taught us how to gouge a man's eyes and punch out his windpipe. Caroline and I both learned Renee's lesson well.

And Joe? When no one was looking, he stuffed the cleats into the trash. He took a long shower that night and went to baseball practice as usual the next morning. He'd lost his cleats, he told Coach Marty, probably left on the bus, and Marty shrugged and said, "Okay, Joe," and found him another pair. For Joe there was no lesson from Renee, only her gratitude. He was her savior. She thanked him later that night and again the next morning. In a way Renee thanked Joe every day for the next sixteen years.

But not once did she worry about what the man in the car had done to Joe. She never wondered what those kicks required of him. What that bloodied face told our brother about himself.

* * *

"I'LL NEVER LEAVE you," the man said again to his wife. "I'm staying right here."

Renee hung up the phone. "They're ready for her upstairs," she called to Jaypa.

Jaypa nodded at Renee and then waved her away. "I've got this," he said.

Renee fell back to the nurses' station and let Jaypa get on with it. Her thoughts had moved past the man in the car, that episode banished from her mind in a self-preserving efficiency she'd perfected years earlier: the ability to replace one strong emotion with another. Now a familiar frustration rose up. The blood, the urgent fear in the man's voice, the pregnant woman's screams—all so easily avoided. You want to give birth at home? Try time travel. Try a return to colonial America, where one in ten women died in childbirth. For most emergencies there was no warning, but for this one they'd had forty weeks of warning.

It was the same frustration she felt with Joe. His drinking, the drugs. How does a man genetically predisposed to heart disease justify the regular use of cocaine?

Last week they'd met at a coffee cart outside the hospital. Recently Joe had suffered some chest pains. A moment when he felt his heart buck. That's how he'd described it to Renee: "Like a horse, like a horse kicked me right here"—he placed his palm in the center of his chest. She'd immediately called a cardiologist friend and arranged for Joe to have a workup.

But the tests came back normal. No cause for concern.

"Just stop, Joe. Just stop using," Renee said, holding her coffee in two hands, blowing the steam into the frigid autumn air. "It's a risk."

"I don't do it that much," he replied. He ate a glazed doughnut in three bites, licked the sugar from his fingers. "It's fun. It helps me stop thinking about work. You know, unwind."

"I'd like to get you into some kind of treatment."

He laughed. "Renee. I love you. But come on. You heard your friend. The tests were normal. I just got freaked. That's all. I have it under control."

"I wish you would stop hanging out with Ace."

"Ace? He's harmless."

"He's a drug dealer."

"That's a bit of a stretch. He's got some connections, that's all. He's a good person to know."

"Well, I wish you didn't know him." Renee paused and then asked gently, "And, Joe—have you seen Dad again? Or any other hallucinations?"

Joe looked up at the sky and then down at Renee. "It wasn't a hallucination," he said.

"Okay, fine. But have you seen him?"

"No, Renee. I haven't. I'll let you know next time it happens. Okay?" He gave Renee a tight smile.

Renee took hold of Joe's elbow and pulled him toward her. "Hold out your arms," she said. "Please."

"What? Why?" said Joe, but he did it, he held out his arms.

Before he could pull them away, Renee grabbed his left arm, pushed up the shirt cuff and examined the interior forearm. She saw a smattering of small purple bruises, each no bigger than a dime, with a vicious point of red in the center. Renee inhaled sharply. "Joe," she said.

"Renee. *Relax*. It's not heroin. Coke is so much better when you inject it. I've only done it a few times. It's okay. Really." And then, suddenly contrite, "I'm sorry you saw that. Listen, I'll stop. Okay? I will. I promise. I can stop the coke. It's not a big deal."

Joe's phone had started to buzz then, and he'd angled away from her to answer it, mouthed a good-bye, and turned down Lexington Avenue.

Afterward Renee had been so agitated she'd walked and walked, from New York-Presbyterian on East Sixty-Eighth all the way downtown. What could she do? Stage an intervention? He was working, he was in love, he was getting married, he was living a responsible, productive life. Maybe she was overreacting. Maybe she was being hysterical. But no autopsy had ever been conducted on their father; they never knew why he suffered the sudden cardiac arrest that killed him. Cardiomyopathy was one possibility, or ventricular fibrillation. Renee made sure that Joe had routine physicals; the tests had all been normal. Still, she worried.

From behind the blue curtain came another moan from the pregnant woman. Her husband wept softly.

"She's going to be okay, right?" the man asked. No one answered.

Jaypa spoke low into the phone on the wall and caught Renee's eye but did not smile. And then a tall, formidable nurse sheathed in the peach scrubs of the delivery room arrived and took charge. The curtain swiped open, and the whole enterprise, woman and man, doctors and nurses, gurney and IV, moved swiftly down the hall toward the elevators like an urgent traveling circus. The massive swinging doors that separated the ER from the hospital proper shut behind them with the slightest sucking noise—Renee always thought of a submarine pulling closed its portal—and they disappeared.

The ER returned to calm. The electronic blip of a blood-pressure monitor. The soft chatter of the triage nurses.

* * *

RENEE NEVER CONSIDERED herself a prude. She liked to think about sex. She masturbated, each orgasm a small, perfect miracle, and found herself aroused equally by the sight of Mr. Quigley's firm, round buttocks in math class and the kissing scenes in *Top Gun*. And yet by the age of eighteen she had never had a boyfriend, never dated, had kissed only one person—a pimply high jumper at a postseason track conference—and found it pleasant but not pleasant enough that she wished to repeat the exchange. She didn't blame the man in the car for her ambivalence, not exactly. The line of causation was not so straight. But an unease rose up in her throat, the slightest taste of disgust, whenever she felt herself the subject of male sexual attention. Plus, she was busy. So busy! Track meets, academic decathlon, four AP classes, part-time work at the lab in New Haven, tutoring on Saturday afternoons, volunteering at the soup kitchen on Sunday nights. This was the reason she didn't date, Renee told Noni, who offered her wholehearted approval.

"There's plenty of time for dating," Noni said. "High-school boys are Neanderthals anyhow."

But then, toward the end of Renee's senior year, Brett Swenson asked her to prom.

At eighteen years old and 205 pounds of pure muscle, Brett had been the star of the high school's championship wrestling team.

Thick, dark brows, a full, sensitive mouth, ears flat to his square head. Brett was cute, at least that's what her friends said, and Renee appreciated certain aspects of his physique: the wide shoulders, the hard, flat stomach that he displayed often—in the lunchroom, in biology class, passing in the hall—by lifting the hem of his shirt to wipe his face or lips as though the simple task of carrying his prodigious muscles was enough to raise a sweat.

Yes, Renee liked the flash of that stomach. But she did not particularly like Brett. He laughed too loudly and too often and strode the halls as though the high school were his home and all the other students and teachers merely guests enjoying the whims of his hospitality. Stories circulated about Brett: the college girl he'd dated, the night he slept with two girls at the same time. Jennifer Garrit had slept with him, Renee heard, and Sarah Cooper and even a freshman, coltish Julie Farley, with her long legs and braces. All of these girls became marked by him, carrying with them through the halls a badge of experience and allure and tawdry knowledge. Brett never had a girlfriend. Such official couplings generally happened within the school band or the chess club, involving people without the wealth of opportunities that presented themselves to young men like Brett. He had a social obligation, it seemed, to spread himself around.

It was a distinct surprise when Brett asked Renee to the senior prom—a shocking event, thrilling to her friends but nausea-inducing for Renee. Weeks of back-and-forth communications ensued: his friends talking to her friends, handwritten notes, chats beside her locker. He called her once at home to detail the limousine his parents had rented, its long sunroof, its television and white leather seats. Renee had been swayed, almost, by these shows of consideration, but in the end she said no—Renee always said no—

and spent prom night at the movies with her friend Gabby watching *Pretty Woman* and eating sticky Raisinets.

Two weeks later she passed Brett in the hall on her way to class, her arms full of books, hair unwashed and pulled up in a ponytail. He said, looking straight at her, his voice an undertone but the words distinct, "What a fucking waste." He shook his head. Gone were the affection and attraction that he'd put on display during those fervent weeks before prom. The look he gave her was dismissive, with a whiff of disgust.

Renee pulled back as though slapped and did not reply. She kept walking.

What a fucking waste.

Later that night, at home in bed, Caroline snoring faintly in the bunk below, all Renee's life choices arrived for her in stark relief. She was eighteen years old, six weeks away from high-school graduation, five months from starting at the University of Connecticut in an accelerated premed program for which she'd won enough scholarship and grant money that Noni would pay nothing. Renee had worked so hard to excel academically, to keep her body lean and strong for cross-country, to keep an eye on Joe and her sisters, to watch Noni for signs of relapse into depression. Had she expended so much energy and time on these pursuits that something precious had slipped away? Her adolescence was nearly over—what did she have to show for her teenage years?

Caroline, Renee knew, had not wasted a minute of her time. She and Nathan were practically married already. They held hands in the hallways and on the street. They went to movies together, Nathan driving the ratty green Volkswagen Bug he'd been given by a dying uncle, Caroline installed in the passenger seat like a queen. Caroline had been on the pill for a year now. All the nights Renee had stayed in to study, all the parties she'd missed, all the beers she had failed to drink—these choices struck her now as safe and, yes, wasteful. And whatever it was she had wasted, she would never get it back.

That night Renee thought about the tan, smooth stomach of Brett Swenson and the senior prom that she did not attend and the ways in which she had already closed herself in. One small voice in her head wished she could go back and say, *Yes, Brett, bring me to prom and feed me schnapps and vodka and take my virginity in the slippery, heated backseat of that rented limo.* But the louder voice wished she could go back to that hallway and punch Brett Swenson in the face for making her question herself like this.

*   *   *

A BUZZ CAME from the triage nurse: a new walk-in patient designated urgent but not life-threatening. A thirty-eight-year-old white male in overall good health. No medications. Laceration on the left palm with persistent blood loss.

"Sorry, Renee, you're the last doc standing," the nurse said.

Renee groaned. "On my way."

When Renee pulled open the curtain, the patient was sitting on a gurney holding his left hand with his right. His name was Jonathan Frank and it was the tenacity of his bleeding that struck her first.

"What happened?" Renee asked. Jonathan's left hand was wrapped in a dish towel soaked with blood. Brilliant drops of red fell to the floor as Renee unwound the cloth to get a better look at the cut.

"Just a bread knife. Newly sharpened," Jonathan answered. He looked pointedly at the woman standing beside the gurney. "No one told me."

The woman rolled her eyes. She wore a long green dress under a longer black coat. A large diamond sat on her ring finger, throwing a tiny rainbow onto the blue curtain that divided this examining space from the one beside it. "Who decides to have a bagel after five courses at Jean-Georges?" she said. "Who?"

"Are you on any medication?" Renee asked Jonathan.

"No."

"No blood thinners?"

"No."

"And when did this happen?"

"Thirty minutes ago."

"More like an hour," said the woman. "I'm worried about him. He's such a bleeder."

"When have you seen me bleed, Simone? When, in the last ten years?" Jonathan Frank's face was tight and neat, with short dark hair that rose in a little crest over his forehead. He was tall, over six feet, Renee guessed by the length of thigh that extended past the gurney's edge, and thin as a pole vaulter. His whole person seemed drafted by an architect: it was precise, efficient, self-contained.

"Maybe your wife should step outside," said Renee.

"She's not my wife. She's my sister. My older sister."

The woman sighed dramatically. "Fine, bleed to death, see if I care. I'll be in the waiting room."

Renee continued working on the cut. The sister was right: Jonathan bled copiously. Renee was concerned about his inability to clot, and so she recommended he be admitted for further tests.

"Admitted?" he said.

"I'm afraid so."

"I'm sure you're very good at your job. But I'll be fine."

Renee released his hand. "Hold it up like this," she directed. "Listen, at the very least you'll need stitches. Quite a few. And probably physical therapy so you can keep full mobility. A wound like this can cause the hand to curl inward as it heals." Renee made her hand into a horrible claw shape. She was exaggerating, but she hated this brand of skepticism. Sometimes male patients asked how old she was or if her superior was available to give his opinion.

"What do you do for a living?" Renee asked.

"I'm a carpenter. I make furniture," Jonathan answered.

"So you work with your hands."

"Yes, but I have an assistant. A really excellent assistant."

"Tennis, then?"

"Do I look like a tennis player?"

Renee stepped back. "You do, actually."

"No tennis. I box."

"Box?"

"I've broken my nose twice."

Jonathan's nose was straight as a blade. "Doesn't look broken to me," Renee said.

"Okay." Jonathan smiled. "But I've always wanted to be a boxer. Real tough-guy stuff."

"You don't look like a tough guy."

"I do have a bleeding hand."

"True," said Renee. "But it's from cutting a bagel."

In six months' time, Renee would learn that Jonathan liked to pretend, to put on characters the way other people put on clothes. He wore a fake mustache three days a week. He entertained casual friendships with at least a dozen people who knew him as Fodor Leyontiev, an émigré from the former Soviet Union, a poor violinist who still longed for the borscht of his childhood. This was not to say that Jonathan was dishonest. To the contrary—he was honest to a fault, and this was precisely the sort of complexity that later Renee would value so highly in him. Renee arrived at honesty through the usual route—a good heart, a sensible mind, a fear of making mistakes—while Jonathan's route meandered, stopped to photograph the view and buy some candy. But their ultimate destination remained the same.

After Renee's jab about the bagel, Jonathan quieted down. He coughed into his good hand.

Renee regarded the bloom of blood on his trousers. The frayed laces of his running shoes. The wound was his own doing, yes, but not one of reckless disregard. A hunger pang, a newly sharpened knife, a wily bagel. Simply an accident. No one was to blame. Certainly not Jonathan. He wasn't the sort of person to act carelessly. Already Renee knew this about him.

She pulled Jonathan Frank's chart from the slot at the end of the bed.

"You may have reached a tendon," she said. "I'm going to hold off on the suture until we know if you'll need surgery."

"Trust me," he said. "I don't need anything."

Renee had been writing in his chart, but now she stopped. "Nothing?" she said. "There's nothing you need?"

"Not a thing," said Jonathan Frank. He blinked. "Except your phone number."

Renee had been hit on many times in the ER. The place had an air of perpetual disorder and diminished expectations, and there were some people who believed that such conditions also required sexually inappropriate behavior. These kinds of people always ended up in Renee's care. She'd been mooned, flashed, asked out, grabbed by patients more times than she could count. Never before had she reacted to it with anything other than a quick shake of the head or, on a few notable occasions, a call to security.

But with Jonathan Frank she hesitated. He was holding his injured hand up as she'd instructed. The discarded dishcloth was stained a deep red and edged with little yellow ducks.

On the day she met Jonathan Frank, Renee was thirty-four years old, a fellow in general surgery with top marks from the attending physician, already in talks for a transplant fellowship next year. Brett Swenson was sixteen years behind her, the man in the car twenty-one. Jonathan was attractive and intelligent and had asked for her phone number. The fact that he was her patient should have prompted Renee to answer with a simple, straightforward no.

Instead she wondered if there was any Chinese food left in the staff fridge. She wondered if Jaypa's girlfriend, the nurse from Arkansas, had ever wanted to be a doctor. She wondered if she wasn't the kind of person who did better on her own, someone who was meant to lead a solitary life. Someone for whom a profession, the most noble of professions, would provide a vast, singular joy. She realized that this man here was not Brett Swenson or the man in the car, but someone else entirely. Someone who perhaps, with his neat, clean hands and dark, intelligent eyes, might widen her world, not because it needed to be wider but because the opposite, a narrowing, might otherwise be inevitable. And she did not want that. Alone or not, Renee wanted to expand. She had always wanted more than herself. Medicine gave her that; maybe this man could, too. One did not necessarily preclude the other. For a brief, blazing moment, she hoped that this was true.

Without looking at Jonathan, Renee ripped a scrap of paper from the chart and wrote down her name and phone number.

"A nurse will take up you up to X-ray," she said, and handed him the paper.

* * *

IT HAD BEEN a Sunday morning in April when Joe called Renee from the Alden College dean's office. Renee was a second-year medical student and had slept four hours the night before. She'd been study-ing for the national board exam, a punishing full-day test.

When she picked up the phone, Joe said, "Renee, I need your help." His voice was rough and low.

Renee did not speak. Briefly she considered hanging up on him, turning the phone off, returning to her books. Her roommate Lydia was still asleep; Renee could hear faint snores emanating from the closed bedroom door.

"What is it, Joe," Renee said without inflection. "What's hap-pened?"

Joe explained the situation: the party, the alcohol, the police. Renee said very little. She whispered, "Okay, okay, I understand," trying not to wake her roommate.

"You need to come here," Joe said. "They wanted to talk to Noni, but I told them you."

"Yes," said Renee. "That was the right thing to do. Don't let them call Noni. I'm leaving now."

At Alden College she was greeted by Joe's coach, the college reg-istrar, and, she realized only as he introduced himself, the college dean. The meeting was tense but photogenic, held in a room of wood-paneled walls and chairs upholstered in supple leather. The large leaded-glass windows offered a view of the grassy quad cut through with the silvery gray of paved walkways.

The baseball coach began. As he spoke, Renee gazed just above his head, out the window. She watched a knot of tousled young people shouldering serious backpacks travel from one corner of the quad to the next. There were four of them, all deep in conversation, hands working as they spoke, debating, it seemed, some question of great significance. Each appeared so clean and shiny-haired, so focused and brilliantly backlit by the late-morning sun that Renee wondered if perhaps a photographer followed them, taking snaps for the college brochure.

The students drifted beyond her field of vision, and Renee turned her attention back to the room. Joe had been showing up for practice drunk or high or not at all, the baseball coach was saying. He wasn't bench-pressing enough, couldn't run the nine-minute mile required of all players. He was barely passing three classes and flat-out failing a fourth. His teammates felt like they didn't know him. Worse, they couldn't trust him. Yes, he'd had a decent freshman season, their hopes had been high for his sophomore year, but Joe's behavior now was intolerable. Beyond the pale.

The registrar followed in a similar vein but focused on academics, reading comments from Joe's professors and passing to Renee copies of Joe's underwhelming schoolwork.

Finally it was the dean's turn. There were the team problems, the academic issues, yes, but the most serious incident had occurred two nights before at the frat party.

"He was appointed the bongmaster?" the dean said, unsmiling. "Something like that. Neighbors complained about the noise, and let me tell you, neighbors of a frat house are accustomed to noise." Still he didn't smile, though he did raise one dark eyebrow and gazed at Renee with something that suggested a wryness, an ability to see humor in this situation. Or maybe he was just flirting with her; it was always difficult for Renee to tell.

When the police arrived, they found a dozen fraternity brothers passed out in the common room, numerous others on the grounds of the frat house in various states of intoxication and undress. A dozen people were taken to the ER with alcohol poisoning; one girl was still hospitalized. Her stomach had been pumped, she'd briefly stopped breathing on her own, but she was now out of intensive care. Her parents were at her bedside.

"She's an eighteen-year-old freshman," the Dean said, his cheeks coloring. "She could have died, Ms. Skinner. The university is facing possible legal— Well, let me just say that it's a very troubling, very difficult situation all around."

When the police arrived at the party, three young men were seen running out of the building. One of these men had been Joe. He'd been carrying nearly a pound of marijuana on his person, the dean told her. One *pound*. Additional drugs and drug paraphernalia were confiscated from the fraternity house: cocaine, tabs of Ecstasy, PCP, various other pills that had yet to be identified.

It was at this point in the meeting that Renee mentally left the room. She opened the heavy door and floated out over the polished oak floorboards and down the wide, curving staircase to that brilliant emerald quad where she'd seen the students. *Wait!* she yelled. *Wait for me!* Renee had never applied to Alden College; after receiving the scholarship from the University of Connecticut, a school located within driving distance of Bexley, it made no sense to apply anywhere else. Throughout those four years of college, Renee had continued to live at home, sharing a room with Caroline, eating Noni's food, working part-time. She'd never had the occasion to walk across a quad like this quad. She wondered if such an experience would have changed her.

Renee floated back into the meeting. The dean was still talking. The police had agreed to release the men into his custody. No charges had been filed. Yet.

"But you must understand, Ms. Skinner, the seriousness of the situation." The dean gazed at her without blinking.

That year Renee was twenty-four and looked eighteen. The men in the room had cataloged Joe's egregious errors as though this were primarily a subject of university concern. Today did not represent, for them, the dissolution of thirteen years of dreams and family sacrifice. It didn't signify anything more troubling than the payment of legal fees and a rejig of Alden's baseball team, the unexpected need for a new center fielder, maybe that kid from Gainesville, someone who might have more staying power than Joe Skinner, the disappointment from Bexley.

"Under normal circumstances Joe would be a candidate for expulsion," said the dean. "His academic record alone is grounds for that. The fraternity party only worsened his position. The other two young men caught with drugs in their possession, both with academic records similar to your brother's, have already been asked to withdraw."

The baseball coach shifted in his chair. "But because Joe's a scholarship athlete, we don't want to go that route."

"We're looking for some kind of assurance from you," the registrar contributed. "From Joe's family." He raised a pair of remarkable gray eyebrows.

All three men gazed at Renee. Waiting.

"Well, you can't expel him," Renee said. She paused. Then, in a rush, "You know, our father died when we were young, and then our mother became clinically depressed and basically didn't leave her bedroom for three years. It was really hard on Joe. He's still recovering in a way."

Renee felt the tenor of the room change. A tentative relief settled over her, alongside a pure revulsion at what she'd done. To use their father's death like that, to betray Noni. Joe would hate her for it. Though of course he would never know; she would make sure of that.

The coach cleared his throat. "Yes, well. Apparently he was talking to the police about his father."

"To the police?" Renee asked. "What do you mean?"

"Ask Joe about it," the coach said, not meeting Renee's gaze. "I think your brother may need some additional . . . assistance."

The coach's demeanor put Renee on high alert. Why would the man not look her in the eye?

Renee turned now to the dean. "Please. What about academic probation?" she said. "Something like that. He'll do better. I'll make sure that he does."

"He will have no other chances," said the dean.

In the end the panel agreed to a two-year academic probation, during which Joe would be required to maintain a B average and be the subject of no disciplinary hearings. The fraternity was prohibited from hosting parties for the remainder of the year and would require a school administrative chaperone at all parties the following year. Joe Skinner was off the baseball team, effective immediately.

Renee shook all the hands, and then she left the wood-paneled room and vomited neatly into a tall trash can in the hall.

"Don't tell Noni," was the first thing Joe said when he opened the door to his room at the frat house. A girl, elfin and blond, slipped from behind Joe and past Renee. Her eyes were red.

"Bye, Joe," she said tearfully, with a quick wave of a tiny hand.

Renee ignored the girl. "Of course I won't tell her," Renee said. "Listen, we need to talk."

In the common room, they sat on a sticky leather couch. The only other furniture was a wide-screen television and three battered beer kegs.

"Will they take away the scholarship?" asked Joe.

"No," said Renee. "They will not take away the scholarship. You played for the first half of the season. You're lucky. They could have taken it away. They could have expelled you."

"Oh, that's such a fucking relief," Joe said, and he began to laugh.

"But, Joe," Renee said sternly, "you have to clean it up. Stop messing around." She explained the probationary terms offered by the college.

Joe stretched his neck to the left and right. "Don't worry," he said. "I won't get in trouble like this again."

"You can't get into *any* trouble."

"Promise." He held up a hand like a Boy Scout and winked. Renee nearly slapped him.

"And baseball is over," she continued. "You're off the team." This part of the deal she felt in her stomach, an achy nausea left over from the meeting. She had no idea how Joe would react; he'd played baseball nearly every day of his life since their father's death.

But the look on Joe's face was pure relief. Nearly joy. "Oh, thank God," he said. "I didn't want to play anymore. Renee, I haven't wanted to in years. My throwing arm isn't what it used to be. I just didn't want to tell you. Or Noni."

For a moment Renee watched her brother: the clear blue eyes, the dimples. For the first time, she noticed the faintest trace of sagging purple beneath his eyes, the swell of a belly beneath his T-shirt, a puffiness to his cheeks. His familiar features looked older, altered. She could almost see the kind of man he was becoming.

"You can't tell Noni you want to quit baseball," said Renee. "I've already talked to Caroline. We'll tell her you had a knee injury. That's why you're off the team. I don't want Noni to know about the party or the drugs. None of it, okay?"

Joe nodded and moved in to hug his sister. "Thank you," he said into her hair.

"You're welcome," she replied.

"Renee," he said, still in the hug, "have you ever seen Dad?"

"What?" She pulled away from him.

"I mean, have you ever seen him? Like a ghost. Or spirit. What-ever you want to call it."

"Dad? No, Joe. I haven't." Then Renee remembered the coach's comment. "Have you? Seen him, I mean?"

"I saw him the night of the party. 'Joe, your throwing arm isn't what it used to be.' That's what he said to me. Isn't that wild? And he's totally right."

Joe's face shone with an innocent wonder. *He believes this*, Renee realized.

"Joe, what were you on?" During Renee's pharmacology class, she'd read about hallucinations induced by all sorts of drugs. Talking animals, aliens, dead people—all the result of chemically altered neurons firing in unexpected ways.

But Joe shook his head. "It wasn't the drugs. Really. It wasn't. Dad was standing outside on the back lawn of the frat house, talking to me just like we're talking now. Really, Renee. It was amazing. I had been hoping for it for so long. And finally it happened." Joe smiled with such calm satisfaction, such a clear sense of relief, that Renee did not know how to respond.

"Maybe you should talk to someone about this," she said.

"Someone? You mean like a counselor?"

Renee nodded.

"I don't need a counselor, trust me. I'll talk to you about it. You and Caroline and Fiona, but that's it. You're the only ones who would understand anyhow." Joe smiled again: the same relief, same joy. "It's a good thing, Renee. Don't look so worried. Someday it'll happen to you, too. I bet he visits all of us." Joe yawned. "I better get some sleep," he said, and hugged Renee again and then disappeared into his room.

When Renee returned to Boston, her roommate told her the news about Caroline.

"Your sister's in labor," Lydia said, not looking up from a text-book on the table.

Renee called the number that Nathan had left. His sleepy voice confirmed that little Louis had arrived. Everyone was delirious, relieved, happy.

"I'm so glad everything went well," said Renee. "Noni will be thrilled. We all need some good news right about now. We all need a distraction."

Joe kept his promise to Renee. He graduated on time and in good standing from Alden College, certainly not an A student, but did it matter? A degree from Alden was a degree from Alden, whether you worked as hard as you could or you slacked off, drank beer, cy-cled through girlfriends as fast as you changed your jeans, climbed the roof of your frat house, and shouted Beastie Boys lyrics until the hazy dawn light hit the trees and the grass and made everything look like a mist-filled dream. Joe took his degree and accepted a job offer from Kyle Morgan, an Alden alum and former fraternity brother two years older than Joe. His family ran a boutique invest-ment bank called Morgan Capital Ltd. The year was 1996.

"We're getting into tech," Kyle explained at Joe's first and only job interview. "There's a lot happening in that sector. Lots of po-tential. You can start as an analyst. Go from there. Bonuses, baby." Kyle smiled broadly, teeth white as a new baseball, and held out a hand for Joe to shake.

* * *

NORMALLY RENEE WOULD not visit an ER patient once he or she had been admitted to the hospital. But the failed home birth stayed on Renee's mind. Soon after the woman left the ER, a baby girl had been delivered. Everything had gone as well as it could go, Jaypa told Renee as she was packing up to leave. Even so, the mother remained in intensive care. She'd labored at home for over forty-eight hours and lost a large amount of blood. The baby, deprived of oxygen for an unknown length of time, was in the NICU. There was the possibility of cerebral palsy, epilepsy, autism, developmental delays, any number of disabilities.

"What can you do?" Jaypa had said to Renee with a shrug, and then he returned to the ER for the remaining ten hours of his shift.

After Renee scrubbed the blood from beneath her fingernails and changed into street clothes, she traveled via three separate elevators to the neonatal intensive care unit. There she found the baby splay-legged and purple inside an incubator that bristled with white tubes and black cords. BABY GIRL DUSTIN read the card on the incubator. Most of the infants here were preemies, some weighing no more than a pound or two. Baby Girl Dustin looked freakishly large in comparison, but the size differential only underlined the problem. At least you knew what you were looking at with the others. But this baby girl—it was impossible to say. Perhaps she would be fine. But perhaps she would not.

Renee's phone buzzed. A message from Fiona: WHERE R U? Renee groaned. She did not reply. She was now an hour late for Joe's party.

The baby's father, the man from the ER, was not in the room. Baby Girl Dustin sighed audibly into her respirator. She clenched and unclenched her toes. For a moment Renee considered pushing her hands into the built-in black rubber gloves the nurses used for feeding and changing and cleaning. The gloves that were also used by parents to hold and caress. But again came the insistent buzz of her phone. How would she explain to Joe and Noni, to Sandrine and Fiona and all of Joe's friends, all of Sandrine's family, why she was late? *I could not step away from an infant without a name.*

This baby was one of hundreds, perhaps thousands, that Renee would treat over the course of her career. Renee was not sentimental. Years ago she had decided never to have children. It was precisely these kinds of moments—when she hesitated about what was best to do, when she blanched at the possibility of creating connection—that showed her just how ill-suited she was for motherhood. When Renee had visited Caroline at the hospital after baby Louis was born, she had felt only inadequacy. Caroline's face was exhausted, her hair a mess, the hospital gown slipping off her shoulders, but she shone—literally glimmered—in that hospital bed like some beautiful consumptive.

"Isn't he perfect?" Caroline had said, and Renee could only nod. She had leaned over her nephew's small body and observed his beauty and newness, but she could not bring herself to touch him.

Renee left the NICU without touching Baby Girl Dustin. She texted Fiona: BE THERE SOON.

Outside, the dusk smelled like frost and chestnuts, and Renee breathed to clear the chemical stench of the hospital from her lungs. With her arm outstretched, she walked one block, two, but no cabs stopped. It was that busy early-evening hour when people had plans, places to be. Renee was considering how long it would take to walk all the way to Kyle's apartment when her phone buzzed. She was expecting Fiona again, but the number was unknown. Renee answered; it was Jonathan Frank, her patient with the cut hand.

Renee explained that she was late, she couldn't talk. She'd already overstayed her shift and would be late for her brother's engagement party, and now she couldn't find a cab and would probably have to walk or wait for a crosstown bus, which would take nearly as long.

"Why didn't you leave earlier?" Jonathan asked. "I thought I was your last patient."

"I had to check on someone in the NICU," Renee answered. "A new baby."

"What happened?"

Renee paused. What had happened? Why had she visited a baby who was not her patient, whom she had not treated, to whom she had no connection whatsoever? Renee told Jonathan about the parents' entrance to the ER, the failed home birth, the preventability of certain situations. Why were people so stupid? she asked him. Why did they put themselves and the people they loved at risk? She was talking about the home birth, but more than that she was talking about Joe. She never mentioned his name, of course, and this man Jonathan Frank didn't know anything about her, didn't know about her father's death, didn't know she had a younger brother whom she felt sometimes she'd done more to raise than their mother had. That her kid brother had grown into a man who appeared in all material respects successful and happy and blessed and yet who carried around within himself a sense of absence and loss, and for whatever reasons—he refused therapy, he didn't talk about it with friends, he liked to preserve the illusion of strength—this emptiness had become his core. Renee remembered Joe's fury with the fireplace poker on the day of their father's funeral. Part of Joe was still that boy, still raging through the yellow house, still destroying the image of the family that would never exist again.

"I'm sorry," Jonathan said. "About the baby."

"Thank you," Renee replied.

She wondered who he thought she was. The kind of woman who swooned over babies? Maybe she should tell him a story: Once, Renee had gone fishing with her father on the Long Island Sound. He'd rented a cruiser, a big boat, but he'd taken only Renee with him. *Just you and me kid,* she remembered him saying in a funny, scratchy voice that seemed an imitation of someone, though she didn't know who. The voice had momentarily confused Renee, made her wonder if perhaps her father expected a certain kind of response. She didn't want to disappoint him, not on such a momentous day, and so she'd bounded aboard and with concentration began to thread worms onto the hook. She sat in the sun with her father, who had packed salami sandwiches, her favorite, and cans of Coke, and she held that fishing pole until her arms ached, and she'd wished the day would never end. She was nine years old then, maybe ten.

"When will they know about the baby?" Jonathan asked. "I mean, the long-term effects?"

"Well, it could be tomorrow," answered Renee. "Or it could be years. This kind of early trauma, we don't know when or how it might show up."

She thought about her father and that day of fishing, the bloody worms on the hook, the cans of sweet Coke, and about her brother Joe. *I can stop, Renee. Don't worry,* he'd said to her. Why didn't people understand the responsibility that came with being the subject of someone's love? It made her so angry. How easy it would have been for that man and woman to keep their baby safe. How easy it would be for Joe to stop what he was doing. He wasn't an addict, not the strung-out, desperate kind. Maybe he was addicted now, but it was pure laziness. Pure stupid indulgence and privilege. He could get high when and how he wanted, and so he did. It felt good, Joe had told her, like excitement, like sex, almost like falling in love.

"You're a fast walker," Jonathan said then. "I can barely keep up."

Renee stopped. "What did you say?"

"You walk very fast."

"How do you—" Renee looked around her. Directly across the

street stood Jonathan Frank, holding his phone to his ear. He waved at her with his good hand.

There was some traffic on the street, and at that moment a white van rolled past, obscuring Jonathan, but then it passed and there he stood, smiling at her. Still waving. Renee waited for the light to change, and then she crossed the street.

Chapter 7

KYLE MORGAN LIVED in one of those mammoth gray stone buildings on Central Park West that evoked scenes of women in dresses nipped at the waist and men wearing spats. A timeless building that would outlast us all. I'd been here before—Kyle and Joe had been friends since college—but the gravity of the place still stunned me every time.

The doorman wore a long black coat and gave a slight bow before leading me through a dim marble reception to the old-fashioned elevator with its brass buttons and clanking, accordion-style door. Up, up, up we went, the tinkling sound of music and conversation growing louder as we ascended. At the top the door opened directly onto Kyle's apartment.

Inside was an expanse of richly polished wood floor and rugs patterned with giant yellow roses and blue, heady hydrangeas. Paintings hung on every wall, each lit by a brass oblong light. A young woman wearing a tuxedo handed me a champagne flute. Waiters circulated with trays of pink and white and green food: mini lobster rolls, salmon sashimi, shrimp on bamboo spears. Somewhere, someone played a piano. I saw no one I knew, just men in suit jackets and jeans, women in tight complicated dresses, all of them buffed and polished to a high shine. Along the far wall stretched a wide bank of windows filled with the greenery of Central Park.

I was nervous. Standing on the edge of Joe's party, I worried about the poem I had written. Was it too sentimental or not sentimental enough? Too edgy, too sexual? Caroline had clapped her hands at the end, but I didn't know what Joe would think, or Sandrine.

I scanned the crowd looking for Noni and Renee. And where was Joe? In the week since helping Caroline in Hamden, I'd wondered often about my brother. He hadn't returned any of my calls or e-mails. I wanted to believe that Renee was overreacting, that Joe was fine, but small incidents kept creeping to mind: Joe late for a lunch, Joe distracted, Joe and Sandrine talking in urgent whispers. His bloodshot eyes, uneasy smile, and always the same explanation: *I'm tired, that's all. Just tired.*

Finally I spotted my brother. He stood behind an ornately carved and painted screen pushed close to the wall. The screen created a small shadowed space, inside of which Joe was talking to a woman. I saw them only because of my position beside the elevator; from all other points in the room, the screen would have shielded them from view. I did not appreciate this at the time. Only later.

The woman was young and pretty, with long strawberry-blond hair tucked behind an ear, a high flush to her cheeks. She smiled and laughed, throwing her head back to expose a thin white throat. She looked vaguely familiar, but I couldn't place her. I started toward them, and at that moment Joe rested a hand on the woman's forearm. One hand, the fingers circling bare skin. He leaned in—he was so animated, was he telling a joke?—and put his face beside hers. And then he pulled away, removed his hand. Again she laughed.

Then Joe directed his gaze out toward the party. His eyes met mine. There was no shame or hesitation, just a full smile as he moved smoothly away from the woman to greet me.

I thought nothing of the scene. It wasn't until weeks later that I remembered the woman, the delicious rose-gold color of her hair, the lily white of her throat. She had not looked uneasy or bothered in any way by Joe's attentions. No, she was comfortable, happy in the glow of his company.

"Hi, little sister," Joe said, and hugged me. At thirty, Joe still had the bearing and biceps of an athlete, though he hadn't played sports in years. Tonight he wore a pale blue shirt that glimmered like a cool liquid beneath the dim party lights. He was half drunk—I could see it in the ruddiness of his cheeks and the slightest slur of his voice—but it made him soft, not sloppy.

"I can't wait to hear the poem," Joe said. "Sandrine is excited, too."

Joe took my coat and wrapped his arm around my shoulders, and together we walked into the party. Joe greeted friend after friend, introducing me to people I hadn't met before, stopping to chat with old teammates from the Bexley Mavericks and fraternity brothers from Alden College, their wives and girlfriends.

"Tore my Achilles," said Langdon, a friend of Joe's from work, who wore a clunky black orthopedic boot. "Marathon training. But next year, Joe, how 'bout it?"

Joe nodded. "You bet," he answered. "Let's do it."

To stand beside my brother like this, in a room so grand, was not like being Cinderella at the ball but close. It was to absorb the radiant goodwill reflected off him, the headiness of all this love and adoration. I felt myself stand taller, hold my face as the wives and girlfriends held theirs, with crescent smiles, cheeks sucked in to accentuate the bones.

Joe wandered deeper into the party, pulled forward by his

friends. For a brief moment, I was alone, watching him, my heels unbalanced on the thick carpet.

And then from behind me came a voice. "Fiona? Is that you?"

I turned. The man was skinny in the knobby way of a kid who'd grown too fast. His face held some of that boyishness, too—freckles, green eyes, hair the color of a rusty ten-speed—but he carried himself with adult confidence, easily holding not champagne but a beer bottle. He leaned forward to kiss my cheek, and without thinking I offered it up.

"I *thought* that was you," he said.

"It's me," I said, and stepped back. I recognized him, but a name and context escaped me.

He saw my uncertainty. *"Fiddler on the Roof?"* he said. "'Tradition'?"

"Tradition." And then it came back: a pink-and-blue sky, the Bryant Park outdoor-movie season just begun. We had a mutual friend, was that it? Or a mutual friend's cousin, one of those connections that was entirely circumstantial and forgettable. After a brief flirtation, we had pulled our blankets together to share a bottle of wine.

"Poor Tevya," he'd whispered as the movie played. "All he wants is to keep his daughters safe."

"And marry them off to old men," I whispered back.

The T-shirt he'd worn felt soft as skin.

That night I'd pretended to be a philosophy grad student at NYU, a waitress on my off days at a Mexican place in Chelsea, a relatively new arrival to New York, still starstruck by the skyscrapers and wide avenues.

Afterward what had I written about this man? He was, I believed, number twenty-three.

"What's your connection?" Man #23 asked now, circling his finger in the air. "Bride?"

"No, groom," I answered. I looked toward Joe but saw only his tall back rising from the crowd. This was the first time my worlds had collided in this way, and I didn't like it. At some future point, yes, I would tell Noni about the blog, I would show my siblings and explain the feminist underpinnings, read to them the many comments I received, the discussions that were sparked by my posts—my words! my experience! *Time Out New York* had featured *The Last Romantic* the previous month in a piece about virtual communities and feminist blogging. *Watch out, men of New York,* the journalist had written. *The Last Romantic might make you her next subject.* In the days after, I'd received a few tantalizing e-mails from literary agents sent to the blog's general address. But I hadn't returned any of them. I wasn't ready yet to lose my anonymity.

As I stood with Man #23, I was jittery and distracted, wanting only to escape him before Joe or Noni saw us talking. And before he formed some connection between our night together and the blog. Did he read it? Had he recognized himself? Generally my posts revealed personal details about the men I slept with. Never names, of course, but there were other ways to identify a person. Tattoo, birthmark, snaggletooth, scar. I was candid when evaluating my partners' sexual techniques, their understanding of a woman's body, their kissing, their intelligence. More than one commentator had called me cruel.

But Man #23? The details of our encounter were escaping me. What had I written? As he smiled at me, his green eyes reflected spots of gold. His eyelashes were the same rusty red as his hair.

"It's great running into you," I said now to the man. "But I . . . I have a boyfriend, and he's here, and this is a little awkward." I flashed him what I hoped was a winning, sincere smile. These days I never hesitated to lie; I'd even stopped recognizing them as lies.

They were simply a part of the project, as necessary as my keyboard or computer.

"It's Will, by the way," he said. "It's okay, I forget people's names all the time. Good luck with that boyfriend." And Man #23—Will—turned away and disappeared into the crowd.

*   *   *

DURING THOSE FIRST years after the Pause, my siblings were busy with after-school activities and friends and homework, but I was home promptly at two forty-five with nothing to do, no one to play with, and so Noni hired our neighbor, Iris Durant, to look after me. Iris had brown eyes set very close together and a quick, high-pitched laugh. She was eighteen, just graduated from Bexley High with atrocious grades and a disinterested mother. She agreed to take the babysitting job until something better—anything, really—presented itself.

This was in the mid-1980s, the Reagan era of Just Say No and a blond Tipper Gore warning us about the corrupting effect of dirty song lyrics. Since the Pause had ended, I'd become the kid who was always asking questions. Probably this had to do with attention seeking or trying to make sense of Noni's vivid return. I never asked about anything useful—how does the television operate, say, or why do we catch colds?—but only questions that were elusive and unanswerable and always about people. Why do some people get married and some not? Why do women carry their wallets in handbags and men in pockets? How long can a person go without talking? How long does it take to fall in love?

I suppose this is how the game with Barbie began. Perhaps I asked Iris a question about sex. Or perhaps it was just boredom. Bexley on a sodden spring weekday afternoon was no place to be.

We had Barbie dolls by the dozens, not bought by Noni—perish the thought!—but handed down by the friendly parents of older girls who had moved on to other games. Barbie ballerinas and Barbie stewardesses, Barbie nurses and singers and brides. One wore a green sequined sheath that curled up her plastic body like a giant snake. I thought of Barbie's hard, jutting breasts as some sort of weaponry, torpedoes, perhaps, or small bombs, and the denuded, squared-off space between her legs as a mysterious slot into which a mechanical tab might fit.

For years Barbie was my example of womanhood. Noni was not a woman; she was our mother, too much and too close. Our friends' mothers were irritated carpoolers, bleary-eyed pancake makers. A quick, dark ride to the movies. A hatted figure clapping lazily at a soccer game. But Barbie wore frilly dresses and pliable plastic heels. Barbie stared dully from blue eyes painted beneath a crescent of long, pretty lashes.

It was Iris who took it upon herself to teach me the mechanics of sex. For this exercise she used the Barbies.

"First they get married, then they do it," Iris would say.

I dutifully marched Barbie the bride down an imaginary aisle toward our lone Ken. Ken had fewer clothing options than Barbie; his limbs were not as supple.

"Does she *have* to marry him?" I asked.

Iris shrugged. "That's usually how it works, but it's not like there's a law or anything."

Iris showed me how to make Barbie have sex missionary style with Ken and I soon extrapolated from her examples. Over time the couplings I conceived grew increasingly complex and difficult to arrange. I might include the adolescent Skipper, for example, or the small, posable figure of Batman's Robin, though he was burdened with painted-on clothing. I don't know where this erotic imagining came from. Iris herself was surprisingly conservative.

"Why don't you have a boyfriend?" I asked her one afternoon. "Your mom works nights."

Iris was polishing her nails a brilliant bubblegum pink, and the acetone stench filled the kitchen. This was generally how the afternoons with Iris progressed: I returned from school, she pulled a snack from the refrigerator—salami, cheese, yogurt—and I ate while watching her perform some act of personal decoration. Hair braiding, makeup application.

Now Iris paused in her polishing to consider my question. "Oh," she sighed, "boyfriends are too much work. All they want is for you to go places with them and put your hand on their you-know-what. It's disgusting, actually." She resumed her nail polish with a little shiver.

I was prepubescent, no breasts to speak of, still two years away from pubic hair and a first period, but of course I knew the implication of a you-know-what. Why disgusting? I had never in my life seen pornography or a naked man other than my brother, but I had glimpsed the covers of the girlie magazines displayed on the high shelves at the pharmacy. Once I had spotted the high-school calculus teacher, Mr. Louden, standing at the rack, flipping casually through the pages as though it were his birthright to look at naked women under the pharmacy's fluorescent glare while the rest of us passed through with our cough-syrup needs and prescriptions for eardrops. I watched as he tilted the magazine, pulled out an oversize page, raised his eyebrows. A small, secret smile.

Years later, after I began *The Last Romantic* blog, I would remember those magazine covers. They suggested something so alluring, so corrupting that they were safe only on the highest shelf, where children and women could not reach. Female sex appeal was dangerous. Sexual desire something expressible exclusively by men. My friends' fathers, male teachers, older brothers. All of them, reaching for that high shelf.

Where, I asked myself even then, was my high shelf? And what wonders would I find there?

*　*　*

WITH WILL GONE I searched in earnest for Noni, worrying that she had seen us speaking and that I would be forced to explain. Noni did not recognize boundaries when it came to us, her daughters, our skin problems or boyfriends or job prospects. Her questions were always frank and pointed, designed to elicit answers that contained enough salient information for her to critique. Dodging Noni's questions had become a sport for my sisters and me, a verbal tennis match with Noni always retaining the serve. I could only imagine what she'd do with Will and the kiss he'd delivered.

But I didn't need to worry. When I found her, Noni stood alone at the edge of the party, looking out of place but not uneasy in her black cotton dress and chunky hippie necklace. In late middle age, Noni carried a mystical sort of self-possession that set her apart from all the showy money here. She never wore makeup, and had let her hair grow long again, curled and crazy like mine.

"It's about time," Noni said as we hugged. "I was thinking you'd forgotten how to get uptown."

"I'm not *that* late," I said, feeling chastised and annoyed and then silly for feeling chastised and annoyed. I was a grown-up. I could come and go as I pleased.

"I was trying to talk wedding details with Sandrine's mom, but she kept asking me about the feral-cat problem." Noni rolled her eyes. Sandrine's mother, Jacinda, bore an eerie resemblance to Iggy

Pop: blond and bland, thin as a racing dog. She spent the majority of her time serving on the boards of various charities related to pets. It did not surprise me that she and Noni had trouble communicating.

"What did she say about cats?" I asked, remembering the ones from Caroline's new house. I had in the end taken them all to a shelter in Queens. My feckless roommates hadn't wanted a kitten, not even the smallest one with the white-blue eyes, but I had lied to Caroline and told her I'd found homes for them all.

"Apparently it's a huge problem in the suburbs. All these dirty, skinny cats wandering around. Jacinda wants to tour some pet place when she comes to Bexley." Noni had invited Sandrine's parents to stay overnight with her later in the week, a decision she regretted deeply once she learned that Jacinda was gluten-intolerant and abstained completely from alcohol.

For a moment Noni and I stood at the window, gazing out as one by one the streetlights flared on in Central Park. Standing so close to this wall of glass induced in me a sense of vertigo, as though the trees and lights and people moving sludgily along the park path were all traveling toward me, or me toward them. Inside and out, up and down. I closed my eyes and turned away.

"And where is Renee?" Noni said, looking at her watch. "Her shift ended an hour ago."

"It'll be a miracle if she makes it," I said. Renee's job was demanding, complex, the justification for any number of late arrivals and missed events. I always expected Renee to be engaged in more important work than spending time with us, her family.

"She'll come," Noni said. "She promised Joe. Send her one of those phone-message things."

"*Text*, Noni. It's called a text." I took out my phone and typed, WHERE R U?

"Are you nervous to read your poem?" Noni asked, looking around the room. "This is a big group."

"A little," I said. I didn't tell her that it wasn't the crowd that worried me, it was the presence of Will, Man #23, and how he might somehow reveal my identity as the Last Romantic here, in front of Noni and my siblings. Probably Noni had never before read a blog, but undoubtedly she had her views on them. Especially a blog about female sexuality researched and written by her youngest daughter.

Noni must have seen the discomfort on my face; she took hold of my hand. "You'll do great, Fiona," she said. "You're a firecracker." Her palm was dry and warm, and the weight of it startled me, the give of the fingers as they circled mine. Noni was not generally a toucher, a hand-holder, a you'll-be-okayer. What I'd learned about self-reliance I'd learned from her. Now her unexpected touch calmed me down more than I expected. It was exactly what I needed.

"Fiona, you're here!" It was Sandrine's voice behind me. I released Noni's hand and turned in to Sandrine's skinny hug.

"You look beautiful," I said. This was what I always said to Sandrine, because this was what she always wanted to hear. Tonight it was true. Sandrine's dress was the color of cream, short and tight at the waist with a flared little skirt and a wide neck that showed off clavicles thin as chopsticks. Fat diamonds sparkled on her ears.

She smiled. "Can't wait for the poem. Just watch for Kyle. He'll start the speeches." She winked. "Oh, and, Fiona," she said, pulling me and Noni closer to her. "I already told your mom, but I'll have my hairdresser do you both for the wedding." Her eyes rested briefly on my hair—curly, loose, still wet from the shower. "That way we can all be on the same page. Okay?"

Noni looked at me with wide eyes and shook her head the slightest bit. *No, Fiona, do not make a fuss, not tonight.*

"Sure, Sandrine," I said, smiling brightly. "Whatever you want."

Flutter, flounce, ripple, bony, toothy, tart, brittle.

For a few uncomfortable minutes, Sandrine remained in our small circle while Noni issued compliments about the food, the view, the very nice waiters. Then Ace appeared beside us.

"Fiona Skinner, how the hell are you?" he said, and leaned in to kiss me on the cheek. "You look fantastic." Ace made a show of looking me up and down in a way that was not flattering but appraising, the look you'd give to a length of wood you were considering for a fence post. Was I durable? Would I need two coats of paint or three?

Ace had expensive shoes and impressive biceps from sessions with a personal trainer, but he still laughed with the same sharp bark I remembered from the pond. To me he would always be that little boy: not necessarily someone who acted with bad intent, merely one too weak and careless to follow through on the good. Now Ace worked in the music industry—not the creative side, something related to marketing—but still it lacquered him with a certain artistic patina when placed alongside Joe's college friends in finance and law. He wasn't a drug dealer, I learned later. It wasn't that simple. He was the guy who knew how to get things, lots of things. People invited him to parties not because they liked him but because he was glamorous and useful. In Joe's demographic no one was an addict. No one was losing their hair or teeth or sleep over the drugs, but they wanted them at certain times, and there was no way they'd hail a cab or walk down a seedy street to meet some stranger in a back alley. This was where Ace fit in.

"Thanks for being here," I said carefully.

Ace grasped my hand and held it even as I began to pull away. "I love your family, you know that. I'd do anything for Joe. And I hear you wrote a poem for the happy couple." He smiled. "Good for you, Fiona." He released my hand and patted me on the cheek like a poodle.

There was a moment of silence, Ace and Sandrine standing stiffly side by side, and I suddenly realized they might not know each other. "Joe and Ace are friends from the pond," I explained.

"Oh, I've already met *Ace*," said Sandrine with a flap of her hand. "I've met all of Joe's friends." She paused. "But what's the pond?"

"The pond?" I said. "Joe hasn't told you about the pond?"

"Noooo." Sandrine shook her head. "Is there something I should know?"

"Nothing," Ace said smoothly. "There's nothing you need to know about the pond."

I opened my mouth to contradict him, to explain how much the pond had meant to us growing up, how that time was the foundation of Joe and Ace's friendship, but before I could speak, a woman long and sleek as a heron moved in to greet Sandrine. "Look at *you!*" the woman said loudly, and then Ace sighted someone else across the room, and Noni and I were left standing alone.

I wish now that I had been more aware of the dynamics of that small interaction. Noni, Sandrine, Ace, and I, all of us positioned beside that mammoth, glorious window as the night descended and the view turned to shadows and sparkle. I had never seen Ace and Sandrine together, although I should have known they'd already met. Perhaps they had met many times.

From across the room, Man #23 was trying to catch my gaze. I studiously ignored him. What had I written about him? The sex itself had progressed according to convention: kiss, kiss, touch, stroke, clothing dropped, bodies positioned, give, slide. Nice, sweet, unremarkable sex. Afterward pale moonlight fell across the sheets. The city breeze and distant street noise drifted in like smoke. It was then that I looked at him, really looked. Freckles marked his entire body, up and down his legs and arms, across his shoulders. On his lower back, where the skin was smooth and hairless, lay a constellation of freckles. I traced those freckles with a finger. Yes, that's what I'd written about for TheLastRomantic.com: Man #23, the freckles at the small of his back, their position nearly identical to the constellation of Andromeda.

*　*　*

HOW TO DESCRIBE the blog? It was a project that began innocently enough as the product of my healthy libido and a newfound sexual attractiveness that took everyone by surprise, myself most of all. What happened was that I became thin. I was twenty-four years old, newly arrived in New York City, still without health insurance, and I began to run. There was no grand plan, no Twelve Steps to a New You. The running was simply a free activity that took place outside the cramped apartment I shared with college friends of similarly pinched circumstances. Along with the exercise, I maintained a strict weekly budget that allowed for only two meals per day. Or one meal and alcohol. The combination led to the initial weight loss—some twenty pounds in two months—and by then I was hooked. Cheekbones emerged, an ass and a waist. It was fun, like shifting your image in a funhouse mirror to see the shapes you could make.

With my new body came a certain kind of power. Men's heads flipped like Ping-Pong paddles as I walked past. Taxis were easier to come by, and good tables at restaurants, and drinks, so many drinks, sent my way by well-wishing, generally far older men. At first I felt uncomfortable. I didn't trust it. I didn't trust the men. I asked Renee, "How do you deal with it?" This was before she met Jonathan, when I believed my oldest sister to exist on a plane beyond the base needs for sex and affirmation.

"I just ignore it," Renee said. "I never make eye contact, and I don't wear makeup. And I have a can of Mace in my bag."

But Renee and I had different perspectives. I didn't want to think about risk or violence. I knew how to be careful; I'd learned the lesson of the man in the car. Now I only wanted a free martini. I only wanted to have some fun.

So I did. It was the grand transformative fantasy of every pudgy teenage girl who'd been overlooked, taken for granted, ignored by the many and diverse objects of her affection. Over the next year, I flirted and slept with every type of man I'd lusted after in high school and college—the jocks, prom kings, bad boys, stoners, and class presidents—and then I moved on to all the others. I dated some men for a few weeks here and there, but I happened upon a relationship only once: Eli, a tall and earnest publishing intern who broke his leg in a spectacular bike accident that required a twelve-week convalescence. During this time I brought him groceries and toilet paper. I held his cast outside the shower curtain to keep it from getting wet. Something about this vulnerability and need made me want to stay, plus the knee-to-thigh cast and the pulleys installed above his bed made the sex interesting and acrobatic. But once Eli's physical therapy ended and he was walking again, I broke up with him. Eli cried.

"If you'd put up with all of that," he asked, "why leave now?"

He had thick, sensitive lips and dark eyebrows marked on the right side by an unexpected shock of premature white. He was in fact a good guy.

"I don't know exactly," I said at first. And then I realized the problem. "I guess I just don't want things to be normal."

It was natural that I'd take my experiences into my poetry class. I wrote almost exclusively about sex, because sex was the most interesting thing that was happening to me.

My poetry teacher's name was Kevin Kealey.

"I like the sex poems," said Kevin.

Emma, an almost-model, almost-artist in the class, sighed extravagantly and rolled her eyes.

"But?" I asked.

"Listen, the idea isn't *entirely* new. You've got Anaïs Nin, Erica Jong . . ." Kevin looked confused.

"Sylvia Plath," I reminded him. "Sharon Olds, Eileen Myles."

Kevin was nodding. "Yes, yes, of course. And . . . others. And your work is *appealing*. I mean, it's fresh. It's very honest."

Again Emma sighed, louder this time, and was joined by a distinct groan from the back row. I ignored them. My class was composed of fourteen antagonistic strangers with day jobs and the kinds of literary ambitions that grew from personal torment and a scattershot idea of what might make it all feel better. Their critiques were not kind. (*Soulless. Demeaning. Empty.*) They all seemed to hate me, or maybe they just hated my work. Only Kevin thought I was onto something.

I submitted my sex poems to and was summarily rejected by ninety-nine literary journals and poetry magazines, and I told Kevin that was it. The number one hundred was simply too demoralizing, too symbolic. How would I ever recover from a hundred straight rejections?

One night I stayed late with Kevin after the others had trickled out. The class was held in an NYU building in what appeared to be an abandoned classroom designated too drafty and dangerous for tuition-paying NYU undergrads. There was some halfhearted graffiti on one section of the blackboard and what looked very much like asbestos pushing up the floor tiles beneath the room's only window, which was cracked. We all kept our coats on during class.

"Kevin," I said, pulling up a chair beside his desk, "why do I even care about getting published?"

"I don't know. Why do you?" He was peeling an orange, and the fresh smell of citrus filled the room.

"Because people tell me I should care. *You* tell me that!"

Kevin looked wounded. "Fiona, I am all about the purity of the process. Don't listen to those bozos at the *Paris Review*. Just write what you want to write." He paused. "Maybe you should start a blog."

"What did you just say?"

"A blog!" Kevin's mouth was full of orange.

"Bog?"

He chewed and swallowed. "Have you been living under a rock? A *blog*. It's like if you put your diary online and invited people to comment on it. Not for the faint of heart, Fiona."

I considered his words. "I've never fainted in my life. Really."

"I mean, I love these lines." Kevin picked up the poem I had submitted for that night's class. "You could turn this bloggy. Easy as pie."

Kevin wrote down some website addresses, and I took the subway home. The year was 2003. I spent the weekend taking notes on *Gawker, Dooce.com, Belle de Jour,* and *The Daily Dish.* By Sunday afternoon I figured I had read enough. I downloaded Movable Type version 2.6 onto my iMac and, after an all-nighter of mouse manipulation and profanity, became a blogger.

Because I was a little bit chicken and because I didn't quite trust that Kevin totally knew what he was talking about, I did not use my name. I called myself the Last Romantic.

On the blog I described the project like this: "The Last Romantic aims to record in Full Truth the Sex Life of a Young Woman in a Great City, the woman being myself, the city being New York. Or, in other words, the process of providing myself with a sentimental education, unsentimentally."

My first post, an earnest and semi-erotic poem about kissing a man with a mustache, drew 7 hits. My next post, a wryly detailed account of oral sex with the same mustachioed man, titled "Ticklingus," drew 288 hits. I was hooked. I could say anything in a few short paragraphs, and anyone with a computer could read it. I told only Kevin when I posted something new, and yet week by week, month by month, my audience grew.

Before *The Last Romantic,* dating had always seemed like a purpose-driven exercise—date men, sleep with men, to find one man—but now it became process-driven. There was no one man, I realized, waiting at the end of this rainbow. The project itself served as both pot of gold and rainbow. I applied all the five-cent homilies I'd ever heard about the journey and the destination and not investing in the outcome into this, my sex life. And it was so interesting! What was more interesting than personal foibles and predilections related to sex? Because related to sex meant related to self and self-esteem and esteem of others. How a person behaved on a one-night stand spoke volumes. After I warmed up to the basic project mechanics (flirtation, initiation, fulfillment), I liked to shake it up. I would play a woman searching for commitment, or one heartsick from a bad breakup, or (once) a prostitute, or (twice) a virgin. Dabbling in the emotional specifics varied my partners' responses and, most interestingly, changed my own physical outcome in ways that always surprised me.

Of course, the sheer number of encounters required that I look beyond the men themselves, their personalities specifically. They became for me a sequence of responses, physical, emotional, behavioral. Perhaps I should have taken anthropology in college as well as women's studies, because the project seemed a melding of the two. Gendered in its consciousness and goals. But those who read the blog didn't really care about the theoretical underpinnings, what I believed about gender expectations and sexual politics, the traps of marriage and motherhood, the need for women to claim their own personal freedom and expression, sexual and otherwise. Young women read my blog about sex because my experiences matched their own and my words provided confirmation that they—the furiously typing, horny, sexy female *they*—were not alone.

On the night of Joe's engagement party, I had been writing the blog for ten months. I had 5,188 followers, averaged fifty to seventy-five comments per post, and was on the way to becoming the unlikely sexual guru to a certain group of single, primarily hetero-sexual young women with Internet access and complicated love lives.

Since the blog began, I had slept with seventy-six men.

*   *   *

"HELLO? HELLO OUT there?" said Kyle Morgan. He rapped a microphone. A small platform stage had been installed against the wall facing the windows, and Kyle now stood upon it, looking down at his party guests with the amused expression of a calm and indul-gent host. Kyle had a louche authority about him. As vice president of Morgan Capital under his aging father, he was the de facto man in charge, the one who enforced the rules, but also the one who most frequently broke them.

"Children. Children, please," Kyle said over the din. "It's circle time now, so let's listen up."

All heads turned toward the stage. An expectant silence fell.

"Good, now you'll all get a nice treat after class," Kyle said, and grinned. "I first wanted to thank you all for being here tonight to celebrate Joe and Sandrine." A few whoops, a smattering of ap-plause. "I think I speak for many of Joe's friends when I say thank you especially to Sandrine for taking Joe Skinner off the market so the rest of us have a chance." Laughter, more hoots. "And I'm sure Sandrine's friends would say the same. You're a vision tonight, darling, really." In the crowd Sandrine tipped her blond head.

I'd always liked Kyle more than many of Joe's other college friends. Maybe it was his own brand of camp, heterosexual but not entirely. Maybe he was in love with Joe, or with one of the other fraternity brothers, or with all of them. Before Alden he'd gone to Dayton Academy, an all-boys boarding school where he was captain of the tennis team and voted Most Likely to Be Arrested for Tax Fraud. His lifestyle was paid for by his father's bank, but Kyle wore his privilege lightly and enjoyed spreading it around. I'd gotten concert tickets from him, invitations to benefits and parties that Kyle couldn't attend, a job interview (but not the job) at a liberal think tank. Because I was Joe's little sister, Kyle folded me into the loose web of his concern and generosity, and it was a nice, warm place to be. For Joe, after so many years, it must have felt like home.

Kyle talked in a sweet, meandering way about his and Joe's time together at Alden College, those years of magic and dreams, he called them, and the camaraderie of the fraternity, the enduring love these men had for one another.

"We never saw a finer bongmaster," Kyle said. "Am I right, Joey? Am I right? We had some crazy ones."

Joe raised his arm and yelled "Kyyyyy-le!" in a loud, gravelly voice. He broke the name into two distinct sounds—Ky-ULL—and repeated it again and again in a kind of chant. Kyle laughed and raised his arm in return, and soon all the other fraternity brothers—thirty at least—in the room followed. As the sound persisted, it warped and changed and became not a man's name but something else. Something animal and of the moment. A sound distorted by the element in which it was issued.

Gradually the arms lowered, the chant died down. But Joe continued. Alone, he chanted at the same volume, the same rhythm: "Ky-*ULL*, Ky-*ULL*." From where I stood, I could not see Joe; I only heard his voice.

Kyle looked uneasily out at the crowd. "Sandrine," he said into the microphone, "are you out there? I think your man may need a glass of water." He laughed nervously, and then Ace stepped to the stage and began to introduce the next speaker, his voice loud enough that it drowned out Joe. And then Joe's voice abruptly stopped and the next speech began, this one from a friend of Sandrine's.

The entire episode lasted no longer than five minutes, but it changed the tenor of the room. The party now felt unsettled, on edge, as though the chanting had contained a message that everyone but Joe had understood.

And then it was my turn. Kyle offered a brief introduction. There was a moment of ruffled silence as heads turned to look for me in the crowd and I made my way to the small stage. I delighted in the weight of all those eyes on me, the attention of Joe's friends and colleagues, the looks of surprise from his old fraternity brothers: Here was Fiona, no longer tagging behind athletic, smart Renee and dreamy, beloved Caroline. No longer chubby and awkward, now a full-grown woman. *You look fantastic,* Ace had said.

"This is called 'He and She,'" I announced, and pushed a curl away from my face.

I began to read. I didn't think about the crowd, or Man #23, or Joe, or Sandrine, or Noni, or the poem as a whole, its meaning, or the feelings I wanted it to evoke (longing and hope and lust and pride), but only about the sound of each indivisible word, the musicality of each, the rhythm. I leaned into the pa-pa-*pa* of the poem in the way I'd seen other poets, powerful amazing poets, read their work.

I was nearly halfway through when the noise began. It came from the very back of the room, a ripple of conversation, not loud but loud enough for me to hear a distinct word—*boring*—said with a laugh. I looked up, and there at the back was a tall, handsome man: my brother, Joe. His body was only half turned toward the stage. Another man stood with him, the two of them swaying, bending slightly, then straightening again as they talked and laughed. Joe's cheeks were shaded a startling red, and he threw back his head and uttered a loud, sharp *Ha!* in response to something the other man had said.

I resumed reading. I ignored Joe and put my mouth closer to the microphone, spoke louder and faster. But a general rustling began. The noise moved forward from the back of the room, slowly at first, a tickling, nervous kind of sound, and then in an instant a switch flipped, an organic process was triggered, and the entire crowd erupted into conversation. I looked up again, and people were turning into groups, chatting and drinking. I saw a hand rise from the crowd to summon one of the waiters who hovered at the edge of the room.

I didn't know what to do. I wasn't finished with the poem. I tried to speak louder into the microphone, but my voice fell beneath the din. I paused in the middle of a line. I looked for Joe, but I didn't see him. The only person I recognized was my mother, charging toward me through the crowd. She stepped onto the stage with her glass and a spoon and tapped violently.

"Quiet! Quiet, please!" Noni said. "Fiona hasn't finished yet. She's still reading."

No one noticed her. No one paused in his or her conversation.

"Be respectful!" Noni called, her voice shrill, her face red. "This is Joe's sister!"

A few people looked up at Noni then. Their faces showed a tinge of guilt and embarrassment as they turned their backs to the stage. I was nearly as surprised by Noni charging onstage as I'd been by her handholding earlier in the evening. Perhaps the emotion of Joe's impending marriage had affected her. Perhaps she'd had too much wine. Either way, Noni coming to my rescue was the last thing I expected. But here she was, standing beside me.

"I'm so sorry, Fiona," Noni said. "It's a lovely poem. May I read it?" Dumbly I nodded and handed her the page.

As Noni read the rest of my poem silently to herself, I scanned the crowd. Only one face was still turned toward the stage. It was Man #23, Will. He looked at me quizzically, a half smile on his face that was amused but not ungenerous.

"Fiona," he said, enunciating carefully. "I liked your poem." I couldn't hear his voice, but I made out the shape of the words.

A waiter obscured my view of Will, and my sight line shifted. Now I noticed, standing far at the back of the room, Joe and Kyle. Kyle was talking very fast, his hands moving emphatically, but I couldn't make out Joe's face, only his stance, which was one of re- sistance. He leaned away to exit the conversation, but Kyle grabbed Joe's arm above the elbow and held it, the two men locked in some private struggle. Only a few seconds passed, and then Kyle released Joe and turned abruptly away, as though in anger or dismissal. For a beat, Joe remained by himself. He let his head hang toward the ground. Still he didn't look at the stage. He didn't seem aware of what had happened, that he had started the avalanche of noise and disregard that drowned out the poem he'd asked me to write.

Noni pulled gently on my arm. "It's a wonderful poem," she said to me. "Joe will appreciate it eventually."

Together we stepped off the stage. It was time to leave. I moved steadily through the crowd, head down, to retrieve my coat, my bag. I pressed the elevator button and waited as the tuxedos circulated around me: more champagne, more shrimp.

At last the elevator pinged, the doors opened, and there was Renee.

We looked at each other in surprise.

"Am I too late?" she asked. "Is everyone leaving?"

"Not everyone," I said. "Just me."

"So I missed the reading," she said with dismay.

"Everyone missed it. Don't worry, it's okay."

"Did Joe love it?"

I didn't know how to answer. I didn't want to cry, not here. She watched my face. She must have seen something, my disappointment and anger and embarrassment, because she leaned forward and grabbed my hand.

"What did Joe do?" Renee said. "Do you get it now? Do you *see?*" There was concern in Renee's voice but also anger. Anger directed at me.

And then Renee's face changed into a wide, automatic smile, and I knew without looking that Noni had come up behind me. It was then I noticed a tall man standing beside Renee. His left hand and arm were wrapped in a pristine white bandage and supported by a sling.

"Fiona, Noni," Renee said, still smiling. "Meet Jonathan."

Chapter 8

AFTER THE SPEECHES and my failed reading, the party shifted into a higher, more potent gear. There was more alcohol, louder music, dancers in the living room, smokers on the terrace. People laughing behind closed doors. A long, snaking line at the bathroom. Ace on his phone.

"I should get home," Jonathan whispered into Renee's ear. He'd met Noni and Joe and watched Renee greet some old Bexley friends.

Renee nodded. "Just give me a minute," she said. "I need to talk to my brother."

She found Joe outside on the balcony. The view stopped Renee for a moment: the sky so clear, Central Park West like a sparkling red artery separating the neat empty block of the park from the glittering mess of the West Side. It amazed Renee how desolate the park looked from up here, the black heart of the city gouged out, scraped clean, a crater.

Joe was smoking a cigarette with two of the waiters, college students both, who ducked away as Renee approached. The night had turned cold, and Renee shivered without a coat, but Joe was sweating. Dark stains marked his blue shirt under the arms and down the back.

"Having fun?" Joe asked. He exhaled smoke over the balcony railing.

"No, I'm not," Renee answered. "We need to talk about your drinking. And the drugs, whatever it is you're taking now. Should I ask Ace?"

Joe snorted. "You've had it in for Ace ever since we were kids," he said.

"That's not true."

"He's not a bad guy."

"He's a bad influence. He's not your friend."

"Jesus, I'm not ten years old anymore. I can take care of myself."

Renee took a step closer to Joe. "I want to get you some help," she said.

"Oh, Renee. Help?" Joe held out his arms wide like a T, as though to indicate all of it: the balcony, the city, the park, the sky. "I'm fantastic. Did you see Sandrine? Isn't she fucking gorgeous? I can't believe this is my life. Here. This. I'm doing great."

"I'm worried about you."

"You worry too much." He smiled, and the dimples came up. In the dim light of the balcony, he did look like a kid, an oversize kid dressed up in his father's clothes. "Go home, Renee. I don't want you here. I've never wanted you here, hovering over me." Now he fluttered his hands like moths. "You're not my mother."

To the east a plane descended toward JFK, its red lights blinking steadily, without urgency, and Renee thought for a moment of all the people contained inside. Eating, sleeping, listening to music, staring out at the night, waiting to arrive. The interminable descent and how shocking it always felt, how impossible, when the plane landed with a jolt and the transition from sky to earth was complete. There were moments in the ER that stretched on like that, past the end of Renee's shift, past a four-hour night of dreamless sleep, into the next day and the next, on and on until another moment replaced it. Over the course of her medical career, there would be hundreds of these eternal moments. A girl with two black eyes, one broken arm, no shoes. The young woman, a lump in her breast the size of a lemon, the texture of stone. A boy, his name was Alexey, his right hand plunged into boiling water. He is very bad, the father said. How else to teach a lesson?

Here with Joe on the night of his engagement party, looking past him to the glittering lights of Manhattan and the plane, obscured now by a ragged scrap of cloud, was not one of those moments. Her brother was right: look at all that he had. There was pain in the world, so much, and she had the capacity to ease some of it. Just a fraction, but still.

Renee turned and left our brother on the balcony. She found Jonathan and rode with him in a cab first to a twenty-four-hour pharmacy and then to his apartment, where she watched as he took his medicine. Then she put him to bed, and then, finally, after thirty-one hours of wakefulness and half doze, Renee was home in her own bed. Asleep.

* * *

HOW LONG WAS it before Joe called me? Perhaps two weeks, perhaps three. Every day that passed felt like a slap. Every day a reminder of the reading. Those minutes on the stage in Kyle's apartment played again and again in my mind, hot and embarrassing.

When Joe finally called, I was getting ready for work. Sitting on the edge of the bed, I held the phone in my hand and watched Joe's number flash on the screen. For me to accept an apology, I thought, it must be lengthy and sincere, perhaps even tearful. The poem was long gone, the paper thrown away, the file deleted from my computer. I would never write another word for Joe. Nothing for the wedding, nothing for a christening or graduation. This was what I planned to tell him, as though it would be the greatest insult, the harshest punishment.

I answered the phone. "Hi, Joe," I said, the syllables curt and sharp.

"Fiona—" Joe's voice sounded strange, strangled, as though he were trying to swallow but could not.

My roommates had already left for work. It was 9:30 A.M., Monday. I had keys in my hand, my coat on.

"I think I'm in trouble," Joe said. "I hit someone."

"Hit? You were driving?"

"No, hit with my hand. I hit Kyle. I punched him."

"You punched Kyle?" All at once the morning fell away. "Why?"

"He fired me. He threw me out of the building."

"What? Where are you?" I heard a wail of sirens, but I wasn't sure if the sound came from the phone, where Joe was, or from the street outside my apartment building.

"I'm at the library." Again the strangled sound. He was crying, I thought. A real cry, a sound I recognized from that long-ago day at the pond when I had almost drowned, when Joe cursed his own foolishness, his role in making something wonderful turn to sorrow.

"Stay there," I said quickly. "I'll come to you."

* * *

I MET JOE on the stone steps of the New York Public Library, but it started to rain, a heavy, drenching shower, so we ran to a nearby deli, where we sat on plastic chairs and drank watery coffee from paper cups. Joe wore no coat, only a short-sleeved polo, and held no briefcase. Rain darkened the shoulders of his shirt, and his hair shrank to his scalp, making him look cold and small. I shivered at the sight of him.

"I didn't mean to hit him," Joe said. "It just happened. I was just so, so . . . angry."

"But why did he fire you?"

"My numbers haven't been great. And I'm expensive, Fiona. Kyle is worried that things are getting ready to turn."

I remembered the exchange I'd witnessed at the party. "And what else, Joe?"

Joe paused and rubbed his face with his hands. "He thinks I need to straighten up. Too much . . . I don't know, partying." Joe paused. "You know, I was pretty wasted at the engagement party. Did you read your poem, Fiona?" He looked at me with an open face, innocent.

All at once the anger I'd held since the party faded. "No, I didn't," I said.

"Send it to Sandrine, okay? She'd love to see it."

I nodded. Then I said, "Joe, do you think you have a problem?"

"No," Joe answered quickly. "Of course I don't." There was another pause, this one longer. Then he said, "And Kyle mentioned something about a harassment allegation. My old secretary, Sierra."

Sierra? My mind searched for a face, and then all at once, of course. A dawning recognition, a connection between two disparate points. Sierra, the strawberry blond from Joe's engagement party.

"She said you harassed her?"

"Something like that. Kyle said she wouldn't press charges. If they fired me. Otherwise she might. She threatened him. I think she wants more money, better office, better job. She isn't that great on Excel, which is the God's honest truth, so she got moved downstairs into HR. There are no windows down there, none."

I did not respond immediately. My brother's face was red, still wet and raw from the rain. At last I said, "So she's lying about sexual harassment as leverage for a better view? Is that what you're telling me?"

Joe slowly shook his head. "Fiona, Fiona, don't be so naïve. People do things like this. Women do them. It isn't uncommon."

"I saw you," I told Joe, "with Sierra. At your engagement party."

"What?" He looked genuinely confused. "Oh, behind the screen. Is that what you mean?"

I nodded.

He sighed and looked at the floor. "I love Sandrine, I really do. But it's so hard to say no. Why would I say no? You understand that now, don't you, Fiona?"

"What are you talking about?"

"Look at you," Joe said. "Look at how you dress. Look at how you talk to guys. I've seen you flirt. You're practically a different person since you lost weight."

This was a new Joe regarding me. A starkly serious Joe with a cold calculation in his eyes. He was judging me, assessing me. And suddenly my brother became a stranger. I recognized in Joe the kind of man about whom I wrote most viciously on the blog, the kind who carried himself with an entitlement that masqueraded as confidence. Joe believed that he deserved whatever he wanted— Sierra, Sandrine, an annual raise, a six-figure bonus.

"This isn't about me," I said.

He rolled his eyes. "I did not harass Sierra. I didn't. We've flirted, yes. She's a very attractive woman. Once we kissed, a long time ago. We made out, at an office party. Okay? Happy now, Fiona? This was before Sandrine and I were serious. Way before."

"Before you were *serious*? But you were already dating?"

"Yes. Before we were serious." He put his face in his hands, and then he sat up straight. "I need to call Kyle. I just need to talk to him. We're *brothers*, for Christ's sake. I know we can work this out."

He punched a number into his phone. I watched his face as the line rang and rang and rang.

Joe hung up. "I'll call Derek," he said.

And so he did. On and on, friend by friend, fraternity brother by fraternity brother, the wide circle he shared with Kyle: Kevin, David, Lance, Kurt, William, Xavier, Mike B., Mike H., Mike S., Hank, Matt, Camden, Bobby, Logan, Cal. Joe would often bring one or two or five of these boys back to Noni's house on weekends or breaks, for home-cooked meals and movies. Generally they holed up in Joe's room or piled themselves in front of the television with beers and bags of Doritos. To me, adolescent hormonal Fiona, they were like great cats, sultry and sleepy, launching into quick, explosive motion before languishing again into blurred half sleep. Eyelids lowered, voices so deep, grunting at one another in monosyllables, like the language of some ancient tribe. They moved with a certainty about their place in the room, their place on the planet. I marveled at it. I wanted it.

I remember writing in my book, *Muscle, tooth, solid, sex, skin, languish, stubble, power.*

No one picked up Joe's call. His face drained. "They all know," he said, his voice thin.

"You can't be sure."

"Yes I can. It's been . . . what? Two hours since I left. That's enough time. They all know."

And then Joe's phone rang with an unidentified number. With a small, hopeful smile, he picked up.

"Hello? Yes, this is Joe Skinner." I leaned forward to hear the other side of the conversation, but I caught only a deep, ominous babble.

"Uh-huh, okay. . . . Yes. . . . Okay, I will," Joe said. "Okay. . . . Yes, thank you, Officer." He hung up. "Well. Kyle reported me to the police. They're investigating an assault charge. I have to go down to the Seventeenth Precinct and turn myself in."

"Oh, Joe," I said. "I'm so sorry. Let me go with you."

"No. Absolutely not. But can you call Sandrine? I can't talk to her. Not right now."

I nodded.

"But don't call Noni, okay? Don't tell Caroline or Renee either, not until . . ." Joe paused. "Not until I know what to tell them."

I nodded again. I waited for Joe to make the first move toward departure, but he just sat in the deli's flimsy plastic chair, legs crossed at the ankles, back curved, folded into himself as though seeking to protect some tender inner spot. Once I would have said that I knew my brother better than any other person. At the pond we would play gin rummy for hours, barely speaking, and then rise together at the exact moment when the heat became unbearable, run into the water, and then return, dripping and cool, to the game. Now I didn't know what to say, how to comfort him, or if comfort was what he deserved.

"Fiona," he said without looking at me, "do you think it's unfair that we never had a chance to know Dad?"

"I don't think about it very much," I answered.

"I wonder if Noni really loved him," he said. "I don't think she did."

"Why do you think that?"

"She never talks about him."

It was true: Noni rarely talked about Ellis Avery anymore and, when we were younger, only in relation to her regrets.

"Maybe it hurts Noni to talk about him," I offered. "He was there for her, and then he was gone, so suddenly."

Joe shook his head. "I don't think so."

"Well, it's not like it makes any difference. Does it? He's been dead so long. I don't even remember him."

"I remember him," said Joe. "I loved him."

"That makes sense. You were older."

"Fiona, sometimes I think I see Dad," Joe said.

"See him?" I repeated. A memory of that day in the yellow house came back to me. Standing in our parents' old bedroom. I'd thought it was silly, almost a joke. But Joe had been waiting for our father. Maybe Joe had been waiting his entire life. I remembered what Caroline had told me about the night of the frat party, Joe's disillusionment with baseball: *Dad told him to stop playing.*

"Usually it's when I'm high," Joe continued. "Really high. Or drunk. When my mind is . . . elsewhere. When it's relaxed. It's not a hallucination, it's not. I've been trying to do it without the drugs. To relax enough, like meditation. So I can see him when he's here."

"You don't see him," I said.

"You'll see him one day, Fiona. We all will. I told Renee too."

"You don't see Dad," I repeated.

But Joe wasn't listening to me. He was looking at the floor, appearing to examine the dirt-filled cracks of the linoleum.

"Joe?" I said.

He lifted his head. "What?"

"Should I be worried about you?"

Joe smiled. "Me? No. Don't worry about me. I'm great. I'm always great."

* * *

JOE CAUGHT A cab downtown to the police station. I took the subway to my office. That morning I edited a press release about the upcoming UN climate-change conference in Buenos Aires and posted some website copy. I ate lunch at the bagel place down the block. I walked back to the office and saw on the way a man without legs scooting himself along the sidewalk on a dolly, his hands black with the filth of the street. I remember these details exactly. Some days continue to exist year after year, decade after decade, as though they are happening inside you concurrent with the present. A persistent, simultaneous life. One that you consider and wish more than anything that you could change.

I returned to the office, and I picked up the phone. I called Sandrine. I said hello and how was your weekend? And then I began.

"Something happened today, and Joe wanted me to call you."

"Oh," said Sandrine. "What?"

I told her what Joe had told me: the bad numbers, the partying, the anger, the punch.

"Where's Joe? Why isn't he calling me?"

"He had to go to the police station. Kyle is pressing charges. Assault."

Sandrine began to breathe shallowly into the phone.

"Sandrine, I'm sure it'll all be okay," I said. "They're like brothers, remember?"

"Will Joe get his job back?"

"Job?" I asked, surprised. "I doubt it."

"But why? What *happened*?"

I wanted to say it and I didn't want to. I had never liked Sandrine. I didn't like the way she appraised and quantified, looking over Joe's suits, his apartment, the menu at every restaurant. After he proposed—on bended knee, a champagne picnic in Central Park—she'd asked to exchange the ring for diamond earrings, Joe had told me. More carats, he explained. Two instead of one. He'd ended up just buying her the earrings for her birthday later that month.

"There's been a claim of sexual harassment," I told Sandrine in a rush. "Against Joe. That's what Kyle said."

"What?" Her voice was now a whisper. "Who did he harass?"

I paused. "Sierra. His old secretary."

"Sierra." Sandrine breathed the name. "Of course. She' so pretty. Have you met her? She's very, very pretty."

"But he says he didn't do anything." I inhaled, exhaled. "I mean, nothing serious. Not recently."

For a moment there was complete silence from Sandrine. "Fiona, I know we've never been friends," she said slowly. "I know you don't like me. None of you do. I'm not good enough for your perfect brother, Joe. But what are you trying to tell me?"

The moment stretched forward, branching, lifting, dividing. There were many things I wanted to tell Sandrine: That it was true, she wasn't good enough for my brother. That I didn't like her or her friends or her cadaverous mother. That I wished Joe had chosen someone more like us, his sisters. And what did that say about his regard for us, that he had selected the exact kind of person whom each of us would despise equally, but for different reasons? Did he want to push us away?

Yet I said none of these things to Sandrine. I thought about the Joe I'd seen in the deli, the person he'd become at his Alden College fraternity and then at Morgan Capital. Sandrine seemed part of this. The unraveling of Joe Skinner, my brother who had loved Celeste, who had taught me to swim, who would play Battleship late into the night, ignoring his homework and all the phone calls, who could knock a ball straight out of the park as though it were as easy as breathing. What should I tell Sandrine? Was it worth the betrayal? In that moment I believed that it was.

"Something happened with Sierra," I said. "Something more than a flirtation."

Sandrine again went silent. I was telling her the truth, just as I did on the blog. I was speaking the truth about all those men, some of them honest, some of them unfaithful, some of them sweet and lovely, others calculating and mean, driven by a need to dominate, to make a woman, any woman, feel inferior. I was telling Sandrine the truth about Joe. I was telling her what she needed to know.

Sandrine said something more, but I can no longer recall what it was. We said our good-byes, the tones less pleasant now, the words crisp and fast. That was the last time I ever spoke to Sandrine Cahill.

* * *

WHAT HAPPENED NEXT was predictable, as sentimental tragedy often is. Sandrine left Joe. She began a relationship with Ace McAllister, moving from Joe's apartment on the Upper East Side into Ace's on the Upper West. Joe swore they had not been having an affair, and perhaps this was objectively true, but something must have passed between them. Perhaps Ace made the first move. Perhaps Sandrine. It didn't matter.

"She wanted a certain life," Joe told me. "It wasn't really about me. I was incidental. Once I couldn't give her that life, that was it."

We were drinking gin and tonics at a noisy bar near his apartment. George W. Bush had won again, and Caroline had decided not to host Thanksgiving at her house, opting instead to visit Nathan's sister in Vermont, and Renee was suddenly and miraculously in love with Jonathan Frank, an event that caused considerable heartburn for Noni, who now believed it inevitable that Renee would leave her transplant fellowship despite all the years she'd put into her training. Caroline had made Noni gun-shy about what her daughters might give up for a man.

That night with Joe, my stomach ached from my own sense of irreversible disruption. I sat unsteadily on the barstool, sipping my drink. I wasn't worried *about* Joe. My worry was that he knew about my conversation with Sandrine. I waited for Joe to raise the topic and had already developed a defense—*She would have found out eventually, she had a right to know*—but he never did. He simply ordered another round of cocktails, and then I had to get home, and we said our good-byes on the sidewalk.

Kyle, in the end, dropped the assault charges. He was too busy, Joe said. He didn't have time for the hassle of lawyers and police. And Sierra dropped the harassment claim, if indeed she'd had one in the first place. Perhaps it had been a pretense for Kyle, an easy way to relieve himself of the obligation of Joe Skinner, merely a fraternity brother, the two of them thrown together by chance so many years ago. Who could blame Kyle for not honoring that commitment? He wasn't married to Joe. Kyle was running a business, and he couldn't carry around deadweight forever. Joe had been lucky and charming, he looked the part, he talked the right kind of talk, but he was a man in need of something. What? Counseling, drug treatment, a less stressful job, a cheaper lifestyle, a better girlfriend, better friends, a more developed sense of self. Or maybe something entirely different, something that no one could name.

We didn't see much of Joe in those following months. After that night on the balcony, Renee released him. It was no longer her concern, she told us, what our brother did in his free time. He was old enough to take care of himself. Caroline was so busy with the new house, the kids, getting them settled in their new schools. And of course she heard about what had happened at the party, my poem and Joe's dismissal of Renee. It was easy for her to cut Joe off.

Joe stayed in New York for another six months, but there was nothing left for him here, that's what he told me. He never looked for another job. He was too embarrassed, he said, and no one would hire him anyhow. Everyone knew what had happened with Kyle and Morgan Capital.

"I'm leaving New York," Joe told me on a Wednesday night. "Do you remember Brent, the Mavericks shortstop? He's got an ad company down in Miami. Online stuff, banners. He offered me a job, and I'm going to take it." We were again sitting on barstools, Joe drinking his usual gin and tonic, me a Diet Coke. I had recently been promoted at ClimateSenseNow!, surprising everyone, myself most of all, and now was attempting to make up for five years of lukewarm employment by arriving early to the office, fulfilling my responsibilities as conscientiously as I knew how.

"Miami? But you hate hot weather," I said.

"Well, I'll learn to like it."

"I hate it, too."

"Don't use that as an excuse not to come visit." For a moment Joe smiled one of his old smiles, both dimples engaged, a happy glimmer to his eyes. But just as fast as it had arrived, the smile disappeared.

"Have you told Renee?" I asked.

"Not yet," he said. "She'll be happy to get rid of me. One less thing to worry about."

"No," I said. "She'll miss you. We'll all miss you." Even to me my words sounded false.

"It's the kind of thing I should have done years ago."

"But you'll be all alone down there," I said. "No family. None of your old friends. No one who knows you."

Joe drained his drink. "That's the point, Fiona."

I've often thought back to that conversation. Could I have stopped Joe from moving? Could I have persuaded him to stay in New York, to get help, to start again? Would the right words, the right level of concern, a new insight, a patient voice—would any of that have altered the outcome? For years I asked myself these sorts of questions.

I believe now that certain events are inevitable. Not in a fateful way, for I have never had faith in anything but myself, but in the way of human nature. Some people will choose, again and again, to destroy what it is they value most. This is how I saw my brother. This is why I now believe that the accident would have happened in New York or Miami, with Luna or without her. The accident was searching for Joe, and eventually it would find him.

PART III

Miami

Year 2079

"HEY—MS. SKINNER?"

It was a man's voice, a young man who stood very close to the stage. Somehow I'd missed his approach, and now here he was, only a few feet from where I sat beside Henry. The man was tall, thin, his head shaved, a small hoop earring in one ear that gleamed in the yellow safety lights. He had a roughness about him, as though he worked or slept outside.

"Ms. Skinner, I've got a question," he said.

Where was Luna? My eyes scanned the crowd, and I found her, sitting in the front section, an aisle seat. She had her shoes off, her legs stretched forward, feet in red socks. She was watching the man intently; they all were. It was surprising to me that more people hadn't left the auditorium for home by now. Perhaps with the electricity still off, there was some trepidation about what might be happening outside. I felt it, too.

I turned my gaze to the young man. "Yes?" I said.

"I was wondering—" He stopped speaking to scratch vigorously at his scalp with one hand. As he did, I noticed something off about him. Not quite right. A way he moved his body, as though he were on a boat and the rest of us on dry land. A drifting, an unsteadiness. Without lifting my gaze from the man, I reached for Henry's hand and squeezed once.

"I was wondering," he repeated, "what you think of the current state of affairs. You know—what's happening in this world, all the *bullshit*. All the corruption. Rich getting richer while we struggle and scrape and barely have a chance to make it, to do anything." He paused. "What do you think of that?"

"Well." I cleared my throat. "I think it's appalling," I said. "The current administration. What's happening to the environment, what's happening to minorities. I think it should stop."

"You do?" The man squinted up at me, his mouth curling into the suggestion of a smile. "So why don't you use all of this to do some *good*?" He waved his arms around to indicate the auditorium, the audience, the cameras. The gesture was made excessively large by the length of his reach, his thin, bony fingers. "Huh?" he said. "You've got all these people listening to you, and all you do is tell us a story about a family? The failures of love, isn't that what you said? Visions and hallucinations?" The man snorted. Again he scratched his scalp.

This was not the first time I'd considered or responded to this kind of critique, although it was generally delivered with more acuity. Given what was happening in the world of late, I had devoted more than passing thought to becoming involved in politics. My work at ClimateSenseNow! ended decades ago. In recent years, I'd attended rallies, donated money, private actions of a private citizen, but publicly I hadn't done much at all. No op-eds, no speeches, no social media, no fund-raising efforts or lending my words to a campaign, although I'd been asked to take part in all these various ways.

The dilemma was that any words I might say at a lectern or in the pages of a newspaper would never achieve the same strength as the words I wrote as a poet. Inspiration, calls to action, can take many forms. It is not so much the persuasive force of an argument that prompts engagement, but a feeling that inspires it. A sense of injustice, a longing for redemption, empathy, rage. What better to provoke any of these than a poem?

I thought of how best to explain this to the young man, but he had started to yell—at full volume, with profanity and frustration. What was I to do? The flame-haired woman in the front row shifted in her chair. Luna watched the man impassively, as though she were accustomed to this sort of display. I considered the balance of public engagement and private protection. I considered the power of poetry, of art. I considered my sources of inspiration and what might have moved Luna's mother to select her daughter's name from the last line of a poem written by me seventy-five years earlier. It took a madman to believe that individual involvement might change a system. It required a miracle, it required magic. Or maybe not. Maybe all it required was the alchemy of individuals who believe first that they can change themselves.

"—fuckin' imbeciles, assholes, how dare you try to do that, and then you can't even—" The man was still yelling. I had lost track of what he specifically wanted from me. Henry and I watched him as he raised his hands and shook a fist.

"He's an angry one," Henry said, leaning into me. "Times like these I'm happy the Second Amendment didn't make it."

At last the young man quieted down. His face was red, sweat running from his temples. I glanced around, saw no security guards. They must have long since wandered off, perhaps to address the lights or to venture outside; or perhaps they'd been called by a higher authority to assist with a more pressing emergency.

"My dear man," I said. "Come up here. Please. Come onstage."

Henry turned to me. "Fiona, *no*," he whispered. "This isn't wise."

But I ignored Henry. I waved the man forward. After a brief, confused hesitation, he climbed the steps to the stage two at a time. There was a folding chair propped against a wall, and he pulled it, legs squeaking, to sit beside me.

"Come closer," I said, and he did. I heard the rapid rhythm of his breath.

"Give me your hand," I instructed.

It was very quiet in the auditorium. I saw Luna watching the scene with her head tilted as though watching a minor but deadly event unfold in nature, a bird pulling a worm from the ground or a cat toying with a mouse. Something of morbid interest that had nothing at all to do with her.

"Did you know I trained as a palm reader?" I said to the man. "After the accident I searched for many years for reason and truth in a variety of different disciplines. I wanted to understand why people put their faith in things like palm readers, clairvoyants, mediums. Was it simply desperation, or was there something we didn't quite understand? Magic or God or whatever you want to call it, something that explains those events that science cannot."

"Well?" the man said.

"Well. I never found an answer. Only that people are gullible. And playing on that gullibility has given rise to a great number of professions. But"—I held up a finger—"I don't believe there is anything wrong with offering a gullible person hope, so long as that person believes it to be genuine. In fact, I think hope, even if premised on a falsehood, can be a thing of great power."

I took his hand gently in mine and turned it palm up. My fingers were wrinkled sausages, the nails unpainted, my own palm unreadable now, though I can tell you what my reading once said: A long and eventful life. Love and pain and love again.

This man's skin was rough, pocked with calluses, flaky and dry. I smoothed it with my fingers, rubbed my palm against his to warm it. I felt those calluses, like a clutch of small pebbles fetched from the bottom of a pond.

I put my glasses on my nose. "Let me see here," I said, and peered first into the man's eyes—which had gone from wild to calm and beseeching—and then at his palm. Yes, there it was: the lifeline. It curved and cracked and started up again and cracked a second time.

"Your life has been hard," I said.

The man grunted, shrugged his shoulders.

"But the future holds much promise. Your love line is strong. See here?" I traced it with my index finger. Beneath, I felt the pulse of the man's blood.

What I wanted to say to this man was that the greatest works of poetry, what make each of us a poet, are the stories we tell about ourselves. We create them out of family and blood and friends and love and hate and what we've read and watched and witnessed. Longing and regret, illness, broken bones, broken hearts, achievements, money won and lost, palm readings and visions. We tell these stories until we believe them, we believe in ourselves, and that is the most powerful thing of all.

But before I could begin, the man leaned forward, his head nearly touching mine. "Really?" he said. "A strong love line? You see that?"

I straightened. On his face I saw the faintest, brightest tremor of hope.

"Oh, yes," I said. "I do."

Chapter 9

JOE LIVED IN Miami for fourteen months before he met Luna. Later he would consider those days a series of trials, like the stories of a besotted knight who must first steal a horse or battle a horde of ogres or spin a hundred spindles in a day before the king would allow him to marry his daughter. That was what Joe had been doing: suffering through the trials of his days without Luna.

On the day he first met Luna Hernandez, Joe left work early. He walked with the goal of putting sufficient distance between his drinking and the office. It hadn't been a bad day; he just needed out. That grinding-of-teeth feeling, the sweat rising along his hairline and inside his shoes, the headachy drone of too much talking. Outside, the sidewalks heaved with people, and a car with its stereo volume turned way up sent its gut-thumping bass line straight into the space between Joe's eyebrows. Some days Joe yearned for New York in a way that before he'd associated only with sex, but today he lifted his gaze to the Miami sky, the Miami sunshine. They felt familiar and nice. They felt almost like home.

Joe slung his jacket over his shoulder and crisscrossed block after block until the stream of tourists thickened, seagulls circled overhead, and he tasted the saltwater tang. He'd been walking for about twenty minutes when he saw a discreet, low-hanging sign: REVEL BAR + RESTAURANT. Joe stopped. He'd never noticed the place before, never heard of it, but he stepped inside.

A long, darkly polished bar faced a half bank of windows that looked out toward Biscayne Bay. The floors were black, the couches black, too. Beyond the bar Joe glimpsed a vast restaurant area with shiny glass-topped tables, all empty at this hour. The place had the feel of a deep crevasse lit by a slash of sun glittering far above.

"Tanqueray and tonic," Joe told the bartender, and he pulled out a stool. The man worked fast, a flash of bottle, the sharp patter of ice. Then the glass set before Joe, the bitter spill down his throat. One swallow, another.

Better.

Yesterday Joe had played baseball, and his body hurt in the most satisfying way. He rolled his head and massaged his right shoulder, then the left. After thirteen years away from the game, Joe was starting up again. Center field had always been his position. The length of him, the reach and stretch of his arms with those extra two inches of webbed, stinking leather, transformed him into an unbreachable wall of grace and muscle. Now he played on a team of middle-aged men with bellies and mortgages, but still Joe could reach. He'd felt it again, the delicious tension of the pitcher's preparation, head snapping at ten-degree angles, staring down the hitters at first and third, shake, shake, nod to the catcher. And then the ball itself, a blinking blur of white speed, and crack? Would the batter hit? Joe's legs springing, arm reaching before his mind registered an answer. *Thunk* into the glove, and the ball's trembling weight thrown immediately away. Second base. *Out.*

Sip, swallow. Sip, swallow.

Why had he ever quit? He remembered pressure, the taste of vomit at the back of his mouth. That coach at Alden College, every at-bat like a goddamn audition. His throwing arm would have come back. After college Renee had told him to start again. *It's never too late,* she'd said. *Not with something you love.* At twenty-two, at twenty-five, at thirty, he had not believed her. But on that field again, now, thirty-two years old and slack in every single way, Joe realized that Renee had been right. It wasn't the same. Of course it couldn't be the *same,* but it was still something.

"One more?" came a woman's voice, and he looked up. The bartenders had changed. Dark eyes, long black hair, a pea-size mole high on her right cheek. Her gaze was impatient and closed, not even a suggestion of helpful or nice or sympathetic, nothing to generate a tip.

Joe nodded, and he watched her, watched her ass, as she made the drink. He felt that at-attention kick of interest—his own, certainly not hers. The drink landed on a napkin, her back turned again before he could even mumble thank you. Charming? Maybe once. That had been a long time ago, too.

* * *

LUNA GOT TO work late and shook out her hair. Rodrigo the restaurant manager was always telling her to wear it up, but she liked it long, liked to feel the swing against her back. Dima was out there already, pouring for a man who seemed gray and sad, hunched over on the stool, not looking at anything. Luna tied her apron, squinted into the small mirror she kept in her purse, and rubbed a mascara smudge away from her lash line.

Dima passed her on the way to the kitchen. "More limes," he said.

The man drank fast, three swallows, maybe four. The ice rattled.

"One more?" Luna asked, and he raised his head. His face was puffy, pink around the edges, the eyes a clear blue. Their brightness took her by surprise. He didn't strike her as a drunk, not a true drunk, but he looked tired and habitually sad, or perhaps ill. A depleting illness, Luna thought. Or a poisoned diet. She'd been reading recently about pesticides, BPA, the casual infiltration of chemicals into organs and muscle.

The man nodded, and Luna turned to make him the drink. He was eyeing her up and down, she could see him reflected in the mirror behind the bar. Luna knew men looked at her like that, they always had.

Luna deposited the drink and turned away to cut the limes that Dima had delivered. By midshift they were always running out of limes.

"Um, miss?" the man said. "You dropped something."

She turned and faced him. "What? Where?"

"There. It looks like a flower."

It was. It was a sprig of blooming thyme she'd cut from her herb box. She'd dropped it into her purse because she liked the smell and because it gave her comfort to carry something she had cared for and grown, though it had become mashed and bent in the jumble of her bag.

"Oh. Thank you," she said, and she picked up the thyme and put it back into her purse.

"Was it a flower?" the man asked.

"Yes," Luna admitted. She felt embarrassed, as though she'd been revealed to this man in some small but complete way. She faltered. She smiled.

* * *

ON THEIR FIRST date, Joe took Luna to a restaurant on the top of a tall building made of pale green glass. Everything in the place shone and flickered. Over their artful, tiny meals, Luna asked Joe about his work.

"It's nothing. Boring. Selling stuff. Gathering information. It's a job." Joe shrugged and ate a forkful of steak. He'd been lying about the Miami job to Noni, trying to make it sound better, make himself sound better, but why? He was sick of pretending to be someone important. In New York he'd been able to justify it—the money, his office of glass and chrome, conferences and trips and bottles of fifty-year-old scotch. All that had disappeared, most of the money, too: bad investments, bad habits, Sandrine. Now he was a salesman, pure and simple, hawking banner ad space on websites. Click here for whiter teeth, cheaper mortgage, better life.

"So tell me about Revel," he asked.

Luna told him about the restaurant, the hookers and the wannabes, the manager—Rodrigo—whom they all hated, the other bartenders, the Cuban chef, the French busboy. "It's a great place to work. The money's great for now," she said. "I've also started modeling. Just a few gigs, but my friend Amanda says things will take off soon."

They were on their second bottle of wine and a shared crème brûlée. Joe cocked his head. "You don't seem like a model. I mean . . ." He laughed. "You're beautiful, but you seem . . ."

"Too short? Too *old*?" Luna asked.

Joe looked down, and now Luna laughed.

"I'm twenty-five. You know, I probably *am* too old to be a model. I was saving for college, but maybe I'm too old for that, too."

"No. Twenty-five? I don't think so."

Luna reached across and grabbed Joe's hand and the look on her face was not flirtatious but determined.

"I'm growing plants on my windowsill," she said. "Small things. Herbs. Three tomatoes, and they are beauties."

* * *

AFTER HE TOOK Luna home, Joe sat on the balcony of his penthouse condo, one he had rented unseen from an online broker seventeen months before, and lit a Cohiba. Writing the rent check each month made him shiver, watching the money go, go, go. He didn't need all this space, the fancy kitchen, the whirlpool tub, but the view he'd come to see as essential. The balcony faced east toward the beach, and he could faintly hear the sound of waves breaking sixteen stories below. Joe loved the way the blanket of city lights ended sharply at the shoreline and the black of the ocean stretched upward and back to the faint line of the horizon and the black of the sky, one black bleeding into another until the lights began again, pinpricks of stars leading up to the white glare of the moon. Tonight it seemed circular and right to him—a city, an ocean, a sky—and himself in the middle, observing it, existing within it.

In New York it was easy to forget you were surrounded by something as elemental as water. It was easy to lose yourself in all that concrete, surging crosswalks, taxi honks, steam and grit. But here in South Beach, the ocean reminded you every day of its authority. Whenever Joe thought about New York or Sandrine or Ace or Kyle, he experienced a small deadly drop in his stomach. Nausea and a sense of shame and shock about what had happened. Remembering was like riding a familiar roller coaster, feeling an agony of apprehension as you climbed the slope even though you knew what was coming. He'd heard from none of his old fraternity brothers, but Joe found himself unsurprised. All those years of friendship burned up and floated away, whoosh, like a pile of dry, dead leaves. He had never belonged among them, not truly. That's what Joe thought now, and he felt a certain relief at not having to pretend anymore.

Maybe, Joe thought, he should call the guy Felix. Felix wore expensive suit jackets over T-shirts and jeans, half a head of ratty red hair hanging to his shoulders to compensate for the baldness on top. Felix sold mediocre pot but perfect cocaine in tiny glassine envelopes. Most nights Joe went to him—the guy charged more for house calls—but a few times Joe hadn't planned ahead and he'd ended up on the phone in the darkest hours. Felix traveled with a large brown case that he'd set up on a table and open with a small silver key. Inside, boxes and packets, powders and pills. *I'm your friendly traveling salesman,* Felix would say, and count the cash and close the case back up again. He was part greasy adolescent, part circus ringmaster, part savvy businessman, and each time Joe decided that he never wanted to see him again.

But tonight the urge was there, that niggling *want, want, want* that flashed out from Joe's stomach in ever-expanding circles of light, like sonar. Joe almost picked up the phone, but he reached for the cigar instead. It was more than two years since he'd made that promise to Renee on the sidewalk. *I'll stop,* he'd said. *I'll stop the coke.* Joe hadn't meant it then, but he meant it now. He would take one thing at a time. One thing, and maybe the rest would follow. He knew this wasn't the way you were supposed to do it—sober or not, clean or not, no in between—but this was all he could manage. One thing.

Joe exhaled, and the smoke curled lazily above his head and dispersed out over the chrome railing as the wind took it down and away. He thought about Luna, about her long black hair and the way she talked about the place where she was from: Matapalo, Nicaragua. He liked the way the words felt in his mouth, the exotic lilt of the rounded vowels and trailing end. Joe remembered the way Luna had rolled the *r,* and he finished his cigar and practiced until he could say it right.

* * *

TWO WEEKS AFTER Luna met Joe, Donny started coming around the bar, trying to talk to Luna as she worked. They had dated for six months, maybe a little longer, but that had been over a year ago, during a period she recalled only as a hazy muddle. The details she had chosen to forget.

But now Donny on a barstool, talking to her, drumming his thick fingers along the side of a brown bottle, brought it all back. Hyped-up nights, the highs shorter and shorter, the want more and more. Donny was good like that: he pushed things through, always had money, knew who to call. She'd only smoked crack the one time; it tasted dirty, and afterward her hands wouldn't stop shaking.

That night Luna had imagined her younger sister, Mariana. Five years ago Mariana had run away from home, disappeared, gone. *Where are you?* Luna had asked into the darkness of Donny's bedroom. *Are you here?* But Mariana hadn't answered; she'd smiled her smile with two dimples and thrown back her head and laughed.

One morning Luna woke up beside Donny and wanted it over. *Your eyes follow other women. I can't trust you,* she told him, but she was thinking of the plain fact that there was nothing real between them, only the fleeting rush of skin against skin, only a cheap companionship founded on weakness.

Now, at the bar, Donny talked as though Luna had wronged him. "You broke my heart," he said after two beers. "I miss you so much."

At first she acted as though he was joking. "Cut it out Donny," Luna said. "Go bother your real girlfriend." But he kept coming back. Every shift there he was, slumped on the same corner barstool. Drink after drink until she wondered how he could stay upright. Once he grabbed her wrist as she cleared an empty glass. She pulled away, but he held tight, a smile carving up his cheeks, and then he released her. A tattooed bat circled his wrist; it must be new, she'd never noticed it before.

He usually came on a weeknight when the bar was slow. Luna tried to stay light with him, answer his questions with few words, laugh as she walked away, but the sight of him made her pulse surge. She knew he watched her as she delivered drinks to other customers, bent to retrieve the ice, unloaded clean glasses into careful rows. His eyes were a muddy brown, and Luna wondered why she hadn't been more careful. Why she hadn't seen him for what he was.

* * *

ON THEIR THIRD date, Joe told Luna this story about Sandrine:

Joe sits on his couch watching the Knicks game, a collection of empty Beck's bottles at his feet. He was fired three weeks ago and, in that time, has left the apartment only once. He is waiting for Sandrine to come home, and he is drinking beer after beer in solidarity with his boys getting lashed by the Celtics and with all men everywhere in love with their absent women, wondering who they might be fucking, wondering why love isn't as soothing and life-affirming as they had always thought it would be.

Finally the game ends, the Knicks have lost, Joe has another beer and another. It is past midnight, 2:00 A.M., 3:30. The key turns in the door, and Sandrine's heels click across the kitchen floor, her keys and bag hit the countertop with a jangle and a thud, a moment of silence as she removes her shoes, and then she steps, small and stocking-footed, into the living room.

"My God, you're still *up*?" She is drunk, even Joe can see that, and he is drunk, probably drunker than she is, but still he can gauge the alcohol in her voice, the slight sway in her movements.

"I was waiting for you," Joe says. "Were you with Anna?"

"No, just some people from work." They've been busy recently with resort wear, or was that last month? It's hard for Joe to keep track—Sandrine doesn't talk about it much.

The TV plays an *ER* rerun, a doctor is breaking down on-screen, there are tears from a young woman in green scrubs.

"I can't do this anymore, you know, Joe," says Sandrine. She speaks in one great breath, staring at the screen. Her eyes are unblinking, and she folds her hands across her stomach like she is ill or trying to hold something inside. She has such small hands, such delicate fingers, Joe thinks. Sandrine's collarbone juts out sharply from the neck of her blouse, and Joe wants to kiss it, kiss this hard, angular part of her.

"Joe, I just don't want to do this!" and Sandrine's voice is suddenly raised, as though he has said something to dispute her, convince her. "I don't want to have your *children*. I don't want to go on *vacation* with you. I don't want to have *dinner* with you. I don't want to watch you brush your *teeth*. I don't want us to get all old and stupid and *jiggly* together." She raises her arms now and shakes them, and the small fillet of flesh on the back of each arm shakes.

Joe remains in his chair in front of the television. He does not say a word. He cannot think of a single thing to say.

"I don't think you're a bad guy, it's not that." She is definitely slurring her words now, Joe notes mechanically. "I think you're sad, and I think you're *boring*," and she drags out the word: *boooooooring*. "Look at you—watching the *Knicks*, drinking *beer*. This is not what I signed up for." She pauses. There is a large shuddering intake of breath. "I've had it, Joe, really, this is it. You're not who I thought you were. I'm sorry, but it's true." Sandrine looks out the window where the sound of the early-morning garbagemen can be heard, the drag of metal cans across pavement. "I deserve someone more . . . more . . . more . . ." Joe is waiting for her to finish her sentence—what more does he need to be?—but she turns away from him, walks to their bedroom, and slams the door.

Joe can hear her pushing something—is it the dresser? the TV table?—in front of the door and then the flinging of various things against the wall, the run of water in the sink, then the shower, and again more banging and flinging, drawers opening and closing, their closet door slamming repeatedly. Joe remains seated and stares at the TV screen: the ER bustles now with some medical emergency; electric paddles are placed on a man's hairy chest, and his body lurches with the jolt.

Joe sleeps that night on the couch, and the next morning he leaves the apartment early. He goes to the gym, where he lifts weights and runs on a treadmill until he is light-headed and drenched in sweat. His muscles shaking, breath on fire. He showers at the gym and returns to find Sandrine gone, her clothes and shoes, knickknacks and DVDs cleared out, the apartment as empty and clean as a sand-polished shell washed up with the tide.

"So that was it," Joe said, looking at Luna across the table. "Sandrine wanted *more*. More what? I didn't know there was a score-card. Like a point system or something."

"Fifteen for flowers," said Luna. "Fifty at least for jewelry." She was on her third margarita, the salt heavy along the rim. This woman Sandrine seemed to Luna an exotic animal, one rarely sighted in the wild but the subject of much study and anxious calculation. The last man Luna slept with had been married, with two young children at home, and he liked to drip hot wax onto her back. He'd seen it in a movie, he told her, and the small, bright burn on her skin transformed almost immediately to warmth.

"I'll give you twenty points for dinner tonight. Another ten if we go dancing after," Luna said.

Joe smiled. "Deal."

The waitress brought their meals. They were at a Mexican restaurant, and the smell of warming corn tortillas made Luna momentarily ill. When she was a child in Nicaragua, her mother had made tortillas—grinding the corn, rolling the dough into disks, frying them over the open fire in the yard. It took all day, the tortilla making, and by the end of it her mother's shoulders would curl forward, her back nearly parallel to the floor.

Luna sliced through the fancy dish and chewed without tasting. She hadn't seen her mother in five years, her sister Mariana in five and a half. Now Luna bought her tortillas from the Cuban grocer on the corner where they wrapped them in plastic and charged by the pound.

After dinner Joe took Luna dancing. They drank Moët and slipped small pills the color of sky into their mouths and felt a universe of sensation expand with each driving bass note and shudder of strobe.

"Fifty points!" Luna called above the music. "One hundred," she whispered into his ear.

At dawn Joe checked them into a suite at the Betsy Hotel, a quiet, cool space larger than Luna's apartment. They left the lights on, but the solid raft of Joe's back and his long-reaching arms surrounded her in darkness, and afterward she closed her eyes and slept as though she were at the bottom of the sea.

* * *

JOE TOLD LUNA everything. It was mundane and it was tragic. He'd fallen in love with Sandrine completely. After all the women, all the girlfriends, all the dates and hookups and one-night stands and never thinking it was enough. The more, more, more of it, skin, tongue, breast, pussy, my God, so many women, how could he choose just one? But everything about Sandrine was enough. Enough because hadn't it become exhausting? It came down to the smells, the multitude of smells, all of them *on* him, bodies and perfume, the way a woman had one smell at her neck, another under her arms, another between her legs. And each woman was different! How could he keep up? He worried that he was losing it, his sense of smell, that soon every woman would register as the same, which seemed the worst kind of fate. With Sandrine he focused on each specific part of her: he knew what to expect on the inside of her wrist, her hair when they were going out. He found comfort in knowing with certainty who was beside him. In knowing what she wanted and what she could do. The knowing became more important than the surprise. He understood at last—at last!—what was enough.

But he had been wrong.

* * *

ONE NIGHT DONNY followed Luna to the parking lot after her shift ended. It was 4:00 A.M., and a slight chill moved off the water. The restaurant's dumpsters pulsed with stink. Usually Dima or Jorge walked her to her car, but tonight she'd been slow to clean up, slow to count her tips, and so Rodrigo left her the keys to lock up. Had Donny been watching the bar? How had he known?

"Luna," he said. "It's nice to see you."

"Donny. It's late. I'm going home. I'm tired." She kept her voice steady. Donny's gaze held a clear purpose that scared her, a sharpness that cut her into tiny, separable pieces. Behind her back Luna slid her hand into her purse and felt for her keys. Donny was roughly ten feet away, a distance covered in seconds if you moved fast. Luna remembered him as someone who worked out every day, and he still looked it: biceps that popped, thighs that pulled his jeans tight.

"You should get home, too," Luna said. "Don't you have work tomorrow? I'm sure you do." Her hand closed around the keys, and she began to step backward to the car, a dented Subaru she'd bought last year. Two hundred twenty thousand miles, and still it ran like a dream.

"Nope," Donny said, his voice friendly. "No work tomorrow. I'm partying all night. Come with me, Luna. Remember? Our parties?"

"Sure. I remember." The key slid into the lock, Luna turned it and eased the door open a crack, then turned quickly and slid inside. He did, he ran, but she was faster. She slammed the door shut and pushed the lock, and all Donny could do was throw up his hands and say, "Come on Luna, come on."

She waved at him through the window glass. He didn't wave back but kept his hands raised, palms up, shaking his head. The bat on his wrist rose and fell. Luna's hands were trembling so violently she had trouble putting the car into drive, but the gear dropped into place and the car jumped away.

* * *

JOE AND LUNA are asleep. They do not go to Joe's condo on South Beach, which he is embarrassed to show her because of the mess and the unpacked boxes, but again to the Betsy, to a suite that Joe cannot afford yet books nonetheless because it is the biggest and the best. Once he could have afforded it, and his habits have not changed. The bed is king-size, a raft of white cotton and silk duvet, down pillows that sink slowly beneath the weight of their heads. They sleep without trouble, dreamless, Joe's right hand clasped loosely around Luna's right wrist. She twitches and turns, and Joe turns with her.

* * *

ON THEIR TENTH date, Luna told Joe this story about her mother and her sister:

Mariana has been gone for three weeks when Luna's mother first talks about going back to Matapalo.

"Back?" Luna asks. She's eighteen years old and a senior in high school.

"I miss home," Luna's mother says. "Maybe Mariana did, too. Maybe she went there."

Luna is getting ready for work, pulling her hair into a ponytail, slipping into the loose black trousers she wears in the kitchen. "She would never go back," Luna says. "Never." She knows what happens to women and girls there. Mariana is younger; she doesn't remember as much, but she remembers enough.

Her mother has just come home from her job cleaning rooms at the Betsy Hotel and is standing by the door, still in her uniform with the frilly white skirt. She sighs extravagantly and kicks off her shoes, then sits on the couch and stretches her legs long, spreading her bare feet with their thick yellow nails and calluses.

"Mami, put your feet away," Luna says, and her mother slides them off the couch.

"But maybe for the jobs," her mother says. "Tourism—everything is changing now. Rosa keeps telling me. Or maybe for Papi. She loved him, it didn't seem to matter what he did. And she had that friend Sofía, remember her? They were like sisters."

"I'm her sister," Luna says, but her mother seems not to hear.

"I don't know, it's harder there, but it's easier, too. Do you understand?"

Easier in that you had no choices, that your future was the same as your mother's, and her mother's, on and on. They call you *bruja* if you try for something different. Say that you have no respect or love for your family or your friends, say that you deserve all the bad luck God will deliver upon you. Go back to that?

"No, I don't understand," Luna replies, but she does in a small, secret way. There is a smell she remembers from Matapalo, a dry burning, tortillas cooking, gas from the stoves, a collection of different odors that together form one, and it is not immediately attractive, but it is specific. It is home.

The last time Luna saw Mariana, the bruises on the girl's face had shaded already to yellow. Mariana spent a week on the couch, watching cartoons and sipping milk shakes through a straw. Her boyfriend, Davie, claimed she fell out of the car, not that he'd pushed her, and who could say? Mariana herself had been so high she barely remembered the night, only the flashing lights and the handsome ER doctor who handed her pamphlets on drug addiction and alcohol abuse. They pumped her stomach, took her blood, and told her all the things they'd found there. Mariana was fifteen years old.

"I don't think Mariana wants to go back," Luna tells her mother. "She wants . . ." Luna doesn't finish the sentence, because she doesn't know what Mariana wants, only that it is something she doesn't yet have.

"Did the police call today?" her mother asks.

"They'll only call if they have something new to tell us. Remember?"

"Oh," says her mother. "Yes."

"There's nothing new," says Luna, and she is suddenly angry at her mother, for her job and her feet and the way she lets the TV blare all day and all night. Luna picks up her bag, heavy with her

American-history book. This quarter they are studying the American Revolution, George Washington crossing the Delaware, no taxation without representation, *liberté, égalité*. Without saying good-bye, Luna leaves for her 6:00 P.M.–to–2:00 A.M. kitchen shift at Revel.

One month later Luna's mother asks for the savings-account passbook. "I need to go back home," she says. "I don't know what else to do. I can't just sit here. If she comes back, you'll see her. If she goes back to Matapalo, I'll see her. It's better to spread out." Her mother's face, since Mariana disappeared, has fallen into itself, like her cheeks are the roof of a house that has lost its beams.

Luna sees many flaws in her mother's logic, but she does not describe them. She merely nods. Spread out. Like they have lost a dog in the greening sesame fields of Matapalo. Spread out, call her name, promise her treats and kisses. Luna has been saving for college, but she hands over the passbook. The college money never felt real anyhow. Luna has watched the number grow over the years to a figure that seems impossible. And it is. An impossibility. Luna has a 3.95 GPA, plays varsity softball, and works nights in the kitchen at Revel Bar + Restaurant. Her school counselor, Ms. Jasmine, tells her she has a shot at a good school, maybe UVA or UFlorida. *Stay southern, only state schools with lower tuition. Study for your SATs, don't get into the drug scene. Go straight home after work at night.* Ms. Jasmine knows Mariana, knows the kinds of things she was doing before she disappeared.

"Okay then, go back," Luna says. "I'll stay here. I'll keep looking."

On the morning of her mother's departure, Luna helps her pack. "Where will you stay?" Luna asks, sliding small plastic bottles of shampoo into a larger plastic bag.

"With Auntie Rosario at first. Then I'll find a place."

"Will you see Papi?"

Her mother shakes her head. "Not if I can help it."

"I'll send money," Luna says. Her mother nods, as if this is expected, as if this is nothing.

Luna folds up a thin towel, *Miami Sexy Baby!* printed in curling pink script across the fabric, and places it in the suitcase.

"I've paid up rent here until May, and then you'll have to move," her mother says. Luna watches her click the suitcase closed. "You'll be okay, Luna," her mother says, and kisses her forehead. "You are always okay. I know."

Joe listened to Luna's story without comment, only a few nods, head shakes. This was rare, Luna speaking this way about her family. He did not want her to stop.

At the end he took her hands. "Your mother sounds very wise," he said. "She knows you. You *are* okay."

Luna shrugged. "Actually she's a fool. Mariana never went back there, and I can't find her here." She paused. "My mother had two daughters. *Two.* And now she has none."

* * *

JOE THOUGHT OFTEN about his sisters. He missed them. He knew he had fucked up, but he couldn't identify the how or why of it. He kept telling himself he would visit them, he would apologize for everything, that whatever it was they wanted him to say, he would say it. He would throw himself at the feet of his family. But he wasn't ready, not yet. Before you can lie down, you first must stand up. Didn't someone say that once?

Maybe Miami had been a mistake. All the partying, the job about which he felt only ambivalence. He was alone, with no one's expectations bearing down on him or assumptions buoying him up. He could do anything, and no one would care. He could fall, and no one would pick him up. This was terrifying, but clean in a way. Honest. Every morning he woke in a dark room, the alarm rattling, and wondered what would happen. Would he drink to-day? Would he call Felix? Would he call Renee? Would he find his strength? Joe considered these questions with a detached, clinical curiosity, and then he pushed himself out of bed and into the day.

Before Miami, Sandrine had formed part of the picture in his head of what his life should be. Within a gold, ornate frame, she stood beside him, beautiful, blond, with a neat, clean smile and fingernails painted pink. But that picture had disappeared completely: there was no Sandrine, there was no gold frame, there was no life as he'd previously imagined it. There was only Joe alone surrounded by sea and sky.

And into this space came Luna. Joe held no picture in his head of their life together. Every day Luna became something different, something altogether unexpected. She didn't care what he'd done, the good or bad of it; she knew him only now, in this moment of drift. She was drifting, too, he could see it, and yet when he stood beside her, he felt anchored, secure. Even on the days they were at their worst, the days he saw them both as weak, he felt there was more to them than the weakness. Luna made him feel a potential. *Hope* was too sentimental a word for it. *Faith* was too sanctimonious. But it was something like that. Something grand.

He wanted to explain all of this to Fiona. Of his three sisters, he always felt the most comfortable with her. But she was writing a sex blog now, not poetry, and sleeping with dozens of men, describing their weaknesses and flaws, all the things they'd done wrong. How was that empowering? he wondered. How was that art? It tore people down. It was Caroline who sent him the link, no comment, just the word *Fiona*. He'd felt a jolt of happy surprise to hear from his sister, swiftly undercut by the contents of the blog. *The Last Romantic.*

And so, two days after the e-mail arrived from Caroline, Joe picked up the phone and called Fiona. She was surprised to hear from him, she said, but glad he had called. For a spell he considered telling Fiona about Luna, but no. He wasn't ready to share her. His sisters had judged Sandrine so harshly; he didn't want to subject Luna to their scrutiny, not yet.

Joe had always liked the lilt of Fiona's voice, the way she told a story, and so he listened for a bit to updates on her job, her revolving cast of housemates. Then he asked:

"Fiona, have you heard of *The Last Romantic*?"

"Sure. I've heard of it. New feminism. I read it every week." Fiona's voice had shifted. Now she was carefully casual, on guard, and immediately Joe knew it was true.

"Who do you think writes it?" he asked.

"It's anonymous. Who knows? It could be anyone."

"I think I know who it is."

"Yeah?"

"I think I know her pretty well."

Silence from Fiona. Joe knew that at this moment his sister was twisting a curl around an index finger. When she was a kid, the hair twist happened in any circumstance of stress or discomfort. Scary movie, fight between Caroline and Noni, studying for a math test. The memories washed over him all at once, a composite picture that made his chest contract. But Fiona was not a kid anymore.

Joe said, "Fiona, why are you doing this blog?"

"Me?"

"I hope you're being careful." A surge of his old protective impulse, a need to shield Fiona, to help her, came rushing back. He hadn't felt it in years.

A pause. "Who told you?" she asked.

Joe decided not to give Caroline up; it would hurt Fiona to know. "Those guys don't know what you're doing," he said instead.

"Of course they don't. That's the point."

"It seems unfair. They trust you."

"Trust? I'm the one at risk! I'm trusting *them*." And then she said, "I trusted you. You kept secrets from me. The knee injury, Sierra, Ace. Remember?"

"Come on, that's different."

"Not really."

"Fiona, the whole thing is cheap, taking cheap shots at these guys." Joe paused. "People make mistakes. It's not right to punish them like this."

"I'm not punishing anybody. I'm just telling the truth."

"Well, I think it cheapens you."

"You don't understand the project."

"I don't need to."

"How's the coke habit, Joe?" Fiona asked with ice in her voice.

A hot flush of shame came down on him. He didn't want to tell Fiona the truth, but he couldn't lie to her, not anymore.

"I just want you to find someone you love," he said.

"Love? What would you know about it?" Fiona laughed. "I can't talk about this with you, Joe. Good-bye." And then she hung up.

Luna was watching Joe as he spoke on the phone. It was mid-morning, a Sunday. Newspapers and sunshine on the bed. She heard the name Fiona, she knew the significance of Joe speaking to his sister after all this time. But his face was opaque.

"So?" Luna asked.

"It's okay," he answered. "She's still mad. We'll work it out later."

* * *

JOE AND LUNA drive south, following the coast until they reach a new beach, a narrow strip of South Florida sand that isn't packed with tourists, where no radios ricochet noise, no volleyballs arc skyward. It is high tide, and Luna bends to retrieve a shell, a slice of small white conch that forms a ring. She slips it onto her finger.

"Joe, look!" she says, and puts out her hand for him to see. With the solemnity of a prince, he bends and kisses it.

At the far end, they scramble over an outcrop of tall, slippery rock. Here they are alone on the sand. The sun beats down, and Joe builds a tent of sorts from their two towels and a battered fishing pole he finds on the ragged tide line. In the small triangle of shade, Joe traces a finger across Luna's tan stomach. A circle. A figure eight. A heart. She lies back, and the feeling is of a creature, smooth and cool, looking for a home in her skin.

* * *

SOMEHOW DONNY AND Joe had never crossed paths. Luck, or maybe Donny knew that Luna had a new boyfriend. Luna sometimes believed that Donny was watching her, through the windows of the bar, at her apartment as she walked up the front steps, even at the Betsy as she waited with Joe for the room key. After that night outside Revel, he'd been back only once, perched on the corner stool, not talking to her. Luna wanted to forget about her time with Donny. Back then he had seemed like all she was good for, all she deserved. Donny inhabited a dark place that was familiar to her, and she knew how familiarity could sometimes feel like comfort.

At 2:00 A.M. on the last night, Joe picked Luna up from work and they went to a nearby bar. They drank shots of tequila, then ordered pints of beer and sipped and talked, their heads close together. "Smile!" the bartender called, and they looked up: he held an old-fashioned Polaroid camera, and *thunk*, pressed the button. Out slid a photo, the image sticky and white. The bartender pointed to the side wall, which was festooned with Polaroids of smiling customers, but Joe said, "Can we have it?"

Together Joe and Luna watched as the paper surrendered its image, ghostly and pale until the colors surfaced: their faces, smiles, shoulders touching. Joe held the photo and turned to Luna. He kissed her, and as she disappeared into him, a hand descended on her shoulder.

"Hey, who's kissing my girlfriend?" a voice said.

Luna pulled away from Joe. "Donny," she said. "What are you doing here?"

"Luna, fantastic to see you." Donny spoke only to Luna. "You look beautiful."

Joe stood to face him. Joe was taller than Donny by a head, but he had none of the other man's bulk. Or youth—Donny was closer to Luna's age than Joe's.

"You know him?" Joe asked Luna. She nodded and looked away, embarrassed. Donny wore an idiot's provocative grin, looking from Joe to Luna and back again. His wide shoulders pulled the T-shirt tight.

"Leave her alone," Joe said. He sounded like a heavy in a bad movie, but Joe was no tough guy, and anyone could see that: flip-flops and old jeans, the short-sleeved button-down shirt with tails hanging out, a man trying to dress younger than he was.

Donny smirked. "Luna, looks like you've found a hero."

"Donny, go home," Luna said. "Please just leave me alone."

Luna became aware of others at the bar, the bartender who watched Donny steadily, the drinkers paused in their conversations, their attention directed onto the scene: Donny, Luna, Joe. Luna saw Donny begin to falter. He blinked, and the grin faded.

"Is there a problem here?" the bartender called.

Donny was losing interest, he was going to leave them, Luna realized with relief. She grabbed Joe's hand.

"Come outside, asshole," Joe said then, and Donny whistled.

"No," Luna whispered to Joe. *"Don't."*

"You better fuck her good. For her, you gotta be a man," Donny said, and laughed.

Joe swung, but he was not a fighter. He didn't gather himself or aim or steady his breathing; he clenched his hand into a fist and directed it with all the force of his six-foot-four frame into Donny's head. They stood two feet apart, the distance of sparring boxers, and had the fist landed, it would have toppled Donny. But Donny ducked smoothly away from Joe, the smile never leaving his face. Joe's weight followed his fist, and the momentum turned him fully around and then slammed him down toward the floor, where he sprawled on his back, his arms and legs tangled in fallen barstools.

"Joe!" Luna screamed, and the entire bar hushed. She crouched to him. "So stupid! You are so stupid!"

"I'm calling the police," said the bartender. "Miss, get your boy-friend out of here."

Donny was backing away into the crowd. As he did, he locked eyes with Luna and nodded. A sense of futility gripped her then, the idea that she had already lost. Donny knew the truth: he was all she deserved. She was a twenty-five-year-old bartender, alone, her apartment so small, her tip money sucked away by rent and drink and clothes and food. Maybe Luna would return to Donny after all. The familiarity, the comfort, the ease of giving in. Maybe she would disappear just like Mariana.

Joe pulled himself up to standing, and Luna slapped him across the face and left the bar. When he followed her outside, she slapped him again, first across the face and then against his stomach, his shoulders and chest, not with her full strength but hard enough.

"Why did you do that? Who do you think you are?" she shouted. Dimly she was aware that a restless Saturday-night street crowd was watching them with the halfway interest of people who are drunk and bored and waiting for something better to happen to them.

"Stop it, Luna," said Joe, holding up his hands to shield himself. "I'm sorry. It's just— The way he looked at you. I couldn't help it."

Luna stopped hitting.

"Let's go home," he said.

*   *   *

THE ELEVATOR DEPOSITED them at the penthouse floor. Wall sconces made of smoky glass and shaped like flaming torches lined the elevator landing. Luna's heels clicked on pale gray marble, and she wondered why Joe had never brought her here before. Joe took her hand, and she leaned into him. The scene with Donny faded, a reverse Polaroid of an image undone. With the warmth of Joe's arm around her shoulders, the night seemed to Luna like a hurricane, some natural disaster that neither could be blamed for, that together they had survived.

Joe opened the door, and they stepped into darkness. He didn't turn on the lights. The far wall was all window, and the bright gray of night light filled the room, reflecting off the television screen and the glass of photo frames lining a bookshelf, so that for an instant the room seemed full of winking eyes. Luna's sight adjusted, focused, and there they were: framed photos of Joe's three sisters, Renee, Caroline, Fiona, and their mother, Antonia, whom they all called Noni for reasons that Luna still did not understand. Photos of children, too, Joe's nephew, Louis, and two nieces, Beatrix and Lily. Twins, he'd told her.

It was only then that Luna noticed the piles of clutter crowding the floor and the tabletop, the boxes stacked against the walls. *Oh, she thought, so this is what he's been hiding.* She said nothing about the mess and went straight for the photos.

"Who is who?" she asked. "Tell me."

Joe picked a frame off the shelf and angled it for Luna to see. Here Joe was younger, thinner, his hair thick and brown. "This is Renee, the oldest," he said, pointing to a tall, slim woman with bare shoulders, even teeth, a wry smile. "Caroline, middle sister. She's the one with kids." Caroline was pale, with pink cheeks, a bright orange shirt, mouth open as though she was laughing or calling out to the photographer. "And here's Fiona, the youngest. She writes that blog I told you about." Fiona's hair reached to her shoulders, curly and a rich dark brown, and her face was plump, her body easily double the width of Renee's. "She's lost a lot of weight since then," Joe said. "She's almost a different person now. I haven't looked at this in a long time." He said the last almost to himself and tilted the picture more toward the light. "This was Louis's birthday, I think. Louis, my nephew, Caroline's son. This was his fifth—no, sixth birthday. The twins were still toddlers. We were all back in Bexley." He started to place the photo back on the shelf, but Luna stopped him.

"May I?" she asked and he handed it to her.

"Sure. Let's go sit on the balcony. Light's better out there anyhow." He took her hand and carefully led her through the mess of the room, out the sliding glass doors, and into the cool, fresh night. "I'll make us some drinks," he said, and turned back inside.

Luna studied the photo in her hands. The sisters. She was younger than them all, though in this photo Fiona seemed about Luna's age. There was something in Fiona's stance that interested

Luna, a forcefulness, an aggression, and also a sadness in her eyes. The other two—Renee with her confidence and polish, Caroline with her kids and long hair—seemed members of distinct female tribes that Luna had seen before: women with money and careers, women with children and husbands. These two would undoubtedly decide that she was too young or too poor or too something for Joe. Only Fiona seemed like she might accept Luna.

Joe returned with two gin and tonics.

"I've been wanting to ask you," he said. "Come to Bexley with me. I want you to meet my family. And it's time I went back for a visit. It's Louis's birthday soon. Caroline always throws a big party at their place in Hamden. He's turning twelve. Jesus, that means I'm old."

Luna sipped her drink and gazed out at the night sea. "Do they know about me?" she asked.

Joe tilted his head to the side. "Well, not exactly."

Luna lifted her eyebrows. When she didn't respond, Joe said, "Just consider it. I think you'd like them. I really do."

"Mmmm," Luna said, not quite a question, not quite a statement. Joe continued talking, but a vision of her own sister came to her then, from the night before Mariana disappeared. Mariana had been lying on the couch watching TV. A children's program, some cartoon played out in manic color. "See you for breakfast," Luna had called, and Mariana's eyes stayed fixed to the screen as Luna left for her shift at the restaurant. What cartoon had Mariana been watching? Luna realized that she could no longer remember. A vicious ache for her sister and mother overcame her. She put down the drink and closed her eyes.

"Why don't you move in here?" Joe asked suddenly.

The question could not have surprised her more. Luna opened

her eyes and looked at Joe. He sat leaning forward, elbows on knees. He took her hands into his. "Move in with me," he said.

"But . . . but what would your family think?" Luna said.

"My family? Oh . . ." He smiled with relief as though the answer to a vexing riddle had just been revealed to him. "Luna, I don't care what they think. And they'll love you anyhow. And even if they don't, we live here, they live there. It doesn't matter."

"I don't know," Luna answered slowly. "Are you sure you want a roommate?"

"I don't want a roommate."

"Are you sure—"

"Yes," Joe interrupted. "I'm sure."

Luna bit her lip. "But my hours at the bar suck. I'm not back until three, sometimes four A.M."

"I know. It's okay."

"And I snore."

"I know." Joe smiled. "Me, too."

"But—"

"But what?" asked Joe.

Now Luna went quiet. What if she broke her lease, moved in here, and then Joe decided he wanted someone else? What if he decided to move back to New York? Living alone was easier, safer. She knew where everything was kept, she knew what food to buy. Living alone was the daytime; Joe was the night. Joe was drinking and sex, the clubs, the constant side-to-side motion of the bar and behind her the brilliant glistening bottles lit up like vaudeville girls. During the day Luna tended her plants, she cooked sometimes, and watched her tiny color TV; she sewed the rips in her clothes with a long needle and black thread, the short, fine stitches her mother had taught her how to make.

The day and the night together, in one place, here, and in this moment Luna wanted it with a raw longing that terrified her.

Luna smiled. "Okay, roommate," she said. "Go get us another drink." Joe leaned in to kiss her, but she pushed him away, and he stood up too quickly and swayed, or maybe Luna's own head initiated the movement, an unsteady mixing of sky and balcony, city lights and sea, the horizon, the railing, tall Joe, his arms held up to right himself, and then he was gone, opening the glass doors, disappearing inside.

The dawn was coming, and Luna wondered what it would look like from up here, the first smudge of pink over the ocean streaking into a fiery red and then the glorious sun. Her plants would thrive on this balcony, so much larger than her own. She and Joe would eat fresh tomatoes with basil and dill. Every day she would set her alarm so they could watch the sun rise.

From inside came the sound of Joe's footsteps on the kitchen tiles, glasses retrieved from a cabinet, the fridge door, and a scatter-shot of ice cubes, and then a loud *whomp* as something heavy and soft fell or dropped to the floor.

Luna turned her head from the view. "Joe?" she called. "Joe? Are you okay?" There was no answer, no sound from the kitchen, so she stood and walked inside, her sight momentarily gone as her eyes adjusted to the darkness.

In the kitchen Joe was lying on the floor, his arms by his sides, his legs open in a V as though he were midway through marking an angel in the snow. Briefly he opened his eyes and issued a tired half smile, motioned for her to join him on the floor, and then began almost immediately to snore.

Luna made her way back to the living room, where she found a pillow and a throw blanket on the couch, and returned, crouching to lift Joe's head and slide the pillow underneath. She curled up beside him, her head on his chest, and spread the blanket over them both. Lulled by the rhythm of his breath, the firm pillow of his rib cage, she almost fell asleep, but the marble floor was cold and hard against her hip, and she remembered that she had to be at work early that afternoon to check stock and she still hadn't slept since the night before.

Luna lifted her head and kissed Joe on his open mouth. She thought about waking him to say good-bye, but no, he was tired, he should sleep, and so she stood up, straightened her skirt, and grabbed her purse. She rode the elevator down to Collins Avenue, and now, at last, she saw the first sun, the light rising with each passing moment, washing the street and buildings around her with pinks and yellows. Luna marveled at the beauty available each and every day with a simple dawn.

Chapter 10

THREE DAYS LATER Luna stood behind the bar spearing maraschino cherries through colorful little plastic swords. It was 4:00 P.M., still an hour before opening. She looked up as two men walked through the door. They wore plainclothes and showed no badges, but they looked like cops, even with the jeans and, on the shorter one, a sleeve tattoo.

Luna's manager, Rodrigo, was sitting at the table closest to the door, working on next week's schedule. "How can I help you gentlemen?" Rodrigo asked.

The tall man's mouth moved, and she recognized the shape rather than the sound: Luna Hernandez. Rodrigo turned, and then they were all looking at her from across the expanse of set, empty tables, the knives and forks gleaming, ready for a feast.

Rodrigo glanced nervously toward the black curtain that hid the doors to the kitchen. Michel, Dima, Pablo, Tikki, Jorge—were any of them legal? Luna was, though Rodrigo didn't know that; he'd never asked for a Social Security card—the tips were her pay. But she'd never filed a tax return, and now she remembered with a jolt that a half-smoked joint was zipped inside the internal compartment of her handbag.

"Luna," Rodrigo was calling to her. "These men would like to talk to you."

The cops sat at an empty table, the chrome-and-black chairs creaking as they settled their powerful bodies into place. Luna slid in and crossed her arms against her chest. She remembered her visit to the Miami Beach station house six years ago when she first reported Mariana missing. *Does your sister have any tattoos? Birthmarks?* That cop had been old and white, with long gray hair pulled into a ponytail, and she'd thought how different he was from her idea of a cop. But these two, with their burly necks and thin lips, looked exactly as you'd expect.

Rodrigo, Luna noted, had disappeared into the back. He would be telling them all to go home—the dishwashers, the busboys, the sous-chefs. Who would work the kitchen tonight?

"I'm Detective Castellano," the short cop began. "This is Detective Henry. We want to talk to you about Joe Skinner."

"Okay," Luna said. She waited. This was not what she had been expecting.

"You know him?" Castellano continued.

"He's my boyfriend."

"When was the last time you saw him?"

"A few days ago." Luna did not volunteer her unreturned calls. Maybe Joe was busy at work, his mysterious and demanding job full of meetings and presentations, clients to woo, proposals to write. Or maybe he regretted asking her to move in. This was how men operated: back and forth, forward and back, a dance of intimacy, and maybe she would never hear from him again, though she didn't think so. She would bet, she would put good money, on Joe walking in here tonight, his tie already off, and she would nod and smile, pour him a gin, and wait for her shift to end.

"How many days?" Henry's eyebrows rose. He had been staring

at her steadily. Good cop, bad cop, Luna realized. This was really how it happened.

"Three, I think. Yes, three."

"You haven't heard from him because he's dead. Joe Skinner died three days ago." Castellano was trying to be gentle, but the words came out like hammers.

"What?" Luna's eyes fixed on the detective's lips, which were chapped and cracked. "Joe?"

"Subdural hematoma. Brain injury. We think you were there when he died." This from Detective Henry.

Luna shook her head. A slow reveal was working on her memory, a curtain pulled to show a different view. The whoosh, Joe on the floor, the scattered ice cubes. They had both been so drunk.

"He was breathing," Luna said. "His chest was going up and down. I lay down with him. He was *sleeping*."

"He was dying."

Again Luna shook her head.

"Did he fall?" Castellano asked.

"Yes. I think so. I didn't see it, but I heard him."

"And then what?"

"I went back there, into the kitchen. He was on the floor. He looked at me and then he closed his eyes and started snoring. I got a pillow and a blanket and I lay down with him."

"And?"

"I put my head on his chest. I started to fall asleep, but the floor was so cold. So I left."

"You *left*?" Castellano asked.

Luna nodded dumbly.

"Did you call anyone? Did you think about calling for help?" Now it was Detective Henry.

"No," Luna whispered. A horrible dawning, a sickening drop in her stomach. She hadn't called anyone.

"Maybe you were afraid to call? You didn't want to get the police involved?" Detective Henry leaned forward as he asked this.

"No. That's not what happened."

"Was there anyone else there in the apartment with you?"

"No, just us. Me and Joe."

"Maybe an old boyfriend"—Detective Henry looked down at his notebook—"Donald Linzano?"

"Donny? Of course not." Luna wondered why—and then she remembered Donny's arrest for armed robbery, years before she'd known him.

"Or did you let someone else into the apartment? Maybe after Joe fell?"

Luna looked at Detective Henry, his unblinking gaze, and felt a new emotion. Not shock or sadness but fear. She shook her head no.

The detectives looked at each other, and each nodded as though they'd reached an agreement.

"We'd like you to come down to the station with us," said Castellano. "Just to talk. We need to ask you some more questions. To rule out any foul play."

"But . . . I need to work. This is my shift." This seemed the only item to cling to, the only thing that would keep her from drifting away. Her job, the bar, the people who knew her, routines and hours, tips and drinks.

"I'll talk to your manager." Detective Henry pushed up from the table, went to Rodrigo, who had reappeared behind the bar. Rodrigo nodded and shrugged his shoulders. *What do I care?*

Luna folded herself into the backseat of the cop car, and immediately it pulled from the curb and screamed away. She wanted to put her hands to her ears, but it seemed a childish gesture, a sign of weakness, so she kept them clasped in her lap. Within the padded dark blue of the car's interior, the shock of Joe's death was settling into her, and inside it took on a new shape. Not *death*, which was definitive, conclusive, inarguable, the end. This was a question. An uncertainty.

Luna remembered the cop with the ponytail, how he'd squinted as he typed her description of Mariana into a computer. No tattoos, one mole low on her back, long black hair. *Ethnicity? Um, Nica. We're Nicaraguan. So Hispanic, then? Yeah, I guess so.* The cop had disappeared for a long time, and Luna wasn't sure if he was done with her, if she should go or stay, but then he'd returned and said, *A young Jane Doe was brought in last night. She might be your sister. Are you prepared to identify the body?*

Prepared? Luna repeated. It seemed an odd word for such a request, as though a test or some type of specialist training were needed to perform the act. Luna had undertaken no such preparation.

Yes, she told the police officer.

Downstairs they went, deep into the bowels of the building: water-marked concrete walls, scuffed linoleum floor laid upon an uneven base, harsh overhead lights. Luna followed the cop's squeaky shoes, his ponytail swinging with the cadence of his step, along a hall, past closed doors, and finally into a white-tiled room. Another man waited for them there, and it was this second man who took her through another door, this one metal and thick, and lifted a sheet laid atop a table.

No, Luna said. *This is not Mariana.*

Are you sure? the man asked.

Luna looked straight at the face, once a woman's face, now a mask or something shaped from clay. Rough pink abrasions rose on the left cheek as though painted on with a brush.

Yes, Luna had said. *I am sure.*

Perhaps Joe's death was like that, a mistake. A guess. Luna's belief that no one knew anything for sure, no matter what kind of badge they wore or how much money they had, took hold of her as she watched from the backseat the thick necks of the two cops. This death could not be trusted. It was death in word only, spoken by two men (nothing but ordinary men) who didn't know her, didn't know Joe. Foul play? The term itself seemed laughable. Fowl play. Chickens at bat.

More than anything Luna wanted to pick up her phone, wedged now in her back pocket, and call Joe. Hear the deep calm of his voice, the funny little hiccup that came when he really, truly laughed. She would explain this to him: *And I missed you, I was worried, I thought I had done something wrong when I didn't hear from you, and then these cops came in and said you were dead! Dead! I didn't believe them, and I'm so glad to hear your voice. Come back to the bar. I'll pour you a gin. It's okay. Everything will be okay.*

* * *

INSIDE THE STATION house, Luna filled out some forms and agreed to be fingerprinted. The ink felt cool against her skin, and then the detectives led her to a room with a table, a few chairs, a window that looked onto the blemished white wall of another building. Luna sat with her back to the window, Detective Henry next to her, Detective Castellano across the table from them both.

"So," Henry said. "Tell us about Joe Skinner."

Luna began to speak. She told them about meeting him, what she'd liked about him, how he'd made her laugh, the drinking. She did not shrink from describing that, not his or her own. Detective Henry scribbled as Luna spoke, the ballpoint moving smoothly against the page. As she described Joe, she smiled, she relaxed, forgetting in an insubstantial way why she was here. She willed herself to focus on this rush of talking about Joe.

"Did you ever fight?" Castellano asked.

"No. Not really. Joe's not a fighter."

Detective Castellano tilted back his chair and yawned. Luna heard the bones of his back crack.

"Did Joe ever hit you?" Detective Henry asked.

"No. Never."

"Did you ever hit him?"

"No. Of course not."

"What about a recent altercation outside the Lotus Bar?"

Luna didn't respond for a moment. "I— Yes. I slapped him then. He started a fight with Donny. I mean, he swung at Donny. Donny was bothering us."

"This is Donny Linzano, your ex-boyfriend?"

"He was never my boyfriend."

"Could you take off your shirt, please?"

Luna shook her head. "Excuse me?"

"Your shirt." Detective Henry pointed at Luna and circled his finger in the air. "We'd like to see if there are any signs of a physical altercation between you and Mr. Skinner. Bruises, scrapes. We need you to take off your shirt."

Both detectives gazed at her with bored, cold eyes.

"Don't I get— Can I have some privacy?" Luna asked.

"Sure." They glanced at each other. "We'll give you a couple minutes," said Henry, and they left the room.

Luna stood up. In the room's new silence, she heard the muffled sounds of men talking, a restrained laugh, footfalls, a sudden guttural shout. She walked to the window and gazed out at the wall of the building opposite. Down and to the right, a stretch of windows revealed rows of women sitting at computers with complicated telephone headsets attached to their scalps, making them look insectlike and vaguely dangerous. They all appeared to be talking or listening. They looked straight ahead at their computers.

Luna began to unbutton her shirt. Across the alley the women shifted and tilted, all those heads and talking mouths seeming to form a singular unit rather than disparate, individual parts—like a cornfield or a stadium crowd. Today Luna had worn her black bra, the push-up that tended to generate more tips when she bent over the ice maker or leaned forward to deliver a glass. It wasn't something to be proud of, but every bartender did it, the men rolling up their sleeves to show their tanned, veiny biceps, the women and their tight tops, short skirts. But now the bra seemed to mark her as manipulative, dishonest, guilty of something: Why else parade yourself like that? Behind all that skin and seduction, what were you trying to hide?

Luna folded her shirt carefully. As she placed it on the table, there was a quick, short knock, and then the detectives reentered the room before she had time to respond. With them was a uniformed woman who stood to the side of the door and looked in Luna's general direction without looking at Luna.

The female officer stayed where she was as the men approached Luna, their eyes fixed on her torso, her naked middle, the black bra, and her breasts barely concealed within it. Luna shivered and crossed her hands on her stomach.

"Please uncross your arms," said Detective Henry, not unkindly, and he walked around her, inspected her. Up and down the two men's eyes traveled.

"Okay. That's it. Thank you, Miss Hernandez."

Luna pulled on her shirt. She focused on forcing each pearly white button through its seamed hole. She kept her eyes lowered to the task. More intimate than the act of standing before these men half naked was their witnessing of this, Luna rebuttoning her shirt. The female officer, Luna realized, had silently left the room.

"We apologize for any inconvenience," said Detective Castellano. "We have a bus token for you."

Detective Henry deposited a gold token on the table and waited for Luna to pick it up, and then the policemen ushered her out of the room, out of the building, and deposited her on the sidewalk in front of the precinct. Luna stood there for a spell, staring at the gold disk in her palm. It was early evening now, the sky streaked with orange, the day's heat starting to pull away. She'd been with the detectives for just under an hour, and in that time the news of Joe's death had become something else; it had become his death. This time there was no mistake, no false identity. In his apartment, on the floor. A brain injury. The horrible thud of Joe's fall: Why hadn't she realized? Why hadn't she called someone?

A grain of doubt and regret, horror and sadness, lodged then deep within her, an oyster's piece of grit, and it would remain with Luna for the rest of her life. Year after year it would grow layered, polished, and it would with time become something beautiful—a testament to Joe, a cautious tenderness that Luna would apply to her future choices. But in this moment, remembering the office full of talking women and the detectives' cold eyes, Luna experienced these feelings only as sorrow, as the falling away of Joe's life and of her own.

The bus token was warm from the heat of her palm, and she threw it onto the sidewalk where it landed with a flat and tinny sound. Luna began to walk.

Chapter 11

AN X OF yellow police tape ran corner to corner. DO NOT CROSS DO NOT CROSS DO NOT CROSS. The grim sense of purpose that had been building within us all day—on the flight from New York, meeting with the detectives, the hot, breezy taxi ride from downtown Miami to South Beach—now faltered. No one moved to open the door.

"Just rip it down," Caroline whispered at last, although it was unclear if she was speaking to me or Renee or to herself. Behind us the elevator doors clanked shut. There was a subtle whoosh as the box descended, and its absence made the hallway quieter, the air thicker.

I stood behind my sisters. The floors were pale gray marble, sconces glowing gold on the wall. Above our heads cool air spilled silently from a silver vent. The shimmering heat of the street outside, the blue fuzz of the sky, the Atlantic's salty tang existed in a different city, a different state.

Joe's front door shamed us. Behind this door, with its yellow X and rude command, was the apartment where our brother had lived for two years. We had never seen this place before today. Only Noni had ever visited Joe, and this week she'd refused to return.

"I'm never setting foot in that state again," she'd declared from her bed, as though humidity and alligators had killed her son. I'd been the one to speak with her about the trip, not because I volunteered but because Caroline and Renee had not yet come home to Bexley. Renee held up at some medical conference in Denver. Caroline unable to find an overnight sitter, Nathan traveling for work. She didn't want to bring the kids, she'd said. It was too much.

Noni had been propped up in bed with pillows, wearing a yellow bathrobe, hair frizzed and crazy around her head. For one hallucinatory moment, she'd looked like a sad, oversize Easter chick.

"You can't blame all of Florida for Joe," I told her.

"Well, what then?" Noni had answered. "Tell me, who *can* I blame?"

"Sometimes there's no one."

"You don't know what you're talking about."

"I loved him, too," I said.

"Ha! Everyone loved him," Noni had replied. "*Everyone.* Look where that got him."

"I'll do it," Renee said now. In one swipe she ripped down the tape with a raw tearing sound, and then she balled it up and threw it onto the floor. "Key?" she said, turning to Caroline.

I watched as first Renee, then Caroline disappeared into the apartment. Now that I was here, in the city of Miami, inside Joe's building that strained like a silver rocket above the wide and busy Collins Avenue, I didn't want to see where Joe had lived. I only wanted to see Joe. I closed my eyes and imagined him: exiting the elevator, fishing for his keys, walking through this door. Again and again and again. Two years of bringing home groceries, girlfriends, DVDs, furniture, magazines, mail. Pizza deliveries, Thai food from the place we'd seen on the corner. Tall Joe, golden Joe, in suit and tie, his oxfords on the marble, gripping the brown leather case he used for work. Joe in running shoes and nylon shorts, the kind he wore in high school for baseball practice. Joe returning late from a work event or a party. Maybe he'd had too much to drink. Maybe he was unsteady on his feet. Joe stumbling, Joe falling.

"Fiona, what are you doing?" Caroline stood in the doorway.

I stayed where I was. I did not move forward.

"Come *on,*" she said with force. I recognized this voice: it was the one Caroline used on her children. Irritated and firm, capable of shifting swiftly to anger.

Normally I would have bristled at Caroline's command, but now I was grateful for it. Step inside Joe's world. Do it. Do it now. You will never have the chance again.

* * *

THE SMELL WAS pervasive. A closed-in, moldy, sickly kind of smell. Not strictly of organic decay but more general: mess and inattention, grime and dust and forgotten food.

Hazy sun streamed through the floor-to-ceiling glass doors that lined the far wall of the apartment. For a moment I saw nothing but then began to make out individual items: the cardboard boxes against the wall, full garbage bags tied with yellow twists, dirty dishes, cast-off clothing. Sofa cushions on the floor. One green beer bottle balanced precariously atop a Frisbee on the corner of a coffee table. I saw neither of my sisters.

"Renee?" I called. "Where are you?"

"Here," came a small voice.

Renee was sitting on the floor a few feet in front of me, her back against a long, low, black couch that had melted into the darkness of my vision. Now I saw her. I saw everything.

"Jesus Christ," I said. I sank down beside Renee. "Joe."

"I didn't realize," said Renee.

Tentatively Caroline was making her way across the cluttered floor. She removed a pile of books and unopened mail from the couch and sat down. "What happened?" she said. I could tell from her voice that she was crying; we had all been crying so much this past week that it seemed unremarkable. Neither Renee nor I moved to comfort her.

"I can't believe he lived this way," said Renee. "Ever since the Pause I can't stand mess."

Caroline nodded.

"I loved the Pause," I said.

"I hated the Pause," Renee answered.

Caroline tilted her head. "Well, there was Nathan."

"I wonder if Noni ever thinks about it," I said.

"Nope. No way," answered Renee. "Once it was over for Noni, it was over." She picked up a beer bottle and began peeling back its label. "Do you remember Dad's funeral? Remember Joe with the fireplace poker?"

"Of course I remember," I said.

"Me, too," said Caroline. "And do you remember how we hugged him? We surrounded him. He almost fell over." She smiled. "Remember that?"

* * *

THE NEXT DAY we returned to Joe's apartment with cleaning supplies and a roll of large black garbage bags. We fanned out, each of us intent on a separate corner. Renee went first to the balcony's glass doors and pushed them fully open, letting the sea air and the distant thrum of traffic and crashing waves work their way into the apartment. Sixteen stories below, the precarious body of a surfer bobbled atop a gray wave. Renee closed her eyes and counted to ten. Then she started on the pizza boxes.

Caroline declared that she'd focus on the kitchen. This was the cleanest room in the apartment though also the worst, because on these tiles, this floor, Joe had fallen. Tentatively she entered, expecting a taped silhouette on the floor or a roped-off area like she'd seen on TV. But there was nothing to suggest tragedy. Sunlight streamed through the large windows, bright and insistent, glancing off the black floors and black countertops and silver appliances. It looks like a showroom in here, Caroline thought, not like a kitchen where anyone had ever prepared a meal or worried over bills.

Her sandals made a soft sucking noise as she moved about the room, wiping, sorting, tossing. The fridge contained one desiccated lime, brown and shrunken, and a large bottle of gin. On the counter lay a tall pile of catalogs. Caroline picked one off the top: Hammacher Schlemmer. A heated massage chair, remote-control attack helicopters, noise-canceling earphones. What would Joe have wanted in here? And what should she buy Nathan for his birthday? Or for Louis—the helicopters? At twelve, was he too old for toys like this?

Since learning of Joe's death, Caroline had been able to do this: disappear into pockets of concentration like a gopher dropping down into its comfortable hole. She had coasted through the last few days, distracted from the reality of a Joe-less world with the sudden adrenaline of crisis planning: contacting family, contacting friends, the funeral, the memorial service. Plus the nagging specifics of her regular life: meal preparation and helping the kids with their homework and loading the dishwasher and folding the sheets. Caroline found that she could pretend, in the shadowy corners of her consciousness, that Joe was in a work meeting and could not be disturbed or had embarked on a lengthy, impressive business trip.

Caroline picked up another catalog, and a photo fell out, an old-fashioned Polaroid of Joe, his arm around a pretty young woman with dark hair pulled back from her face, a mole high on the right side of her cheek. They were sitting at a bar, the glint of bottles to their left flaring white from the camera's flash. Joe and the woman were smiling, skin a little flushed, eyes bright.

Oh, Caroline thought. *Joe looks happy.*

* * *

DRAGGING A BLACK garbage bag, I walked along the shadowy hall toward the bedroom. Inside, Joe had tacked towels over the ceiling light and windows. Sunlight edged in, but the room was dank, murky, as though it existed within an algae-filled pool. There was a king-size bed, unmade, a grayish white duvet swirled up in the middle. The floor was littered with clothes, shoes, socks, a long snaking belt. Inside the closet hung a few dark suits.

We hadn't talked about Joe's clothes. Furniture, all the household effects would be donated, apart from the few specific items that various family members had requested. Joe's bicycle would go to Nathan. Renee wanted the vintage *Casablanca* poster she had given him years ago for Christmas. Caroline wanted Joe's old guitar, for Louis, she had said, who'd been talking about taking it up. Noni wanted Joe's baseball glove, the first one from Coach Marty.

"Are you sure he kept it?" Renee had asked her gently, the day before we left for Miami.

"He's got it. I know he does," Noni replied. Now in grief our mother was sure and stubborn. We no longer worried about a return of the Pause; at least there was that. "If you can't find the glove, then you're not looking in the right place."

Only I didn't know what I wanted. I couldn't remember what Joe had, which of his possessions would mean something to me. I wanted everything of his, and yet I could not bear to take a thing.

"What are we doing with his clothes?" I yelled over my shoulder, though weakly. Neither of my sisters answered. I pulled at the towel on the window until it came down with a flurry of dust, and raised a hand to my eyes with the sudden influx of light.

A tall chest of drawers was pushed inside the closet. All those drawers, and I both did and did not want to see what was inside. I had no right to uncover Joe's secret self, and yet I felt an obligation to protect him from embarrassment; anything bad, anything Joe wouldn't want Noni to see, porn or drugs, I would take it away and destroy it. Flush it down the toilet, stuff it into my bag, and drop it into the sea. I felt a sudden, urgent nausea to think of what Caroline and Renee would find in my bedroom were I to die unexpectedly, unprepared.

But I found only boxer shorts and socks, white T-shirts still wrapped in plastic, belts, jeans, shorts—so many shorts, plaid, canvas, and khaki. And then, deep in the last drawer, my hand closed around a small box. I brought it out into the bedroom's new, tentative light. It was a pale blue, the color of a perfect sky. Across the top, in black letters, were etched the words TIFFANY & CO. The box looked brand-new, the edges sharp, the surface unmarked.

I sat on Joe's bed holding the box in my hands. It seemed almost to emit light, to glow deeply, bluely from within. I opened the top. Inside was another box, this one covered in a deep navy velvet. Carefully I lifted the hinged lid, and there, nestled in a crack of velvet, was the most beautiful ring I had ever seen. A diamond, large and round, smaller than Sandrine's, but somehow more brilliant, positioned on a band set with smaller diamonds. The whole thing took the light from the room and flung it back at me magnified a hundred times, a thousand. The ring seemed on fire, and I threw it down onto the bed.

* * *

AFTER A SPELL I returned to the living room.

"What were you doing back there?" Renee asked.

"Cleaning. Joe's bedroom." I held the box loosely in my hand and considered for the briefest, rashest moment just tucking it into the pocket of my jeans, taking it home with me to New York. But that, I knew, would be cruel.

"Look what I found," I said, and held out the box on an opened palm.

"Tiffany blue," Caroline remarked as she walked in from the kitchen. "What's inside?"

"A diamond ring. An engagement ring."

Renee dropped her half-full garbage bag. "Sandrine's?"

"No," I said. "This one's brand-new."

"Are you sure?" asked Renee.

"Yes. I'm sure. Sandrine kept hers. Remember? And look at it. Look at the box." I held it up but did not move toward Renee. She stepped forward and plucked it from my palm. She lifted the lid and whistled.

The three of us remained still, eyes trained on the ring. All silently asking ourselves the same question.

"Is it . . . ?" Caroline breathed. "The woman who was with him?" The detectives had told us about Luna Hernandez, the woman who'd left him alone that last night.

"The detectives said she hadn't known Joe for very long, just a few months." Renee turned toward Caroline. "And he wanted to *marry* her?"

"I . . . I don't know," said Caroline, and then she held up a hand.

"Wait—" She darted out of the room, into the kitchen, and returned with the polaroid. Caroline placed the photo of Joe and Luna on the coffee table, and we crowded around to look. For a moment no one spoke. The muffled clang of the elevator reached us from the distant interior of the building.

"Look at them," said Renee. "How old do you think she is?" My sister appeared to vibrate ever so slightly, like a rocket in the seconds before liftoff. "So the woman who *leaves* him, leaves him to die, he was going to *propose* to her?" Renee's hands were shaking. She sat down on the couch. Her garbage bag hit the floor with a splinter of glass. "Does Joe have a will?" Renee said. "We need to get in touch with that lawyer. This is important." She was looking directly at the ring, as if she were speaking to it and the ring was talking back. "Did this woman know? I mean, did she know how *serious* Joe was?"

"Renee, do you think . . . she *did* something?" Caroline asked. She peered first at Renee, then at me with the look of a confused passenger who has just been told she's boarded the wrong train.

"The police talked to her. They let her go," I said. "Don't even think about that. He fell. He slipped. There was water on the floor, that's what the police said. It was a horrible, horrible accident."

"I don't know, Fiona," Caroline whispered.

I saw Renee's paranoia taking hold of Caroline, the wheels spinning as they often did, with Renee alerting us of danger. Don't put plastic in the microwave. Exercise twenty minutes every single day. No trans fat. We should have listened to her about Joe and the drugs, I knew that, but that didn't mean we had to listen to her now. The idea that Joe had loved Luna made me feel just a tiny bit better, and this seemed reason enough to believe. Here before us was the most magical of fairy tales: a secret ring, an innocent girl, a true love.

"Renee, you always assume the worst," I said. "They were in love.

She made a mistake, that's all. She was in shock when they told her—you heard what the police said."

"Fiona, did Joe ever tell you he was dating someone?" Renee asked.

Joe had called me early on Sunday morning, just a week before he died. Somehow he'd found the blog and deduced that I was the Last Romantic. *I think I know her pretty well,* he'd said. And then, *Why, Fiona? Why are you doing this? It cheapens you.* This was what seemed the most intolerable: his judgment, his dismissal of the entire project. *Find someone you love,* he'd said at the end, and his voice was earnest and sincere in a way I hadn't heard before. Perhaps it was this moment of vulnerability that provoked my anger. Joe had cheated on his fiancée, lied to his sisters, kept secrets from me, from everyone, distanced himself year after year while we were living in the same city, and then just left, left us all behind as though we meant nothing. As though his sisters occupied the same position as his fraternity brothers and work colleagues. Who was Joe to advise me about love? I hadn't wanted to hear his voice or his judgment, so I hung up on him.

And that was the last time I spoke to my brother, Joe. The very last.

"The last time I spoke to Joe—" I began. Maybe he'd intended to tell me about Luna. *Find someone to love.* But maybe it was something else entirely.

"What is it, Fiona?" Renee asked. "What did he say? Did he mention Luna?"

I shook my head. "No, he didn't mention anyone." I looked around the room, at the newly open spaces of dusty floor, the taped-up boxes and bulging bags of trash. "But I never asked him. We only talked about me."

"Well, I don't buy it," Renee said, her voice fierce. Her suspicion filled the room. "There's something going on here. There's motive."

"Okay, Miss Marple, let me go get my magnifying glass," I said, and I began to cry.

"I want to meet her. I want to look her in the eye and ask her why she left him," said Renee.

Caroline clapped her hands fast. "Yes, we *should* look her in the eye. We should give her the ring!" She said the last with the conviction of a missionary. "That's what we should do. That's what Joe would have wanted us to do." She nodded once with finality.

"I agree with Caroline," I said, wiping my tears. Of course, fulfill the last wish. Bestow the ring upon its rightful owner. There was a simplicity to it, a clarity of purpose. "Yes, that's exactly what we should do."

For a moment Renee was silent. She recognized that she was losing ground. Her anger, so vivid on her face just moments before, had gone slack.

"We should not give her the ring," Renee said.

"It's hers," I replied. "Renee, don't you see?"

Caroline nodded emphatically. We sat together in our dead brother's apartment, and we waited for our big sister to decide.

"Okay," Renee said at last. In her hands the diamond ring flared and sparkled in the room's reflected sunlight. "Give it to her. But I want to be there. I want to see her face."

For five more hours, we cleaned Joe's apartment. Once the windows were washed, the garbage bags deposited in the dumpster, three runs made to the Goodwill, Renee told us that she was going for a drive. "I just need some air," she said. "I won't go looking for Luna. Don't worry."

It wasn't until after Renee had left that I wondered about her words. Why reassure us like that? I tried my sister's phone, but she didn't answer.

"Caroline," I said. "Where's the ring box?"

Caroline was eating a piece of pepperoni-and-pineapple pizza; we had ordered from a place one block away. "The usual for Mr. Joe?" the man on the phone had asked. "Yes," I had answered. "The usual, please."

Now Caroline stopped chewing and swallowed. "Let me look." She began searching around the coffee table, under the couch. "I don't see it," she said.

"Do you think . . . ?" I began.

"Renee doesn't like carelessness," answered Caroline. "Sometimes she forgives people. Other times she doesn't. It's hard to know when she will or won't."

Caroline and I looked at each other. "We should go down to that restaurant," I said.

Chapter 12

RENEE DROVE ACROSS the causeway from Miami Beach, with its all-week weekend of skin and flash and thumping noise, to downtown Miami, which was slower, more restrained, particularly now, 4:00 P.M. on a Tuesday before the office buildings emptied.

Inside Revel Bar + Restaurant, the tables were empty. It was possible to see Joe here, Renee thought as she paused just inside the front door. This seemed like Joe's kind of place. Slick, expensive, but homey, too, comfortable. The bartender was a tall man with hard, pale arms and sharp, straight-edged planes to his face. He looked vaguely dangerous, like a Russian gangster or a struggling actor who auditioned for those kinds of roles.

Renee strode to the bar and asked brightly, "Hi. I'm here to see Luna, Luna Hernandez?"

The bartender was drying a glass with a clean white cloth. He continued the motion, but his eyes rose to meet hers. "Luna? She's not on till later."

"Oh. What time?"

The man stopped polishing and set the glass down somewhere behind the bar. "Are you police?"

"No. Just a . . . friend." Renee forced a smile, and with that one small lie her posture caved, her certainty crumbled. She tried to relax her shoulders, to radiate the goodwill that a friend to Luna Hernandez would surely exhibit. She must have some friends, this unknown woman who had left Joe alone; she must even have family. Had they met Joe? Did they know that he had died? A lump rose in Renee's throat, and she could not swallow, she could not speak, so she looked down, busying herself with her purse to hide her face from this man.

"Well," the bartender said, and he cleared his throat. "Just a moment." He traveled the length of the bar to check on two men drinking red wine, who shook their heads—*No, nothing more, thanks*—and then the bartender disappeared.

* * *

DIMA PUSHED THROUGH the swinging chrome doors into the kitchen, where the pre-dinner service hum was just beginning to sound. A prep cook chopped red peppers in a corner, the dishwasher thrashed through a cycle. Jorge, the sous-chef, was squinting at a packing slip, crates of condiments piled in the narrow space between the walk-in cooler and the service entry.

"You seen Luna?" Dima asked him.

"No. Not yet." Jorge gave him a long look. "Police?"

All the kitchen staff knew about the detectives who had taken Luna away, though only Rodrigo had been on the floor to see it, Rodrigo whom they all despised because he ran the waitstaff with cruel efficiency, refused to hire more busboys or change the table allotment to a more sensible, fairer arrangement. He watered down the well bottles, dealt small packets of coke from the back men's room on Saturday nights, never including any of them in the cut. They all wished they'd been there that day to advise Luna. They knew about police, what to refuse, how to behave. *I want a lawyer.* This they could all say, no matter how poor the English. If it had been any of them—any save Rodrigo—they would have been able to help Luna. Their Luna, beautiful and sad, who stayed after hours to eat a meal, have a drink. They'd seen Luna age from a sixteen-year-old still talking about college to now, twenty-five and the first fine lines blooming at her eyes when she smiled. That awful night Luna had returned from the police station shaking. Jorge gave her a cup of tea and a plate of pasta; Dima covered the whole bar for the hour it took before she was ready to go out there.

Now Rodrigo came bustling in from the prep area, holding a celery stick in one hand, a clipboard in the other, chewing. "Get out there, Dima," he said. "What are you doing back here?" A fine sheen of sweat covered Rodrigo's forehead, and he set down the clipboard to swipe at it with his palm.

"Someone is here for Luna." Dima hesitated to say this, but he was not a good or a fast liar.

Rodrigo rolled his eyes. "Police again?"

"No, a woman. She says she's a friend, but she doesn't look like a friend of Luna's."

"A friend? And how is this part of your job, Dima? You're a part-time messenger for Luna now? I hope she pays you well, because if you're not out there in ten seconds, she will be your only employer." Rodrigo smiled benignly and bit the celery with his big, yellowed front teeth, and Dima was reminded of the TV character Bugs Bunny, the show he'd watch for hours when he was a child, just arrived in Miami from the Ukraine, when the new English words had sounded to him like gunfire, like heavy rain: a harsh staccato that hid a meaning rather than unveiled it.

Dima turned and reentered the restaurant floor, poured two more glasses of expensive cabernet for the two men in gray suits, and then returned to this tired-looking woman.

"Is Luna here?" she asked. "I have something I need to give her."

Dima shook his head. "I'm sorry. I didn't see her." He shrugged and began cutting limes into neat wedges with a short, very sharp knife.

The woman exhaled. "Sorry, but what time did you say Luna was coming in?" she asked.

Dima sighed. He considered honesty his single greatest flaw. "Seven o'clock," he answered. "You want to leave it, the thing for Luna?"

The woman shook her head. "No. I'll wait." She settled on a barstool and took out her phone.

"Can I get you something?"

"Gin," she said. "I'll have a gin and tonic."

* * *

AS RENEE WAITED at the bar, Luna arrived for work through the back service entrance. She squeezed past the boxes of ketchup and sriracha, sidestepped the tower of just-delivered fresh white napkins and tablecloths tied with string, and then she searched inside the dry-storage room for a clean black apron, which she found and wrapped around her waist as she exited to the kitchen. She called hello to Luis, the dishwasher Riley, the waitresses Estella and Sue, and was on her way out to the bar when Jorge said her name.

"Luna, stop." He walked around the order-up line of heat lamps, their bulbs not yet turned to hot, and met her by the doors.

"What is it?" she asked. Jorge rarely crossed into the service area; his realm was the kitchen, where he was king.

"There's someone looking for you, Dima said. I don't know . . ." Jorge shrugged. "Maybe just take a peek before you go out."

"The detectives?"

"No, not police. Dima said a woman."

A tepid flare of hope: Mariana? But Jorge saw it and shook his head. "No, not your sister."

"Thanks, Jorge," Luna said, and he winked, this gray-haired man, small and wrinkled, his eyes heavy with concern and affection.

Jorge returned to his post behind the order-up line, his apron fresh and white, his fingers nimble, and began the delicate process of deboning a skate. Luna pushed open the swinging door and paused, shielding herself behind the black velvet curtain that separated the restaurant from the kitchen. The bar stretched to her left, just beyond the curtain and the swinging chrome doors, the doors that divided calm from chaos, leisure from work, rich from poor, and they would swing ceaselessly—enter to the right, exit from the left—until the kitchen closed at midnight.

Dima was polishing wineglasses with studious concentration. One customer sat at the far end of the bar. Luna saw the woman in profile, her face half obscured by a phone pressed to her ear. She seemed agitated, twisting and shifting on the stool, her free hand shredding a white cocktail napkin into little rough-edged scraps. But even in this disturbed posture, the woman gave an impression of confidence and low-key affluence: two thick rings on the hand that held the phone, the precise cut of her dress, shoulder-length dark brown hair that shone and rippled as she moved. Luna recognized the woman from the photographs: it was Renee, Joe's oldest sister.

Dima looked up and saw Luna standing there. His eyes grew wide, and he angled his head toward Renee. "I'm not here," Luna mouthed. But Dima didn't understand. He squinted at her, shook his big leonine head. Oh, Dima. Luna waved him over.

"I don't want to see her," she whispered, feeling meek and small, but the idea of talking now to one of Joe's sisters cut her down. She wasn't ready. "If she asks, tell her I called in sick. Tell her I'm not coming in tonight."

Dima nodded. He didn't ask why, and Luna squeezed his arm. Once they had slept together, in the first months after he'd started working here last year, and it had not been horrible, it had not been great, but they shared that knowledge of each other, and now Luna was glad for it.

Renee called loudly, "Excuse me? Bartender?"

Luna met Dima's eyes. "Go, go," she said, and he turned back to the bar. Luna retreated farther within the curtain. She didn't want to go into the kitchen, where Rodrigo would undoubtedly tell her to get to work. Until Renee left, Luna was trapped here, and she sank to the floor, pulled up her knees, and closed her eyes.

* * *

THE BARTENDER APPEARED again. "Yes, ma'am? What can I get you?" He balled up the bits of napkin Renee had shredded. The sight of them embarrassed her, a sign of her unstable mind. She had called Detective Henry again to ask questions she was sure he had not yet considered. But the detective had answered with a maddening calm.

No reason to suspect . . .

No evidence of . . .

No motive for . . .

All valuables still . . .

Let me assure you . . .

And then: "I've seen this sort of thing before. You're looking for someone to blame. I get it. I understand what you're going through. It's a hard truth. Sometimes bad things happen to those we love, and it's no one's fault."

No one's fault. It seemed impossible to Renee that an event as momentous as this one, a happening so profound, could occur without a push. And a push needs a pusher. Someone, something, somehow. A finger on the trigger. A bad heart. A mutating virus. Years of neglect. But an ice cube? An ice cube melted, evaporated, disappeared. An ice cube was not enough.

Throughout the conversation with the detective, Renee had felt dulled and misunderstood, her every utterance cut short by one of his breezy responses. Now she wished she could do the whole thing over again. Her interior belief in the suspicious intent of Luna Hernandez wobbled only the slightest bit with the detective's certainty. An orchestra of scenarios played out in Renee's head: Luna quietly opening Joe's front door to allow another man (men?) inside; Luna tiptoeing behind and bashing Joe with a . . . what? a brick? Luna and her accomplices ransacking Joe's apartment, carting away as-yet-unidentified items of immense value. Or maybe: Luna whispering into Joe's ear about life insurance and designated beneficiary (where was the policy? Renee knew they would find it eventually). She entertained these scenes obsessively, painfully, like picking at a scab. Her fingers were bloody, but she could not stop.

As Renee picked up her phone to call Detective Henry again, the bartender placed another clean white napkin on the bar. "Another G&T?" He looked directly at Renee and then quickly flicked his gaze away; his cheeks flared pink as he shifted from one leg to the other.

"Luna's here," Renee said, and it was not a question. "And she doesn't want to see me." Her conversation with Detective Henry had left her primed, ready for rage, and here it was, unmitigated by her sisters, unfiltered by the sadness that inhabited Joe's apartment. She didn't intend to give Luna the ring; no, she intended to hurl it into her face, slap her across the cheek, yell and kick. She wanted to punish Luna, to hurt her.

"Don't lie to me," Renee said to the bartender. "She's here, isn't she?"

The bartender wouldn't meet her eyes. He only shrugged in a vague, dismissive way and began again to cut the limes.

Renee inhaled and then yelled, "I know you're here!" She pushed her stool away from the bar and stood, enjoying the power in her voice and the way the bartender cringed as he set down the knife and stared at her. "Luna Hernandez, I know you can hear me!" Inhale, exhale, inhale. "I know you're back there, so let me tell you this." Inhale. "Even if the police say you're innocent, I *know* that you're guilty." Inhale. "Guilty of leaving Joe to die." Inhale, exhale, cough, swallow. Her hands were shaking. Inhale. "*You* are the one to blame here." Inhale, exhale, lump rising, swallow it down, *swallow.* "And I hope you think about that every day for the rest of your life. I hope—"

Renee stopped. A group of people had appeared beside the bar, standing in front of a long, plush curtain that Renee hadn't noticed before, so seamlessly did it blend into the shadowed spaces at the edge of the room. A dark old man wearing a long white apron and loose, black-and-white-checked trousers approached her, his rubber shoes squeaking over the polished floor.

"Ma'am, we need you to leave the restaurant," the man said. "We'll call the police if you don't go right now." He did not look at her with anger. Renee sensed a certain sympathy, but his voice was firm. "You're causing a scene," he told her.

Yes, Renee was. She was causing a scene. There was no one here to see it, except these few kitchen workers, but she was indeed making a spectacle of herself. Renee gazed at the group: a young woman, pretty and heavily made up, a man who looked barely out of his teens with a thin, wispy mustache, a muscular man with his head shaved clean. All gazed at her with apprehension and resistance and an unmistakable hostility. They were defending Luna, she realized. They were protecting her.

The old man's eyes were mild, his voice restrained, and yet Renee almost hit him. She almost kicked him. She pondered for one long moment the relief that delivering these blows would bring her. Perhaps he would hit her in return with his small fists—he was shorter than she was and older, frailer. Or maybe the bartender—the strength of those arms, the unyielding force of his mammoth knuckles. Wasn't that what she really wanted? To be obliterated?

"Please," said the man again. "Please leave."

Renee became aware of the dim sound of a woman weeping. Or was it her own? Had she started to cry again, as she had so many times these past six days, without realizing it? The sound reminded Renee of herself, the alternating restraint and release, the familiar low moans. Who was crying?

"I . . . I . . ." Renee said, and shame came down like a sack thrown over her head. Shame and guilt, loyal partners until the end. What had Luna done to Joe that Renee hadn't done herself on that balcony two years before?

"Renee." Renee turned and saw Fiona and Caroline standing in the doorway. She remained motionless, unsure which way to turn—toward the old man, the bartender, or back the way she had come, toward her sisters. Turning around felt like a retreat, like an acceptance of the worst possible outcome. *We did all that we could.* Her own voice droned in her head with the words she'd been taught to say after a patient's death. *I am sorry to inform you . . . So sorry . . .*

Renee felt strong, capable hands on her shoulders. Here were her sisters.

"I'm sorry I took the—" Renee began, but they both shook their heads.

Renee always thought of her sisters as they'd been during the Pause: so little, so in need of care. Caroline with her nightmares, Fiona walling herself away in her own fantasy world with her books and notepads, her lists of funny words. All that time Renee had worried that she was failing them, that some irreparable damage was being wrought. But her sisters had become women, and their strength was all around her. Renee could lean against them, and now, at last, she did.

PART IV

After

Year 2079

THE YOUNG LUNA had moved up to the first section, a few rows back from the stage. Absently she played with a necklace, a simple silver chain that fell against her chest, heavy with some sort of charm. A circle, perhaps. Or a ring.

"So there *was* a real Luna," the girl said. "My mother was right."

"Yes, there was a real Luna."

"What happened to her?"

The auditorium remained full. Hours it had been now, the power still gone, generator humming steadily along. We'd heard the sirens twice more, but without the evacuation signal. It seemed inevitable that it would come. This was why I stayed at my house in the mountains. Why I avoided crowds.

The flame-haired woman in the front row had shifted from her partner. She was leaning forward, her body pulled away from his, the two like magnetic opposites. Abruptly he stood and stretched his arms above his head. I heard the muffled crack of a joint, one vertebra colliding against its mate. Why had they fought? I wondered. They shouldn't argue now. Now is when they should come together.

The sirens began again, that awful wail. It seemed louder, longer this time. I waited motionless for the noise to end. At last came a brief, delicious pause. Silence cool and smooth as silk. And then the evacuation signal sounded. At first no one moved. The series of short, sharp blasts was well known—there had been enough public education, the billboards, radio announcements—but we'd heard them only in the context of a test. This, apparently, was no test.

Henry took hold of my hand. "I'll get the car," he said into my ear. "Wait here."

With Henry gone I was alone on the stage. I stayed where I was, the watched now the watcher. I don't think I could have stood in any event. My knees have a mind of their own.

A large man in the second row audibly groaned and began the process of extricating himself from the clench of the auditorium seat. The flame-haired woman and the man came together again, holding hands, their faces tense, and moved toward the exit. It was satisfying to see them reunite, but then I felt an abrupt sorrow at their departure. We had all been through something here, I thought, a joint experience that bound us. But the dispersal had begun. Moment by moment, as the signal went on and on, the audience rose up like a wave gathering force. The room's sense of calm order transformed into a fractured potency. Each part buzzed with a new energy, the latent potential for chaos.

And then the stage creaked with an added weight, and Luna was standing beside me. The young Luna, the girl who would not be put off. The mole was on her right cheek. The charm around her neck was a diamond ring.

"Ms. Skinner, are you okay?" she said. "Let me help you up. We need to evacuate."

She took my left arm across her shoulders and braced her foot against the chair in a posture of strength and an odd intimacy. Our heads came together, her dark hair falling on my temple, my gray across her shoulder, her left hand holding my left. Intertwined, interwoven, knitted, linked. And then—*heave*—Luna pulled me to standing.

"The knees. Just you wait," I said. "You should be thanking those young pliable knees of yours every goddamn day."

Luna smiled. "There's a shelter not that far from the auditorium," she said. "I can help you." She was yelling to make herself heard over the blare of the signal. The auditorium was largely empty now, the last stragglers making their way outside.

"Thank you, dear, but there's no need," I said. "Henry is bringing the car around. I won't last long in one of those bunkers, I'm afraid." An impulse to protect this girl flared again in me, just as it had when the lights first went out. Only this time the idea made its way into voice. "But why don't you come with us?" I offered. "Our complex is entirely self-sustaining. You'll be totally safe. There's a guest cottage on the east side of the main house. And Mizu, our cook, makes the most delicious blackberry scones."

Just then the evacuation signal stopped. The silence took possession of the hall in a way the people had not. It touched every corner, every inch. It was then a soldier appeared. His face covered with a protective shield, a weapon at his side.

"Everyone out," he called to us.

"We're coming," Luna called. "I'm just helping Ms. Skinner."

The soldier waited as we made our way off the stage, down the row toward the emergency exit. Luna pushed open the door, and the rush of cold, fresh air made me forget my knees, forget the soldier.

The exit opened onto a side alley in which stood a few large dumpsters, wooden crates piled high, and people, so many people,

262 • TARA CONKLIN

all of them moving incrementally out of the alley, toward the street. The sky was clear, a full moon, and the light illuminated the scene starkly but without color, as though we had all been washed clean.

How will Henry . . . ? I thought, but of course he would find me. He always did.

We reached the street. A few cars moved along with the push of the crowd, going no faster or slower than the bodies around them. I searched for Henry's—an old Prius sedan, a dark blue—and saw it across the street, half a block south, Henry standing on the hood. He was searching for me. I reached up an arm to wave. "Henry!" I called, and his gaze was pulled by the sound. He came down off the hood and entered the crowd to reach me.

A third type of siren began, a sound I did not know. Fast, piercing. It roused people to hurry. The pace quickened, I felt Luna pulling me forward, and then, at the moment I thought I could not walk any farther, that I might fall, Henry was there to catch me.

"Thank you," he said to Luna, "thank you for getting Fiona out of there. Let me pay you."

"Henry, no," I said. "I've invited her to come with us. Home."

Henry looked at me quizzically. The noise of the new signal rang in my ears and in my head, a thudding that I felt on the inside.

"Ms. Skinner," Luna said. "Thank you, but I can't."

Henry opened the car door and motioned us inside. In the backseat of the car, the signal was muffled, distant. Tinted windows shielded us from the view. People were moving faster now, some breaking off and running. Henry slid into the front seat.

"I think it would be best if you came with us," I said to Luna. "Really, my dear. It's the most sensible course. The shelters will be so crowded, and they're hardly protection. You do realize that."

I wanted Luna to stay with us, with me. I wanted to look at the ring around her neck, to ask her questions about her mother. An old ache returned. Age had not lessened its force.

But Luna shook her head. "My husband, he's at home with our son. I need to get back to them. But please, Ms. Skinner, tell me what happened. Tell me about the other Luna." She leaned forward. "I want to know the story so I can tell it to my son someday. The great Fiona Skinner! It will be such a thrill for him when he's older. I've started reading some of your poems to him before bed. 'The Last Tree' is his favorite. He's a climber."

Her fingers played with the ring around her neck. So many years had passed, it was impossible to say if it was the same. Perhaps if I looked at it closely, in better light with glasses on my nose.

"My sisters and I searched for Luna Hernandez," I began. Henry was turned halfway around in the seat, listening. He had not heard this part before. "I told myself it was because of the ring, but of course it was more than that." I paused. "Where are you from, Luna?"

"Oh, around here," she said, and circled a finger. "About twenty miles north, a small town. But originally, years ago, long before I was born, my great-grandparents lived in the Pacific Northwest. The islands, the ones that disappeared in the western tsunami—"

"Yes, I remember that storm. Horrible. No one had expected it. And then everything gone."

Luna nodded. "Everything."

I considered telling Henry simply to drive, to take us away. A desperation seized me. The crowds had thinned enough that he could get through with some care. The doors had driver-operated locks. But of course I couldn't take her away from her family, I would never do that. I looked at this Luna and thought how much I would miss her when she opened the car door, exited to the street, disappeared. Lost and found and lost again.

A buzz came from Luna's pocket, and she retrieved her device. "Excuse me," she said, and answered, her face breaking into a smile. "Yes, I'm okay. I'm safe." She listened for a few moments, nodding. "Good," she said. "I'll be home soon. I love you."

Luna turned back to me. "It's an elevated practice drill, that's what they're saying on the channels. Can you believe it? All this, for practice?"

Henry looked relieved. "Consider the alternative," he said, and then regarded me with a short shake of the head: he was telling me to give her up. "Luna, would you like me to drop you somewhere?" Henry asked. "With the crowds gone, I should be able to pass through."

And so we drove through the city streets, still busy with people, but their movement had changed. It was relaxed, relieved, almost giddy. Danger confronted and surmounted. The worst had been imagined and now had passed.

It's so difficult to let some things go, to watch them walk out a door, get onto a plane, make their way in a dangerous unpredictable world. I didn't ask more about Luna's family, I did not reach out to examine the ring around her neck. Questions arise no matter how hard you strive for certainty. On the remainder of our drive, I told Luna and Henry the rest of the story. I told them about Luna, the first Luna, and about the secret I kept from my sisters. Henry listened without comment, though I could sense from the tenor of his coughs, the tension in his shoulders, that he yearned to discuss it. There would be time enough for that; we had a long drive home.

We arrived at Luna's address, a narrow old brick building, not one of the newer builds, and sat for a few moments outside. The blue-black sky was just beginning to color with the dawn.

"Fiona, will I see you again?" Luna asked me.

"Perhaps," I said. "Though this has been enough excitement for me for a while. Henry and I will stay put in the mountains. You're always welcome to come visit of, course, but it is a journey."

Luna demurred in the polite way of someone with the best of intentions. I would never see her again, this I knew.

"Good-bye, my dear," I said as she opened the car door.

Luna hugged me awkwardly, a grasping sort of hug, the ring pushing painfully into the soft spot at the base of my throat, and then I released her into the morning.

Chapter 13

AFTER WE RETURNED to Bexley from Miami, after we organized Joe's memorial service and wrote thank-you notes and assured ourselves that Noni was okay—she was attending the grief support group, she was meeting regularly with her doctor, she was going to be *okay*—Caroline and I agreed to contact Luna. Our plan was to meet her—possibly in Miami, possibly bring her to Bexley—and give her the ring in person. We wanted to watch her open the blue velvet box and see for the first time the brilliant diamond that Joe had intended to place on her finger. It seemed important that Caroline and I be there to witness Luna's reaction. To stand, in a way, in Joe's place. I imagined the scene as well lit, cinematic, dramatic gasps and happy tears.

After that day in the restaurant, Renee wanted no part of it. She refused to discuss Luna Hernandez. Joe had died alone, Renee said. This was the truth, and it was all that mattered. This was what we, his sisters, had to live with.

Renee and Jonathan began to travel. Work, it appeared, was her antidote to grief. They went first to Chiapas, Mexico, where Renee volunteered at a rural medical clinic and Jonathan apprenticed with a seventy-four-year-old master carpenter who built intricately carved *retablo* altarpieces that stood taller than a man. Jonathan learned how to inlay mahogany, teak, and bone into oak, to bend the wood into fantastic and sacred shapes. At the clinic Renee conducted routine exams, set broken bones, and administered vaccines, but primarily she taught local doctors how to perform corneal-transplant surgery. Ocular surgery wasn't her specialty—she worked with lungs and kidneys—but she'd received training in New York, and the procedure was fairly simple: *cut, lift, slide, suture.*

Renee's patients arrived from distant, remote villages, on horseback, tractor, or foot. Causations varied: untreated infections, vitamin-A deficiency, trauma. But whether the patient was child or adult, female or male, the reaction to the bandage removal was always the same. The patient would blink, blink again, and reach out a hand to touch Renee's face. The new eyes would fill with tears. *Gracias. Gracias.*

"I'm not sure when we're coming back," Renee said on a scratchy call from Mexico. "Some days the line at the clinic stretches so far I can't see the end. The transplants—it's like recycling. Tragic, intimate recycling."

The idea of good arising from bad had always appealed to Renee. The senseless imbued with sense. After Joe it became for her an urgency. Luna she saw as a coward, possibly even a criminal. Nothing would be gained from meeting her, in Renee's view, only regret.

Caroline and I believed otherwise. Why did Luna become our focus? Perhaps because we needed something to do. We could not return to the normalcy of our old lives, the stupid luxury of believing that Joe would always be there on the other end of a phone line. Luna gave us a focus, a distraction, but one that did not strike me as false. We were not hiding from anything; we were seeking.

Or perhaps it was the trace of what came later that prompted our search for Luna. A shiver of future knowledge that I did not understand, not yet. All I can say is that Caroline and I pursued Luna with a sense of unreasonable purpose. Luna was the answer to a question we did not yet know how to ask.

Day after day I called the Miami phone number given to me by Detective Henry, but it rang and rang. No answering machine, no voice mail, no Luna.

"No, we haven't heard from her," the detective said when I called him from New York. "She's supposed to notify us before she leaves the state." He paused. "But now that we've completed the investigation, I can't devote any resources to finding her."

I searched online with Google, visited Myspace and Bebo. The year was 2006, when an escape from the Internet was still entirely possible. The name Luna Hernandez gave me teenagers in Texas and Massachusetts, middle-aged women in Ohio and Arizona; none was the Luna from Joe's Polaroid.

I called Revel Bar + Restaurant, but the hostess said that Luna Hernandez no longer worked there. How long had it been? I asked.

"Oh, two months?" she said. "Maybe three." She didn't know how to reach Luna, and no, she could not give out any personal numbers. "I need to go now, ma'am," the woman said. "It's a Saturday night."

Caroline's theory was that Luna's inadvertent role in Joe's death had provoked in her an inconsolable sadness. "She's hiding," Caroline said. "We have to go find her. Remember the Pause?"

In my apartment I was broiling a tuna melt in the toaster oven. In Caroline's house in Hamden, she was picking the woody needles off a rosemary stalk for the chicken she would roast that night. Both of us with phones pinched between shoulder and ear.

"If someone had wanted to find Noni," I said.

"They'd go to the gray house," Caroline finished.

"Okay." I straightened up. "I'll go back."

* * *

AND SO, THREE months after that first trip to Miami, I returned alone to search for Luna. I took a cab straight from the airport to the address that Detective Henry had given me. A short, squat apartment building, three stories high, each floor with a small, crowded balcony and windows lit from within. On the second floor, Luna's floor, I saw slow movement behind a gauzy curtain.

I climbed the stairs and rang the bell. I carried my suitcase in one hand; the coat I had needed in New York was tied around my waist. It was early evening, overcast, the light low and colored the dull pink that in Miami seemed to infuse everything, all the time. Again I rang the bell, and this time a woman answered.

"May I help you?" she said. The door opened directly into a small white kitchen. Behind her I glimpsed a man and a boy seated at a table laid for dinner. Tortillas, a plate of beans, one glass of milk.

Luna Hernandez? No, they had never heard of her.

"When we moved in, the place was empty," the woman said. "Very clean. The landlord lives in Ohio. We've never met him. Just send the checks." And then she held up a finger. "Oh—but there were some plants on the balcony. Some tomatoes. Beautiful. Just delicious."

I only nodded; I couldn't speak. I had been so sure I would find Luna here. I didn't move from the doorway. I couldn't even remember the name of the hotel where I was staying. This would be the first of many such moments, a hint of Luna, a near miss, a sense that she was close but never found.

The woman, sensing my distress, said, "Wait here," and then she was gone, darting from my vision. From his seat in the kitchen, the little boy watched me with wide, gold-colored eyes. The woman returned and handed me a fat red tomato. "See?" she said. "You can eat it, just like an apple. Enjoy." And then she closed the door.

Back on the ground floor, I stood on the grass outside Luna's old apartment building. The tomato felt heavy in my hand, overripe. Just below the window was a large shrub awash with pink flowers that shook and twittered as small dark birds flew urgently in and out, in and out, as though some great trouble were erupting deep within the interior. I ate the tomato as the woman had suggested, holding it in my right hand, biting directly into the flesh as juice dripped down my chin. I didn't taste a thing.

The next day I returned to the restaurant where Luna had worked. The manager, Rodrigo, told me that after the scene with Renee, Luna missed her regular shift. He hadn't seen her since.

"There was no one to cover for her," Rodrigo said. "Dima called in sick again. So I fired his ass. I had no bartender for three hours. *Three*. You know how much money I lost?"

I asked to speak to any staff who had known Luna. Rodrigo shrugged and looked at me steadily. "What's it worth?" he said. I realized with a start that he was asking me to pay him, and so I pulled forty dollars from my wallet, then another forty, and he led me into the kitchen. There was the smell of steam and onions and a sense of manic but ordered activity. And then, person by person, I was noticed. A stillness descended, and, person by person, the staff moved away.

Only one of the chefs waved me over. He remained behind a long stainless-steel table, attending to various pots on three different stoves, and spoke to me without once making eye contact. He told me about Luna's mother, the sister who had disappeared, and that Luna deserved a fresh start. "I know it's not what you want to hear, but you should leave that girl alone. Maybe she went home to Nicaragua?" He shrugged. "She talked a lot about home."

For the next week, I stayed at a hotel on South Beach not far from Joe's old apartment. I met again with the detectives; again I went to Luna's apartment building and wandered the surrounding streets. At sunset I watched the sky shift through a kaleidoscope of color before darkening into night. At dawn I watched as fiery reds and pinks painted the sand and the white sides of buildings and laid a golden path across the top of the sea. I walked the nearby beaches. I visited the Betsy Hotel, where Luna and Joe had stayed. With me I carried the Polaroid.

"Have you seen this woman?" I asked at every location, to every person who would meet my gaze.

But everywhere people shook their heads. *No,* they said. *I'm sorry, but no.*

* * *

AFTER MY RETURN from Miami, Caroline began arguing in favor of a private investigator. We needed someone certain, trustworthy, systematic, and skilled.

"I think we should try someone . . . alternative," I said. "Someone unusual."

We were in the Hamden house, the kids at school. I had taken another day off work, the ever-tolerant Homer once again permitting me endless sick days, answering only with a sigh and his wish that I get better soon. Since moving to Hamden two and a half years ago, Caroline had overseen a kitchen remodel, refinished the wood floors, and replaced the downstairs shower stall with a full bath. The front picture window was framed with curtains that Caroline had sewn herself from a colorful print of hummingbirds and fat red dahlias. The couch was low and long, covered in turquoise velvet, bought for a song at an estate sale. The Skinner-Duffys were not rich, but Caroline knew how to spend their money well.

"Alternative?" Caroline asked.

I told my sister that I'd been visiting palm readers, clairvoyants, mediums, anyone I could find who would look into my eyes and tell me something new. Women waiting behind beaded curtains and flimsy sliding doors, jewels on their foreheads, henna tattoos, diaphanous scarves, and always the musky, dusty smell of incense. I remembered Joe and his sightings of our dead father. *You'll see him, too, we all will,* Joe had told me that day in the deli. I'd been so dismissive, but Joe's words struck me now as a clue. A promise. I wanted to believe what Joe had believed. If Joe had seen our father, then perhaps I would see Joe. The search for Luna was one messy part of this. We had to give her the ring. It was the fulfillment of Joe's last wish, the symbol of their love. It was irrational, illogical, obsessive, unhealthy, and absolutely necessary.

"Oh, Fiona," Caroline sighed. "This sounds crazy. I don't like it."

I had expected this response. Nathan was a man of science, cause and effect, hypotheses and evidence, and Caroline was, too, in her crafty, practical way. Canned peaches for winter, homemade pumpkin costumes for the twins, beetles kept by Louis in a glass terrarium and released back onto the grass after a night's observation. She did not teach magic to her children. She did not even take them to church.

"Please, Caroline," I urged. "I think there's something to it. I don't know how to explain." My face became hot, I felt my eyes fill. "Please trust me on this."

Caroline stood up and pushed the curtain back from the window. It was March. A mammoth pile of dirty, crusty snow sat on the front lawn, build-up from the town plow's repeated road clearing that winter. The house looked so different from when I'd first seen it. What, I wondered, had happened to all those cats?

"Okay, okay," Caroline said, still looking out the window. "We can do whatever it is you want, psychic woo-woo, medium, whatever. But *you'll* have to set it up. I just can't. Beatrix started seeing a reading tutor. Louis hates junior high. And we need a new roof, did I tell you? I just don't have any more time, Fiona."

"Will you pay?" I asked. My finances remained messy; the money given to me by Noni and Renee kept me afloat, but barely.

Caroline sighed again, louder this time, then nodded.

I assured Caroline I would take the lead. I would find someone suitable, brief him or her, handle the communication. Invoices would be sent to Caroline's home address.

On TV the clairvoyant Mimi Prince looked wise and kind in a grandmotherly way, with big, wet eyes and a jowly, creased face. She appeared regularly on a cable show that followed a photogenic police team as they searched for missing persons. The show consistently used the same formula: First the detectives met with the bereft family members, lovers, and friends to get an impression of the missing person. An aspiring ballerina who loved her pet cockatoo and homemade pizza. A quirky computer scientist with dreadlocks and a fondness for bridge. The team then employed the tools of science and technology—fingerprint analysis, cell-phone tracking—in the search; these would inevitably fail. And it was always at this point in the program when Mimi Prince arrived. As family members looked on, she would hold an item belonging to the missing person—a sweater, say, or a hairbrush—in one hand, and the other she would place over her heart. *The vibrations of love are strong,* a voice-over would intone. *They travel through space and time. Some say they even connect the living and the dead.* The camera would zoom to her fiercely concentrated face, and then a dawning would occur, an epiphany. She would open her eyes with a start, and before the next commercial break the missing person would be found, sometimes dead, sometimes alive, but always with a photogenic ending of tears, catharsis, closure.

It was unclear to me if the stories depicted were entirely fictional or based on fact, but it didn't matter. At the end of every episode, I too was moved to tears. Here was what we needed, I thought. Someone who would understand the sensitivities and complexity of our interest in Luna. Someone who would feel the vibrations of love.

Mimi Prince in person differed from her television character. This Mimi Prince was shorter, wider, more abrupt. This Mimi Prince required payment up front in cash and Caroline's signature on a ten-page contract that released Clairvoyant International LLC from all liability and offered no guarantee as to outcome.

Caroline signed the contract. Mimi Prince closed her eyes and began to hum at a low, even pitch, dreary as a dial tone. We were sitting in Caroline's living room, Mimi and Caroline on the big turquoise couch, me on a three-legged wooden stool that Beatrix used for cello practice. Items related to Luna and Joe were arranged on the coffee table: the Polaroid, a crinkled receipt from the Betsy Hotel, a hair elastic with one lone black strand caught in the metal fastening. In one hand Mimi gripped the velvet ring box; the other hand rested on her heart.

I was too antsy to be comfortable. One window was cracked open, and the faintest breeze stirred the curtains. I watched it move and thought surely this was a sign of significance, an indication that Mimi's efforts—strenuous, as evidenced by the uptick in her humming—would bear fruit. *Luna Hernandez, where are you?* I thought fiercely, and closed my eyes.

We sat like that for a long spell. The hum continued with only the briefest pauses to mark Mimi's inhalations.

Then, after forty-five minutes, Mimi Prince went silent. She opened her eyes.

"The trail is cold," she declared. "No vibrations, no voices. That usually means the subject's dead."

"What?" I said. I felt myself go cold, a sensation that began at the base of my spine and spread upward and out through my chest and limbs and fingertips. Luna could not be dead.

"This doesn't always work out, honey," Mimi said in a practiced, soothing way as she patted my hand and then Caroline's.

"So that's it?" Caroline asked.

"Yes, dear, I'm afraid so." And then Mimi Prince looked at her watch and announced that she was late for her next meeting.

Without a word Caroline showed her to the door. When Caroline returned to the living room, she said, "Okay, Fiona, we tried it your way. Now we need to get serious. We're hiring a private investigator, end of story." Caroline began pacing the room, straightening and tidying things with quick, efficient movements. Folding a blanket, picking up a doll, dropping an old magazine into the trash. Today Caroline was wearing a pale blue pullover sweater and a jean skirt that went to her knees, her hair brushed and up in a neat ponytail. In all respects she appeared put together, but I registered an unsteadiness.

Caroline stopped and turned to face me. "We need to find Luna," she said. "We need to give her the ring."

I nodded. "I'll get someone to really help us," I said. "Let me do the legwork."

Caroline held her arms in front of her, hands cupping opposite elbows. I noticed a series of small round holes in the hem of her sweater. Moths.

"Thanks," she said. "I can pay, I'll find the money, but I just don't have the time. The kids—"

"It's okay," I said. "I know."

* * *

I FOUND GARY Lightfoot, private investigator, online. He had a slick website featuring grateful testimonials from a host of articulate, attractive clients. Gary himself was very attractive. On the site he appeared in a short promotional video where he tilted his head slightly to the left and spoke with an accent that moved between English and Australian. His office was located in an old redbrick building overlooking Grand Army Plaza. The plaza's formidable stone arch was just visible from the reception window. There was no secretary. Gary himself opened the office door.

"Ms. Skinner?" Thick eyebrows, lifted. Neat suit, shiny shoes, teeth that dazzled. The palm of his hand grazed the small of my back as he ushered me into his office. The room was small but well appointed. Leather chairs. A wide, weighty desk.

For two hours I told Gary Lightfoot about Luna, Joe's accident, my trips to Miami. He nodded with sensitivity, asked the occasional question, and took detailed notes by hand on a yellow legal pad. His office smelled masculine and spicy, like cinnamon or cloves. The accent made every word sound charming and insightful.

How much did these details sway me? At the time I would have claimed not at all. But afterward I recognized their pull. I was no longer writing the blog; I had not slept with anyone since Joe's accident, but I was beginning to miss the heady thrill of attraction and flirtation. It was Gary Lightfoot's job to persuade me. And he did.

"I'm thinking one month or two," he said. "I may need to travel. Of course I'll run that past your sister before making any arrangements." He smiled at me, each white tooth nestled soundly within the gum, and I smiled back.

Outside, I stood before the stone arch and studied the sculpture at its top: the winged goddess of victory, a horse and chariot straining forward. It was spring, the earthy flowerbeds pungent and soft with thaw. Traffic flowed around me on Flatbush and Vanderbilt Avenues, but the green northern edge of Prospect Park dulled the noise and fumes. That day it seemed not that the world was right again but that perhaps the possibility of rightness would return. Gary Lightfoot's calm confidence, the loping curl of his script across the page, the long haughty *Ah:* for the first time since Joe's death, I did not feel crushed by the weight of his absence. The idea of Luna filled me like helium, and I ran down the subway steps and toward home.

But Gary Lightfoot did not find Luna. After four months he announced that Luna Hernandez was almost certainly dead.

Caroline and I met him in his little Brooklyn office. Rain fell heavily against Gary's one window, which shook and rattled with the wind. The room appeared shabbier and smaller than I remembered.

"You're *almost* certain she's dead?" Caroline said. Already she had paid him sixteen thousand dollars.

There were no credit-card records, no travel records, no rental cars or car purchases, Gary explained. Internet searches turned up nothing. The last known address for Luna and her mother proved unhelpful, as had the national databases. "She's a naturalized citizen, but she never applied for a Social Security number," Gary said. He had found no death certificate, but this meant very little. Thousands of people died every year in the United States without identification or family to claim them, their bodies summarily cremated, the ashes scattered at sea. "And those are the ones who are found!" Gary exclaimed. "Imagine how many people stay where they fall. Those people are just *gone.*" I thought he said this with rather too much gusto. "Luna has effectively disappeared," he concluded, waving his hand with a sharp downward chop.

"But we knew that already," Caroline said. "That's why we hired you." A sudden flash of sun entered through the rain-spattered window and cast speckled shadows over the papers and books on Gary's desk. *The Best of Raymond Chandler,* I read on one spine. *Fingerprint Analysis for Dummies* on another. I felt a mild responsibility for this situation, but it was dull and distant. Gary had done his best. Look at his sharp suit, the shirt cuffs white and starched stiff. Listen to the honey pour of that voice.

"Well," Gary said to Caroline, shrugging, "disappeared and dead are versions of the same thing. I'm not a miracle worker, Mrs. Duffy."

Outside on the street, Caroline turned to me. We had no umbrella, only our coats. I shivered. The rain plastered Caroline's hair to her head and darkened it into rivulets of brown that streamed rainwater down her shoulders and chest. Her blue eyes blazed. "Fiona. What was *that*?" She pointed a finger in the general direction of Gary Lightfoot's building. "Why didn't you find someone better? That was all you had to do. That was it. I told you to find someone to help us. You have nothing else going on. You barely go to work, you're not even writing anymore. You have all this time. I paid that man so much money. So much! Nathan and I can barely afford it. And for what?" She paused for the briefest moment, too short for me to formulate a response.

"You are always taking advantage, always using me," Caroline continued. "Using us, me and Renee, for money or meals at fancy restaurants or help with whatever. And Joe. You used Joe, too. Why don't you have your own life? Why are you never in a relationship? Why do you always say you hate your job but never look for another one? You're the youngest, sure, Fiona, but you're thirty years old! Nothing is serious for you. Everything is a game. And why did you pretend you knew what was going on with Joe? Why did you lie to me that day before his party? Why did you say he was okay?

That he didn't need help? Maybe Renee and I . . . maybe we could have helped him. Maybe—"

Caroline stopped speaking. She shook her head and looked at me through the rain.

"Caro, I'm sorry," I said. "I thought—"

"What did you think, Fiona? What? That the detective was cute? That he might fuck you?"

"No." I knew that Caroline was upset; she was angry, she didn't know what she was saying. "I thought he could help us."

"That ridiculous man?"

"I thought it would be okay."

"It's not okay. It will never be okay."

The rain had infiltrated my coat and spread steadily across my shoulders and down my back. I felt it as a stain, a mold. "Caroline—" I said, and stopped.

Caroline shook her head one last time and then turned and walked very quickly along the sidewalk away from me. Within a block she hailed a cab and ducked inside.

I stood on the wet pavement, thinking that perhaps Caroline would return. We had arrived here together; her car was parked outside my apartment building—but no. My sister was gone.

* * *

I DID NOT see or speak to Caroline for another five years. My calls and e-mails went unreturned. Nor did I speak to Renee, not really. She remained busy, traveling, always out of phone range or forgetful or uninterested, and I made no special effort to reach her. It was Noni who kept me informed about my sisters. Renee and Jonathan were in India, Venezuela, Zaire. Jonathan's work appeared frequently in home-design magazines. Madonna had ordered a chair; Robert

De Niro a twelve-foot-long dining table. Caroline isn't doing well; Nathan is working so hard; the kids are great. Noni provided information in a straightforward way, withholding any advice or judgment, reporting the facts of my sisters' movements and moods as though discussing the weather. I took the information in the same way. I did not respond with emotion or questions, only an acceptance of these facts.

During this period I considered myself an emotional vagrant. I did not reside in a specific place over which I might exert control—repaint the kitchen, say, or knock down a wall—but in a relentless state that remained absolutely the same regardless of what I did, where I traveled. I did not live in Queens, New York, with a rotating cast of underemployed roommates. Caroline did not live in Connecticut with her family and pets. Renee was not treating patients in Chiapas while a subletter watered her plants and gathered the mail in New York. Each of us occupied the same boundless space of a world without our brother. Each of us gazed at the same horizon that would never appear closer or farther away, that merely underlined the enormity of our solitude. Friends and family milled around us, and yet each of us stood in that space alone. It was as though the care we had shown each other as children had been revealed as faulty, flawed, riddled with holes. Now we avoided any interaction that reminded us of what we once had assumed ourselves to be.

I continued to search for Luna. In a way we all did. Even Renee. We searched for Luna as we searched for ourselves, the people we were forced to become.

Chapter 14

ONE SATURDAY I took the train from Long Island City, switched at Court Square, and rode the subway to Bed-Stuy in Brooklyn. I exited to the quiet bustle of early-morning Bedford Avenue. The last big storm had hit two weeks before, and icy piles of gray snow remained in front of unused doorways, marking the sides of abandoned cars. It was cold, a dry, brittle cold that stung my lips and made my eyes water. The year was 2008, two years after Joe's accident, a year since I'd last spoken to either of my sisters. The Iraq War dragged on, presidential candidates won and lost in state primary elections, but I barely read the news anymore. World events, even climate change, were happening elsewhere.

I often walked the city. On weekends or afternoons when I left work early, for hours, in all weather. At the beginning I used these walks ostensibly to look for Luna Hernandez. After the fight with Caroline, I gave up searching in any methodical, focused way. I used what was close to hand, what was free, what I could do myself. Perhaps Luna had come to New York, I thought. So many did. Why not her?

The walks, too, were part of my new project. After Joe's accident I wrote nothing at all—not a blog post, not a poem, not a line—

but after my fight with Caroline I began again. She was right: I did nothing of value, I cared deeply for nothing, no partner, no profession. Friends came and went; men, too, with the frequency of trains, loud and heavy, leaving behind only a blessed silence. And so, slowly, cautiously, I began to write again, not as a poet or a woman but as a sort of record keeper. A witness. The only thing I thought about was my brother, but putting words to paper about him was impossible. Too raw, too hurtful. And so I wrote around him. I began to record in detail the last world that existed when Joe was still alive. The last meal I'd eaten, the last book I'd read, the last pair of shoes worn, the last earrings. Soon it became a tic, almost an obsession, to document all these final occurrences. There were so many of them. Once you begin to precisely identify every action and event, every building, every tree from a particular moment in time, they become countless, they stretch on and on. And so it was with the Lasts.

At first I wrote them down not as poetry—I could make nothing beautiful then—but as simple lists. Items, colors, smells, sights, speech, weather: an echo of the lists I'd kept as a child. I fixed on paper every element of the old world so that I might remember and return to it when the present world—where my brother was gone, where things happened anew for the first time, and the second, and the hundredth—became too much. I created the old world in specific detail so that I might hide there.

Last breakfast:

Mushroom and Swiss omelet
black coffee
brown toast, one-half foil packet of butter
two sips water
New York Times, Arts Section

Counter, third stool from right
Uniform stitched with Paige
Old Adidas sneakers, blue stripes, hole in toe
White socks

I posted the lines first to Twitter, which was brisk and new then and provided me with the same sort of anonymous public platform as the blog. Later *The Lasts* became my first published work, but at the time I wasn't thinking about career or recognition or art. It was catharsis.

On my walks I was always searching for a last. I carried a notebook, and I let Joe lead me. When a sight, a smell, an overheard conversation prompted a memory of Joe, I would follow it. Once I sprinted after a truck emblazoned with JOE'S EATS until I lost it to the BQE. For an hour I stalked a man wearing a T-shirt with JOSEPH AND THE AMAZING TECHNICOLOR DREAMCOAT splashed across the front. I'd followed him into the park, down an alleyway, in and out of a restaurant, until finally the man let himself into an apartment building in Carroll Gardens and I gave him up.

My brother was leading me, I believed, to Luna or to something else entirely. It was up to me to quiet down, to listen wisely and well so that I might hear him. Joe had seen our father—now I believed him! Of course he had seen Ellis Avery. After the disappointment of Mimi Prince, I became more, not less, convinced of this. Mimi was a hack, but the vibrations of love endured. My brother had tried to catch our father with drugs and alcohol, but these produced in me only a fuzziness, a blunting. I needed the brisk, brutal force of sobriety to catch the signs. I needed to notice, not to fade.

As I walked, I counted the rhythm of my steps to my brother's name:

Joe, JOE, JOE, Joe. JOSEPH. JOSPEPH. *JOSEPH PATRICK.*

JOSEPH PATRICK SKINNER.

Joe

Joe

Joe

JOSEPH

Joe

Today, as most days, my last conversation with Joe played in my mind as a scramble of words and images.

Don't, cheap, why, please, careful, someone, love.

Sunday morning. A hot wind blowing through my open window. Man #82 in the shower. Joe on the phone: "Fiona, have you heard of *The Last Romantic*?"

"Sure. I've heard of it. New feminism. I read it every week."

"Who do you think writes it?"

"It's anonymous. Who knows? It could be anyone."

"I think I know who it is."

"Yeah?"

"I think I know her pretty well."

Pause. I twirled a curl around my index finger. Curl, release, curl.

"Fiona," Joe said, "why are you doing this blog?"

"Me?"

"I hope you're being careful."

Curl, release, curl. "Who told you?"

"Those guys don't know what you're doing."

"Of course they don't. That's the point."

"It seems unfair. They trust you."

"Trust? I'm the one at risk! I'm trusting *them*. I trusted you. You kept secrets from me. The knee injury, Sierra, Ace. Remember?"

"Come on, that's different."

"Not really."

"Fiona, the whole thing is cheap, taking cheap shots at these guys. People make mistakes. It's not right to punish them like this."

"I'm not punishing anybody. I'm just telling the truth."

"Well, I think it cheapens you."

"You don't understand the project."

"I don't need to."

"How's the coke habit, Joe?"

Pause. Curl, release, curl.

"I just want you to find someone you love."

"Love? What would you know about it?" And the anger I'd felt mounting as the conversation progressed, my anger at Joe for leaving New York, for lying to me, for hiding so many parts of his life, rose up in my chest and throat, making it difficult to breathe. I couldn't speak, and so I hung up on him. The last conversation I had with my brother ended when I pressed my phone to off and set it on the floor.

The shower stopped and Man #82 entered my room, towel around his waist, hair wet, skin flushed. "Who was that?" he'd asked. "Everything okay?"

"Fine," I'd answered. "Family. Don't you wish sometimes they'd just disappear?"

I began to walk very fast, only vaguely aware of my direction. I thought of the last words Joe had said to me and also of what had not been said. The sounds beneath the words. What had I heard? The in-out of a woman's breath. A creak of floor beneath a slender, bare foot. A door closed, a door opened. Had Luna Hernandez been there with Joe?

I traveled deep into Crown Heights, arms flapping at my sides to keep myself warm. Down unfamiliar streets, past parks where children played unfamiliar games, past shops selling goods that seemed unusual and oddly specific: pet toys and carrier cases; dog food, cat food, birdseed; rabbit hutches, rabbit runs. Celeste?

I stopped. Joe? I asked, scanning the signage atop storefronts for something, anything.

Joe?

Joseph?

Joe—

Blam—a man ran flat into me and dropped what he was carrying. He spun around and looked at me, and despite my shock and pain—he quite literally knocked the wind out of me—our eyes held for a moment, and I saw that his were black, bottomless, containing an empty wildness.

"Fuckin' A, lady!" he said. His hair hung lank and greasy around his pale face, purple shadows beneath his eyes. A stench of unwash and urine.

"You dropped—" I said, and when I bent to pick up the package, I saw it was a woman's purse, brown and large and battered.

The man looked at the purse, looked behind me, and began again to run. There were distant shouts drawing closer, and at last I understood what was happening. The man turned the corner and disappeared. From the opposite direction came two figures: one man, one woman, both coming quickly but neither seeming of an age or condition to run. I held the purse with both hands and looked up to the sky, where there was no suggestion of Joe, only sparse clouds, wan sun, and a blue, brittle sky.

"You . . . you got it!" the woman called from half a block away. "You've got my bag!"

I held up the purse. "I've got it!" I called back.

The woman smiled at the man, both of them seventy, or perhaps eighty years old. Old in the way that for me back then was difficult to gauge specifically. When hair and bodies have fallen, when every step trembles.

"Thank you," the woman wheezed as she reached me. "I can't thank you enough for stopping that man."

I handed her the purse. "He just kind of ran into me," I said. "I didn't really do anything."

"Oh, but you did," she replied. "You were right here. Standing right here. Thank you."

"You okay now, Mrs. Diaz?" the man asked the woman. She closed her eyes briefly and breathed yes. He clasped her hands, gave me a curt nod, and then headed back the way he had come.

The woman bent to the purse and went through it quickly, with sharp eyes, taking stock of its contents. She sighed, satisfied. "Now let me give you something, dear," she said. Her breath came in plumes of frost as she removed from the purse a long wallet with a tarnished bronze clasp.

"That's okay," I said. "Really, you don't have to do that."

"But I want to. That young man was high on something. Did you see his eyes? What a waste. What a godawful waste of a life."

"I don't want anything. Really." I put up my hands. "Thank you anyhow. I'm glad you got your purse back."

I turned away from the woman and retreated quickly, not wanting any further gratitude. My left side hurt where the man had crashed into me, and my right hip, which had struck a mailbox as I spun, now throbbed. I forced myself to keep a steady pace. There were no other people on the cold sidewalk. The only sounds were the dull thumps of my sodden boots striking the pavement and the slushy splash of a car passing on the road. When I had walked two full blocks, I allowed myself to pause and look behind me, but the woman was gone. She must be on her way home by now, I thought. Rattled but okay. This would be a story she'd tell

288 · TARA CONKLIN

her husband, her friends and neighbors, a cautionary tale to watch out for hollow-eyed young men with fleet feet, to hope for dazed young women who do not look where they are headed, who search the skies and rooftops for signs of dead brothers, lost worlds.

I continued walking. I remembered then a hardware store somewhere in Brooklyn. Where? A hardware store where Joe had purchased for me a beautiful hammer with a solid red handle, heavy, strong. *You need essential tools,* he had told me. *Nothing fancy. A hammer, a screwdriver. Preferably a wrench, too, though that can wait.* The hammer. The last gift from my brother. Where was the hardware store?

The last conversation. *Please, cheapen, love, someone.*

Joe

Joe

JOE

Joe

JOSEPH

Joe

Four more blocks, maybe five, and there was no hardware store, nothing at all familiar. I stopped because my hip now pulsed with pain. I'd made several turns and seemed to have crossed over into a different neighborhood. The smell of cooking was stronger here, a steel-drum kind of music spilled down a stoop. I hobbled a bit, testing out my range of movement. Ouch, *ouch.* Looking up, I realized I was blocking the doorway of a coffee shop. I considered for a moment the possibility of entering: inside, the walls were painted yellow, and a black woman with long glossy braids stood at the counter. Perhaps she could direct me to a hardware store, I thought. There was a glass case laden with swirls of pastries, fat round bagels, bottles of juice in sunny colors, and it seemed a world away from the grim sidewalk, the bitter cold, my feet, which were damp in my old boots and had begun to ache from my wandering. My throbbing hip. I could feel the rise of a bruise.

I placed a hand on the door and stopped because there was Will. Man #23. The man I saw at Joe's engagement party. That night had marked the last of so many things I couldn't possibly name them all. Everything returned to me: Kyle, Sandrine, Ace, the poem, the woman with strawberry-blond hair, the window and its impossible expanse of green smack in the middle of a gray, cold city.

Will sat alone at a small, round table. I stared at the reddish curl of hair around his pale neck, at the yellowed paperback he was reading. The white cup and saucer on the table. His freckles. His strong, square shoulders. The book was *Catch-22* by Joseph Heller.

Will did not look up, he did not see me, and a woman pushing a stroller bumped up behind me with a small grunt of impatience. I apologized. I turned and moved farther onto the sidewalk, where I lingered in the dismal winter sun, staring at Will through the café's wide front window, watching him turn his pages, sip his drink.

I didn't know what to do. Panic rose from the pavement and through my old, tired boots, panic that I was imagining all this. Had I truly lost my mind, after all these months of wandering? Did I hit my head, did that man knock me harder than I thought? I had never attended a grief support group meeting, though Noni had urged me to. All these months I'd kept my distance from Caroline and Renee. But now I wanted desperately to talk to my sisters, because they would tell me the truth. *Have I lost my mind?* I wanted to ask them. *Will I ever be the way I was before?*

Again I looked through the window. Will. Yes, it was him. I couldn't leave him here, nor could I go inside, and so I waited and I stared, silently urging him to look up, to remember my brown curls and my half-read poem. And finally, after what felt like a lifetime of waiting, Will lifted his head from the book, and he saw me.

Chapter 15

CAROLINE WAS ROAMING her house. It was 3:00 A.M. The TV played a news report of international financial collapse, a housing market gone to hell. Caroline was holding an apple in one hand, the remote control in the other, when Nathan walked into the den.

"Caro," he said. "You're up."

"Yep," she replied. She took a bite of apple.

"Can I fix you something?" Nathan asked. "There's chicken. Betty cooked some chicken for the kids." Betty was the unemployed school nurse Nathan had hired to help with "household organization" once it became clear that Caroline would not be organizing anything for a while. As far as Caroline knew, Betty had assumed the role of housekeeper, nanny, chef, tutor, driver, and whatever else Nathan asked her to do. What else *did* Nathan ask Betty to do? Caroline had no idea but found that she didn't really care one way or the other.

That year, as Will and I were falling in love, Caroline was falling into a period of despondency. It was as though the grief that she had refused to acknowledge after Joe's accident had waited for the second, lesser apparent death of Luna Hernandez to descend. And descend it did. Every last ounce of effort and resolve departed

Caroline's body like the contents of a bottle emptied into the grass. For nine months, through the financial collapse of 2008, the closing of Lehman Brothers, bankruptcies and foreclosure and demonstrations, Caroline lay in her bed and languished. She slept and cried. She ate whatever it was someone brought to her or things she'd pick up in the kitchen—a piece of bread, an apple—that required no preparation or heat. At night she roamed the house, reading a page or two of a book, watching ten, fifteen minutes of television, checking over homework left out on the kitchen counter. And then, just as the sun was beginning to rise, as the colors of the house moved from dark to dusky, Caroline would return to her bedroom (this was her bedroom now; Nathan slept in the guest room down the hall), pull the duvet up over her head, and fall into an agitated sleep.

Nathan was still teaching a full course load at Hamden College, still publishing further conclusions about his beloved Panamanian golden frogs, a species that seemed to offer a boundless wealth of data and insight despite the animals' negligible size and, if Caroline were being honest with herself, annoyingly high-pitched croaks. Tonight Nathan wore his monogrammed blue pajamas, the ones Caroline had given him for Christmas two years ago. She'd ordered them for the whole family, though, she realized now, she hadn't seen her *C* pajamas in months.

What had happened to her *C* pajamas?

"Caroline," Nathan said, "I'm worried about you."

This, Caroline had to admit, was fair. Ever since she'd returned from that meeting with the private investigator, Nathan had drifted at the corners of her peripheral vision, an apparition on the horizon that did not approach. *I'm sorry,* Nathan would call across the distance. *I'm so sorry.* And she knew what he meant: that he had kept Caroline away from her family all those years with their various moves, that she had lost her brother long before he fell on that kitchen floor. But Caroline didn't blame Nathan, not for this; she blamed only herself for allowing it to happen.

"You know how sorry I am about all this," Nathan said now. "But please come back to us. The kids miss you. I miss you." He folded his arms around her. Instinctually she pulled away but then stopped. She felt his hands on her back, drawing her closer, and she relaxed. She laid her head against his chest and remembered the feel of this, being close to someone. He kissed her on the neck and lingered there, his breath warm on her skin.

All at once Caroline wanted Nathan to fuck her. She wanted nothing but that. It was the smell of him, sweaty and sleepy, a bit of musky deodorant, and the softness of the pajamas, these stupid, sentimental flannel pajamas. Slowly she traced the cursive N stitched in shiny white thread across his chest and then began to unbutton his shirt, and then she was pulling off the shirt, pulling off his pants. His hands were under the T-shirt she wore, had worn for days now, and he backed her onto the couch where their children watched TV and played video games. Where now a scattering of Lego pieces lay across the upholstery.

"Ouch," Caroline said, and reached beneath her to sweep the toys onto the floor and pull down her sweatpants. Nathan waited, and then he was on top of her, and she arched her back, her legs went around his waist, and he was inside her. Her apple, one bite taken from the flesh, sat on the arm of the couch; it fell to the floor as Nathan grasped for a better position.

It was over quickly, both of them coming with a speed and force that startled her. Afterward Caroline lay against the couch, stunned more than sated, as Nathan stroked her stomach, her breast, her cheek.

"I love you," he said.

Caroline nodded. "I know," she replied.

After that night on the couch, Nathan tried to entice Caroline back to life. Sex. They returned to it as though they were newly-weds again in those short, fevered months after the wedding, before the first move, when the idea that they could do this without secrets or lies or shame acted as the greatest aphrodisiac. Nathan changed his office hours and began to return home by two o'clock on Mondays, Wednesdays, and Fridays.

And so on Mondays, Wednesdays, and Fridays, Caroline waited for him. She wore satin negligees or matching bra-and-panty sets in electric reds and pinks. Sometimes she greeted him at the door in nothing but a pair of stilettos or a short, frilly apron. They began an affair that was similar to their honeymoon in sexual intensity, but now the sex was slower, smarter, better. Now they came to each other with an unapologetic, unembarrassed understanding of what they wanted and what they could do. Nathan attended to Caroline with such precision that she forgot everything else. She was left only with a crystalline awareness of how he touched her and moved within her.

Soon Caroline had left her bedroom and began again to ferry her children from this place to that, soccer games, doctors' appointments, play dates. To make dinners and load laundry into the machines. She cut and colored her hair into a sharp-edged bob the color of honey, lighter than her natural color ever was. She fired Betty.

The twins, eleven years old now, seemed satisfied by Caroline's renewed presence, by these acts of going through the normal motions. Only Louis, fifteen and taller already than Nathan with angry raw patches of acne on each cheek, looked at Caroline askance. He spoke to her as though she were a child. Or, worse, a disappointing pet. Louis, Caroline suspected, understood her secret. That even as she went about her maternal duties, even as she cooked and joked and brushed her teeth, her essential self remained upstairs in that bed, underneath the down duvet, wrapped in darkness.

Every so often Caroline wondered what we, her sisters, were doing. If we were okay. If Renee was still angry, if I was still searching for Luna under the guidance of some shaman or raven-haired witch. Sometimes Caroline dreamed of Luna, and it was as though she, Caroline, entered the Polaroid picture and stood beside Joe at the bar and watched him but did not touch him. Caroline studied Joe's face, and then she turned to Luna and examined her as you might a piece of art. Looking for meaning. Joe and Luna remained still and silent for these examinations, and then, as though charged with a sudden electric pulse, they began to move and talk. Caroline stepped back and watched them together. She recognized the way Joe and Luna looked at each other and touched, fingers lingering, gazes held, because once she had done the same. It was clear to Caroline that Joe and Luna were in love, and in the dream this realization brought her a great upswell of joy and also unspeakable regret.

One morning after Nathan left for work, the kids at school, Caroline sat alone in the humid, ticking house and wondered what it said about her that she mourned for her brother by fucking her husband until she was raw and senseless. "What do you want?" Nathan would always ask before they began. "Caroline, what do you want me to do?" Caroline always offered a detailed reply. Nathan's imagination only got them so far. But she and Nathan seemed no closer. Nathan operated on her, he made her come night after night, but there was no corresponding transcendent intimacy. If anything, the sex pushed Caroline deeper into herself. She sailed away during their lovemaking to someplace fast, primal, dark. Afterward she would fall immediately asleep, exhausted, and Nathan did the same. In the mornings, when he kissed her and smiled and placed a hand on her cheek or stroked her hair, she felt doll-like, an empty-headed body responding mechanically to another empty head.

Today Caroline sat at her dining-room table, the long one they used at holidays and for Sunday family dinners and the parties they threw—or once had thrown—and she examined her hands. *Caroline, what do you want?* The veins were risen, the skin spotted faintly with irregular freckles; her wedding ring, scuffed and scratched, cut into the pink, swollen flesh of her finger. Her nails were raw and bitten, though she could not remember biting them. The mysterious failings of her own body, Caroline thought. Like the nightmares that had fallen upon her as a child, and she powerless to make them stop. Now her body again seemed consumed by its own set of principles and needs, divorced completely from what she herself, Caroline Skinner-Duffy, wanted. She wanted to laugh. She wanted to feel like things mattered. She wanted her brother back.

* * *

NATHAN'S PROMOTION TO chair of the biology department of Hamden College surprised no one. But still, when he told Caroline, she gasped and felt tears spring to her eyes. It seemed the appropriate response.

Nathan wanted to host a party, something for faculty, administrators, a few standout graduate students. "You know how much I hate these things," he told Caroline. "But I think it's important. A new day in the department. That kind of thing."

"Of course," Caroline replied. "Shall we do steak or salmon?"

Caroline had been "better" (Nathan's word) for over a year now.

She had not spoken to me since that rainy day in Brooklyn four years before. Renee communicated with us all via the occasional group e-mail with subject lines of "Update from Jo-burg" or "Notes from the clinic in Port-au-Prince." Personal phone calls were difficult to arrange, unreliable, and expensive, Renee told us. Caroline did not bother inviting either of us to Nathan's party, and I understood why: it had been too long, it seemed too risky, as though a chemical reaction might occur. Without Joe our atoms did not know where to rest, how to behave. We were free radicals, spinning in our own small orbits, dangerous, poisonous, causing invisible but elemental damage to anything we touched.

Will. Thank goodness for Will. After three months of dating, we moved in together. He tolerated my aimless walking, my obsessive list making. Sometimes he walked with me, wending our way to the Cloisters or over and up to the boat basin on the West Side. The High Line had recently opened, and it was often crowded, but we began early in the morning and occasionally had the path to ourselves. I showed him the Lasts, which now sounded something like poems, and he read them and smiled and said, "Well done, Fiona, these are beautiful." I still worked at ClimateSenseNow!, where I had steadily advanced in title and position. After Caroline's outburst that day, I had thought about my job. Why was I there? What was I doing? I no longer called in late. I took only my allotted vacation time. Improbably, I was becoming an expert on the slow-moving disaster of global warming.

"We are watching it happen, day by day," I would say in the talks I gave to classrooms and boardrooms. "We all see the signs. What can be done, you ask? It is a conundrum so overwhelming in size and scope that no one can bear to acknowledge it. Around the globe I hear only a startled silence. A nervous, cowardly hush. But we must acknowledge it. We have no choice but to face it head-on."

* * *

ON THE DAY before Nathan's party, the twins woke with fevers. They weren't truly sick—no vomiting, temperatures hovering at 101—but cranky, achy, and demanding, with raw, rough coughs and watery eyes. Caroline saw no choice but to keep them home from school.

Today was not a good day for sick children. Caroline had the party preparations to contend with, and today—of all days—Noni was stopping by with her friend Danette on their way to the airport. Noni was going to Europe.

"Juice!" Beatrix yelled from her bedroom. Caroline was downstairs in the kitchen.

"Water for me!" That was Lily. The two shared a room, the large west-facing bedroom where once long ago an orange tabby had birthed ten kittens.

"What's the magic word!" Caroline called back up to them, and a chorus of *pleases* came down.

Dutifully Caroline brought the drinks. After Beatrix drained the last of the juice and handed the glass back to Caroline, she said, sniffling, "Thank you, Mommy." Caroline looked down at Beatrix's pink face, and for a moment she was overcome by a spasm of love so pure that she couldn't see, and she nearly dropped the glass.

"You're welcome," Caroline said, and pulled the covers up under Beatrix's chin and kissed her on the forehead where the skin was hot and tender. Then Caroline crossed over to Lily's bed and leaned over to kiss her, too, and cup her palm around Lily's puffy face. Lily opened her eyes and emitted a small sigh. Lily was six minutes younger than her sister, a span of time that she wore like a stamp on her forehead. Always she trailed after Beatrix, who was bossy but gentle, and Caroline often wondered what would happen when her daughters split into separate bedrooms, separate lives. Perhaps they would always stay close. She hoped that they would, but there were no guarantees. Once she had believed her relationships with her sisters would never falter, but look at them now.

A car door slammed, and then Caroline heard the unmistakable sound of Noni tipping a cabbie: "Thank you so much. Good luck with your surgery, Oscar. You take care, now."

Caroline removed her hand from Lily's face. Both girls had closed their eyes, and her mind shifted from this obligation—tending to the girls, bringing them water, loving them—to the next: our mother.

Caroline headed downstairs. Already they were standing on the porch, waving at her from behind the screen door: Noni and her friend Danette, a woman Noni met the previous year at the grief support group. Danette had lost her only child, a teenage daughter, seven years earlier. Car accident. Somehow the girl had ended up in a lake, the car submerged for three months and four days before the police found her. "Can you imagine?" Noni had asked Caroline over the phone last night. "Not knowing all that time?" "No," Caroline had answered. "I cannot imagine."

Danette's husband was an airline pilot, and consequently Danette traveled free of charge to any destination. "What adventure!" Noni had said. "What freedom!" Last month Danette had invited Noni to join her on a tour of Europe's great cities: London, Paris, Rome, Vienna, Madrid.

"I've never even been to Europe," Noni told Caroline in the hushed tone of a confession, although Caroline knew as much; Caroline had never been there either.

"Noni, you should go," she said, feeling a tremor of envy. "You can't *not* go. It's Europe."

And so Noni had said yes.

"Hello, Caroline!" Noni called, and hugged her on the doorstep.

Caroline felt her breath leave her body and wondered when her mother had become a hugger.

"Caroline, it is so wonderful to finally meet you," Danette said, and then she, too, leaned in and hugged Caroline fiercely, pinning her arms to her sides so that Caroline could return only an approximation of a hug, more a light slapping of Danette's torso with her hands. Danette stepped back, gripping Caroline's shoulders. "You are the image of your mother," she said, looking from Noni to Caroline. "The very *picture*. Thank you so much for inviting me to your lovely home."

The force of Danette momentarily paralyzed Caroline. She'd been expecting someone sadder, older, more beaten down. Noni and her new friend were joined by grief, members of the worst possible club. But Danette looked easily ten years younger than Noni. She was African-American, her hair sprung up in a high Afro, pinned away from her face with a multicolored band. Everything about her was a study in contrast: dark skin, white teeth, long skirt, sleeveless tank, a battered pink suitcase resting beside an expensive-looking black leather handbag. And Noni, rather than fading away in comparison to Danette, seemed herself more vibrant, the lucky recipient of Danette's reflected glow. Noni wore traveling clothes in earthy colors and wick-away fabrics, but her hair was longer and her face made up, a tint of lipstick that looked good.

"Hi, Noni," Caroline said. "You look great." Noni smiled but said nothing in return; she stepped past Caroline and into the house.

"Sorry it's a little chaotic in here," Caroline said. "We're getting ready for Nathan's party tomorrow." Stacked lawn chairs crowded the entryway and living room; they'd been delivered that morning, but Caroline hadn't been ready for them out back.

When Noni gave her a puzzled look, Caroline added, "His promotion? I told you about it last week. We're having a party to celebrate."

"Congratulations!" Noni said. "I'm so pleased for Nathan. How nice of him to host his own party."

Caroline felt her pulse elevate. "We've both been working very hard for this," she said, and then she excused herself from the room.

The kitchen was full of the insistent smell of a cooked quiche. Caroline pulled it from the oven, and her index finger slid past the pot holder and touched the hot metal of the pan. She yelped in shock, dropped the pan onto the stove top with a clatter.

"Are you okay?" her mother called from the dining room. Caroline heard a murmured comment from Danette. "Can we help?" Noni added.

"I'm fine!" Caroline called back. She sucked on her finger, the burned spot raw and tender in her mouth, and she began to cry in a hot, childish way. Why had she let her mother come here today? She should have told her to eat lunch at the airport. She should have ordered food from Pepe's.

Danette appeared in the doorway. "Caroline, what happened?"

"I'm fine," Caroline said. "Just a little burn."

"Oh, dear. What a shame," said Danette, and she reached to examine the finger. She said nothing about the tears but abruptly enveloped Caroline in another paralyzing hug, this one longer and fuller than the one bestowed at the door. This embrace went on and on, and Caroline breathed in Danette's scent (gardenia? or was it lily?), felt the tangy, sweaty heat of her, and found it all strangely and deeply comforting. This near suffocation by her mother's unknown friend was the most comfort she'd accepted in years.

Danette at last released her, and Caroline stepped back. "I'll be right in with the quiche," Caroline said, wiping at her eyes.

"No, let me," said Danette, and she carried the dish into the dining room.

* * *

THEY ATE LUNCH. Danette and Noni told Caroline about their plans, the hotels they'd be staying at, the sights they'd see. After clearing the quiche away, Caroline checked on the girls (still sleeping) and made coffee. Another half hour remained until she needed to pick up the table linens. She returned to the dining room with the coffee pot and mugs on a tray.

"Laurie loved, I mean *loved*, linzer torte," Danette was saying. "I have to tell you, Antonia, that's really why I put Vienna on our list. I mean, it is a beautiful city, you will just adore it, but we are going to eat us some serious amounts of linzer torte."

"Joe's cake is more cinnamon," Noni said. "He never really liked *sweet* sweet, but my God, he could have eaten that cake breakfast, lunch, and dinner. The first time I made it for him, he ate nearly half the thing in one sitting."

Both Noni and Danette were smiling, talking about their dead children in an easy way that made Caroline uncomfortable. It was like talking about God, like talking about love: you needed to do it with a certain amount of reverence, in hushed tones, or on your knees. Caroline didn't care for her mother's breeziness. Plus, Noni was wrong.

"*I* made that cake the first time," Caroline said. "Remember? That Christmas, I wanted to make something new?"

Noni tilted, then shook her head. "It was Easter 1984. Joe was ten years old. You were eleven then—I don't remember you being a baker at that age."

"I was. I was always a baker—I always made cakes," Caroline said, feeling irritated and righteous. "I started when I was . . . I must have been seven or eight." Caroline began to bake during the Pause, following the recipes printed on the backs of yeast packets and sacks of flour. Renee would prepare all the family meals, but she said that dessert was too much work. Memories of scorched cookies and undercooked cakes came back to Caroline, blistered fingers, struggles to reach the oven knob. "Noni, you weren't there when I first started," she said. "You wouldn't remember."

Noni narrowed her eyes and gazed at Caroline as though she were a distant figure whom Noni was trying in vain to identify. "No, Caroline," she said finally. "I think *you're* remembering wrong. It was Easter. I made the cake."

There was a beat of silence, and then Danette remarked with great good cheer, "Well, whoever made it, it must have been a doozy of a cake. I need to get down that recipe. Laurie was never much of a baker herself, though she did like to eat the results. That girl had a sweet tooth, just like her mother." Danette spooned sugar into her coffee, looking to Noni with raised eyebrows. And Noni nodded once, a short downward clip of her chin, and a look of understanding passed between them.

"I need to use the bathroom," Noni said, and left the room.

"I did make it," Caroline said weakly to Danette. "I did."

"It doesn't matter. You both made it," Danette replied. "You all made it, really. You all made that cake for Joe."

Danette's tone was soothing, and Caroline wondered if Danette would hug her again, which she both longed for and feared. But no, Danette stayed where she was, gazing at Caroline across the crumby tablecloth with a look of frank pity. "Your mother's told me that you've taken it the worst. Joe's death."

Caroline bristled. "Me? I think Fiona's still a wreck."

"You know, I don't have any other children," said Danette. "Laurie was it. As much as her father and I hated that—I mean, we lost everything when we lost her—I did think it was easier, in a way. Her father and I took it all. We didn't have to worry about anybody else. Your mother, she's got to get on without Joe, *and* she's got to watch you and your sisters get on without Joe."

Caroline had never looked at it this way before. She had always thought of us as Noni's greatest consolation; Noni had lost her son, but at least she still had three daughters. And Caroline was taking care of Noni. Ever since Joe's accident, Caroline had grouped Noni alongside Louis, Beatrix, and Lily, the four of them crammed into a sack that Caroline slung over her shoulder and carried around. It was heavy, but there was no safe place to put it down.

"Caroline. Listen to me. You have to decide what you love," Danette said. "Joe wasn't the only one. You have to decide *now* and hold on. Start small. Begin with the small things and work up from there."

Noni's soft-soled shoes entered the room with a small sucking noise. "Is Danette telling you about the place we're staying in Paris?" Noni asked, still standing in the doorway. "It's got a view of the island, that tiny one? Caroline, we will have to go next time. Next time I'm taking *you* to Europe."

Caroline looked from Noni to Danette and then pushed herself away from the table. It was as though a deep, dark secret, the secret of her life, had been suddenly revealed to all, the curtain pulled, and Caroline stood there alone, naked and shivering. She recognized what was happening here, and she was exhausted by it. Maybe Danette *was* telling her the secret to overcoming one's grief. Maybe Danette's own acute suffering (every time Caroline began to think of that girl in the car, she shuddered and shook her head and sang a little song to clear away the image) made her wise, and she was sharing this wisdom with Caroline, the most precious gift Caroline would ever receive. Yet even if that were the case,

Caroline could not muster the strength to focus. To file away Danette's words in some empty drawer of her socked-out brain for later reference. The little things? What did that even mean? Everything was big. Everything was monumental.

Caroline left the dining room and stood, dazed, in the center of the kitchen. Dirty dishes filled the sink; her phone was ringing on the counter; someone knocked at the front door. She listened for the girls, to discern their small voices from amid the din, but no, they were quiet. The girls were okay. The girls were sleeping. Caroline could leave, and so she walked out the back door and into the yard. Eight round black metal tables filled the back lawn, looking ugly and industrial without tablecloths or chairs. A long, narrow folding table backed against the west-facing flower bed; this was where the caterer would lay out the buffet of poached salmon, Swedish potato salad, grilled asparagus, arugula salad with balsamic dressing, a cheese plate, a Meyer lemon cake that Caroline had almost baked herself, almost, but decided at the last moment to pay someone else to make.

Noni and Danette remained inside. Caroline heard the delicate sounds of silverware and dishes pinging against one another, the barely detectable suck of the refrigerator door opening and closing. They were cleaning up after the meal, Caroline realized. Good.

She noticed then heaps of new compost that dotted the flower beds, deposited there yesterday by the gardener, who said she would return this morning to finish, but where was she? The backyard, Caroline realized, was a mess. The gardener late, the caterers waiting for her to confirm final numbers, the flowers probably wilting in the back of the florist's van.

Caroline didn't care. Nathan's party. It didn't matter.

Start small.

A plastic Coke bottle lay on its side in the grass. She picked it up.

A flattened buzzing noise emanated from the bottle's open neck: inside, a furious bee bumped against the sides. The plastic interior was dotted with condensation, moist and slippery, and the bee moved urgently but ponderously, as though this were a fight it had been waging for many days, so long that it had already given itself up for dead, but instinct drove it still to make the motions of escape.

Holding it carefully, Caroline carried the bottle down the back slope to where the lawn stretched out, a bit rougher and more ragged than the area closer to the house. They hadn't landscaped this part yet, though every spring she and Nathan talked about doing it up. In truth Caroline liked the wildness, the sparse grass stretching to a row of towering firs that darkened the property line, separating them from those horrid Littletons next door, the boy who played tuba and the anti-vaccination wife. Here dandelions poked up from the grass, fearless or just oblivious to the anti-dandelion campaign Nathan waged every spring on the upper lawn with his fork-tongued extractor.

It was here among the wayward dandelions that Caroline tipped the bottle and tapped it gently once, then again. The bee stopped its buzzing and crawled toward the neck, emerging after a brief rest at the bottle's lip, as if saying a quick, fervent prayer for its resurrection, and then flying off in a boozy, looping route away from Caroline and the site of its imprisonment. Caroline watched it circle up toward the house in the direction of the tower. How she loved that tower! From the moment she'd first seen the house, nothing had mattered but that. The romance of its delicate spire and mysterious curved window. Rapunzel, Rapunzel, let down your hair. A grown woman falling for a fairy tale.

Caroline snorted. She headed back to the house and dumped the bottle into the green recycling bin by the back door. For a moment she paused to listen, like an interloper, to the soft murmur of voices from inside: Noni and Danette, perhaps bent together over a map or compiling a list of the sights of Vienna. She should go inside to them; she should assure them that she would be fine, she was just having a bad day, temporarily overwhelmed by the myriad imperatives of sick girls and a party.

Perhaps it *was* Noni who first made that cake for Joe. Caroline rarely thought of what Noni had done for them, only what she hadn't.

It came to Caroline then, the memory: One Easter, Aunt Claudia sent Noni an old Skinner family recipe. It was German, or maybe Austrian, a cake that called for a pound of butter, heaps of cinnamon, almonds, raisins, powdered sugar dusting the top. Noni doled out careful slices. Everyone ate slowly, reverently. The cake was very good. After we finished, Joe sat for a moment, agitated, a finger tapping the table, and then he pulled the cake plate toward himself. He picked up his fork and pried off an enormous piece, opened his mouth as wide as he could, and stuffed it in. "I love it," he said, only his mouth had been full: "I wuff it" was the sound. He kept eating the cake as quickly as he could, and Noni began to laugh. Joe had powdered sugar all over his face and hands, even in his hair. She laughed and laughed, and we did, too, laughing until we cried as Joe ate the entire beautiful cake.

With the memory Caroline began again to laugh: Noni had been right after all. She bent over in hysterics. She could barely breathe. Her eyes filled with tears. And suddenly Caroline longed to see her sisters. The desire hit her with a whack to the chest, strong enough to make her stumble. She could no longer recall the details of her fight with me or why Renee had reacted so vehemently against the search for Luna.

Start small.

Caroline wandered again between the tables, to the flower beds, which were lovely and messy. Dirt gathered in her flip-flops, gnats at her neck, the trodden-down grass and discarded sprinkler hose and the long-forgotten sandbox that was now choked with weeds and smelled distinctly—even from this distance—of cat piss. All this earth and wood, the house rising from the mossed and molded foundations, spreading itself wide. All the small items dotting the lawn—old Lego blocks, paper fans, tennis balls, a bath towel, a wooden spoon, a ruler—that spilled from the doors and windows like a fat woman who's discarded the wrappers of her eaten bonbons. All these things she should tidy up—the party, the party!—but instead Caroline admired each with a vicious ache. She loved this house, this yard, this rusting swing set and decaying apple core, her son's teeth marks visible on the flesh. She loved this life, but did she love him? Caroline inhaled sharply. Could it be possible that she was not in love with Nathan? Maybe she did not love him at all?

Loving Nathan required so much of her. She'd never thought of it before, not exactly. The frogs, the faculty potlucks, the research trips, his eternal search for publication, for validation. And what about loving Noni, loving the kids, loving Joe—even more now that he was gone? It all required so very much of her. What would happen if she put the sack down? Maybe carrying all these people around wasn't strictly required of her. The twins were nearly teenagers, Louis now in high school. Noni had bought hiking boots for her trip and foldout maps of each city they'd be visiting.

Caroline stopped in the shadow of the house, the neighbor children's voices reaching her, glad shouts and then some crying, and she realized that it had never occurred to her to try another way. To try *not* loving Nathan. To try loving herself. What would happen? It had never before occurred to her, but now—yes, now it did.

Chapter 16

RENEE FIRST MET Melanie Jacobs at a Monday-morning intake appointment, one of the first in her new office at New York-Presbyterian Hospital. Renee and Jonathan had recently returned from their travels, Renee to accept a permanent position as a transplant surgeon, Jonathan to focus on private commissions for the *retablo* pieces he'd first developed in Chiapas. This was nearly four years after Joe's death, during the time Renee, Caroline, and I weren't speaking. Did Renee miss us? Later she told me no, she didn't think about us; she was too busy to miss anyone, and that was precisely her objective.

Melanie was one of Renee's first new patients, a twenty-seven-year-old woman with cystic fibrosis, already on the lung-transplant list. A sprite of a thing, barely five feet tall, married to a longshoreman named Carl who towered over his wife. Shoulders nearly as wide as Melanie was tall. Dark hair receding in a sharp widow's peak. A kind, gentle smile.

As they entered Renee's office, Carl held the door for Melanie and pulled the portable oxygen tank behind them. Clear tubes ran from the tank over Melanie's ears and into her nostrils. Melanie held out a hand to Renee, the long fingernails painted a brilliant aqua blue. "Matches the hospital gowns," she said. "I've got mascara the same color, too."

Renee laughed.

Since Melanie's diagnosis, her doctors had managed the disease, but her condition had worsened in the past year, and she came to Renee for a new evaluation to move her position up the transplant waitlist. Because of Melanie's small size—105 pounds at the height of good health—her potential donors were limited: a man's lungs, for example, would not fit inside her chest.

"My heart is so full!" Melanie told Renee. "My rib cage just doesn't know it."

Renee advised her to keep exercising, to be ready to come to the hospital at any moment, to travel no more than an hour from the city, to stay healthy, to eat well. They'd shaken hands again at the door, and Renee felt vitality in the warmth and press of Melanie's palm.

Over the course of the next six months, Melanie Jacobs grew sicker and sicker. After she was admitted full-time to the hospital, Renee would find herself lingering in Melanie's room, talking and laughing with her. On paper the two could not have been more different. While Renee was graduating magna cum laude from college and pursuing her medical degree, Melanie worked as a receptionist at a Toyota dealership, as a packer at a vegetable-canning facility, and as a waitress. She met Carl when she served him a piece of chocolate cream pie and he offered her a bite. But like Renee, Melanie had been raised by a single mother. Like Renee, she'd worked her way through college, though Melanie had stopped one semester shy of graduation after another hospital stay.

Month by month Melanie's name rose higher and higher on the national transplant list until finally Melanie Jacobs was the sickest lung-transplant patient in the country.

"A dubious honor," she croaked to Renee, who had seen her diminish from the bright, blond smart aleck to this, a frail shell beneath a sheet. Carl would arrive every day straight from work with Thai food and DVDs or a *People* magazine or a thriller that he would read aloud to her. After Melanie fell asleep, he would leave and then return the next day to do the same thing all over again. His union provided excellent benefits, Carl told Renee. The work was punishing, the shifts long, but he couldn't quit now. Not until Melanie was better.

"We're having a kid when this is all over," Carl told Renee one afternoon as she conducted a routine exam. By now Melanie had been waiting ten months for a lung donor.

"I just want one," whispered Melanie through the oxygen mask. "Boy or girl, doesn't matter. I'm going to spoil that kid rotten. Carl's not a carrier, so we won't pass on the CF, thank God." Here she crossed herself over the sheets. "I've got good eggs in a freezer. We were getting ready for liftoff before things turned bad."

Later Renee couldn't remember how she had responded to this information. *Good luck,* she had probably said. *My mom had four, and let me tell you, we were a handful.*

The call came at 2:00 A.M. Renee immediately jolted awake; Jonathan, accustomed to her call buzzer, slept soundly beside her.

Car accident, the nurse said. A twenty-two-year-old Caucasian woman, five foot five, slight, small-boned, blood type O. A fit.

Slipping into her clogs and coat in the kitchen, Renee called Carl's cell.

"It's time," she told him.

At first the surgery appeared successful. It had taken nine hours, and Renee felt the exhaustion in her bones and core as though wet, heavy clay had been pumped inside her. She'd briefed Carl, telling him that Melanie was already out of the recovery room and in the

ICU, that he should go home and get some sleep. Renee herself had gone home, remembering only from Jonathan's note on the kitchen table—*See you tomorrow, love you*—that he had meetings in L.A., and fallen into bed.

Five hours later she woke to the buzzing of her phone. Ten missed calls flashed on the screen. Never before had Renee slept through a call buzzer. She cursed herself as she stumbled through her apartment, trying to reach the on-call attending, pulling on jeans and shoes. A thickness rose in her throat. A dread.

Heart failure was the official cause of death. Melanie had lasted three hours in the ICU and then unexpectedly crashed.

Renee found Carl alone in the hospital's small chapel room. He'd already been told, but Renee wanted to see him, ask if he needed anything, if there was anyone she could call. If there was anything she could do, anything at all.

"Melanie was simply too weak to recover from a surgery of this magnitude," Renee explained. These were words she had said before, but for the first time she felt the true weight of their delivery. "The team did everything they could to save her, but her heart wasn't strong enough."

Carl did not meet Renee's gaze. "Her heart was strong," he said. "It was her body. And the fucking transplant list. Why did she wait so long?"

It was a question that Renee had been asked before. The lung-transplant list operated on a system of need and perceived chance of recovery and pure dumb luck, she explained now to Carl. It was a complicated calculus, imperfect and unjust, but it was the system they had. Some people were saved. Some had to wait too long. Some died waiting. There weren't enough donors, it was that simple.

Carl listened. He nodded, dry-eyed. He'd already done his cry-

TARA CONKLIN

ing, he said. "Thanks for everything, Dr. Renee." Into his pocket
he stuffed the thriller he'd been reading to Melanie before the surgery, and then he left the hospital.

* * *

RENEE DIDN'T HEAR from Carl for seven months. Every so often she
thought of him, but she had new patients, all with their own families and stories, and the memory of Melanie Jacobs faded. A smart
aleck. Brightly painted fingernails. The only child whom one day
she'd spoil rotten.

And then Carl knocked on Renee's door at New York-Presbyterian.
It was an unseasonably warm day in April, and Renee had her lab
coat off, her shoes off beneath her desk. It was near the end of her
workday, but the door was open, and she waved him in.

"Carl," she said, surprised at how glad she was to see him and also
how the sight of him alone, no oxygen tank, no Melanie, shifted a
weight in her chest. Rising from her desk, Renee hugged him.

Renee took Carl down to the hospital cafeteria, where he insisted on paying for their coffees. They sat at a small table overlooking a paved courtyard where fat pigeons fluttered and clucked.
It was 4:00 P.M. The cafeteria was empty and overheated, smelling
of pasta water and Windex. Across the room one lone window was
open, and brief, tantalizing bursts of fresh air washed over them.
With each one Renee breathed more deeply.

"Dr. Renee, you ever want kids?" Carl asked her.

Melanie would often ask Renee personal questions—What's
your favorite movie, Dr. Renee? Do you ever smoke pot?—but Carl
never had, and for a moment Renee was taken aback. She sipped
her coffee and considered Carl's question. Had she ever wanted
kids? She remembered a discussion with Jonathan not long after
they'd met. This was shortly after Joe's engagement party, still al-

most two years before the accident. Jonathan's no to kids was as emphatic as Renee's own, though she admitted to him one point of ambivalence. On a practical level, she liked the idea of creating newer, fresher, better Skinners. Our mortality weighed on Renee. Given our father's example, it seemed any of us might disappear at a moment's notice. With our bad luck and genetics, how would the Skinners continue? The pressure had lifted a bit with Caroline's three, but those children were Duffys, not Skinners. It was clear even then that I was unlikely to become a mother, so it had to be Joe or herself, Renee, keeping her maiden name, procreating with a certain degree of independence or an extremely understanding partner. When she explained this to Jonathan, he had smiled and said, "Joe is a born father. Look at him. I bet he'll have three wives with two kids each. At least. Don't worry. We're off the hook."

Renee had laughed, but she'd also felt relief. Jonathan was right: the Skinners would endure.

But now, here in the institutional hush of the empty cafeteria, sitting across from her dead patient's husband, Renee realized with a small, terrible shock: Joe will never have children. Renee felt loss again, not of Joe, her brother, but of possibility. Of the future.

Renee still had not answered Carl's question. She was forty-two years old. It was no exaggeration to say that she and Jonathan had everything they'd ever wished for.

"No, I've never wanted kids," Renee answered at last. "Not really."

Carl shifted in his chair, gripped the coffee cup but did not drink. "Well, Melanie wanted me to give you her eggs. That's what she said. She said she wanted to donate them to you. She didn't have any sisters. And her friends—it's hard to maintain friendships when you're in the hospital for so long. She admired you, Dr. Renee. She cared about you."

Carl's phone began to beep. "Oh, shit," he said. "I'm late for work. Overnight shift. Dr. Renee, think about it, okay? You and that boyfriend of yours. Kids. I'm not having any, not without Mel around, but she'd love it if a part of her was tumbling around the playground. Or learning how to play the violin or be a doctor or whatever. I'd really love it, too. I wouldn't bother you. We could make whatever kind of legal agreement you want. Anyhow, I gotta go. Think about it, Dr. Renee. Just think about it."

Carl left the cafeteria, but Renee sat for a while. Perhaps twenty minutes, perhaps an hour. She held on to her coffee until it grew cold.

Renee told no one about the eggs. She filed away their existence into a compartment that contained the things she did not want to think about. The man in the car. Luna Hernandez. The ring. Those bruises on the thin, fragile skin of Joe's forearm. That night on the balcony at the party. And so Melanie Jacobs's eggs remained frozen in a basement laboratory in New York-Presbyterian Hospital while, fourteen stories above, Renee went about her profession. She transplanted lungs and kidneys from the dead into the living, she taught medical students and residents about cross matching and pulmonary function tests. Her patients were young and old, responsible and careless, and grateful, all of them, grateful beyond words for what she and her team had granted them. Time.

*　　*　　*

I WAS AT work when Caroline called to invite me to lunch. It was two days before an environmental conference on the Paris Accords, and I had been spending long hours at the office, writing speeches for Homer, researching our position papers. At night I was working on a new project, the Love Poem, about a man and a woman who lived in a hot climate, who in many respects appeared

THE LAST ROMANTICS • 315

different in background and aspirations, but who had discovered in each other something rare.

My assistant, Hannah, put the call through. "Caroline something," Hannah said. "I didn't catch the last name."

I paused. "Masters?" I said, referring to one of our major donors, heiress to a shipping fortune and, thankfully, dedicated to ocean preservation. She was fifty-five years old and looked thirty, as was the job of an heiress.

"No," said Hannah.

I thought of other Carolines I might know.

"Duffy?" I said.

"Yes! I think that was it. Duffy."

"Hm." The line was blinking red; Caroline remained on hold.

"Who's Caroline Duffy?" Hannah asked.

"She's my sister."

"Sister? But I thought her name was Rachel."

"*Renee.* Renee is one sister. Caroline is the other."

"Oh, two sisters! That's a lot of sisters. You're so lucky to have sisters! I only have a brother, and he's younger and totally ridiculous."

I had hired Hannah, but there were times when I deeply regretted it. "Yes, very lucky," I said. "Okay, put her through, please."

And then I was hearing Caroline's voice for the first time in nearly five years.

"Fiona," she said without preamble, "I'd like to see you. Lunch, with Renee, too."

"Oh," I said. "When?"

"Maybe, gosh, I don't know. Tomorrow?"

I had a meeting tomorrow at eleven o'clock, another at one that was sure to go late. In the lull before I answered, I heard Caroline's breathing, the delicate in-out of my sister's lungs.

"Okay," I said. "Where?"

We met in the city, at an Italian place that none of us had been to before. Only half full on a Friday afternoon, with plastic flowers on the tables and a balding waiter who stood at the back of the room and jiggled change in his pocket. The kind of restaurant frequented by lost, footsore tourists or illicit lovers looking to hide.

I cancelled all my afternoon meetings. We stayed three hours and drank two bottles of wine.

Caroline told us she was leaving Nathan—had left him, in fact, although they both still remained in the Hamden house. He was looking for another place, but these things took time. They had told the kids, who were understandably upset but coping, she said, as best they could. There was a counselor, the school had been notified, the parents of their best friends.

"But why?" I asked Caroline. The table had been cleared; we awaited our dessert of tiramisu and affogato. Caroline's marriage had always seemed immutable, incontrovertible as a law of physics. Till death do us part. The happily ever after.

"Nothing *happened*," she explained. "I mean, nothing dramatic. No affairs. No drug habits or porn habits or anything like that. I just couldn't become the person I wanted to be. I couldn't even figure out who that person *was*. With Nathan I could only be the same old Caroline." She took a sip of wine and then shook her head, flapped her hand to signal a change in topic. "And listen, you won't believe it, but yesterday I saw someone who looked like Luna Hernandez. On the train platform, just as the train was pulling in. She got onto a different car, and I wanted to go look for her, but I hate stepping between cars when the train is moving." Caroline paused. "I'm sorry we never found her," she said.

"I'm sorry, too," I said.

Renee rolled her eyes.

"Don't *do* that," said Caroline to Renee.

Pointedly, Renee did it again.

"I know it's silly," Caroline continued, shifting her attention fully to me, "but . . . I think about Luna a lot. I joined that thing Facebook. Have you? It's so easy to look for someone. I looked for her, but maybe she changed her name. Or maybe she's not on it yet."

"I think about Luna, too," I said. I considered telling my sisters about my walks, my lists, my belief that Joe was leading me somewhere, that I would see him again someday. This was the place, this was the time to talk about these kinds of things. Finally together again, a blanket of otherworldly calm thrown over us by the wine and the dim lights. If I didn't tell them now, I never would. But I stopped myself. It seemed too unreasonable, too self-important. Selfish, almost. Of course they missed Joe, too. Of course they had loved Joe, too. But hadn't I loved him the most?

"Please stop. I don't want to talk about Luna," said Renee. "I can't talk about this." Her face was drawn. As she pushed hair behind an ear, I saw her hand shake.

I grabbed Renee's hand to steady it. "How's work?" I asked. "How's Jonathan? Tell us."

Renee gave me a half smile. Jonathan's *retablos* were selling well, almost too well, she said. He could barely keep up with production. He'd been invited to a residency in Rome by the American Academy; she would lecture at a hospital there, returning to New York every other week to consult with the lung transplant team. This was when we first heard the name Melanie Jacobs, thrown by Renee into the discussion as an example of how punishing the transplant surgery was on the human body, most of them ravaged already by disease and months of waiting.

"Melanie was so funny," Renee said. "Like stand-up-comic funny.

She'd had cystic fibrosis since she was thirteen, and I suppose humor was how she coped." Renee paused. "I hate losing any patient, but I really hated losing Melanie."

There was a certain degree of melancholy in her voice, but I didn't view it as extraordinary. It had been too long since I'd communicated with Renee for me to judge what was normal professional concern and what suggested something deeper. Later I came to understand that Melanie Jacobs had been different for Renee.

Renee told us that she and Jonathan had recently bought the apartment next door and were planning to knock through the dividing wall, expand Jonathan's studio, add a guest bedroom. And they were building a sauna, a small room of cedar.

"You guys will have to come over," Renee said, leaning forward, grabbing my hand. "I got so hooked on them when we were in Finland last year. Twenty minutes on a winter's day. It's life-changing."

"You're lucky, Renee," Caroline said then, almost like an accusation. "I mean—I know how hard you work. *Lucky* maybe isn't the right word."

Renee shrugged. "I guess I am," she said. "I've been very lucky. In some ways."

Caroline rushed on. "I mean, I know I've been lucky, too. I love my kids. They're healthy, they're happy. But ever since Joe, I have this dread, even more than before. Worse than the normal parenting dread. This terror. What if something happens? It's like having your heart walking around outside your body, no protection, just at the mercy of the world. It's awful." Caroline laughed. "I mean, don't worry. I'm on Xanax. I'm not going to lock them in a closet or anything."

"Can the kids come to my next reading?" I asked. "KGB Bar in two weeks." They were all teenagers now, frequent visitors to the city, Caroline had told us, urbane and generally bored with life in the suburbs.

"Yes, they'd love it," Caroline said, and then she grimaced. "I can't believe I'm the only one with kids."

"Don't look at me," I said, and held up my hands. "Will's already had the snip." I made a scissoring motion with my hand, and Caroline laughed.

We both turned to Renee, but she wasn't smiling. "No," she said, and slowly shook her head. "Jonathan and I decided a long time ago. We're too busy. And besides, I think becoming a parent would limit me." Renee said these words carefully, thoughtfully. She was looking at Caroline with a clinical, cold eye. An appraisal of all the decisions Caroline had made and all that Caroline stood for.

Caroline said nothing, but her cheeks flushed red as though she'd been slapped. There seemed in her a sliver of shakiness, as though one side of her face had been drawn by a child. It would never disappear, never entirely. Today marked the first time I became aware of it.

Renee must have seen it, too. "No." She held out a hand to Caroline. "I don't mean it that way. You've . . . you've adapted to it. The kids are so wonderful. For you the sacrifices are worth it."

Renee was just digging the hole deeper, I thought. Caroline still looked stunned. I worried that she might cry or run out of the restaurant, that we would return to how we'd been—separate, silent, the three of us alone. But Caroline looked down at her lap, shook her head, laughed.

"Renee," she said, and she was truly smiling, a wisdom there. A tolerance. "Becoming a mother is the most expansive thing you can do. But it's an experience you can't really explain. I won't even try."

Then she turned to me and clapped her hands fast and said, "I'm going to plant a tree. A tree for Joe."

"What kind?" I asked.

"Lilac," Caroline said. "It reminds me of Joe. It's tall with these big clumps of flowers that smell so good. Purple and green. Those were the Mavericks' colors, remember?"

I nodded. Of course I remembered. Joe in the Mavericks uniform, tight green pants, purple baseball cap with that slanting *M* in bright green. Yes, a lilac tree. That was perfect.

We left the restaurant, blinking into the light of the day as though exiting a casino, recognizing what we had almost lost. We swayed a bit, from the wine and emotion, and then formed a tripoint hug in the middle of the sidewalk.

"Jesus, ladies," a man barked as he walked around us. We ignored him.

And so three weeks after our lunch, on a beautiful morning in June, Will and I met Jonathan and Renee at Grand Central Station, and together we took the train to Hamden.

Caroline served us all wild salmon and a salad made from lettuces she and the kids had grown in their own raised beds in the yard. We sat outside, the long patio table set with Caroline's colorful napkins and yellow tablecloth. There was wine, lemonade, a cake—Joe's cake—that Noni and Caroline had baked together. Louis, Beatrix, and Lily threw a Frisbee and helped Caroline in the kitchen.

That year I had published my first book of poetry, *The Lasts*, and it had done well, at least by the low-achieving standards for a poetry book. As part of the tree ceremony, I read one poem—"The Last Tree Climbed"—about the locust in Noni's front yard that, at the age of twenty-eight, the last Christmas before the accident, I had climbed with Joe on a bright, cold day.

And then Caroline, Renee, and I took turns with the shovel, digging the hole, maneuvering the young lilac into place. Already it had begun to flower, not the weighty purple clumps Caroline had been hoping for—those would come in later years—but even these delicate blossoms produced the most intoxicating scent.

Chapter 17

FOR A DECADE this was how we were: Renee and Jonathan in their West Village apartment, both of them sought after in their fields, frequent travelers, spending layover weekends in Berlin or London or Hong Kong. They became glamorous, in a sensible, intellectual way, she in medicine, he in design. They spoke at benefit galas and before groups of the young and talented. The travel and work, the possessions and experience—Renee had been lucky, so much luckier than she ever imagined she'd be. Caroline was right.

Will and I remained determined in our careers and committed in our marriage. We moved out of New York City at last and into a farmhouse, of all things, in the quaint commuter town of Croton-on-Hudson. Deer in the backyard, snowshoes at Christmas, a refrigerator in our basement that held only wine. I continued work on *The Love Poem,* the book that would define my career, publishing some pieces first on Instagram, where I found a vibrant poetry community and, over time, hundreds of thousands of followers. After Homer's retirement, I was made editorial director of ClimateSenseNow!, and I felt at home in the role.

Caroline began acting in small regional productions, and then Off-Off-Off-Broadway plays. She excelled. She amazed us. In *Play-*

boy of the Western World, she developed an Irish brogue that convinced us all, and the following summer she turned coquettish and sly as Blanche DuBois. The work paid nothing, of course, but Nathan supported them financially. What else could he do? This was his family. For the first years after the divorce, Caroline cycled through a supply of boyfriends, all of them without fail similar in disposition and looks to Nathan, until she met Raffi: bearded, sarcastic, a chef with a belly who one night prepared for us a plate of pappardelle with spicy sausage and mushrooms that to this day appears in my dreams. Louis went to Wesleyan, Beatrix to Berkeley, Lily to Hamden College on a faculty admission, Caroline confessed. All three of them kind, generous young people who provided their parents with a great degree of joy without ever intending to do so.

It was in the year 2022 that Renee woke one morning to a call from the fertility clinic. She was alone. It was a Monday. That semester Jonathan was teaching at RISD and spent three nights per week in Providence.

"Dr. Skinner, you're listed as the contact for a collection of oocytes harvested from Melanie Jacobs. We check every five years to clear space and renew the storage agreement. Are you planning to use them?" The nurse's voice was calm, routine, but it provoked in Renee a sudden heat that rose to her cheeks.

Renee was fifty-two years old. When she looked in the mirror, she greeted the lines, the bagging around the upper cheeks, the shadowed creases with a clinical eye. Yes, she was aging. Some might even call her old. There on the phone, the nurse waiting patiently on the line, Renee considered the question of Melanie's eggs. When Carl came to see her that day, the idea of potential motherhood had shocked her. Scared her, even. *A heart walking around outside your body.* So soon after Joe's death, Renee knew she could not sustain that kind of vulnerability. It would have shut her down.

But now Renee could assess the idea with distance, with a certain passivity and recognition of her own strength. The limitation problem no longer worried her; she'd already surpassed all the goals she'd set for herself. It had taken decades, but Renee no longer felt reverberations from the Pause. She no longer ached for Joe every single day. And there, as she stood in her kitchen, clutching the phone to her ear, an image of Melanie Jacobs came to Renee, shocking in its specificity. An exchange they'd had soon after Melanie had been admitted full-time to the hospital: Renee leaning in with her stethoscope to listen to Melanie's heart, their faces nearly touching. She saw the lift of Melanie's eyebrows, the collection of small brown hairs, plucked into thin parentheses, and there, just beneath the arch, a white scar on the left brow bone. *Fell as a kid,* Melanie explained, touching it with an index finger, the nail painted a cherry red. *Split it wide open on the curb. My parents were so worried, but look at it, just a little thing.*

Now in the kitchen, Renee saw again that stubborn scar, no longer than the white cotton end of a swab. She heard again Melanie's cracked, husky voice.

Something inside my sister shifted: it was a tectonic, abrupt change that fell upon Renee altogether and all at once. With an urgency that defied all common sense, all rational thought, Renee wanted a baby, Melanie's baby. Those eggs. Good from bad. Intimate recycling.

"Yes," Renee said to the clinic nurse. "I am planning to use them. When's your next appointment?"

* * *

THREE MONTHS LATER Renee lifted groceries onto the counter. Her shoulder ached. Her muscles were strong, her body whole, but the parts did not fit as smoothly as they once had. The joints stuck, the bones complained. Renee, Caroline, and I often discussed the indignity of it, the ambush of aging. A woman's body had so much more to it than a man's, so many more curves and crannies where gravity did its awful work and so quickly! All at once you had fallen.

It was June. Today was a rare day, with no call shift, no meetings, no events. Renee had woken late, eaten a bagel, and walked to Citarella, where she roamed the aisles, examining each item carefully before placing it in her basket. Today Jonathan was due home from a sourcing trip to Bangkok.

Today was the day.

Jonathan had consented to the use of his sperm. Consented, after months of cajoling, counseling, discussion. He agreed, he signed the papers, he jerked off into a plastic cup. ("The porn just made me feel old," Jonathan had said. "It was all stuff I'd already seen.") And then, little by little, day by day, he withdrew. First from their apartment as he took on more international work, more far-flung commissions and residencies, and then from her life: fewer phone calls, e-mails, meals together, events. He was so busy with the *retablo* commissions. Clients flew him to summer homes on Harbour Island to take measurements. They arrived at the initial consultation with personal assistants, girlfriends or boyfriends half their age. One with a small Pomeranian that sat on the man's lap throughout the meeting and watched Jonathan, he later recounted to Renee, as though he would soon be eating Jonathan's face for dinner.

Renee remembered once early in their relationship watching Jonathan work on a chair, a captain's chair made of cherrywood with curved armrests, a low broad seat, a back that carried the swoop of a wave. This had been in those first months after Joe's death, when Renee saw herself as a walking tender bruise. But as Jonathan sanded the wood in clean, even strokes, moving in the direction of the grain, his face intent with the seriousness of the task,

Renee had forgotten, for a few precious minutes, her own distress. The client was a friend of theirs, a woman Renee knew from high school in Bexley, not a close friend but someone who had talked to Noni months earlier about wanting to commission a piece, something special, she said, for her husband. The couple had come to Joe's memorial service. Jonathan had worked for months on that chair. When the woman first saw it, she burst into tears.

Recently Jonathan had finished a large *retablo* for a Greek shipping magnate, a ten-foot-tall wooden secular altarpiece with a series of carvings and small sculptures that evoked the life and family of the client. Finished, it operated more as extravagant spectacle than furniture or art, which Renee supposed was the client's intention. These were the kinds of things Jonathan did now. Gone were the tables and chairs and tall, elegant mantelpieces. Nothing utilitarian, nothing useful, only more and more of these personalized, quasi-ceremonial pieces, enormous and, to Renee's mind, reflective of little more than his clients' own outsized narcissism.

It was nice, Renee admitted, to have the money. Her medical-school loans gone. The entire brownstone theirs. They traveled widely and well, when their schedules allowed, and had offered to help Noni on numerous occasions (*What about a nicer house? You and Danette don't have to stay at youth hostels anymore!*) though she'd always refused.

Renee glanced at the clock. She pulled the milk from the bag. She set the glowing red tomatoes onto the sill. Today the egg (Melanie's beautiful, special egg) would meet Jonathan's rangy, lab-pummeled sperm, and two would become one. Would become four, sixteen, thirty-two. On and on and on. In five days Renee's body would receive the cluster of cells (the embryo, the nurse informed her, the size of a petit pois) and she would be pregnant.

Renee placed an eggplant into the vegetable drawer. She put a hand on the refrigerator door. There were still things that could go wrong. Things could always go wrong.

A door slammed. Jonathan was home.

Renee had bought flowers, a great bouquet of yellow and red tulips. She took them to the door to greet him. "Jonathan," she called, and already he was there in the kitchen doorway. His eyes caught on the flowers, and instantly Renee felt silly. This day was nothing. It might be nothing. Why mark it with so much fanfare? She placed the bouquet beside the sink.

"Hi," Renee said. "How was the flight?"

"Long." He glanced at the bags on the counter. "Did you get wine?"

"Yes. A nice pinot gris. Harold recommended it."

"Great. Tonight, you know. The thing at Nan's."

"Yes. I'm not going. Remember?"

"Why?"

"I need to rest. I can't drink."

"Renee."

His voice was solemn and she paused before answering. "What?"

"I don't want this." Jonathan was still wearing his jacket. His packed suitcase was still in his hand.

"They're just flowers," Renee said, although she knew what he meant. The only surprise, she realized now, was that it had taken this long.

"I mean. This. The egg. The baby."

"It's not a baby yet."

"It will be. You heard what they said. You're a great candidate."

"Still. Anything could happen."

"I don't want it. The change, the disruption. I like us the way we are."

Rene studied Jonathan: graying, a shadow of stubble, older than she was. He still wore the same glasses, the same types of shoes as he had when they first met. Jonathan was loyal, there was no denying that, when the subject of his loyalty remained constant. But Renee: she had changed.

"We've been over this, Jonathan. With Betsy. With Dr. Petarro. This is what I need. But if you want to go, go." Renee waved him away and turned back to the sack of groceries; there were still items to unpack.

There followed a minute or two of silence from Jonathan. Renee refused to look at him as she moved around the kitchen, finishing up. It was his choice to make. She would not try to convince him. On some questions the need for persuasion meant you had already lost.

Finally Renee heard the rattle of Jonathan's keys, the soft tap of his shoes, the whine of the door as it opened and closed again. The quiet that descended.

She emptied the grocery bag and hung it from a knob. She took the flowers from the counter and carefully unwrapped them, snipped the ends, found a vase in the side cupboard, the tall one used for unwieldy things, and filled the vase with water. She slid the flowers in and placed the vase onto the kitchen table, right in the middle. They were lovely flowers, the cups of the tulips just beginning to open. It was spring, and the watery, dank scent of spring—even here, surrounded by concrete—came to her from the open window.

So much remained uncertain, but Renee felt at ease. This egg, hers but not hers. A baby. After eighteen years with Jonathan Frank, Renee was ready to love someone new.

Chapter 18

I SAT AT the computer in the den reviewing my itinerary for the climate-change conference. Three mornings of presentations and meetings in Seattle, with day excursions possible. A trip to the Olympic Peninsula. A ferry ride to various islands, each one appearing on Google Maps as craggy and green, studded with peaks shrouded in mist. I clicked through this link, then that one. Will was upstairs packing for his own business trip, this one to Chicago, when he heard me cry out.

"Fiona?" He pounded down the stairs and stood in the doorway. "What is it? Is it Renee?"

"No," I said. "Not Renee. She's still pregnant and big as a house and bloated, but she's fine. I just talked to her an hour ago." Caroline and I were on perpetual call for Renee: she'd asked us both to be there for the delivery.

"Oh, thank goodness," Will said. "What is it, then?"

"I . . . I found someone," I said.

"Who?"

This of course was the question. I had told Will only the barest information about Luna Hernandez. My brother's girlfriend, the woman who'd been with him when he fell. A terrible accident.

Judgment clouded by alcohol. I had never told him about the ring or our search for Luna, about Mimi Prince, that private investigator, Caroline's fall into despondency. It had seemed a silly, shameful chain of events.

But now. On the screen. I pointed to the website. Will leaned over, pulled reading glasses from his front pocket, and squinted at the page. "Ivy and Vine. Farm-to-table restaurant and grocery," he read. "And?" He removed the glasses and looked at me.

"That woman," I said. "I recognize her. I think I know her. I may look her up when I'm in Seattle."

"An old friend? College or something?"

I nodded. "Yes, college. I haven't seen her in years. Laura Shipka," I read the name off the website. "Must be her married name."

"Sounds Russian."

I tilted my head. "Maybe."

"Huh," Will grunted. "Okay, then. I'm going up to finish packing. You sure you're okay?" He looked at me with his soft gray eyes, his red hair gone white at the crown, the sweet concern of Will, my husband of fourteen years.

"Yes." I nodded and smiled. "Totally fine. Just tired."

Will left the room. I heard the creak of his feet ascending the stairs to our bedroom. I leaned in closer to the computer, then enlarged the photo until the woman's face filled the screen. Short black hair, high cheekbones, a mole the size of a dime high on her right cheek. I had only seen that one Polaroid photo of Luna, although I had imagined her countless times. Was this the woman Joe had loved? The picture fractured into colored atoms, pixels fine as dust.

I picked up my phone and dialed the number on the screen. Luna answered on the first ring. "Ivy and Vine," she said. "How may I help you?"

* * *

I STOOD AT the front door of Luna's house, but I did not knock. I listened to the sounds within. A child's request: "Again, please, Mommy. More." The bark of a good-natured dog. A woman's laughter. The house stood alone at the end of a very long dirt road, up on a low hill that looked to the basin of Puget Sound. Tall pines rose to the east of the house, and mature gardens surrounded it, settled now into late-winter dormancy.

I had not told Caroline or Renee about my discovery. Renee was thirty-seven weeks pregnant, progressing exactly as she should, but still—it was a high-risk pregnancy, and she insisted on maintaining her surgery schedule for as long as possible. Caroline was acting as doula, helpmate, labor coach, and anything else Renee needed. My business trip would be short, only two days. "I am a hundred percent reachable," I told Renee before I boarded the plane. "I'll have my phone on at all times."

Caroline had moved temporarily out of the Hamden house, leaving Raffi with careful instructions as to garden maintenance and care of the chickens, and into Renee's apartment. In the past weeks, Jonathan had made overtures toward a reconciliation, but Renee had rebuffed him.

"I'm fine," she told him. "Honestly, I had no idea how easy it would be to do this without you."

Luna lived on one of those green, misty islands I'd seen on my computer screen. The ferry ride took only thirty minutes from downtown Seattle, but I disembarked into what felt like a different time: a small, tidy town, a slow-moving police car, a woman and her pointer, all of it charming, quiet, and contained. The month was February, and a chill, damp wind blew off the water. No place, I decided, could be farther from the heat and hustle of Miami.

The moments at Luna's door dragged on, but still I didn't knock. Inside my purse was the ring in its velvet box. I also carried a manuscript, a bound advance copy of *The Love Poem,* to give Luna. The book would be published later that year. It would change my life, although of course I didn't know this at the time. I knew only that for fifteen years I had imagined Luna as Joe's last love and his truest. I had written a book of poems about her, about the two of them together. All this time I'd held an idea of Luna in my head, and now it would collide or collapse with the real person who stood on the other side of this door.

The sun was setting. The light was almost gone. I felt the encroaching darkness around me. I rapped the iron knocker. The sound of feet, a pause, and the door opened.

"Fiona, hello," Luna said. "You found us." A toddler hovered at Luna's knee, looking up at me with wide, dark eyes. Luna looked older, of course she did, than in that faded Polaroid, but she still retained the clear skin, arching eyebrows, that mole. I would have picked her out in any crowd.

"Yes, your directions were perfect," I said. "I'm sorry I'm late. I missed the first ferry."

I sensed a hesitation. Perhaps Luna would not invite me in. Perhaps, after all this time, the visit would consist only of a cautious stare-down on the doorstep.

The toddler began to fuss. He reached for his mother. Luna bent to pick him up and then stepped back. "Please come in, Fiona," she said.

As I entered, a yellow Labrador rushed to greet me, jumping up and pushing its nose against my crotch. I backed away, self-conscious, already off balance. "Doggy, no," the child said.

"Come on out back," said Luna. "I made us some tea."

I followed Luna through the house: large woody rooms, floors made of wide scuffed boards, beams visible overhead. A pair of glass-paned doors led onto a large circular room lined with windows through which I saw, dimly in the near dark, a view of the water. Two steaming mugs of tea sat on a square coffee table. Toys lay scattered across the floor, and the toddler scrambled out of Luna's arms and ran to a set of wooden train tracks.

"That's Alfredo," Luna said. "My son. He's two. He looks just like my husband, Dima."

Alfredo had thick blond curls and a little bow mouth. He pushed the train across the floor with his chubby pink hands, chanting, "Chugga-chugga, chugga-chugga." As with all children, I found him intoxicating but also somehow threatening, like a hard drug I'd tried once and knew I should never do again. Although of course I hadn't tried it, not even the once.

"He's adorable," I said. "And I say that about very few babies."

"He's a handful," Luna replied. "And I just found out I'm pregnant again." She laughed in a nervous way, though about the pregnancy or something else, I couldn't say. "We weren't expecting it. I'm forty-one. It's a gift, you know? We haven't told anyone yet, actually."

I felt a small thrill at the sharing of this confidence. "Your secret is safe with me."

"Do you have kids?" Luna asked.

I shook my head. "No, my husband and I decided not to. I'm the editorial director at an environmental NGO. And I'm a writer. I write poetry, I'm working on a lengthy project now. I have a book out next year. Will teaches history." I told Luna about my work, Will's research into indigenous populations of the American Southwest, the strange, desolate quiet of our trips to the desert after the tidy chaos of the New York City suburbs. Behind my streaming monologue sat the disquiet that arrived every time I said these words to a mother: no children. First a small flash of shame and then, following swiftly, defensiveness. It was my own instinctual reaction, irrational and unfair to both of us. Even with Caroline sometimes I still felt it, and now with Renee, large and happy as a house. *Everyone makes different choices,* Caroline had said to me recently as comfort and apology. *Everyone's life is complex.*

"It must be so much easier for you and your husband without any kids," Luna said. "All your traveling?" Her face was curious, without judgment.

"Yes," I said. "The luggage is certainly a lot lighter."

Luna smiled and told me in turn about the business she and her husband ran, an organic farm that supplied produce to restaurants in Seattle. "The farm-to-table movement, what a boon to growers like us," she said. It had taken years to become certified organic, but now they barely kept up with demand. They had five year-round employees and hired dozens of seasonal workers; they delivered produce boxes to homes and ran a store in town.

An awkward silence descended, punctured only by the click-click of the dog's claws on the hardwood floor, Alfredo's singsong whisper as he played with the trains. "In the station here's the house, Mama, Papa, RoRo. Bye-bye, good-bye."

I reached for my purse. I had come here to give her the ring, of course, but now, sitting on this leather sofa, drinking mint tea from the thick ceramic mug, I felt a shyness that registered almost as ambivalence. Finding her had been a deep, interior goal for so long, its significance barely acknowledged even to myself. But maybe this was not the time to introduce Luna into our lives. All the painful memories she would provoke. I wasn't sure. I wavered between giving her the ring, inviting her to New York, and leaving immediately, throwing the ring away, never again speaking her name.

Perhaps the idea to fulfill Joe's last wish now, so many years later, was ridiculous. Perhaps it had always been ridiculous.

But a deep tremor of the old impetus returned to me. Joe's last wish. The very last.

I said, "Luna, I came here to give you something. I found it in Joe's apartment, but I think it's yours." I pulled the ring box from my purse and placed it on the coffee table.

She looked at it but said nothing.

"It's for you," I said.

Luna began to shake her head, but then she reached forward and picked up the box, lifted the lid. She closed it immediately and placed the box back onto the table. "This isn't mine," she said.

I thought for a moment that she didn't understand, and so I explained. "It's an engagement ring. Joe never had the chance to propose, but he loved you, he wanted to marry you."

Luna shook her head. "It's not mine," she repeated. "I don't want it." She met my eyes. "Joe happened so long ago. I'm married now, I have a family. I only want to forget that time."

"Forget my brother?" I felt a sudden crumpling, a collapse, as though a hand had squeezed the internal workings of my chest.

"No, that's not—" Luna stopped. "I made a horrible mistake that day. You should keep this for your family. Your sisters' children. I can't take it."

A disappointment cracked open and grew wider every second that I sat here, Luna across the table from me, the ring between us both. The manuscript of *The Love Poem* weighed down my purse, but I could not give it to Luna. Not now. I had written a book of poems that imagined the truest love, a lost love, a tragedy. But look at all that Luna had now. She was surrounded by love, she was rich with it.

Alfredo was staring at me, his wet, pink mouth open, some food or dirt crusting the corners. I offered him a faltering smile. I needed to leave this house with its shedding, barking dog and domestic mess, the thin lines of dirt beneath Luna's fingernails, the heavy scent of gardenia from the flowers in the hall. My mug of tea was suddenly too hot against my knee, and I set it on the table, where it sloshed messily onto the floor.

"Oh—I'm so sorry—" I said.

And then the sound of the front door opening, footsteps, and little Alfredo looked up, a thunderbolt of joy flashing across his face. "Papa?" he said, and scurried out of the room.

A man's voice answered, but it was muffled, I couldn't make out the words. I turned away from the spill, toward the voice, and then the man entered the room with Alfredo in his arms. "Hi," he said to Luna.

He was Joe. For a blazing flash, this is what I saw. Joe, his wide shoulders, the imposing height of him, dark hair, tawny golden skin, and those blue eyes. For a moment I believed in true miracles, in magic, perhaps even in God. My breath left me, my heart went still, the moment extended into a wondrous stasis of the absolute impossible. I had always known it was true: Joe, still alive, somewhere. Somewhere, and here he was. At last I had found him.

Alfredo broke the spell. "Mommy, RoRo home," he said. "RoRo here."

Joe strode across the room to Luna, kissed her on the cheek, and I realized this was a boy, with dirty sneakers on his feet, wearing basketball shorts and a sweaty T-shirt. Knobby knees, knobby elbows.

"Hi, Mom," he said.

"How was practice?" Luna asked, not looking at me. She took

Alfredo from his arms and reached out to wipe a crumb off his face. "Did you eat already?"

"Just some pizza," the boy replied. "I'm still hungry." It was then he noticed me standing there, like a fool. *I am a fool,* I thought. *What should I say? What should I do?* I calculated in my head. Of course. Fifteen years.

"This is my old friend Fiona," said Luna, turning to me. "And, Fiona, this is my son, Rory."

I didn't meet Luna's gaze, but I held out my hand to the boy. "Nice to meet you, Rory," I said. The boy's palm was hard with calluses, like holding a cheese grater, and I gripped it, feeling those rough spots, not wanting to let go.

I released the boy's hand. For a fleeting moment, his warmth remained on my palm, the ghost imprint of that grip, and then it was gone.

I said, "Luna, I'm afraid I have to leave. I need to get home. My sister Renee is pregnant, did I mention? She could go into labor any day now, really. My sister Caroline was early with her firstborn." I heard myself babble. Every nerve in my body sent raw, urgent messages of escape to my brain and heart.

Luna was studying me. "Rory, can you take Alfredo into the kitchen? Give him a snack, some cheese and crackers?"

"Sure," Rory said, and he left the room, bending to hold Alfredo's hand. I watched them go. I watched Rory's back disappear behind a closed door.

"Fiona," Luna began, "maybe we should talk more."

I lowered myself again onto the couch, but it was more a physical response to Luna's suggestion than a conscious choice to stay. The dog came to sit at my feet, circling once, twice, and then curling its body beside me.

"You said your sister is pregnant?" Luna asked.

I nodded. "Yes. Her first child."

"That's wonderful," said Luna. "A growing family."

"You seem very happy here," I replied.

"It's a wonderful place to raise kids. So much time outside and in the water, swimming and boating. Rory has his own sailboat, a little Sun Cat."

"I always thought Joe should have been a swimmer. But"—I shrugged—"baseball just took over. And that was that."

"We don't always know at the time the significance of our decisions," Luna responded.

"But sometimes we do," I said.

Luna was looking at me, her eyes a clear brown, lines beneath and between, the face of a mother who worked hard at loving her children. "You mentioned you have a ferry to catch?" she said.

I did not answer straightaway. The feel of Rory's callused palm remained on me. And that moment when I had believed he was Joe. I could not undo that moment. I would think of it for the rest of my life. But I needed to return home to my sisters, to Noni, to Will. Yes, I had a ferry to catch, and then a plane and a cab. A dozen possible futures lay before me, each of them fraught, none of them easy. An upheaval, a release. Joy and sadness, regrets of every size and flavor. Only one of these futures was certain, only one future contained the lives we had already built. It seemed a dangerous thing to risk tearing those down. I thought of the Pause and how the four of us came together and then how close we came to destroying everything after Joe died. I didn't want to risk losing us again. And I didn't want to take anything away from Luna, a woman I did not know but whose life had proved for me the greatest inspiration.

"Would you like to say good-bye to Rory?" she asked, and I could see the effort those words demanded of her.

"No." I shook my head. "Will you tell him I enjoyed meeting him?"

Luna nodded, her jaw held tight, her eyes fixed on mine.

"Thank you," I said.

Luna picked up the velvet box and held it out to me.

"Keep it," I said. "For Rory. Maybe someday he'll want it. Maybe he'll want to hear its story."

She nodded and replaced the box on the table.

I followed her along the dark hall, to the front door. "Good-bye, Fiona," she said.

Behind me the door closed with a solid twisting of the lock even before I was down the steps, down the walkway. The wind was blowing strongly now, the trees dancing wildly with its force, so bitterly cold on my face and neck that I was relieved to the point of tears when at last I reached the shelter and quiet of the car.

As I started the engine, a truck was coming up the long driveway; it passed close enough for me to glimpse the interior. A handsome man, with sharp lines to his face, but I saw only his profile in those brief seconds of passing. Then I was beyond the truck, turning onto the main road, heading back to the ferry terminal.

* * *

"IT'S HAPPENING," CAROLINE told me over the phone. "Renee's in labor."

"How is she?" I was back in New York, in a cab driving home from the airport.

"It's not going that well. I think they'll probably have to do a C-section."

"I'll come straight there," I said. "I won't go home first."

"No, that's silly—" Caroline replied quickly, and then stopped. "Yes," she said. "That's probably best."

"Did you call Noni?"

"She's taking the train from Bexley. The kids are on their way, too."

I leaned forward to tell my cabbie the new destination and held on as he pulled abruptly to the side of the road.

"I'm glad you made it back in time," Caroline said, her voice in my ear as the cab swung into a U-turn. "How was the trip?"

"Fine," I replied without hesitation, and was hit by a wave of motion sickness from the car's abrupt change in direction. "I'm glad I made it back in time, too."

The drive to the hospital took ages, the traffic heavy, a battalion of honking New Yorkers inching along the Cross Island Parkway. Thirty minutes in, my phone battery died, and I sat back against the seat and closed my eyes. I tried to doze, but my heart thudded against my chest. An image of the boy Rory kept rising before me like a vision, a ghost.

When finally I arrived at the hospital, it was past 9:00 P.M. A bored receptionist tapped Renee's name into her computer.

"Looks like she's in the maternity ward," she said. "Out of surgery."

"Surgery?"

"C-section." Tap-tap-tap. "I don't see a room number. You'll have to ask on the ward."

But on the maternity ward, I couldn't find an on-duty nurse, and so I wandered, peeking into rooms, pulling my suitcase behind me, with an increasing sense of worry. Where was my family? Had I missed them all?

And then at last I found her.

My sister was asleep, propped up with pillows, her face pale and calm. Caroline sat beside the bed, her two hands holding Renee's right, her head bowed as though dozing or praying. Noni, Lily, Beatrix, and Louis sat in chairs scattered around the room. They were all asleep, breathing lightly, legs stretched before them. And there, within arm's reach of Renee, was a small cot and inside it the compact bundle of a baby. The sight of the small, delicate head, the shock of black hair, even darker than Renee's, delivered to me a hot shiver that moved from my center and extended out to the tips of my fingers and toes. I loved him, immediately and completely. Almost, I imagined, like a mother.

"Caroline?" I said quietly, and she lifted her head.

"Fiona," she said. "You made it!"

I bent down to hug my sister. Since her split from Nathan, Caroline had taken to rubbing lilac-scented oil into her skin—on the pulse points, as she called them—and it gave her a lovely fragrance, as though a summer garden hung around her neck. I lingered now in the hug to enjoy it. I realized I was trembling.

"Fi, are you okay?" Caroline asked.

"Yes, yes," I said. "Lots of traffic. Long drive."

"Your conference?"

"Yes, it was fine, all fine," I answered, looking to the floor.

Our voices had awakened Renee, who began to stir. She opened her eyes and said with a sense of urgency, "Where is he?"

I felt an immediate disorientation. How did Renee know? Had I mumbled it on the phone to Caroline? Was the information so dangerously compelling that it appeared on my face? In that brief moment of Renee's waking, I accepted that already my sisters knew about Rory, and I felt only relief. Here in this hospital room, filled with everyone who had loved Joe, we would discuss what to do about his son. This was not a secret I would carry alone into the future. I began to formulate the words, to start the answer: *Yes, I know where he is.*

But Caroline spoke first. "He's right here, Renee. Here's Jonah."
The cot was beside the bed. Of course, I realized. The baby.

And the room shook and swirled around me, the floor dropped, and into that empty space I threw Luna, her son, the house on the island. I threw it all down, away from my sisters, my nieces and nephews. Away from my mother. I threw it all into the bottomless dark, and the linoleum tiles closed up again, shielding Joe's son from view, protecting him from us and us from him. It was a burial of sorts. A final good-bye.

Renee looked into the cot and inhaled sharply. "Oh, isn't he gorgeous?" she said, her voice sleepy but full. She gently stroked his small head.

I leaned forward to hug Renee. "He takes after his mother," I said.

Beatrix and Lily began to stir, each opened her eyes and issued tired half smiles. These girls. These young women. They were twenty-four years old, the age at which I began *The Last Romantic*. When I thought about it, which was rarely now, the blog seemed almost quaint, idealistic, innocent. What would Lily and Beatrix do with those experiences? Did they ask the same questions now that I asked then? I suspected the answer was no. They were young, fearless women. Intoxicating. Sometimes I wondered what they thought of us. Did they look at Noni, at Caroline and Renee and me and wonder about the dilemmas that had plagued us? Did they wonder why we'd worried so much about children and work and relationships? My nieces assumed that the world was designed for them, the way they wished it to be. They took, they didn't ask. And they made it look so simple. I wondered why we had never done the same.

I was watching Beatrix: her long hair streaked with pink, a pierced nose, her cheeks high and freckled, and suddenly she locked her hazel eyes with mine. She issued a wide yawn and then winked.

And beside her was Louis—still asleep, it appeared. His mouth open, a gentle rhythm to his breath. Maybe he was faking it, but I didn't think so. I knew what fake looked like. Someone should wake him up, I thought. Wake him up so he doesn't miss anything. Wake him up so he knows how much we need him here.

"Hello, Skinners!" It was Nathan, holding two coffee cups, a candy bar stuck in the front pocket of his shirt. Louis startled with his father's entry, blinked and yawned with a wide, luxuriant stretch. Nathan placed one of the cups on the table next to Caroline, and she looked up at him with gratitude.

"Noni, it's good to see you," Nathan said, crossing the room to hug our mother. She and Nathan had a better relationship now, after the divorce, than during his long relationship with Caroline. Now Noni could appreciate him as a scientist, a teacher, a father, rather than as the man who took from Caroline the possibilities that her life might have otherwise contained were it not for children, home, his career, the goddamn frogs. Now Nathan was simply Professor Duffy, an intelligent, middle-aged white man with a poochy belly and silvery gray hair streaking his temples. Almost like a son.

I was considering all this—Nathan and my fearless nieces and mothers and sons—when Jonathan walked through the door. None of us had seen or spoken to him during Renee's pregnancy. He'd been traveling throughout the winter, Renee said, and would send the occasional e-mail but these contained only the barest details about his life and cursory questions about hers. He never mentioned the baby, she'd told me, or his impending fatherhood.

Standing in the open doorway, Jonathan looked sheepish, wiry and old. Older than I remembered him, his hair thinning on top so that the pale skin of his scalp reflected the yellow light.

"Renee," he said, and it was a small hiccup of a sound.

Renee blinked once, twice. None of us said a word.

"Is that . . . ?" He approached the cot. "Can I . . . ?" He looked to Noni for a response, as though the family matriarch controlled the babies here.

But it was Renee who answered. "Yes, you can pick him up. I named him Jonah."

Gingerly Jonathan picked up the sleeping baby and held him awkwardly, like a football or a loaf of bread. Jonah squirmed and screwed up his face, caught somewhere between sleep and wailing.

"Closer to your chest," Renee instructed. "Put his head into your inner elbow."

Jonathan followed these directions. He then began to bounce up and down slightly in a soothing, repetitive motion, and in that moment he looked just like any other new father. The baby quieted, settled against him, and gave a soft little sound of contentment.

"You got it," said Renee.

I knew there would be no grand emotional speeches here, not with all of us in the room. Jonathan and Renee were both too private and formal for that sort of thing. But I could tell. She was watching him. He did not look at her, only at the face of sleeping Jonah. The drooly, mashable face of his infant son, Jonah Ellis Avery Skinner.

*　*　*

I NEVER TOLD my sisters or Noni about the boy Rory. Perhaps this was my greatest betrayal. An unforgivable omission. I wonder now, as you do in old age, how events might have unfolded if I had brought Rory back to New York. If my sisters had seen his young face stamped with the same chin, same nose, same shining eyes as Joe's young face.

What did I give away that night with Luna Hernandez? But what, too, would have been lost?

We would have lost Joe again in a way. He would have become his son, a different boy living in a different time. We would have fought and struggled over that boy with the same ferocity we should have fought over Joe against Ace and Kyle and all the forces that surrounded him. We let Joe slip away, and so we would have held firm to Rory; we would have swallowed him whole. We Skinners are not very good at compromise. We are all or nothing.

There can be no other Joe. There is only one, and he remains as bright and vivid for me as that first day we visited the pond. He pulled me up from the mossy depths, his own head dripping, blinking away the cold, murky water, shaking me back into myself. That feeling endures even today, all these years later. *Joe, you saved me.*

Renee will always remember our brother in that moment after she ran from the man in the car, when she heard Joe's voice calling her name and then the man's weight lifting off her, releasing her lungs so she could breathe again. Her face was sticky with tears, her body shaking with the effort as she pushed herself up from the ground. Somehow Joe had known—how had he known?—where to find her. Joe, solid as a tree, said, *Are you okay?* and he'd taken her hand. He'd looked at her with such concentration, such concern, that Renee felt her fear depart, the knitting back together of the ends of herself that in the past hour of running and hiding and fighting had come loose and flown apart. *Are you okay?* Joe repeated, and Renee had answered, *Yes.*

Renee will see this same tenderness in her own son, first with his friends when he is young, then with his wife and his own children, Renee's grandchildren. Sometimes she will see it, too, in her colleagues and in the families of her patients. A care, a watchfulness, a willingness to accept the burden of another's fear. As a surgeon she will attempt this same degree of humanity with her patients, but to do it absolutely, as Joe did that day, will prove impossible, and she will feel herself over the course of her career falling short. Even as her professional accolades accumulate around her, she will lament her emotional failures.

At age sixty-one—still young in body and mind, still able to perform a nineteen-hour surgery without complaint—Renee will retire from full-time medicine to teach and spend time with her son. Jonah will be nine years old then, and, Renee will say, she's missed enough. Jonah is curious and kind, a violin player, a rugby devotee (though too skinny to play), a lover of the sea and the animals found there, who leaves for his marine-biology program at the University of Washington with a suitcase full of seashells and a framed photo he's kept on his dresser since childhood of his Uncle Joe, his namesake, a man Jonah never met but feels he knows due to the stories his mother tells of baseball and pond swimming and New York and a cake made with almonds and cinnamon.

Jonathan's reentry into Renee's life proceeds slowly after that first day in the hospital. For months Renee will refuse him, not trusting this change of heart or his promises to cut down on travel, to parent alongside her. But then, after nearly a year, she relents. Jonathan returns to their home in New York. He has always loved Renee, Jonathan will tell us that Christmas, all of us gathered around Noni's dining-room table, giddy on champagne and pecan pie. Baby Jonah is asleep in Renee's lap, sucking a pink thumb. "I've loved only her since that day in the ER," Jonathan says, and he holds up his hand, the scar having faded years ago to a thin white line cross-hatched with the ghost of stitches that Renee herself had sewn. Twenty-six years after that Christmas, on the day Jonathan Frank dies of a quick, painless stroke, his eyes will rest on the scar and it will appear suddenly to glow and pulse, a wavering, white-hot mark across his palm that opens again to reveal an image of Renee in her white doctor's coat, Renee gently, seriously holding his hand and healing this small, wounded part of himself.

Renee will outlive Jonathan by twenty years, and her dying image, the last picture she will hold in her head, is an improbable one. It is not of Jonathan, or Jonah, or one of us, her sisters, or Noni or Joe. It is of our father, the long-gone Ellis Avery, and the day he took her fishing on Long Island Sound, just the two of them on a boat long enough for twenty, and how the late-afternoon sun made the water glimmer and glint like a thousand tiny diamonds.

Caroline will always believe that Luna has something to tell us. She will always look for Luna, and it is with Caroline that I will feel the greatest guilt and regret. She is a mother; she would know better than I what it meant for me to walk away from our brother's child.

There are moments, weeks, years when I forget about the boy Rory, but then, after a dinner that Caroline has cooked for us, we sit in her garden with its view of Joe's tree, and she will say the name: Luna. She will ask me, "Why did we never find her? Should we try again?"

"No," I say. Year after year. Decade after decade. "No, we should give it up. Luna is gone."

And so over the course of our life together, I dissuade Caroline from looking for Luna Hernandez. On this question at last I side with Renee. And finally Caroline surrenders.

"What good would've come of it?" she will say one afternoon when we are in our eighties, vacationing in cool, blustery Maine. She grasps my hand. "I'm so glad we never found her. We didn't need another sister."

Caroline and Nathan will not live together again, though they will remain friends, wonderful friends, speaking nearly every night on the phone in the years before Nathan's death. His is a slow-moving cancer, so slow that at first the doctors advise him against treatment—old age will get him first—but then suddenly the disease accelerates as though it has awakened from a long sleep, as though it is reminded of its reason for being. When he dies, Nathan will be single, a beloved father and grandfather, known in perpetuity for a subspecies of the Panamanian golden frog that he discovers while on a research trip in the Cordilleran cloud forest. The *Atelopus duffyi*. This small, glistening amphibian—really more yellow than gold, he's noted in several books, and smaller than its cousin *Atelopus zeteki*—is the last thing Nathan will see when, alone in a hospital room at 1:00 A.M. in the year 2049, he finds himself miraculously walking along a twisting stream on the eastern side of the Tabasará mountain range. The small, brilliant body of the frog hops before him, and he follows it farther and farther into the wet, hot trees.

Caroline will continue with her acting, gaining local acclaim, appearing in all the best regional theaters, Williamstown and Amherst, and then, the year after she marries Raffi, she appears in an Off-Broadway production of *A Doll's House,* a run that lasts ten years and brings her the kind of independent satisfaction and artistic fulfillment that sewing Halloween costumes and directing school productions never could. After Raffi's death she will meet Leo, fifteen years her junior, an esteemed set decorator, and will believe that at last she has found her soul mate, the love of her life.

Caroline and Leo have six years together. It is a simple picture that comes to her one morning in the shower: an image of Joe on the baseball field, a high-school game she had attended only reluctantly and then watched from way up in the bleachers, far from Noni, Renee, and me. She remembers clear as a bell Joe at the plate in his purple-and-green uniform, and he is like that lilac tree she planted so long ago in her backyard: strong, tall, branching limbs, and beautiful, so beautiful, with the perfect arc of his swing. As ball meets bat, the crack of it explodes into light, and Caroline closes her eyes as she, too, falls into light.

Will, my darling Will, follows Caroline one week later. The single-engine plane he is piloting alone crashes over Hopi lands in northeastern Arizona, an accident that is never fully explained. He'd lived a rich and healthy eighty-eight years and his funeral is a celebration, a party, of all that he was and all that we experienced together. But these two absences, Caroline and Will in such quick succession, will topple me like nothing else since Joe. For years I will find myself sitting with eyes closed, one hand around a book, a pencil, an old T-shirt, and the other on my heart. I sit like that old medium Mimi Prince, and I wait for the enduring vibrations to reach me.

I meet Henry when I believe I'm finished with new experiences. I want only to retreat, to hide away and write in peace. To never hear another siren. Everything, I think, has already happened to me, but then there he is. Henry, fly-fishing in those big rubber boots and a floppy green hat in the river on my new land. He's a neighbor who becomes a friend, then lover. My house in the mountains becomes our house and we fill it with books, the barn with horses, the river with trout. Our extended families come when they need respite from their lives in cities—Henry's children and their children, my nieces and nephews, their children and theirs. My sisters never meet Henry, they're gone by then, but I know they would have approved.

And Noni? On the day of Jonah's college graduation, she will fly from New York to Seattle, and in those hours over the vast sweep of the United States something goes wrong. Something fails inside her brain, one blood vessel, a nerve, a synapse that does not connect to its partner. Renee meets her at the gate but senses immediately that Noni is not well. "I'm perfectly fine," Noni says, and waves Renee away, but later in the hotel she'll lie on the bed and pull the covers over her body and she'll talk to Renee, a sometimes nonsensical monologue about her childhood, about the first boy she kissed, the teacher who told her she was too smart for secretarial school, the doctor who felt her breasts with her mother in the room, the summer day she first met our father, and other days, other events we'd never known or thought to ask about. For hours Renee sits and listens. She learns more about our mother on that day than she has ever known before.

And finally Noni will talk about the Pause. "Once," she says, "I went to church. I looked to that dry, ridiculous Father Johns for some kind of wisdom. But after Ellis died, my idea of religion changed. I became a nonbeliever. Your grandmother was turning over in her grave, I'm sure, but the world struck me as stark and unforgiving. There was no plan. No one—no entity, no power, no *God*—controlled a thing. Life was a struggle. Not without its joys, of course"—here Noni smiles—"but a struggle nonetheless to feed, clothe, house, *love* the people for whom I was responsible. My children. You four. I was the only one who would ever love you wholly. I was the only one who would give my life for yours, and this seemed an important and terrible burden." Noni pauses and closes her eyes, opens them again. "It froze me. It did. The Pause, you kids called it. I couldn't face it alone, any of it, but somehow you managed. The four of you, together. You got through and you forgave me. Thank you, Renee. I've never quite forgiven myself, but thank you."

It is not that night that Noni dies, or the next, but two weeks later, after she's admitted to the hospital and rendered mute by

tubes and falls unconscious, long after Jonah's graduation ceremony and our planned returns to the East Coast. We stay. Noni
dies with us surrounding her in a strange bed, a strange city.

And I write. The success of *The Love Poem* grants me a certain degree of independence and I consider leaving ClimateSenseNow!,
but I don't. I stay and do what I can for another twenty-seven years.
Through it all, the floods and the forced migrations. The west
coast tsunami and Asian food shortages and all the talk talk talk
from the politicians. I write and I work. Poetry guides me, guides
so many through these times in a way that would have seemed
impossible when I was a younger woman. Back then, poets seemed
quaint, possibly irrelevant, but there is something about crisis
that returns us to the fundamentals to make sense of an uncertain future and remind us of what we need to know. It's been that
way since humans began telling stories. We sang our poems, we
chanted them. Only later did we write them down: Gilgamesh and
the *Iliad* and *Ramayana*. Akhmatova and Tupac Shakur. In poetry's
stripped-down urgency, in its openness, the space between lines,
the repetition and essentialism—poets can speak in ways that
transcend culture and gender and time. Films and novels remain
rooted in their age, give or or take a century. But poetry? Tell me
The Canterbury Tales doesn't still make you laugh and Keats make
you cry. And, my dear girl Luna, why did your mother name you
what she did?

You asked about the real Luna. You asked about my inspiration.
All of my work, from *The Love Poem* to *The Lasts, The Pond, Mothers
and Fathers,* even *The Last Romantic,* derived from my brother and
my sisters. My first and greatest loves.

For many years love seemed to me not something that enriched
or emboldened but a blind hole into which you fell, and in the fall-

ing you forgot what it was to live in your own light. This was the lesson I took from Noni and Caroline and all those restless young women who wrote to the Last Romantic. My last conversation with Joe, this was what made me so angry. Find someone to love, he told me. It seemed halfway between a cruel joke and condescension, a declaration of my weakness. I didn't know then what the word meant, despite all those men, the flirtations, sex and analysis. But I learned. Perhaps it was Will, or Henry, or Noni, or my sisters or their children who taught me. Perhaps it was Joe and Luna.

I was wrong to tell you that this is a story about the failures of love. No, it is about real love, true love. Imperfect, wretched, weak love. No fairy tales, no poetry. It is about the negotiations we undertake with ourselves in the name of love. Every day we struggle to decide what to give away and what to keep, but every day we make that calculation and we live with the results. This then is the true lesson: there is nothing romantic about love. Only the most naïve believe it will save them. Only the hardiest of us will survive it.

And yet. And yet! We believe in love because we want to believe in it. Because really what else is there, amid all our glorious follies and urges and weaknesses and stumbles? The magic, the hope, the gorgeous idea of it. Because when the lights go out and we sit waiting in the dark, what do our fingers seek? Who do we reach for?

Acknowledgments

THIS BOOK WAS a long time coming. First and foremost my eternal gratitude, admiration, and respect to my agent, Michelle Brower, and editor, Kate Nintzel. These two read more drafts than I care to count, and saw me through personal and professional turmoil, doubt, and some seriously bad writing days. Thank you a million times over. Many people read and offered valuable comments on drafts over the years I spent writing this book (and my apologies if I've forgotten anyone!), particularly: Shannon Huffman Polson, Patricia Smith, Peggy Sarjeant, Katherine Malmo, Marilyn Dahl, Ruth Whippman, Kenna Hart, Elissa Steglich, Art Chung, Beth McFadden, Cynthia Fierstein, and Mari Hinojosa. The idea for this book first emerged from a family tragedy and it was with great trepidation that I sat down to explore it. I would not have been able to write a word without the blessing of my grandmother, Luella Briody Conklin, who passed away in 2014. Thank you, Nana, for teaching me how to say good-bye on the telephone and that real love is always messy. Thank you also to my extended family, all the Conklins, Mills, Stones, and MacLeans who—either tacitly or expressly—supported the writing of this book. I hope that the result does justice to the events and people that inspired it. To my sisters from another mister and partners in crime: Allison Augstyn, Carrie Barnes, Jen Beatty, Margot Kahn Case, Cheryl Contee, Naomi Donnelley, Elisabeth Eaves, Cynthia Fierstein, Heather Jarvis, Jody Lindwall, Susannah Lipsyte, Amy Mushlin, Amy Predmore, Paige Smith, Elissa Steglich, Ruth Whippman—your friendship and support in writing, life, and parenting are invaluable to me. To Arlen Rushwald, thank you for your generous insights into life in rural Nicaragua. To Chris Cain, thank you for the boat and the whisky. To Elisabeth Eaves and Joe Ray, thank you for the desk and the coffee. To Allison Mahaffy and all the folks at Sol Yoga, thank you for the peace and downward dogs. To the doctors in my life, Cynthia Fierstein, Naomi Donnelley, and Laura Conklin, thank you for answering my random medical questions (and it should go without saying that any errors in medical lingo, protocol, or education are mine alone). For professional insight into sibling loss, I relied principally on two excellent books: *Surviving the Death of a Sibling: Living Through Grief When an Adult Brother or Sister Dies* by Dr. T. J. Wray and *The Empty Room: Understanding Sibling Loss* by Elizabeth DeVita-Raeburn. Gratitude to Emily Warn and Peter Mountford at Richard Hugo House where parts of this book were workshopped. To Liate Stehlik, Iris Tupholme, Kate Cassady, Tavia Kowalchuk, Kelly Rudolph, Lauren Truskowski, Vedika Khanna, and the whole William Morrow and HarperCollins Canada teams—my thanks for all that you do to help us scribblers get our work out into the world. Finally to my family, the people who inspire and challenge me, push my buttons, and piss me off, and without whom I would be lost: my children, Freya, Luke, and Rhys Conklin Maddock; my parents, Jay and Christina Conklin; and my sisters, Laura and Riisa Conklin.